Ian Rankin
The International Number One Bestseller

'Taut, dark and expertly crafted tale has plenty to satisfy the most exacting Rebus fan' *Guardian*

'Delightful, impossible-to-fault crime writing from a virtuoso of the craft' *Daily Mail*

'Rankin once again proves himself to be the consummate master of crime' *Scotland on Sunday*

'A thoroughly compelling read' *Mail on Sunday*

'Rebus is one of the most popular fictional characters of our generation' *Irish Times*

'Outstanding . . . very ambitious and very confident' *Sunday Telegraph*

'Rebus is back and he's lost none of his bite' *Independent*

'A chewy, satisfying, thrilling read with a giant narrative switchback when you least expect it' *Metro*

'Gritty and hard-hitting, it's the work of a writer at the very top of his game' *Sunday Mirror*

IAN RANKIN

RATHER BE THE DEVIL

First published in Great Britain in 2016 by Orion Books,
an imprint of The Orion Publishing Group Ltd
Carmelite House, 50 Victoria Embankment
London EC4Y 0DZ

An Hachette UK Company

1 3 5 7 9 10 8 6 4 2

A CIP catalogue record for this book
is available from the British Library.

ISBN (Hardback) 978 1 4091 5940 7
ISBN (Export Trade Paperback) 978 1 4091 5941 4

Typeset by Deltatype Ltd, Birkenhead, Merseyside

Printed in The United States of America by Berryville Graphics

The Orion Publishing Group's policy is to use papers that are natural,
renewable and recyclable products and made from wood grown in sustainable
forests. The logging and manufacturing processes are expected to
conform to the environmental regulations of the country of origin.

www.orionbooks.co.uk

Rather Be the Devil

Day One

Day One

1

Rebus placed his knife and fork on the empty plate, then leaned back in his chair, studying the other diners in the restaurant.

'Someone was murdered here, you know,' he announced.

'And they say romance is dead.' Deborah Quant paused over her steak. Rebus had been about to comment that she carved it with the same care she took when using her scalpel on a cadaver. But then the murder had popped into his head and he'd considered it the better conversational gambit.

'Sorry,' he apologised, taking a sip of red wine. They sold beer here – he had seen waiters delivering it to a few of the tables – but he was trying to cut down.

A new start – it was why they were dining out in the first place, celebrating a week without cigarettes.

Seven whole days.

A hundred and sixty-eight hours.

(She didn't need to know about the one he'd begged from a smoker outside an office block three days back. It had made him feel queasy anyway.)

'You can taste the food better, can't you?' she asked now, not for the first time.

'Oh aye,' he acknowledged, stifling a cough.

She seemed to have given up on the steak and was dabbing her mouth with her napkin. They were in the Galvin Brasserie Deluxe, which was attached to the Caledonian Hotel – though these days it was really the Waldorf Astoria Caledonian. But those who'd grown up in Edinburgh knew it as the Caledonian, or 'the Caley'. In the bar before dinner, Rebus had reeled off a few stories – the railway station next door, dismantled in the sixties; the time Roy Rogers had steered his horse Trigger up the main staircase for a photographer. Quant had listened dutifully, before telling him he could undo the top button of his shirt. He had been running a finger around the inside of the collar, trying to stretch the material a little.

'You notice things,' he had commented.

'Cutting out cigarettes can add a few pounds.'

'Really?' he'd answered, scooping up more peanuts from the bowl.

Now she had caught a waiter's eye and their plates were being removed. The offer of dessert menus was dismissed. 'We'll just have coffee – decaf if you've got it.'

'Two decafs?' The waiter was looking at Rebus for guidance.

'Absolutely,' Rebus confirmed.

Quant pushed a lock of red hair away from one eye and smiled across the table. 'You're doing fine,' she said.

'Thanks, Mum.'

Another smile. 'Go on then, tell me about this murder.'

He reached for his glass but started coughing again. 'Just need to . . .' signalling towards the toilets. He pushed the chair back and got up, rubbing at his chest with his hand. Once inside the gents, he made for a sink, leaning over it, hacking some of the gunk up from his lungs. There were the usual flecks of blood. Nothing to panic about, he'd been assured. More coughing, more mucus. COPD, they called it. Chronic obstructive pulmonary disease. When told, Deborah Quant had formed her lips into a thin line.

'Not so surprising, is it?'

And the very next day she had brought him a glass specimen jar of indeterminate age. Its contents: a section of lung, showing the bronchial tubes.

'Just so you know,' she'd said, pointing out what he'd already been shown on a computer screen. She had left the jar with him.

'On loan or to keep?'

'For as long as you need it, John.'

He was rinsing the sink when he heard the door behind him open.

'Did you leave your inhaler at home?' He turned towards her. She was leaning against the door, one foot crossed over the other, arms folded, head cocked.

'Is nowhere safe?' he muttered.

Her pale blue eyes scanned the room. 'Nothing here I haven't seen before. You feeling okay?'

'Never better.' He splashed water on his face and dabbed it with a towel.

'Next step is an exercise programme.'

'Starting tonight?'

Her smile widened. 'If you promise not to die on me.'

'We're going to drink our delicious caffeine-free refreshments first, though, right?'

'Plus you're going to woo me with a story.'

'The murder, you mean? It happened right upstairs in one of the bedrooms. A banker's wife who enjoyed the odd dalliance.'

'Killed by her lover?'

'That was one theory.'

She brushed invisible crumbs from the lapels of his jacket. 'Will it take long to tell?'

'Depends how abridged you want it.'

She considered for a moment. 'The length of a taxi ride back to my flat or yours.'

'Just the best bits then.'

There was a throat-clearing from the other side of the door, another diner unsure of the protocol. He muttered an apology as he squeezed past, deciding on the safety of one of the stalls. Rebus and Quant were smiling as they returned to their table, where two decaffeinated coffees sat waiting.

Detective Inspector Siobhan Clarke had been at home with a good book and the remains of a ready meal when the call came, the caller a friend called Tess who worked in the control room at Bilston Glen.

'Wouldn't normally bother you, Siobhan, but when I got the victim's name . . .'

So Clarke was in her Vauxhall Astra, on her way to the Royal Infirmary. The hospital sat on the southern edge of the city, plenty of space in the car park at this hour. She showed her ID at the Accident and Emergency desk and was shown where to go. She passed cubicle after cubicle, and if the curtains were closed, she popped her head around each. An old woman, her skin almost translucent, gave a beaming smile from her trolley. There were hopeful looks from others, too – patients and family members. A drunk youth, blood still dripping from his head, was being calmed by a couple of male nurses. A middle-aged woman was retching into a cardboard bowl. A teenage girl moaned softly and regularly, knees drawn up to her chest.

She recognised his mother first. Gail McKie was leaning over her son's trolley, stroking his hair and his forehead. Darryl Christie's closed eyes were puffy and bruised, his nose swollen and with dried blood caking the nostrils. A foam head brace had been rigged up, with further support around the neck. He was dressed in a suit, the shirt unbuttoned all the way to the waistband. There were contusions on his chest and stomach, but he was breathing. He was connected by a clip on one finger to a machine recording his vital signs.

Gail McKie turned towards the new arrival. She was wearing too much make-up and tears had left streaks down her face. Her hair was dyed straw-blonde, piled atop her head. Jewellery jangled on both wrists.

'I know you,' she stated. 'You're police.'

'Sorry to hear about your son,' Clarke said, drawing a little closer. 'He's all right, though?'

'Look at him!' The voice rising. 'Look what the bastards done to him! First Annette and now this . . .'

Annette: just a kid when she'd been murdered, her killer caught and jailed, though not lasting long before he too was killed, stabbed through the heart by an inmate who – best guess – had been put up to it by Annette's brother Darryl.

'Do you know what happened?' Clarke asked.

'He was lying in the driveway. I heard the car, wondered what was taking so long. The security lights had gone on and then off again, and no sign of him, his supper waiting on the stove.'

'You were the one who found him?'

'On the ground next to his car. Minute he got out, they must have jumped him.'

'You didn't see anything?'

Christie's mother was shaking her head slowly, her attention fixed on her son.

'What do the doctors say?' Clarke asked.

'We're waiting to hear.'

'Darryl's not been conscious at all? Able to speak?'

'What do you need to hear from him? You know as well as I do this is Cafferty's doing.'

'Best not jump to conclusions.'

Gail McKie gave a snort of derision, pulling herself upright as two white coats, one male and one female, brushed past Clarke.

'I'm going to suggest a scan as well as a chest X-ray. Far as we can tell, the upper half of the body took the brunt of the blows.' The female doctor broke off, eyes on Clarke.

'CID,' Clarke explained.

'Not our immediate priority,' the doctor said, signalling for her male colleague to draw the curtain, leaving Clarke on the outside. She stood her ground for a few moments, trying to listen, but there were too many moans and cries all around her. With a sigh, she retreated to the waiting area. A couple of uniforms were taking details from the paramedics. Clarke showed her ID and checked that they were discussing Christie.

'He was on the ground at the driver's side, between the Range Rover and the wall,' one uniform began to explain. 'Car locked and the key fob still in his hand. Gates are electric and he'd obviously closed them after driving through.'

'Where are we talking about exactly?' Clarke interrupted.

'Inverleith Place. It looks on to Inverleith Park, just by the Botanic Gardens. Detached house.'

'Neighbours?'

'Not spoken to them yet. His mum called it in. He couldn't have been lying there more than a few minutes . . .'

'She called the police?'

The constable shook his head.

'It was us she asked for,' the male paramedic answered. He was dressed in green and looked exhausted, as did his female colleague. 'Soon as we saw him, we got on to your lot.'

'Hard day?' Clarke enquired, watching as he rubbed at his eyes.

'No more than usual.'

'So his mum lives with him,' Clarke went on. 'Anyone else?'

'Two younger brothers. The mum was going daft trying to stop them getting a close look.'

Clarke turned to the constables. 'Asked the brothers any questions yet?'

Shakes of both heads.

'Professional hit, do you reckon?' the female paramedic asked. Then, without waiting for an answer: 'I mean, lying in wait like that . . . Baseball bat, maybe a crowbar or hammer, and then out of there before anybody's the wiser.'

Clarke ignored her. 'Cameras?' she asked.

'At the corners of the house,' the second of the constables confirmed.

'Well, that's something,' Clarke said.

7

'We all know, though, don't we?'

Clarke stared at the female paramedic. 'What do we know exactly?'

'It was meant to be fatal, or else it was a warning, and in either case . . .'

'Yes?'

'Big Ger Cafferty,' the woman said with a shrug.

'I keep hearing that name.'

'Victim's mother seemed fairly sure of it,' the male paramedic commented. 'Shouting it from the bloody rooftops, she was. And a few choice blasphemies besides.'

'Nothing but speculation at this stage,' Clarke warned them.

'You have to speculate to accumulate, though,' the female paramedic said, her smile fading as she caught the look Clarke was giving her.

Rebus sat on the bed in his flat's spare bedroom. It had been his daughter Sammy's room back in the day, before his wife took her away. Sammy was a mother herself now and Rebus a grandfather. Not that he saw much of them. The bedroom had been cleared of its various posters but was otherwise little changed. Same wallpaper, the mattress stripped, duvet folded in the wardrobe along with a single pillow, ready for use should a visitor need to stay the night. He couldn't remember the last time that had happened, though, which was just as well, as the place was no more welcoming than a storeroom. There were boxes on top of the bed and under it, atop the wardrobe and flanking it. They rose halfway up the window, too, making it impossible for him to close the wooden shutters. He knew he should do something about them, but knew, too, that he never would. They would be someone else's problem – Sammy's probably – after he was gone.

He had finally found the relevant box and was seated with it on a corner of the bed, his dog Brillo at his feet. October 1978. Maria Turquand. Strangled in Room 316 of the Caledonian Hotel. Rebus had worked the case for a short time, until he'd had a run-in with a superior. Sidelined, he'd still taken an interest, collecting newspaper cuttings and jotting down pieces of information, mostly rumours and gossip shared by fellow officers. One reason he remembered it: almost exactly a year before that, two teenage girls had been murdered after a night out at the World's End pub. Their case had seen little or no progress and the investigation was being wound down, but in 1978 there was a last-gasp effort to see if the anniversary jogged memories or stirred somebody's conscience. Rebus's punishment for insubordination: a lengthy and solitary stint on one of the telephones, waiting for it to ring. And it had, but only with cranks. Meantime, colleagues were traipsing through the Caley, pausing for tea and biscuits between interviews.

Maria Turquand had been born Maria Frazer. Wealthy parents, private education. She had married a young man with prospects. His name was John Turquand and he worked for a private bank called Brough's. Brough's was home to a lot of Scotland's old money, its chequebook held only by those with deep and trusted pockets. It was secretive but becoming less so as its coffers filled and it looked for new investment opportunities. Turned out it had even been eyeing up a takeover of the Royal Bank of Scotland, the equivalent of David landing a knockout blow on Goliath's bigger, brawnier brother. Maria Turquand's murder had seen Brough's land on the front pages of the nation's newspapers, and stay there as stories of her tempestuous private life emerged. There had been a string of lovers, usually entertained in a room she kept at the Caley. Some of Rebus's jottings referred to names he'd heard – unsubstantiated, but including a Conservative MP.

Did her husband know? It didn't seem so. He had an alibi anyway, having been in an all-day meeting with the head of the bank, Sir Magnus Brough. Maria's most recent lover, a playboy wheeler-and-dealer called Peter Attwood – who happened to be a friend of her husband's – was on shaky ground for a while, unable to account for his movements on the afternoon in question, until a new lover had surfaced, a married woman he'd been trying to protect.

Decent of him, Rebus mused.

All of which would have been enough to give the story traction, without the incidental appearance of a music star in a supporting role. But Bruce Collier had also been staying at the Caley with his band and management, the hotel being handy for the Usher Hall where he was due to perform. Collier had been in a rock group in the early 1970s. They were called Blacksmith, and Rebus had seen them play. Somewhere he almost certainly still had their three albums. There had been shock when Collier had quit the group to go solo, opting for a mellower sound and covering a slew of 1950s and 60s pop hits with growing success. His comeback gig in his home town, kicking off a sell-out UK tour, had brought with it journalists and TV crews from across the country and further afield.

Sifting through the cuttings, Rebus found plenty of photographs. Collier sporting big hair and skinny jeans, his neck festooned with silk scarves, captured in flashlight glare as he climbed the steps of the hotel. Then out walking in his old neighbourhood, stopping at the terraced house where he'd grown up. Questioned by the press, he'd admitted that the police were readying to interview him. The piece was accompanied by a photograph of Maria Turquand (taken at a party) that had been used a lot in the weeks after her death. She wore a short dress, cut very low, and was pouting for the camera, cigarette in one hand, drink in the other. Plenty of column inches discussed her 'racy lifestyle', the string of lovers and admirers, the holidays to ski resorts and Caribbean islands. Few lingered over her end, the fear she must have felt, the searing pain as her airway was crushed by her killer's hands.

Strong, male hands, according to the autopsy.

'What are you up to?'

Rebus looked up. Deborah Quant was standing in the doorway, dressed in the long white T-shirt she kept in a drawer in his bedroom for the odd nights she stayed over. Almost a year now they'd been seeing one another, but moving in together was something they'd both dismissed – too set in their ways, too used to their own company and routine.

'Couldn't sleep,' he said.

'The coughing?' She pulled her long hair back from her head.

He shrugged in place of an answer. How could he tell her he had dreamed of cigarettes and woken up craving nicotine, a craving no amount of patches or chewing gum or e-cigs was ever going to satisfy?

'What's all this stuff?' She tapped a bare foot against one of the boxes.

'You've not been in here before? This is just . . . old cases. Things that interested me at the time.'

'I thought you were retired.'

'I am retired.'

'But you can't let go?'

He gave another shrug. 'I was just thinking of Maria Turquand. When I started telling you her story, I realised there were bits I couldn't remember.'

'You should try and sleep.'

'Unlike some, I don't have work in the morning. *You're* the one who should be sleeping.'

'My clients tend not to complain if I'm a few minutes late – one bonus of working with the deceased.' She paused. 'I need some water. Can I get you anything?' He shook his head. 'Don't be too long then.'

He watched as she turned back into the hallway, heading for the kitchen. A cutting had slipped from his lap and fallen to the floor. It was from a few years later. A drowning in a swimming pool on Grand Cayman. The victim had been holidaying there with friends, among them Anthony and Francesca Brough, grandchildren of Sir Magnus. There was a photo of the house's elegant exterior, along with a caption explaining that it belonged to Sir Magnus, who was recently deceased. Rebus wasn't sure now why he had added this postscript to the history of Maria Turquand's murder, except that the story had given the newspaper a further excuse to print a photo of Maria, reminding Rebus of her beauty and of how irritated he'd been to be pulled from the case.

He looked at the copies of the *Scotsman* he'd kept from the week of the murder: Vietnamese refugees arriving to start a new life; B. B. King on *The Old Grey Whistle Test* and *Revenge of the Pink Panther* at the cinema; an ad for the Royal Bank of Scotland featuring a photo of the Twin Towers; Margaret Thatcher visiting East Lothian prior to a by-election; rubbish piling up in Edinburgh as the bin strike dragged on . . .

And on the sports pages: *No goals for Scots clubs in Europe.*

'Some things don't change,' Rebus muttered to himself.

Having put everything back in the box marked *77–80*, he brushed dust from his hands and sat for a further moment studying the room and its contents. Most of the paperwork related to cases he had worked on, cases eventually solved – all of it adding up to what, exactly? A policeman's lot. Yet the real story, he felt, remained unwritten, only hinted at in the various reports and scribbled notes. The bald facts of arrests and convictions – these told only partial truths. He wondered who might make sense of it all, and doubted anyone would bother. Not his daughter – she would take the briefest look then put the whole lot in a skip.

You can't let go . . .

True enough. He'd walked away from the job only when told there was no alternative on offer, pensioned off, skills no longer germane or required. *Adios.* Brillo seemed to sense the atmosphere in the room and raised his head, nudging it against Rebus's leg until Rebus reached down to offer a reassuring rub.

'Okay, boy. Everything's fine.'

Rising to his feet, he switched off the light, waiting until the dog had followed him from the room before closing the door. The kettle had boiled and Quant was pouring water into a mug.

'Want one?'

'Better not,' Rebus said. 'I'll only have to get up for a pee in an hour.'

'I'll be gone by then, busy morning.' She nodded towards where his phone was charging on the worktop. 'It's been vibrating.'

'Oh aye?' He picked up the phone and checked the screen.

'I couldn't help noticing the first text is a reminder from the Infirmary.'

'So it is.'

'You're having more tests?'

'So it would seem.' He kept his eyes on the screen, avoiding her stare.

'John . . .'

'It's nothing, Deb. Just as you say – more tests.'

'Tests for what, though?'

'I won't know till I get there.'

'You weren't going to tell me, were you?'

'What is there to tell? I've got bronchitis, remember?' He pretended to cough, while giving his chest a thump. 'They just want to run more tests.'

Having entered his passcode, he saw that there was another text, just below the automated NHS one. It was from Siobhan Clarke. His eyes narrowed a little as he read it.

Any dealings with Cafferty of late?

Quant had decided on the silent treatment, blowing on her tea and then sipping it.

'Need to take this,' Rebus muttered. 'It's from Siobhan.'

He headed into the darkened living room. A half-empty bottle of wine on the coffee table. A glow from the hi-fi system that told him he hadn't switched it off. Last album played: John Martyn, *Solid Air*. Felt like that was what he was walking through as he padded across the carpet to the window. What was he supposed to say to Deb? There's some sort of shadow on my lung, so now it's all about things with scary names like 'tomography' and 'biopsy'? He didn't want to think about it, never mind say it out loud. A lifetime of smoking was doing all its catching-up at once. A cough that wouldn't shift; spitting out blood into the sink; prescription inhaler, prescription nebuliser; COPD . . .

Lung cancer.

No way he was allowing *that* bad boy into his mental vocabulary. No, no, no. Keep the brain active, shift focus, don't think about all the lovely cigarettes smoked at this very spot, many of them in the middle of the night with a John Martyn LP spinning at low volume. Instead, he waited for Clarke to answer, and looked past his own vague reflection at the windows across the street, each one curtained or in darkness. Nobody on the pavements below, no cars or taxis passing, the sky above giving not a hint of the day yet to come.

'It would have waited,' Clarke said eventually.

'Then why text me at four in the morning?'

'It was actually closer to midnight when I sent it. You been busy?'

'Busy sleeping.'

'You're awake now, though.'

'Just like you. So what's Cafferty gone and done?'

'Have you talked to him recently?'

'Two or three weeks back.'

'Keeping his nose clean? Still the respectable ex-gangster about town?'

'Spit it out.'

'Darryl Christie was roughed up last night outside his house. Damage report: a cracked rib or three and some loosened teeth. Nose isn't quite broken but it looks the part. His mother was quick to blurt out Cafferty's name.'

'Cafferty's got forty-odd years on young Darryl.'

'More heft on him too, though. And we both know he'd have hired someone if he felt it necessary.'

'To what end?'

'It's not so long ago he thought Darryl might have put a price on his head.'

Rebus considered this. A bullet aimed at Cafferty's head as he stood in his living room one night, his rival Christie the obvious candidate. 'He was proved wrong,' he said after a moment.

'Got him excited, though, didn't it? Maybe he remembered just how much he missed being the city's Mr Big.'

'And giving Darryl Christie a doing is supposed to achieve what exactly?'

'Scare him off, maybe goad him into some rash action . . .'

'You think so?'

'I'm just . . . speculating,' Clarke said.

'Have you bothered asking Darryl?'

'He's doped to the eyeballs and being kept in overnight.'

'No witnesses?'

'We'll know more in a few hours.'

Rebus pressed a finger to the window pane. 'Want me to broach the subject with Big Ger?'

'Best keep this a police matter, don't you think?'

'Ouch. Speaking of which – you still not talking to Malcolm?'

'What's he been saying?'

'Not much, but I get the feeling his promotion to Gartcosh got you bristling.'

'Then your amazing intuition has let you down for once.'

'Fair enough. But if you *do* want me to talk to Cafferty, you just have to say.'

'Thanks.' He heard her give a sigh. 'How's everything else, by the way?'

'Nose to the grindstone, as usual.'

'Doing what exactly?'

'All those hobbies people take up when they retire. Actually, you might be able to help me with that.'

'Oh yes?'

He turned away from the window. Brillo was seated behind him, awaiting another rub. Rebus offered a smile and a wink instead. 'You got any access to the cold-case files?' he said into the phone.

Day Two

2

Malcolm Fox hated the commute – forty miles each way, most of it spent on the M8. Some days it resembled *Wacky Races*, with cars weaving in and out of traffic, lorries wheezing into the outside lane to crawl past other lorries, roadworks and breakdowns and buffeting winds accompanied by lashing rain. Not that there was anyone he could complain to – his colleagues at Gartcosh, the Scottish Crime Campus, considered themselves the crème de la crème, and they had the state-of-the-art building to prove it. Once you'd found a parking space and proved your credentials at the gatehouse, you entered a closed compound that was trying its damnedest to resemble a new-build university, one aimed at the elite. Plenty of internal space, filled with light and heat. Breakout areas where specialists from different disciplines could meet and share intelligence. Not just the various branches of the Specialist Crime Division, but Forensic Science, the Procurator Fiscal's office, and HMRC's Criminal Investigation wing. All housed under the one happy roof. He hadn't heard anyone moan about how long it took them to get to Gartcosh and then home again, and he knew he wasn't the only one who lived in Edinburgh.

Edinburgh. He'd only been transferred a month, but he still missed his old CID office. Then again, nobody here minded that he was ex-Professional Standards, the kind of cop hated by other cops. But did any of them know the story behind his move? He'd been left for dead by a detective gone rogue, and that same detective had been dragged away by two career criminals – Darryl Christie and Joe Stark – never to be seen again. The upper echelons didn't want the story made public. Added to which, the Procurator Fiscal hadn't fancied taking either gangster to court when no actual body had ever turned up.

'A good defence lawyer would rip us to pieces,' Fox had been told at one of several hush-hush meetings.

Instead they had waved Gartcosh in front of him, and wouldn't take no for an answer. So here he was, trying to find his niche in the Major Crime Division.

And failing.

He recalled an old office saying about promoting mediocrity. He did not regard himself as mediocre, but he knew he had never quite proved himself exceptional. Siobhan Clarke *was* exceptional, and would have fitted in at Gartcosh. He'd seen the look on her face when he'd broken the news – trying not to be dumbstruck or resentful. A brief hug while she fixed her face. But their friendship afterwards had faltered, excuses found not to watch a film or eat a meal. All so he could drive the forty miles here and the forty miles home, day after day.

Get a grip, Malcolm, he told himself as he entered the building. He rolled his shoulders, straightened his tie and did up both buttons on his suit jacket – the suit bought specially. New shoes, too, which had just about softened enough that he didn't need daily plasters on his heels.

'Detective Inspector Fox!'

Fox paused at the bottom of the stairs and turned towards the voice. Black polo shirt, short-sleeved with a zip at the neck; shoulder flashes; two sets of lanyards with photo ID. And above the whole ensemble the tanned face, bushy black eyebrows and salt-and-pepper hair. Assistant Chief Constable Ben McManus. Instinctively, Fox pulled himself to his full height. There were two ACCs at Gartcosh, and McManus was in charge of Organised Crime and Counter-Terrorism. Not the meat and potatoes stuff of Major Crime – murders and the like – but the cases spoken of in undertones and via gestures, the cases that were investigated behind a series of locked doors elsewhere in the building, doors opened with one of the magnetic cards swinging from around McManus's neck.

'Yes, sir?' Fox said. The ACC was holding out his hand, gripping Fox's when it was offered and slipping his free hand over the top of both.

'We've not been properly introduced. I know Jen's been keeping you busy . . .'

Jen being Fox's own boss, ACC Jennifer Lyon.

'Yes, sir,' Fox repeated.

'Settled in okay, I hear. I know it can be a bit disconcerting at first – very different set-up from what you've been used to. We've all been there, trust me.' McManus had released his hold on Fox and was climbing the staircase at a sprightly pace, Fox just about keeping up. 'It's good to have you, though. They speak very highly of you in Division Six.'

Division Six: the City of Edinburgh.

'And of course your record speaks for itself – even the bits we don't want anyone outside Police Scotland to see.' McManus offered a smile that was probably meant to be reassuring but told Fox only that this man wanted him for something and had had him checked out. At the top of the stairs they headed for one of the soundproofed glass boxes that were used for private meetings. Blinds could be drawn as required. Eight bodies could be accommodated around the rectangular table. There was only one there waiting.

She stood up as they entered, tucking a few stray blonde hairs back behind one ear. Fox reckoned the woman was in her early to mid thirties. Five and a half feet tall and dressed in dark skirt and pale blue blouse.

'Ah, they've even brought us some coffee,' McManus announced, spotting the pot and mugs. 'Not that we're going to be here long, but help yourselves if you like.'

Taking the hint, Fox and the woman shook their heads.

'I'm Sheila Graham, by the way.'

'Sorry,' McManus interrupted, 'my fault entirely. This is DI Fox, Sheila.'

'Malcolm,' Fox said.

'Sheila here,' McManus ran on, 'is Her Majesty's Revenue and Customs. You won't have been shown their part of the building yet.'

'I've walked past a few times,' Fox said. 'Lots of people tapping away at computers.'

'That's the sort of thing,' McManus agreed. He had seated himself and gestured for Fox to do the same.

'We work the usual areas,' Graham said, her eyes fixed on Fox. 'Drink and tobacco, money laundering, e-crime and fraud. A lot of it comprises basic forensic accounting, not that there's anything *basic* about it in the digital age. Dirty money can be transferred around the world in the blink of an eye, accounts opened and closed almost as quickly. And that's before we get to Bitcoin and the Dark Web.'

'She's lost me already,' McManus said with a grin, throwing open his arms in a show of defeat.

'Am I being transferred?' Fox asked. 'I mean, I can balance a chequebook with the best of them, but . . .'

'We've plenty of number-crunchers,' Graham said with the thinnest of smiles. 'And right now some of them are looking at a man you seem to know – Darryl Christie.'

'I know him all right.'

'Did you hear what happened last night?'

'No.'

Graham seemed disappointed in his answer, as though he had already failed her in some way. 'He was given a doing, ended up in hospital.'

'Business he's in, there's always a price to be paid,' McManus said. He had risen to his feet and was pouring himself coffee, without offering to Fox and Graham.

'What's HMRC's interest?' Fox asked.

'You know Christie owns some betting shops?' Fox decided not to let on that this, too, was news to him. 'We think he's been using them to clean up dirty money – his own and that of other criminals.'

'Such as Joe Stark in Glasgow?'

'Such as Joe Stark in Glasgow,' Graham echoed, sounding as though he had partway redeemed himself.

'Stark and his boys came barging into Edinburgh a few months back,' Fox explained. 'Joe and Darryl ended up friends.'

'There are others besides Stark,' McManus chipped in before slurping from his mug. 'And not just in Scotland either.'

'Quite an enterprise,' Fox commented.

'It'll almost certainly run into the millions,' Graham agreed.

'We need someone on the ground, Malcolm.' McManus leaned across the table towards Fox. 'Someone who knows the territory, but reporting back to us.'

'To what end?'

'Could be the assault inquiry will throw up names or information. There are going to be a lot of headless chickens running around while Christie recuperates. Meantime he's going to be wondering who he's up against – associate or enemy.'

'He might start to slip up.'

'He might,' Graham agreed with a slow nod.

'So I'm going back to Edinburgh?'

'As a tourist, Malcolm,' McManus cautioned with a wag of the finger. 'You need to make sure they know you're *our* man, not theirs.'

'Do I tell them HMRC have got their bloodhounds sniffing Christie's trail?'

'Better if you don't,' Graham stated.

'You'll be working for me, Malcolm.' McManus had finished his coffee already and was getting back to his feet, meeting over. 'And it's only natural we at Organised Crime should want to know what's going on.'

'Yes, sir. You say he was attacked last night? So the investigation will just be getting started . . .'

'The officer in charge is . . .' Graham sought the name, closing her eyes for a moment. 'Detective Inspector Clarke.'

'Of course,' Fox said, forcing a smile.

'Excellent!' McManus clapped his hands together, made the briskest of turns, and yanked open the door. Fox stood up, making sure he had Sheila Graham's attention.

'Anything else I need to know?'

'I don't think so, Malcolm.' She handed him her business card. 'Mobile's the best way to get me.'

He handed her a card of his own.

'You didn't know about the betting shops, did you?' she asked, eyes twinkling. 'Pretty good poker face, though . . .'

The first thing Siobhan Clarke noticed as she parked outside Christie's house was that it was almost identical in size and design to Cafferty's home across town – a detached three-storey Victorian stone edifice with large bay windows either side of the front door and a long driveway to the side that led to a free-standing garage. The front gate wasn't locked, so she walked up the path and rang the bell. She had already noted the CCTV cameras described by the constable last night, and there was another built into the stonework next to the door buzzer.

Gail McKie pulled open the door. She was standing in a vestibule, the glass-panelled door behind her leading into the main hallway. She didn't look as if she'd slept – same clothes as at the hospital, and her hair drooping to her shoulders.

'Wouldn't have bothered if I'd known it was you,' she offered by way of greeting. Clarke gestured towards the camera.

'You don't use that, then?'

'It's fake, same as all the others. They were there when we bought the place – Darryl keeps meaning to put in real ones.'

21

'How is he?'

'He'll be home today.'

'That's good.'

'There've been a couple of your lot round already, harassing the neighbours.'

'You don't want the police involved?'

'What do you care?'

'Some of us do, though.'

'Then go talk to Cafferty.'

'I'm not saying that won't happen, but we need to piece together the events first, starting with where you found Darryl.'

'Won't do any good. I didn't see anybody.'

'Darryl was out cold?'

'Thought he was dead for a minute.' McKie suppressed a shiver.

'Could your other sons have seen or heard anything?'

A shake of the head. 'Asked them last night.'

'Can I speak to them?'

'They're at college.'

Clarke thought for a moment. 'Shall we go take a look at the driveway, then?'

McKie seemed reluctant, but then headed indoors, re-emerging with a cream Burberry raincoat wrapped around her shoulders. She led the way, pointing towards one of the security cameras.

'Wee red light and everything. Look real enough, don't they?'

'Are there many break-ins?'

McKie shrugged. 'When you've got what people want, you start to fret.'

'Darryl maybe thought nobody was likely to target his house – him being who he is.' Clarke waited, but McKie stayed silent. 'It's a nice part of town,' she went on.

'Bit different from where we started out.'

'Did Darryl pick the house?'

McKie nodded. They had reached the white Range Rover Evoque. It had pulled to a halt next to the rear entrance to the house. There were security lights above both the garage and the back door itself. Clarke gestured towards them.

'Whoever was waiting for him, they'd have tripped the lights, yes?'

'Maybe. But if you're indoors with the curtains closed, you wouldn't notice.'

'Would the neighbours?'

'We get a lot of foxes around here, being next to the Botanics. That's what I always blame if I see a light coming on anywhere.'

There were spots of dried blood on the driveway by the driver's-side door. McKie turned her head away from them.

'He won't want me telling you this,' she said quietly, 'but I'm going to say it anyway.'

'I'm listening.'

'There've been warnings.'

'Oh?'

'One night, Darryl left the car kerbside. Next morning, the front tyres had been slashed. That was about two weeks ago. Then last week, the bin went up.'

'How do you mean?'

'Put it out for collection, and somebody torched it. Take a look for yourself.'

The bin was to the right of the back door, its plastic lid warped and blackened, part of one side melted halfway down.

'You didn't report this?'

'Darryl said it was most likely kids. I'm not sure he believed it himself. No one else in the street got the same treatment.'

'You think he was being targeted?'

McKie gave a shrug, which sent her coat sliding to the ground. She stooped to pick it up, brushing it clean before wrapping herself in it again.

'Have you spoken to him since last night?'

'He didn't see anything. They got him on the back of the head as he was locking the car. Says he dropped like a stone. Bastards must've kept hitting him once he was out cold.'

'He reckons there was more than one assailant?'

'He's no idea – this is me talking.'

'Are you aware of any other incidents or threats? Maybe a note?'

McKie shook her head. 'Whatever's going on, Darryl will find out.' She glared at Clarke. 'Maybe that's what you're afraid of, eh?'

'Your son would be unwise to take matters into his own hands, Ms McKie.'

'He's always been his own man, though, even when he was a kid – insisted on keeping his dad's name for the school register, after the bastard running out on us and everything. Then when Annette died . . .' She paused and took a deep breath, as if controlling some strong emotion. 'Darryl grew up fast. Fast and strong and smart. A lot smarter than you lot.'

Clarke's phone was buzzing. She dug it out of her pocket and studied the screen.

'Answer it if you like.'

But Clarke shook her head. 'It can wait. Could you have a word with Darryl for me?'

'And tell him what?'

'That I'd like to speak to him. That he should agree to see me.'

'You know he's not going to tell you anything.'

'I'd still like to try.'

McKie considered this, then gave a slow nod.

'Thank you,' Clarke said. 'I could come back this evening, maybe see your other sons at the same time.'

'You get extra money for working late?'

'I wish.'

Eventually, Gail McKie smiled. It took years from her, and Clarke was reminded of the woman she'd been when posing for cameras and questions at press conferences back when Annette was still missing. A lot of changes had taken place since, and Darryl had changed most of all.

'Around seven?' Clarke suggested.

'We'll see,' McKie said.

Heading for the gate, Clarke looked at her phone again. One missed call. No message. A number she recognised.

'What the hell do you want, Malcolm?' she sighed, slipping the phone back into her pocket.

3

Rebus stood outside Cafferty's house on a wide, leafy street in
Merchiston, staring at the For Sale sign. He'd already made a
circuit of the garden, peering through any windows that weren't
curtained or shuttered, satisfying himself that the house had been
emptied. He took out his phone and called Cafferty's mobile, but
it just rang and rang. A neighbour across the way was watching
from a downstairs window. Rebus waved and then crossed the road,
meeting the woman as she opened her door.

'When did he move out?' Rebus asked.

'About ten days ago.'

'Any idea why?'

'Why?' she echoed. It was obviously not the question she'd expected.

'Or his new address,' Rebus added.

'Somebody did say they'd seen him at Quartermile.'

Quartermile: the site of the old Edinburgh Royal Infirmary, now
redeveloped.

'Would he have left his new address with anyone?'

'Mr Cafferty kept himself pretty much to himself.'

'Probably didn't go down well, though, when that bullet went
through his window a while back.'

'The story I heard was, he fell against the pane and broke it.'

'Trust me, he didn't. How much is he asking?' Rebus angled his
head towards the house opposite.

'That's not the sort of thing we bandy about.'

'Maybe I'll phone the agent, then.'

'You do that.' The door was being closed again, not hurriedly but with polite Edinburgh finality, so Rebus walked back to his Saab and got in, tapping the solicitor's number into his phone.

'Price on application,' he was eventually told.

'Is this not me applying?'

'If you'd care to make an appointment to view . . .'

He ended the call instead and drove into town. There was an underground car park at the heart of Quartermile, but Rebus stopped on a yellow line instead. The site now boasted amenities such as shops, a gym and a hotel. The old red- and grey-stone buildings of the original hospital had been joined by towers of glass and steel, with the best addresses looking south across the Meadows towards the Pentland Hills. In the sales office Rebus admired a scale model of the site, and even picked up a brochure. The woman on duty offered him a chocolate from an open tin, and he took it with a smile, before asking Cafferty's whereabouts.

'Oh, we don't share that kind of information.'

'I'm a friend of his.'

'Then I'm sure you can track him down.'

Rebus gave a twist of the mouth and took out his phone again, this time composing a text.

I'm outside your new place. Come say hello.

Back at his car, he thought about how he used to fill gaps like this in his life with a cigarette, instead of which he walked to the Sainsbury's on Middle Meadow Walk and queued for a box of chewing gum. He was almost at the Saab again when his phone buzzed: incoming message.

You're bluffing.

Rebus typed a reply: *Nice Sainsbury's, if you can put up with the students.*

And waited.

It was a further four or five minutes before Cafferty emerged from a gate at the side of one of the older blocks. His head was huge, shaped like a cannonball, the silver hair shaved close to the skull. He wore a long black woollen coat and red scarf, an open-necked white shirt visible beneath, exposing tufts of chest hair. His eyes, which always seemed smaller than they should be, had the same piercing quality as ever. Rebus reckoned they had served Cafferty well over the years, as sharp and fearful a weapon as any in his armoury.

'What the hell do you want?' Cafferty growled.

'An invite to the house-warming, maybe.'

Cafferty stuffed his hands into his pockets. 'Doesn't feel like a social call, but last time I looked you were still retired, so what's on your mind?'

'Just our old friend Darryl Christie. I'm remembering the last time we talked about him. You as good as said you had a bit of fight left in you.'

'So?'

'So he's been put in hospital.'

Cafferty's mouth formed an O. He lifted a hand from one pocket and rubbed at his nose.

'Been taking acting lessons?' Rebus asked.

'This is the first I'm hearing of it.'

'And you'll have a cast-iron alibi for last night, I'm guessing?'

'Isn't that the sort of thing a detective should be asking?'

'I'm pretty sure they will. Your name's being mentioned in dispatches.'

'Darryl trying to stir things up?' Cafferty nodded to himself. 'And why shouldn't he? It's an open goal and I'd probably do the same myself.'

'Actually, you did – when that bullet hit your living-room window.'

'Fair point.' Cafferty looked around him, sniffing the air. 'I was just about to have my mid-morning coffee. I don't suppose it would hurt if you sat in the vicinity.'

'Aren't the cafés rammed with people bunking off their lectures?'

'I'm sure we can find a quiet corner,' Cafferty said.

Not the first two places they tried, but the third, a Starbucks on Forrest Road. A double espresso for Cafferty and an Americano for Rebus. He'd made the mistake of asking for a large, which seemed to mean a mug almost the size of his head.

Cafferty stirred sugar into his own tiny cup. They hadn't quite found a corner, but apart from a few students poring over textbooks and laptops, the place was quiet and their table private enough.

'Always music in these places,' Cafferty commented, eyes on the ceiling-mounted speakers. 'Same in restaurants and half the shops. Drives me demented . . .'

'And it's not even real music,' Rebus added. 'Not like we had in our day.'

The two men shared a look and then a wry smile, concentrating on their drinks for a moment.

'I've been wondering when you would show up,' Cafferty eventually said. 'Not about Darryl Christie, but just generally. I had this image of you driving past my house at regular intervals, wondering if you'd catch me in the middle of something, something you could take to court.'

'Except I'm not a detective any more.'

'Citizen's arrest then, maybe.'

'Why's your old place on the market?'

'I was rattling around in it. Time to downsize.'

'And then there was that bullet.'

Cafferty shook his head. 'Nothing to do with that.' He took another sip of the thick black liquid. 'So Darryl's got on the wrong side of somebody, eh? Occupational hazard – we both know that.'

'He's a big player in the city, though, probably the biggest unless you know otherwise.'

'Doesn't make him immune.'

'Especially not if the man he shunted aside decides on a comeback.'

'Nobody *shunted* me,' Cafferty bristled, squaring his shoulders.

'You went quietly then, and you're thrilled to leave the city in his hands.'

'I might not go that far.'

'Any names for me?'

'Names?'

'You said it yourself – he got on somebody's wrong side.'

'It's not your job any more, Rebus. Did they forget to tell you that?'

'Doesn't stop me being nosy.'

'Obviously not.'

'And a man needs a hobby. I can't begin to guess what yours might be.' Cafferty glared at him, and the two men lapsed into silence, focusing on their drinks again until Rebus held up a finger. 'I recognise that tune,' he said.

'It's Bruce Collier, isn't it?'

Rebus nodded. 'Did you ever see him live?'

'The Usher Hall.'

'In '78?'

'Around then.'

'You remember the Maria Turquand murder, then?'

'At the Caley Hotel?' Cafferty was nodding. 'It was the lover, wasn't it? Got his new squeeze to lie through her teeth and dodged a life sentence.'

'You reckon?'

'It's what everyone thought, your lot included. He moved back up this way, you know.'

'The lover?'

'No, Bruce Collier. Think I read that somewhere.'

'Is he still playing?'

'Christ knows.' Cafferty drained the dregs of his coffee. 'We about done here, or are you still waiting for me to confess to thumping Darryl?'

'I'm not in any hurry.' Rebus gestured towards his mug. 'I've got about half a vat left here.'

'Then I'll leave you to finish it. You're a man of leisure after all, about time you faced up to the fact.'

'And what about you? How do *you* keep busy?'

'I'm a businessman. I do business.'

'Every last bit of it above board?'

'Unless your successors prove otherwise. How is Siobhan, by the way?'

'Haven't seen her in a while.'

'She still stepping out with DI Fox?'

'Is this you trying to impress me? Showing you still have your ear to the ground? If so, you'd best get your hearing checked.'

Cafferty was on his feet, adjusting his scarf, tightening it around his throat. 'Okay, Mr Amateur Detective. Here's something for you.' He leaned over the seated Rebus, so that their foreheads almost touched. 'Look for a Russian. You can thank me later.'

And with a smile and a wink he was gone.

'Hell's that supposed to mean?' Rebus muttered to himself, brow furrowed. Then he realised that the song Bruce Collier had just finished singing was a version of the Beatles' 'Back in the USSR'.

'Look for a Russian,' he repeated, staring into his coffee and feeling a sudden need to pee.

Time was, Siobhan Clarke got a frisson just walking through the door of Gayfield Square police station. Each day brought new cases and different challenges, and there might even be something big about to break – a murder or serious assault. Now, though, Police Scotland parachuted in their own squad for high-profile inquiries, meaning the local CID was reduced to a support role – and where was the fun in that? Every day now it seemed there were grumblings and mutterings; fellow officers ticking off the days till retirement or pulling sickies. Tess in the control room was a good source of general gossip, even if the gossip itself was grim.

Clarke had had to park in a pay bay, too, having failed to find a space at the station. So, having put in the maximum amount, she was tapping an alarm reminder into her phone as she climbed the stairs to the CID suite. In four hours she'd have to move the car or face a fine. There was a sign she could use for her windscreen – OFFICIAL POLICE VEHICLE. But she'd tried that once and returned to find someone had scored the car all down one side.

Nice.

The CID suite wasn't big, but then it wasn't busy. Her two DCs, Christine Esson and Ronnie Ogilvie, were seated at their computers, tapping away. With her head angled downwards, only Esson's short dark hair was visible.

'Good of you to drop in,' Clarke heard her comment.

'I was out at Darryl Christie's house.'

'Word is he's had a bit of an accident.' Esson had stopped typing and was studying her boss.

'We all know he's a respectable entrepreneur and everything,' Clarke said, slipping out of her jacket and draping it over the back of her chair, 'but could you find me anything we've got on his activities and associates?'

'No problem.'

Clarke turned to Ogilvie. 'Uniforms are talking to the neighbours. I need to know what they find. And make sure they look at any and all CCTV recordings from dusk till the paramedics arrived.'

Esson looked up from her screen. 'Does Morris Gerald Cafferty count as an associate?'

'Quite the opposite, I'd think, unless we learn anything to the contrary.'

'We're taking this seriously then?' Ogilvie asked. He had started growing a moustache and was running a finger and thumb down either side of it. Pale and gangly, he always reminded Clarke of a long-stemmed plant starved of sunlight.

'According to Christie's mother,' she told him, 'their car and rubbish bin were attacked recently. Looks like a classic escalation.'

'So was last night an attempt on his life?'

Clarke considered for a moment, then shrugged. 'Is the boss in his broom cupboard?'

Esson shook her head. 'But I think I hear his dainty tread.'

Yes, Clarke could hear it, too. DCI James Page's distinctive leather soles, climbing the last few stairs and clacking along the uncarpeted corridor towards the open door.

'Good, you're here,' he said, spotting Clarke. 'Look who I ran into.' He leaned to one side, so that Malcolm Fox was visible. Clarke could feel her spine stiffening.

'And what brings you down from the mountain?' she asked.

Page was squeezing Fox's shoulder. 'We're always delighted, of course, to see our brethren from Gartcosh. Isn't that right?'

Esson and Ogilvie stared at one another, unable to form an answer. Clarke had folded her arms.

'DI Fox needs our help, Siobhan,' Page said. Then, turning towards Fox: 'Or is that putting it too strongly, Malcolm?'

'Darryl Christie,' Fox stated for the benefit of the room.

Page was wagging a finger at Clarke. 'You can imagine how happy I was to be told by Malcolm that the attack on Mr Christie was being investigated by my own officers – news to me, Siobhan.' All the fake warmth left his voice as he glared at her. 'Something you and I will be discussing as soon as we have a minute.'

Fox was trying not to look embarrassed at having dropped Clarke in it. She hoped the look she was giving him wasn't doing anything to ease his discomfort.

'So let's go into my office and have a little chat, eh?' Page said, giving Fox a final pat on the shoulder and leading the way.

Page's inner sanctum was a converted storeroom with no natural light and just about enough space for his desk, a filing cabinet and a couple of chairs for visitors.

'Sit,' he commanded, having got himself comfortable.

The problem was, Clarke and Fox were so close together when seated that their feet, knees and elbows almost touched. Clarke could feel Fox squirming as he tried to put some distance between them.

'Why are Gartcosh interested in a mugging?' she asked into the silence.

Fox kept his eyes on the desk. 'Darryl Christie is a known player. He has direct ties to Joe Stark's gang in Glasgow. Obviously he's on our radar.'

'So you're here to make sure we do our job?'

'I'm an observer, Siobhan. All I'll be doing is reporting back.'

'And why can't we do that ourselves?'

He turned his head towards her. She noticed that his cheeks had coloured slightly. 'Because this is the way it is. If everything's thorough – and knowing you, I doubt it'll be anything but – there's not going to be an issue.'

'You have to understand, Malcolm,' Page interrupted, 'that it can rankle somewhat when overseers suddenly arrive without warning.'

'I'm only doing *my* job, DCI Page. There'll be an email somewhere or a phone message from ACC McManus, advising you of my role.' Fox glanced at Page's laptop, which lay closed on the desk.

'McManus runs Organised Crime,' Clarke commented. 'I thought you were Major Crime.'

'They've borrowed me.'

'Why?'

He held her gaze. 'Until recently, this was my patch. Maybe they thought I'd be welcomed back with open arms.'

Clarke gave a twitch of the mouth.

'And of course you *are* welcome, Malcolm,' Page announced, 'and we'll do our best to accommodate your needs, so you can make your report and we can all get our proficiency badges.' He leaned back in his chair. 'But tell me, Siobhan, is this really anything that should set Gartcosh's antennae twitching?'

Clarke considered her response. 'His injuries aren't life-threatening, but his mother says his car was attacked previously and their bin was set ablaze.'

'Classic escalation,' Fox commented, earning a look from her that he couldn't quite read.

'Reckon he knows who's responsible?' Page asked.

'I've not interviewed him yet. He's being released today; I was going to drop in on him this evening.'

Page nodded. 'No witnesses? Nobody spotted fleeing the scene?'

'We're knocking on doors right now, though a few more bodies would be useful.'

'I'll see what I can do.'

'I'm wondering if we need to offer Christie something,' Clarke went on. 'Maybe a marked car outside his house for a night or two.'

'I doubt he'd thank us for it.'

'An unmarked car then – and he doesn't need to know.'

'He doesn't have bodyguards?'

'Seems to have dispensed with them.'

'Meaning what exactly?'

She shrugged. 'Could be he's trying to save on outgoings. The house he's in won't have come cheap.'

'You think he might be strapped for cash?' Fox's eyes narrowed as he weighed this up.

'How *does* he make his money anyway?' Page was looking at Fox. 'Your lot should know better than anyone.'

'He has his hotel,' Fox obliged, 'and some bars and nightclubs, plus a couple of betting shops.'

'There's other stuff, too,' Clarke added. 'A car wash, I think. Plus a door-to-door operation providing the same sort of thing.'

'Okay,' Page said, his eyes still on Fox. 'And if we scratch the surface?'

'I'm not privy to everything Gartcosh has,' Fox admitted, shifting in his seat again. 'Drugs . . . money laundering . . . who knows?'

'I've got Christine looking into it,' Clarke said. 'So we might have something a bit more substantial by end of play.'

'It's thin stuff for CID,' Page advised. 'People get duffed up all the time.' He paused. 'But as this is Darryl Christie we're talking about, and because our colleagues in Organised Crime are taking an interest . . . fine, let's throw what resources we can at it.'

'Including the watch on his home?' Clarke asked.

'Maybe for a night or two. Better still would be a list of anyone who bears a grudge – you can ask Mr Christie about that when you see him.'

'I'm sure he'll give us a full and frank account.'

Page's mouth twitched. 'Use what charm you can muster, Siobhan. And keep Malcolm fully apprised.'

'Due respect, sir,' Fox interrupted, 'I think I need a bit more than that.' Page looked at him for elucidation. 'I need to be with DI Clarke each step of the way,' Fox obliged. 'I doubt ACC McManus would brook anything less.'

Clarke's eyes were pleading with her boss, but Page just sighed and nodded.

'Off you go then, the pair of you.'

'Sir . . .' Clarke started to complain.

'It's the price you pay, Siobhan, when you don't tell me what's going on under my own nose.'

Having said which, Page opened the screen of his laptop and began hitting keys.

Fox led the way back into the CID suite, but Clarke signalled towards the corridor, and he followed her, stopping as she turned to face him.

'Ask me how happy I am about all of this,' she hissed.

'I did try phoning . . .'

'You could have left a message.'

33

'So you *do* know I tried?'

'I was a bit busy, Malcolm.'

'You've not driven the length of the M8 twice already today – *I'm* the one who should be cranky.'

'Who says I'm cranky?'

'You sound cranky.'

'Livid is what I am.'

'All because the chiefs chose me over you for the Gartcosh posting?'

'What?' She pretended amazement. 'That's got nothing to do with it.'

'Good, because it looks like we're stuck together for the next wee while. And I'm fine, by the way, settling into the new job nicely, thanks for asking.'

'I sent you a text on your first day!'

'I don't think so.'

Clarke thought for a moment. 'Well, I meant to.'

'Cheers.'

The silence lingered until Clarke gave a sigh. 'Okay, how do we work this?'

'You treat me like part of the team, because that's what I'll be.'

'Right up to the point where you scurry off westward to make your report. And by the way, this needs to be a two-way street – anything in the files at Gartcosh, *I* need to see it.'

'That would need to be approved.'

'But you can ask – and you *will* ask.'

'And if I do that, you and me declare a truce?' He was holding out his hand. Eventually she took it.

'Truce,' she said.

Clarke stood outside the tenement on Arden Street and pressed the intercom, then took a few steps back so she could be seen from the second-floor window. When Rebus's face appeared, she waved. He seemed to hesitate before shrinking back into his living room. Seconds later, the buzzer told her the door was unlocked. She pushed it open, holding it with her shoulder as she lifted a box from the ground.

'Am I in for a telling-off?' Rebus barked from above, his voice echoing off the tiled walls of the stairwell.

'Why would ...?' She broke off, realising. 'You went to see Cafferty. Of course you did.'

'Got a confession in full, too.'

'Aye, right. Did he tell you *anything* useful?'

'What do you think?' She had reached his landing and he saw the box. 'Did I forget Christmas or something?'

'In a manner of speaking. Though after pulling a stunt like that with Big Ger, maybe I should reconsider.'

He took the box from her and carried it into the living room. Clarke cast an eye over the place.

'Deborah Quant has been good for you. Tidier than I remember. Not even an ashtray – don't tell me she's got you packing it in?'

Rebus placed the box on the dining table so that it covered the letter from his hospital consultant. 'Deb doesn't like mess – you've seen the way she runs the mortuary. You could eat your dinner off one of her slabs.'

'So long as it wasn't occupied,' Clarke countered. Brillo had emerged from his basket in the kitchen, and she crouched down to give him some attention, scratching at the tight wiry curls that had given the dog its name.

'Is he still getting walked twice a day?'

'Supermarket and Bruntsfield Links.'

'He looks great.' She got back to her feet. 'So you're doing okay?'

'Hale and hearty.'

'Deborah mentioned something about bronchitis . . .'

'Did she now?'

'Last time I was in the mortuary.'

'And you didn't rush straight over here?'

'Reckoned you'd tell me when you were ready.' She paused. 'But knowing you, that's never going to happen.'

'Well, I'm fine. Potions and inhalers and all that jazz.'

'And you've given up smoking?'

'The proverbial ˋpiece of cake. So what's in the box?' He was already prising off the lid.

'Fresh out of cold storage.'

Rebus was studying the name on the topmost brown manila file: Maria Turquand. 'This can't be the whole case?'

'God, no, there's about three shelves' worth. But you've got all the summaries, plus a little bonus.'

Rebus had opened the first file, and he saw what she meant. 'The case was reviewed.'

'By your old friends at SCRU.'

'Not long before my stint there.'

'Eight years ago, in point of fact.'

Rebus was studying the file's covering sheet. 'I thought Eddie Tranter was in charge of SCRU back then. But it's not his name here.' He dug down a little further.

'Enough to keep you going?' Clarke was making a circuit of the room, much as she would a crime scene.

'Stop snooping,' Rebus told her, 'and tell me instead if there's any news.'

'Christie, you mean? Not much. Door-to-door has given us precisely zilch. Interesting, though . . .'

'What?'

'His house is the spitting image of Cafferty's – from the outside, at least.'

'Emulating him, maybe?'

'Or sending a message of some sort.'

'Wonder if Darryl knows Cafferty's changed addresses.'

'Oh?'

'Nice modern flat in Quartermile.'

'Think it means anything?'

'Maybe Big Ger wasn't flattered by the young prince's gesture.'

'Moving into an almost identical house, you mean?'

Rebus nodded slowly and placed the lid back on the box. 'You won't get into trouble for bringing me this?'

'Not unless anyone else goes looking for it in the warehouse.'

'It's really appreciated, Siobhan. I mean it. I'd just sit and stare at the walls otherwise.'

'The dog was supposed to help with that.'

'Brillo seems as keen on exercise as I am.' He watched as Clarke checked her phone. 'Somewhere else you need to be?'

'I'm hoping to speak with Darryl this evening.' She paused. 'And I won't be alone – Malcolm's back in town.'

'Didn't take long for Gartcosh to kick him into touch.'

'He's here as their man on the ground, making sure we don't screw up the case.'

'Seriously?' Rebus shook his head slowly. 'Does every villain who gets a pummelling earn the same level of service?'

Clarke forced a smile. 'Maybe Darryl's gone private.' She watched as what started as a chuckle from Rebus became a cough. With his hand over his mouth he exited the room, and she could hear the fit continuing. When he returned, he was wiping at eyes and mouth

36

both. Clarke held up a small jar filled with clear liquid in which something was suspended.

'Is this what I think it is?' she asked.

'You're not the only one who brings me presents,' Rebus managed to reply.

After she'd gone, Rebus emptied the box, spreading its contents across the dining table. The officer in charge of the cold-case review was a detective inspector called Robert Chatham.

'Fat Rab,' Rebus said aloud as he read. He'd known him by reputation but never worked with him. Chatham had been F Troop, meaning West Lothian's F Division, based in Livingston. Lothian and Borders Police had consisted of six divisions, seven if you included the HQ at Fettes. The coming of Police Scotland had changed all that. There wasn't a Lothian and Borders any more, and the City of Edinburgh was to be known as Division Six, which made it sound like a floundering football team. Rebus no longer attended the get-togethers of cops who had shared various L&B beats, but he heard the mutterings. Early retirements; younger officers giving up after a few short years.

'Well out of it, John.' He got up to make a mug of tea and scoop some food into Brillo's bowl. 'Fancy a walk?' he asked, shaking the dog's lead. Brillo ignored him, too busy eating. 'Thought not.'

Back at the dining table, he got to work. The cold-case review had come about because of a newspaper story, one Rebus had obviously missed. The journalist had interviewed Bruce Collier's road manager, a man called Vince Brady. The piece was about the touring life of the 1970s, a mix of rueful sexism and drug binges. Brady stated that he'd seen Maria Turquand in conversation with Collier in the hotel's third-floor corridor. Brady's room had been right next to Turquand's, while Collier – being 'the talent' – had the suite at the end of the hall.

There was due to be a bit of a party in the suite after the show, and I think Bruce was inviting her. But before the gig even started we found out she was brown bread [dead] so the celebrations were a bit subdued.

The journalist had tried contacting Collier for his reaction, but had received a two-word message that meant pretty much the same as 'no comment'. Chatham and his team had listened to the recording of the interview with Brady, then questioned Brady himself and

Collier. Collier had told them his road manager must be mistaken. He had no recollection of any meeting, however brief.

I had to give Vince the heave after that tour. He was taking the piss over the merch, pocketing more money than I ever saw. This is just him trying a bit of payback, if you take my meaning.

A little later in the interview, Collier stated that he had spent most of his time in the hotel catching up with 'a mate from the good old days'. This mate was a local musician called Dougie Vaughan. The two had played together in a band in high school. Vaughan was still a jobbing guitarist, popping up at folk clubs and open-mic nights around Edinburgh.

He was also one of Maria Turquand's ex-lovers – Rebus had come across him in his own box of clippings about the case. Vaughan had given his story to the *Evening News* a few months after the murder. A one-night fling after Turquand had spotted him playing at a party. He had tried contacting her afterwards but had been rebuffed.

Smashing girl, she was. Terrible what happened.

And yes, Vaughan had been in the hotel that afternoon to see his old school pal. And yes, he'd been questioned by the police, but hadn't been able to help. He'd had no idea Maria Turquand was just a few doors along from Collier's suite. No one had mentioned her.

Rebus's tea had grown cold by the time he finished reading. He rubbed his hands down his face, blinking his eyes back into focus. Brillo was out in the hall, seated and expectant.

'Really?' Rebus asked. 'Well, if you say so . . .' He fetched the lead and grabbed jacket, keys and phone. Arden Street was only a couple of minutes from the Meadows and Bruntsfield Links. There were always dog walkers out and about. Sometimes they even stopped for a chat while the various mutts inspected each other. Rebus would be asked how old his dog was.

No idea.

The breed, then?

Mongrel.

And all the while, he would be thinking about cigarettes.

The sun was already sinking from the sky. He reckoned there would be frost later. While Brillo went for a run, Rebus reached into his pocket, producing his phone in place of a fresh pack of twenty. He was wondering if Fat Rab was still on the force, so he called the one person he thought might be able to help.

'Well now,' Christine Esson answered in his ear, 'here's my second ghost today.'

'Siobhan told me about Fox.'

'He brought flowers and chocolates.'

'Just because I never call, it doesn't mean I don't miss your charm and wit, DC Esson.'

'But it's my other skills you're calling about, right?'

'On the button as usual, Christine.'

'So what is it this time?'

'An easy one, I hope. A DI called Robert Chatham. Based out at Livingston last I heard. I need to talk to him.'

'Give me fifteen minutes.'

'You're a gem, lass.' Rebus ended the call. Thirty feet away, nature was taking its course. Rebus put away his phone and brought out a small black polythene bag, then started walking towards Brillo.

'Who was that?' Fox asked from across the room.

'Nobody.'

'Funny, that's exactly who it sounded like.' Fox approached Esson's desk. They were alone in the CID suite, Ronnie Ogilvie out fetching sandwiches. 'What's this errand Siobhan's running?'

'She told you – it's nothing to do with Darryl Christie.'

'Who's Robert Chatham?' Fox enquired, peering at the note Esson had just made to herself.

'Malcolm, will you back the hell off?'

He held up his hands in surrender, but lingered close by her desk, too close for Esson's liking.

'Does Siobhan ever mention me?'

Esson shook her head.

'Gartcosh wasn't my idea, you know. But I'd have been daft to turn it down.'

'No argument here.'

He was angling his head to look at her computer screen. She gave him the death stare again.

'You must have *some*thing by now,' he complained.

'A whole string of Mr Christie's business interests.'

'Can I see?'

'I'll email them to you.' She hit a few keys. 'In fact, I just have. Now will you leave me in peace?'

Fox walked back to the opposite end of the office, studying his phone and finding her email. Nothing he didn't already know, except that Esson had addresses for the two betting shops. What was it Sheila Graham had said? Christie laundering money through them – how did that work then? Fox hadn't got round to asking. He glanced up at Esson, but couldn't – wouldn't – ask her. She might think him gormless for not knowing the ins and outs. Besides, he had a better idea.

'I'll be back in a bit,' he announced.

'What about your sandwich?'

'It'll keep.'

'Foolish words, Malcolm – you've not seen Ronnie when he's hungry.'

'I'll take my chances.'

'What'll I tell Siobhan when I see her?'

Fox thought for a moment. 'Tell her I'm running an errand of my own.'

Down the stairs and out of the building, taking in a few gulps of the fresh air. He unlocked his car and got in, easing his way out of the parking space, heading for Leith Walk.

Seated in her own car, Clarke watched him go. A text arrived and she studied it with a smile.

Malc's offski – safe to come in!

She wondered how Christine knew. Educated guess, probably. Then a second text: *Might even be a sandwich for you!*

Clarke opened the car door and got out.

4

Fox hadn't been into a betting shop since his late teens. His father hadn't been much of a gambler, but would study the racing form on a Saturday morning and place a bet on four different horses – he called it a 'Yankee'. If Malcolm was at home and Mitch couldn't be bothered with the walk, he would be dispatched to the bookmaker's along the street, despite protestations that a phone call would be as easy, or that his sister Jude could do it for a change. But Mitch wanted the security of a paper receipt, so that he could be confident the bet really had been recorded. Not that Malcolm could ever recall any actual wins – nothing worth bragging about to a son. And Jude was always somewhere else.

He was surprised to walk into Diamond Joe's and find no dishevelled old men nursing the stubs of both pencils and cigarettes. There was a cashier behind a glass screen – as in the past – but the place was filled with shiny machines and wall-mounted TVs. One channel was showing a golf tournament, another tennis, while a further couple showed horse racing. But the few punters in the place were focused on the machines. There was a stool in front of each. Plenty of jaunty blips and beeps and colourful lights. Not just high-tech one-armed bandits, but versions of blackjack and roulette, too. Spoilt for choice, Fox made for one of the most basic-looking models. It had four reels as its centrepiece. He slotted home a pound coin and touched the flashing button. Once the reels had stopped spinning, lights and jingle-jangle sounds told him he should be doing something. But what? He touched one button, then another. Nothing seemed to change, and he was left with one credit. He hit the start button, watched the reels as they clunked to their individual stops.

Anything? Nothing. He tried the start button again, but it wasn't being fooled.

A quid gone in fifteen seconds.

He stayed on the stool, pretending to be sending a text on his phone while getting a feel for the room. The cashier looked bored. She was chewing gum and studying her own phone. Fox walked over to her.

'Can I bet on horses here?' he asked.

She stared at him, then lifted her eyes to the bank of screens.

'How do I do it, though?' he persisted.

'Slips are over there,' she answered, gesturing. 'Or you can do it online.' She waggled her phone. 'The app's free. There's even a tenner credit for newbies.'

He nodded his thanks and went over to the shelf with the betting slips, lifting one and studying it. It reminded him of maths home-work, all grids, symbols and letters that were supposed to mean something to him. His dad used to write down the name of each horse, along with the race time and location, then tear off the scrap of paper and hand it over with his bet.

Next to the slips sat a display of pools coupons. Mitch had done those, too, each and every Saturday, never able – as a Hearts fan – to put his own team down for anything other than a win. Fox smiled at the memory, then heard a sound resembling air escaping a tyre. It was the word 'Yes!' stretched out almost to breaking point and uttered from one of the stools. The punter rubbed his hands together as a slip of paper appeared from a slot. He bounded up to the cashier with it.

'That'll do me for today, Lisa,' he said.

The cashier studied the slip, then put it through a machine of her own before opening a drawer and counting out ten twenty-pound notes.

'I'll take a receipt, too,' the man said. The cashier obliged and the customer stuffed everything in his jacket pocket. 'Nice doing busi-ness with you.' He made his way to the door, but paused with his fingers just brushing the handle. Then he turned back and handed the cashier one of the twenties, receiving pound coins in return. Scooping these up, he made for one of the other machines, settling himself down and feeding them in.

Fox realised he was being watched. He gestured to show the cashier he was taking a pools coupon with him, then made his own way towards the outside world, where he crumpled the coupon, toss-ing it in the nearest bin.

42

He wasn't sure if he had learned anything useful, but with nothing better to do, he drove to the next address. With stunning originality, it was called Diamond Joe's Too. He went in and marched up to the cashier – identical set-up to its sister operation, but with a wary-looking man in his forties behind the glass. He handed over a twenty and asked for pound coins.

'Know about our new app?' the cashier enquired.

'Ten-pound credit,' Fox said. 'Use it all the time.'

'Not quite the same, though, is it?' The man was nodding towards the machines.

'Nothing like,' Fox agreed, heading for a stool.

He was eight quid down but starting to get the hang of things when the door opened and a woman walked in. She slung her bag on to the ground next to a blackjack machine, shrugged out of her leather jacket and got busy, for all the world like someone clocking in for a day on the production line. She hadn't so much as glanced at anyone else in the place, though she gave the machine in front of her a long, slow stroke with one finger, as though she might coax generosity of spirit from it.

Fox bided his time, slowly feeding his own machine. He even notched up a couple of small wins, keeping them as credits. Fifteen minutes to lose twenty quid. He wasn't sure of the etiquette of watching other players from over their shoulder. The glower from the young man next stool along soon put him right, so he wandered over to the woman playing blackjack. He paused next to her, but she kept her eyes on the machine.

'Not interested,' she said.

'Hello, Jude.'

Fox's sister turned her head towards him. As usual, her lank hair needed washing, and her eyeshadow was smudged. Her mouth formed a thin line.

'You keeping tabs on me?'

'Just coincidence,' he shrugged.

'Never took you for the gambling type – always Mister Play-Safe.'

'How about you?'

Her smile showed teeth. 'Chalk and cheese, brother. Chalk and cheese.'

'This your usual spot?'

'You always said I needed something to get me out of the house.'

'Oh aye, it's a good way to meet people, this.'

'Hell's the point of meeting people?'

43

'It's how life's supposed to work, Jude.'

She concentrated on the game for a moment, then turned towards him again. 'Wake the fuck up, Malcolm,' she said, giving equal weight to each word.

'Ever gamble online? Maybe use Diamond Joe's handy little app?'

'None of your business.'

'Except I pay three figures into your bank each and every week.'

'If it's thanks you're after, best find another charity case.'

'I thought I was helping my sister get back on her feet.'

She swivelled on the stool so her whole body was towards him, a furious look on her face.

'No, Malcolm, what you were doing was moving your guilt money around the family. Soon as Dad was dead, you only had me. And you had to give it to *some*one, didn't you, so you could feel that nice warm self-satisfied glow?'

'Christ's sake, Jude . . .'

He saw her face soften a little. But instead of apologising, she turned back to her game.

'Can you shut the yapping?' the punter on the machine opposite demanded. 'Trying to concentrate here.'

'Sod you, Barry,' Jude snarled back at him. 'Five more minutes, you'll be skint and on your smelly way.'

'That really your sister?' the man retorted, eyes on Fox. 'Bet you wish you were a fucking only child.'

'We both do,' Jude stated, feeding more money into the never-satisfied slot.

Robert Chatham's home address was a terraced house on the Newhaven waterfront. A woman answered and Rebus explained he was an old colleague looking to catch up.

'He's working tonight.'

'Oh?'

'Somewhere on Lothian Road. He's a doorman.'

Rebus nodded his thanks and got back in his Saab, retracing his route into the city and parking at a bus stop halfway up Lothian Road. The wide street boasted half a dozen bars, most of which changed their names and decor so often Rebus couldn't have kept track if he tried. The first place he came to, the black-clad doormen were too young, but he stopped anyway.

'Looking for Robert Chatham,' he explained, receiving sullen shakes of the head. 'Thanks for the conversation, then.'

The next bar didn't feel the need for security. It looked warm and inviting, laughter billowing out as the door was opened by a reveller readying to light a cigarette.

One beer won't kill you, Rebus thought to himself. You could settle for a half. But he kept moving instead. At weekends, Lothian Road could be hairy – stag and hen parties colliding; young wage-earners high on drugs, alcohol and life itself. But tonight it was midweek quiet, or else too early and chilly for the pavements to be lively. As Rebus approached the third bar, he noted its solitary gatekeeper. Broad-shouldered in a dark three-quarter-length coat. Shaved head and no discernible neck. Early fifties but fighting fit, ID stuffed into a clear plastic armband around one bicep.

'Seem to know the face,' the man said as Rebus stopped in front of him.

'I used to be a DI,' Rebus explained.

'We ever work together?'

Rebus shook his head, then held out a hand. 'Name's John Rebus.' Chatham's grip was solid, and Rebus returned it as best he could. 'And you're Robert Chatham.'

'My other half phoned to let me know there was a visitor on his way. You're out of the force now, though?'

'I do a bit of work as a civilian. How long since you left?'

'Three years.' Chatham broke off to hold open the door for a pair of new arrivals, allowing Rebus a glimpse of the bar's interior. Too dark for his liking, and a pounding soundtrack.

'Is that called techno?' he asked.

'I call it noise,' Chatham replied. 'So what is it I can do for you?'

'You had a spell at SCRU.'

'A short spell – Eddie Tranter was off sick.'

'I worked SCRU myself not long after.'

'Oh aye?'

'There's a case I've been looking at – Maria Turquand.' Chatham nodded slowly, saying nothing. 'You dusted it off after Vince Brady offered new evidence.'

'Evidence?' Chatham snorted. 'It was his word against Bruce Collier's. Collier got his lawyers on it PDQ. Threatened to sue Brady, Lothian and Borders, and any newspaper we talked to.'

'You reckon he had something to hide?'

Chatham considered this. 'Not really,' he eventually conceded.

'You think it was her lover all along?'

'I take it you've seen the files – what do you think?'

'Any chance we can discuss this somewhere that isn't a pavement on Lothian Road?'

'I don't knock off till midnight. Only place I'm going after that is my kip.'

'Tomorrow morning?'

The doorman stared at Rebus. 'I really don't think I'm going to be any help.'

'I'd appreciate it all the same.'

'There's a café on North Junction Street,' Chatham eventually conceded. 'Best bacon rolls in the city. Ten o'clock do you?'

'Ten's fine.' They shook again, and Rebus headed for his car. He turned his head for a final look at Chatham, but the man was busy with his phone, holding it close to his face as he tapped the screen. Texting or calling? Rebus had his answer as Chatham lifted the phone to his ear. He was staring in Rebus's direction as his mouth started to move.

'Lip-reading, John,' Rebus muttered. 'There's a hobby you could take up.' He unlocked the Saab and got in, turning up the heat. His Marchmont flat was only five minutes away. Brillo would be needing a walk.

Their meeting with Darryl Christie had been arranged for seven, but then changed by Christie to eight. When they'd arrived at his door, however, his mother was ready with an apology that Darryl was 'a bit busy' and could they come back in another hour?

They returned to their two cars, parked kerbside. Fox waited a minute or two before opening the passenger-side door of Clarke's Astra.

'Does it really make sense for us to sit in separate cars?'

'Up to you,' Clarke said. But she didn't look exactly welcoming as he climbed in. She busied herself with her phone while Fox stared through the windscreen at his surroundings.

'Thought I just saw my namesake,' he eventually offered.

Clarke glanced up. 'They do get foxes here.' As if on cue, the security lights came on outside Christie's neighbour's house. A lean shape could be seen stalking past.

'Why do you think they chose this spot? Whoever thumped Darryl, I mean – why outside his actual house?'

'Doesn't need to be any real reason.'

'Is his address public knowledge?'

'I wouldn't have thought so.'

'Which might narrow things down a bit.'

'It might,' Clarke conceded. After a further fifteen seconds, she gave up the pretence of being busy on her phone, and half turned towards him instead. 'But I'm more interested in why he was singled out in the first place.'

'I went to his betting shops this afternoon.'

'Oh?'

'Just for a look-see.'

'Christine told me she'd copied you in on his various businesses. Mind if I ask why you zeroed in on them rather than any of his other interests?'

'Maybe they were at the top of the list.'

'They weren't, though, were they?'

Fox considered for a moment. 'HMRC are interested in him. They think he's laundering money.'

'You mentioned that in Page's office.'

'If he's cleaning up cash for various gangs from all over the country, any one of them could have taken against him.'

'For short-changing them?'

'I don't know.'

'What if I throw Cafferty's name into the ring?'

'Wouldn't put anything past him. But he'd probably only make a move if he thought Darryl was weakened by something.'

'Such as?'

Fox shrugged. 'Maybe we'll get an inkling when we talk to Darryl.'

'*I'll* be doing the talking, Malcolm. You're there to listen.'

'Understood.' He paused for a moment. 'Is this us thawing out here?'

'Maybe a little. Have you asked Gartcosh about intelligence sharing?'

'They're mulling it over.'

'Nice to feel we're all part of the same big happy family . . .' Clarke broke off and watched as Gail McKie padded down the path, opening the gate and making for the Astra. Clarke slid her window down, and McKie's face appeared in the gap.

'He's ready for you,' she said, turning back towards the house.

'Right then,' Clarke said to Fox, sliding the window closed and pulling the key from the ignition.

McKie was waiting for them inside the front door. 'He's in the living room,' she said. 'Told me not to bother offering a drink – you won't be staying long.'

'Are your other two sons around for a quick chat after?' Clarke enquired. McKie shook her head.

'Out with mates.'

'That's a pity.'

'They've really nothing to say.'

'They need to tell me that for themselves.'

Clarke pushed open the door and stepped into the living room. Flower-patterned sofa, almost the entire floor covered with a huge colourful rug, something Persian or Indian. Flowers in vases on occasional tables, and seated in the very centre of the room on a dining chair fetched from elsewhere, Darryl Christie. He was dressed in a shell suit and gleaming trainers, but looked stiff and pained. His nose had been strapped, the eyes still puffy and bruised.

'How are you?' Clarke asked.

'I've felt better.' He spoke quietly, as if each word hurt.

'Cracked ribs, I hear.'

'They've got me in some sort of corset thing.' His eyes had settled on Fox, who stood hands in pockets at Clarke's shoulder.

'You're looking a lot better than last time we met,' Christie commented. Fox's face remained stony. 'If you're wondering about the dining chair, it's better for me than an armchair. But go ahead and make yourselves comfortable.'

They settled side by side on the sofa. Christie lifted a hand slowly, rubbing it across his hair, hair that needed a wash. There was stubble on his chin and cheeks, and the knuckles of his left hand were grazed.

'Lost a tooth, too,' he told them. 'Hence the whistling.' He tried for a grin, so they could see the gap.

'We've asked up and down the street,' Clarke said. 'Nobody saw or heard anything, and the few bits of CCTV we've collected don't seem to have caught whoever did it. That's why we're hoping you can help.'

'Sorry to disappoint. Whoever it was, they were lying in wait, maybe round the back of the house or the side of the garage. Security light was triggered when I drove in, so that didn't alert me. They came up behind me and hit me across the head. I went down and was in the Land of Nod before they got to work.'

'You think it was a pro?'

'Don't you?'

'Leads me to my next question – any idea who might have it in for you?'

'I've not a single enemy in the world, DI Clarke.'

'Not even Big Ger Cafferty?' Fox broke in, earning a stern sideways glance from Clarke.

'It wasn't Cafferty – not in the flesh. I'd have heard him wheezing with the effort.'

'You reckon one assailant or two?' Clarke asked.

'One would have done the job. I'm not the brawniest. Last time I saw a gym was high school.'

'Fallen out with any associates recently?'

The question had come from Fox. Christie looked at him. 'Know why I stopped travelling with a posse? It was because I didn't need them. Like I say, no enemies.'

'Plus everyone knows that if they touch you, they're also messing with Joe Stark and his outfit. I'm surprised he's not hopped over from Glasgow with grapes and Lucozade.'

'Joe had nothing to do with this.' Christie shifted in his chair, his mouth twisting at a sudden stab of pain.

'We know about your car tyres and the bin being set on fire,' Clarke stated. 'If this is an individual who's out to get you, they're probably not going to stop. Best-case scenario: they're just trying to put a scare on you for some reason.'

'That's a real comfort, DI Clarke.'

'You need to think about your family as well as yourself, Darryl.'

'I never *stop* thinking about my family!'

'Then you might want to move them out for the duration.'

Christie nodded slowly. 'I might just do that, thanks.'

'And you may not think you need a posse, but one or two bodies wouldn't go amiss – close by you through the day and sentry duty here at night. We'll have patrol cars tour the neighbourhood at regular intervals, at least for a day or two.'

Christie kept nodding. 'It's almost as if you care,' he said eventually, eyes flitting from Clarke to Fox.

'Just doing our job,' Clarke stated. 'Though without your co-operation, that may not be quite enough to stop another attack.'

'Or even an escalation,' Fox added.

'I thought I *was* cooperating?' Christie pretended to complain.

'Line of work you're in, Darryl,' Clarke said, getting to her feet, 'if you don't have enemies, you're doing something wrong. I know you're hurting right now and probably not taking the painkillers

49

because you want your head clear – that way you can think hard about the list of candidates. So a word of advice: don't start a war. You can bring *us* the names, let *us* check them out. It won't be a sign of weakness, I promise. Quite the opposite.' She was standing in front of him, hands clasped. 'And maybe get those fake cameras switched for real ones, okay?'

'Whatever you say, DI Clarke.'

Clarke made to leave the room, Fox a few steps behind. When he risked a glance in Christie's direction, Christie gave the slyest of winks. Fox's face remained impassive as he followed Clarke out of the house.

'I thought I told you not to do any talking?' she muttered.

'Couldn't help myself, sorry.'

Clarke unlocked her car but didn't get in. She stood on the pavement instead, staring at the house she'd just left.

'Did we learn anything useful?' Fox asked.

'I thought he was maybe trying to become Cafferty,' Clarke obliged. 'Turns out that's not what this house is.'

'What is it, then?'

'Who do you think decorated that room and bought all the chintz?'

'His mother?'

Clarke nodded. 'That's who it's all for. He might have kept his dad's surname, but Darryl's heart belongs to Mummy . . .'

Day Three

5

'You weren't kidding about the rolls,' Rebus said, taking another bite.

'Bacon just the right side of crispy,' Robert Chatham agreed.

They were seated across from one another at a booth with padded seats and a Formica-topped table. Mugs of dark-brown tea and plates in front of them, Radio Forth belting out from the kitchen.

'Sorry if I was a bit ragged last night,' Chatham went on. 'Wasn't expecting to hear of Maria Turquand ever again. You've seen the photos of her? Wasn't she a stunner?'

'She was.'

'Brainy, too – studied Latin and Greek.'

'And Ancient History,' Rebus added, to show that he too had done his homework.

'Probably never should have got married – bit too much wildness about her.'

'Likely frowned upon in John Turquand's world.'

Chatham nodded as he chewed. 'Problem we had was, a lot of the bit-part players had died. No way we could confirm anything by asking hotel staff or guests. And, thirty years having passed, the ones we *did* track down had forgotten anything they used to know. Place was a melee that day, too – comings and goings, reporters who'd booked interviews with Collier or were chancing to luck that they'd get near him. Then there were the fans, who were either standing outside chanting his name or else dodging into the foyer and making for the stairs.' Chatham took a slurp of tea. 'We had a computer guy try plotting a 3D plan of the foyer and all the people who might have seen the killer enter or leave, but there were too many variables. In the end, he gave up.'

'What about the press photographers?'

Chatham nodded slowly. 'We looked at everything we could find. Even got a couple of Collier's diehard fans to hand over stuff they'd shot on the street outside.' He made a zero with thumb and forefinger.

'So if you couldn't place either Maria's lover or her husband at the scene, did you begin to give a bit more credence to Vince Brady's version?'

'All Brady said was that Collier had been chatting to the victim in the third-floor corridor. Collier denied it, and turned out there was some bad blood between him and Brady. He's dead, you know.'

'Vince Brady?'

'Last year. Third or fourth heart attack, I think.' Chatham put down the remains of his roll, wiped his fingers on a serviette and looked at Rebus. 'Why the sudden interest? Has something happened?'

Instead of answering, Rebus had another question ready. 'How about the husband and the lover – did you interview them?'

'Turquand and Attwood? You've seen the files, you tell me.'

'Not everything makes it into the official account.'

Chatham gave a thin smile. 'I did have a word with both, as it happens – off the record.'

'Why off the record?'

'Because we were supposed to focus on Brady and Collier. Top brass didn't think it worth looking much further. But you'll remember that one of the room-service staff said he saw a man who looked a bit like Peter Attwood.'

'He couldn't be certain, though.'

Chatham nodded. 'And Attwood's story was that he had broken it off with Maria – not that he'd told her. Took the coward's way out: left her waiting in her room for him to show up, while he was busy elsewhere with her replacement.'

'He's all class.'

'When I saw him eight years ago, he was happily married with a first grandkid on the way. Said he was "another man" back in the seventies.'

'He's still in the land of the living?'

'No idea. I don't always pore over the obituaries.'

'What about John Turquand?'

54

'Retired and living in a castle in Perthshire. Likes his hunting, shooting and fishing. Always supposing he's not kicked the bucket.'

'Did he ever marry again?'

'Threw himself into his work instead. Made his millions and started to spend them.'

'Life turned out pretty well for the two main suspects.'

'Didn't it though? And Bruce Collier does a bit of touring still, too.'

'I heard he was living back up here.'

'Townhouse in Rutland Square, though you're more likely to find him at one of his other homes – Barbados and Cape Town, I think I read.'

'Rutland Square?'

'I smiled at that, too. Practically next door to the Caley. Reckon it means anything?'

'I don't know. Probably not. Wonder if he still hangs out with his old pal Dougie Vaughan.'

'Ah, there's another thing – according to Vince Brady, Collier made him hand over one of his room keys to Dougie Vaughan.'

'Yes, I read that. Any idea why?'

'So Vaughan could take a nap if the need arose. Hanging out seemed to involve quite a lot of booze.'

Rebus's eyes narrowed. 'Brady had the room next to Maria Turquand,' he stated.

'Right.'

'And Vaughan had a key.'

'Sort of – he said he vaguely remembered a key but didn't know which room it was for or what happened to it. He swears he never went anywhere other than Bruce Collier's suite.' Chatham pushed his plate to one side and leaned across the table. 'You know there were connecting doors?'

'What?'

'Between Maria's room and Vince Brady's. Don't bother checking – the hotel did away with them years back. Solid walls now, not so solid back then.'

'And Vaughan and the victim had had a bit of a fling.'

'He still swears he never saw her that day.'

'How about Vince Brady's alibi?'

'He was running around like a mad thing, backwards and forwards to the Usher Hall to check on the crew and the programme stall. A dozen or more people confirmed talking to him in a dozen places.'

'He must have been in his room some of the time, though.'

'Agreed, but he didn't hear or see anything.'

'Apart from Maria Turquand in the hallway with Bruce Collier.'

'Apart from that, yes.'

Rebus thought for a moment. 'One last thing – did a Russian crop up at all?'

Chatham's brow furrowed. 'A Russian?'

'Anywhere you can think of.'

Chatham shook his head and the two men drank their tea in silence for a moment.

'So what's this all about?' Chatham enquired.

'It's just a feeling I got, right back at the start of the original investigation. The feeling we were missing something, not seeing something.'

'And it's taken you until now to revisit that?'

'I've been a bit busy. I'm not so busy these days.'

Chatham nodded his understanding. 'When I retired, it took a while to change gears.'

'How did you do it?'

'The love of a good woman. Plus I got the doorman job, and I go to the gym.' He gestured towards his plate. 'That's an occasional treat, and I can work it off this afternoon.'

'I've got a dog I can walk.' Rebus paused. 'And a good woman.'

'Spend more time with both of them then. Learn to let go.'

Rebus nodded his agreement. 'This is going to take me a while to digest,' he said.

'Same here.' Chatham thumped his chest with one hand.

'I didn't mean the bacon. Though now that I think of it, that too. Thanks for seeing me.'

The two men shook hands across the table.

'Back so soon?'

Unsure of the protocol, Fox had been loitering in the doorway of the HMRC section, waiting to catch Sheila Graham's eye. It had worked eventually and she was now standing in front of him.

'So you've either brought news,' she began, folding her arms, 'or else decided it's a waste of time.'

'I just think I need a bit more of a briefing. In fact, ideally I'd like to see what you've already got on Christie.'

'Why?'

'So I don't end up telling you what you already know.'

She studied him, her face impassive. Eventually she managed a smile. 'Let me buy you a coffee,' she said.

There was a stall in a corner of the ground-floor atrium, so they queued there, taking their drinks to one of the breakout areas – basically comfy seating separated by a small circular table.

'So what have you learned so far?' Graham asked.

'Christie's been targeted before – car and rubbish bin. There's no CCTV of the attack and none of the neighbours could help. So we're looking for possible enemies, without getting much help from the victim.'

'Is he recovering?'

'At home,' Fox acknowledged. 'I saw him last night.'

'You saw him?'

'DI Clarke went to question him and I tagged along.'

'But he knows you, yes?'

'I didn't say I was working at Gartcosh these days.'

'He couldn't already know?'

'I think he would have said something, just so I'd know he knew.'

'We don't want him to twig that we're digging into his affairs,' Graham cautioned.

'He must have an inkling, though.'

Graham considered this. 'Maybe,' she conceded.

'I also took a look at both his betting shops. Nothing struck me as out of the ordinary.'

'Which two?'

'They're both called Diamond Joe's.' Fox paused. 'Why?'

'There's a third, though you won't find Christie's name on any paperwork. And to be honest, I doubt you'd notice anything unusual, even if money was being laundered under your nose.'

'How's that then?'

'Fixed-odds machines – usually roulette. Losses can be minimised to around four per cent. When you finish playing, you print out a ticket and exchange it for cash at the counter. They give you a receipt, so if you're ever found with a suspiciously large pile of notes, you've got evidence it's legit.'

'So basically the bookie is charging a four per cent fee?'

'A cheap way of cleaning up dirty money. You can send thousands an hour through each and every machine. They're busy trying to change the law in Brussels – any winnings over two thousand euros will need to include the recipient's details. The industry over here is fighting against it.'

'If someone's hogging a machine hour after hour, feeding in thousands, surely the cashier notices?'

'Often they don't, or aren't particularly bothered. Then again, if the person who owns the shop is in on the scam . . .'

'Like Darryl Christie, you mean?'

She nodded slowly. 'But there's a lot more to Mr Christie than that.'

'Oh?'

Her face hardened. 'This goes no further, Malcolm.' She edged forward on her seat, and he did the same. There was no one within twenty feet of them, but Graham dropped her voice anyway.

'The betting shop I'm talking about is called Klondyke Alley. There happens to be a one-bedroom flat above it that is probably also owned by Christie.'

'I'm listening.'

'Do you know what SLPs are?'

'No.'

'Maybe I should show you, then.' She seemed to have made her mind up. Springing to her feet, she grabbed her coffee and told him to do the same. He followed her back to the HMRC section, where they found a spare chair and pulled it over to her desk. There were a few questioning looks from Graham's colleagues, so she introduced Fox.

'Relax,' she said. 'He's almost one of us.'

She got busy on her keyboard until a page-long list appeared onscreen.

'Scottish limited partnerships. Guess how many of them are registered at the flat above Klondyke Alley?'

Fox's eyes narrowed. 'All of these?'

Graham had clicked her mouse several times, and the list kept growing. 'Over five hundred,' she stated. 'Five hundred companies that give their business address as a one-bedroom flat in Leith.'

'I'm hoping you're going to tell me why.'

'They're shell companies, Malcolm. A way of hiding assets and moving them around the globe. Try tracking the actual owners and you usually end up in some offshore tax haven like the British Virgin Islands or the Caymans, jurisdictions that aren't exactly forthcoming when the UK tax authorities start asking questions. There's a new law coming in. UK owners will have to reveal who the real beneficiaries are, though whether we'll be able to trust that information is a moot point. For now though, SLPs are a great way of hiding who you are and what the hell you're doing.'

'And Darryl Christie runs this whole thing?'

Graham shook her head. 'The flat is rented from Christie by a corporate services provider called Brough Consulting.'

'No relation to the private bank?'

'Not quite. Brough Consulting is one man, Anthony Brough, grandson of Sir Magnus, who ran Brough's until it was bought by one of the Big Five.'

'How close is he to Darryl?'

'*Quite* close.'

'So these shell companies ... they're like an extension of the money laundering?'

'That's what we're trying to find out. It's a hideous paper trail that happens to be mostly electronic. So we sit here all day, working our way from one company to the next, one beneficial owner to the next, trying to find real flesh-and-blood people hiding in the margins of a hundred thousand transactions.' She looked at him. 'It *is* proper detective work, you see. Except we tend to call it forensic accounting.'

'Have you made anything stick yet?'

'Against Brough Consulting? We'd be popping the champagne if we had.'

'Getting close, though?'

'We thought maybe Darryl Christie would lead us somewhere.'

'But that hasn't happened.' Fox thought for a moment. 'Could any of these shell companies have some beef with Darryl?'

'We've no way of knowing.'

'You can't intercept his emails and phone calls?'

'Not without the say-so from upstairs. And probably a doubling of resources – has news reached you that we're supposed to be tightening our belts? This is Austerity Britain we're living in.' She swivelled in her chair so her knees brushed his. 'You need to keep this to yourself, Malcolm, remember that. Even if it starts to have some bearing on the assault case, you talk to me before you start sharing with your pals back in Edinburgh.'

'Understood,' Fox said. 'And thanks. It means a lot that you would trust me.'

'There's more I could tell you, but it would probably go over your head – some of it goes above mine.'

'Numbers were never my strong point.'

'But you can balance a chequebook – that's what you said at our first meeting.'

'Maybe I exaggerated a little.' He jabbed a finger towards his cheek. 'Good poker face, remember?'

Graham smiled again. 'You're heading back to Edinburgh?' She watched Fox nod. 'Quid pro quo, then – don't leave me out of the loop.'

'I won't,' Fox said.

'So where does the inquiry go next?'

'That's DI Clarke's call.' His phone was vibrating in his jacket. He dug it out and checked the screen. 'Speak of the devil,' he said, opening the text message. Graham saw his eyebrows arch in surprise.

'Something?' she asked.

'Something,' he acknowledged, turning the phone towards her so she could read what was there.

We've got a confession.

'You better skedaddle, then,' Graham said. 'And be sure to phone me with the news.'

'I'll do that,' Fox said, deserting the remains of his coffee as he headed for the door.

6

A solitary journalist stood guard on the pavement outside Gayfield Square police station. Her name was Laura Smith and she was the crime correspondent for the *Scotsman*.

'I'm freezing half to death here, DI Fox,' she complained as he made to pass her.

'No comment, Ms Smith.'

'It's not like I haven't done you favours in the past.'

'It's DI Clarke you should be pestering.'

'She's not answering her phone.'

'Probably because she's got nothing to say. And isn't a mugging a bit pedestrian for a crime reporter?'

'Not when you bear in mind who the victim is.'

'Local entrepreneur Darryl Christie?'

She smiled. 'Don't worry, my paper's lawyers will make sure I don't say anything that could get us into trouble.'

'That's good, because I dare say Mr Christie has lawyers, too.'

'Just give me a sentence – I can quote you as "police sources".'

'I've got nothing for you, Laura. But I'll put in a word with DI Clarke.'

'Cross your heart?'

'I wouldn't want you suing me for breach of promise.'

He opened the door and went in, past the reception desk, punching in the code for the inner door, then along the narrow corridor to the interview rooms. No doubting which one contained the confessor – a huddle of uniforms had gathered next to it, whispering and listening.

Fox hadn't been lying to Laura Smith – he'd tried phoning Clarke for clarification, but without any luck. Now he asked the most senior of the constables for the story.

'Walked up to one of the beat officers, said he needed to tell him something.'

'Where was this?'

'A Greggs on South Bridge. Carrying a shopping bag and looking like he needed hosing down. Officer played along, asked him what he'd done. He said he'd whacked Darryl Christie around the head, given his ribs a few kicks for good measure.'

'Probably a nutter,' another uniform offered.

'Specific injuries haven't been mentioned anywhere, though, have they?' the older constable said.

'Hospital would know. Family and neighbours, too. Word has a way of getting out.'

'Is there a lawyer on the way?' Fox queried.

'Says he doesn't want one. Not been charged yet anyway.'

'So who's in there with him? DI Clarke?'

'And DC Esson.'

Fox stared hard at the door, with its signage switched from VACANT to IN USE. The surface of the door was heavily scored, its paintwork chipped away. Fox was wondering if he could just march in. He *could*, of course – it was his right. But if Siobhan was getting answers . . . and if the man inside clammed up, spell broken by the interruption . . .

'Has he got a name?' he asked instead.

'Officer he spoke to must have got it, but he's off writing up his report.'

'Will he mention that he was queuing for doughnuts at Greggs at the time?'

'Man's got to eat,' the older constable said, as if dispensing the wisdom of the ages. 'And it was a steak bake, to be exact.'

There was a noise from inside and the door opened, catching them by surprise. Like all the doors, it opened outwards, so that no one left inside could attempt a barricade. The edge of the door caught one of the uniforms a glancing blow to his shoulder. He let out a yelp as Christine Esson emerged.

'Serves you right,' she said, in place of apologising. Siobhan Clarke was right behind her. She spotted Fox and gestured for him to follow as she made for the stairs to the CID suite. Esson meantime was telling the uniforms to make themselves useful – two to keep an eye on the man still seated in the interview room, another to fetch him something to drink and eat.

'He pongs to high heaven,' Clarke informed Fox, sucking in gulps of fresh air.

'Vagrant?'

'Not as such. Lives in Craigmillar. Unemployed. His name's William Shand. William Crawford Shand.'

'And he knows about the cracked ribs?'

Clarke glanced back at him. 'News travels.'

'Unless you happen to be Laura Smith.'

'Laura can wait.' Clarke walked into the office, met Ronnie Ogilvie's eyes and stabbed a finger towards DCI Page's door.

'He's not in,' Ogilvie stated. He noticed Fox staring at his moustache.

'Is that new?' Fox asked. Ogilvie nodded. 'Not sure it suits you, Ronnie.'

'I hate to interrupt a burgeoning bromance,' Clarke said, eyes fixed on Ogilvie, 'but any idea where he's gone?'

'The DCI? Pen-pushers' meeting at Fettes.'

Clarke sighed and pinched the bridge of her nose. 'I need to get his okay,' she muttered.

'Okay for what?' Fox asked.

'There's a civilian Shand wants us to hook him up with. Says *he's* the one he wants to confess to. Bit of history between them, it seems. Not sure I can let that happen without the DCI's say-so.'

Fox was staring at her. 'Your tone of voice makes me think I know who the civilian is.'

Clarke raised her eyes to the ceiling as the name burst from Malcolm Fox's lips.

'Rebus.'

'Tell me Laura isn't still outside,' Clarke said as she led Rebus along the corridor.

'Of course she is.'

Clarke cursed under her breath. 'What did you tell her?'

'Said I was meeting an old friend.' Rebus turned towards her. 'How are you, anyway?'

'I've been better.'

'Two things you need to know, Siobhan.'

'I'm listening.'

'One, everybody knows him as Craw. I doubt he's been called William by anyone other than sheriffs and bailiffs.'

'He's got previous?'

'See, that brings me to my second point – you've been sold a pup. A cursory examination of the records would have told you that Craw's notorious for handing himself in whenever something big hits the news.'

'We ran him through the system – clean as a whistle the past five years.'

'Then he's slid back into his old ways.' They had reached the interview room, where Fox waited. Rebus shook his hand. 'What brings you here, Malcolm?'

'Curiosity.'

'Well, you're in the right place – the gent behind that door is a one-man freak show.' Rebus reached for the handle, then paused. 'Best if I do this on my own.'

'Are you forgetting you're not CID any more?' Clarke said.

'Even so . . .'

'It's a deal-breaker, John. There has to be someone in there representing Police Scotland.'

Rebus looked from Clarke to Fox and back again. 'Then I'll let the pair of you toss a coin.' Having said which, he pulled open the door and strode in.

Craw Shand was seated at the narrow table, toying with a sandwich consisting of two thin slices of white bread and a thinner layer of orange processed cheese. There was an inch of tea left in the polystyrene cup, a scum beginning to form on it. Rebus wafted a hand in front of him.

'Jeezo, Craw. When was the last time you saw soap?' He gestured for the uniformed officers to leave. Without bothering to ask who Rebus was, they did as ordered.

Still got it, John.

'All right, Mr Rebus?' Craw said. His teeth were blackened, his hair – what was left of it – thin and greasy against his scalp. 'Been a while, eh?'

'Best part of twenty years, Craw.'

'Not that long, surely?'

Rebus dragged the metal chair out from the table and sat down. 'Didn't they tell you? I'm retired these days.'

'Is that right?'

'Reckoned it was safe to retreat from the fray – thought the likes of you had got tired of playing games.'

'No games today, Mr Rebus.'

'Then there's a first time for everything.'

Craw Shand's eyes were milky as he stared at the man across from him. 'Remember Johnny Bible, Mr Rebus?'

'Sure.'

'Craigmillar cop shop. You were the one who interrogated me.'

'We don't interrogate these days, Craw – it's called an interview.'

'You were tough but fair.'

'I'd like to think so.'

'Right up to the point where you pushed me to the floor and half strangled me.'

'My memory's not so good these days, Craw.'

Craw Shand offered a grin. 'You remember, though.'

'Maybe I do and maybe I don't. What's that got to do with Darryl Christie?'

Both men turned as the door was opened again and Clarke stalked in. Fox could be glimpsed in the corridor, wanting a view of Shand. Clarke pulled the door closed just as Rebus was offering a wave.

'You've not told me,' Rebus continued, 'why it was me you needed to speak to. As I've been saying, DI Clarke here is perfectly competent.'

'It was that memory of Craigmillar. I just thought I'd like to see you again.'

'In case I dished out more of the same? Sorry to disappoint you, Craw, but we're both in our sixties now and the world's got a new set of rules.' Rebus made show of studying his watch. 'I've a dominoes tournament starting in an hour, so I'd be obliged if we could keep this businesslike.'

'I hit him.'

'Hit who?'

'His name's Darryl Christie. He lives in a big house by the Botanic Gardens.'

'That's good, Craw. Matches every online article about what happened.'

'He was getting out of his car – a white Range Rover. I snuck up behind him and hit him.'

'With what?'

'A length of wood. It was lying to the side of the garage. That's where I waited.'

'In the dark, aye?'

'Security lights came on as I walked up the driveway, but nobody came out of the house.'

'You weren't worried about the CCTV?'

'We all know those things are next to useless.'

'Why did you do it, Craw? Why pick that particular victim?'

'I was just angry.'

'About what, though?'

'People with money. People with too much – the big houses and everything. I'm just sick of them.'

'So you'd done this before?'

'I'd thought about it many a time.'

'But never carried it through?' Rebus watched as Craw Shand shook his head. He leaned back on the hard metal seat.

'You're sure the car was white?'

'Lights went on again as it came up the drive.'

'Were the gates locked when you got there?'

'Gate to the footpath wasn't. Driveway gates started opening as the car came near.'

Rebus looked to Clarke, who raised one eyebrow. So far, the man could not be faulted.

'What did you do with the piece of wood?'

'Tossed it.'

'Where?'

'Inverleith Park somewhere.'

'That's a fair stretch of land, Craw. Might take us a lot of man hours to find it.'

Shand perked up at this thought.

'That's supposing we were to believe you, of course. And I think you're the lying toerag you always were.' Rebus got up from his chair and walked around the table until he was standing behind Shand. He could feel the man tense.

'Same fucking games you've always played,' he growled. 'Just because it gets that chipolata in your manky Y-fronts hard. Playtime's over, pal. Time you headed back to your hovel and your online porn.'

'I'm telling you, I did it!'

'And I'm telling you to get the hell out of this interview room before we have to phone Rentokil!'

'John,' Clarke cautioned. She had been resting against a wall, but took a few steps towards the table. Then, to Shand: 'Can you add to your description, Craw? The house, the car, how events played out?'

'I hit him over the head from behind,' Shand recited. 'Then I leaned over him and gave him a punch in the face. Stood back up and kicked him in the ribs a few times – I forget how many. A last kick to the nose and that was that.'

'Just for being rich?'

'Exactly.'

Rebus placed a hand on one of Shand's shoulders, causing him to flinch. 'We should give the news to Christie. Case closed. We can all go home, and Craw here can go to Saughton nick, where there'll be a small but perfectly formed price on his head.' He paused, leaning in closer to Shand's left ear. 'You know who Darryl Christie is, Craw?'

'He owns a hotel.'

'They said that in the papers too, but what they forgot to mention was that he's taken over from Big Ger Cafferty. Maybe let that sink in, eh?' He straightened up, glancing towards Siobhan Clarke, but she was focusing on the seated figure.

'Anything else, Mr Shand? Anything you specifically remember?'

Shand's eyes widened. 'The bin by the back door – half of one of its sides was melted away!' He looked from Clarke to Rebus and back again, almost in triumph at the memory. Clarke, however, had eyes only for Rebus.

'Give me a reason not to charge him,' she said.

Rebus pursed his lips. 'Seems like my work here is done.' He gripped Craw Shand's shoulder again. 'Good luck, Craw. I really mean that. It's taken you half a lifetime, but you've done it at last. God help you . . .'

Rebus was seated in the back room of the Oxford Bar. Darkness had fallen and the early-evening crowd downstairs at the bar itself was in good humour. Rebus sipped his drink, turning his head to the window when he heard a tapping sound. It was one of the regulars, who had gone outside for a smoke. He was signalling for Rebus to join him, but Rebus shook his head. He'd had a coughing fit in the toilet five minutes back, hawking gobbets into the sink then running the tap, rinsing away the evidence before dabbing sweat from his brow while thinking that next time maybe he'd remember to bring his inhaler. His face in the mirror told its own story, with little to indicate that the ending would be happy.

Clarke had texted, interested in his whereabouts, so he wasn't surprised when she climbed the steps from the bar area and peered around the doorway.

'It's Malcolm's round,' she informed him. Rebus shook his head, his hand resting on the glass in front of him.

Eventually Fox appeared, carrying Clarke's gin and tonic and a tomato juice. They pulled out chairs and sat opposite Rebus.

'What the hell's that?' Fox couldn't help asking.

'It's called a half,' Rebus said, hoisting the small glass and swirling it.

'Denise behind the bar tried warning me, but I thought she was joking.'

'John's watching himself,' Clarke explained.

'Is this Deborah Quant's doing?'

'At least *I* still take a drink,' Rebus said, receiving a mock toast from Fox in response. Rebus turned his attention to Clarke. 'You really think Craw Shand's suddenly become a ninja?'

'How does he know about the bin?'

'Maybe he heard something. Maybe he went over there and checked the place out.'

Clarke savoured the first taste of her drink, saying nothing.

'You're really going to charge him?'

'The DCI can't see good reason not to.'

'Then you have to convince him he's wrong. Does Christie know we've got Craw in custody?'

'He's been informed an arrest has been made.'

'And?'

'Mr Shand's name was not unfamiliar to him.'

'Craw always did like a dodgy pub, and Darryl owns a few of those.'

'He says they've never spoken or had any business . . .'

Malcolm Fox cleared his throat, signalling an interruption. 'Shand says he chose a victim at random, yes? So it's neither here nor there if they know one another.'

Rebus glared at him. 'Malcolm, Craw Shand could no more beat someone up than I could swim the Forth. He's in his sixties, weighs about the same as a scarecrow, and moves like someone's stuck a pole up his arse.'

'Plus,' Clarke added, 'he didn't know about the slashed tyres, added to which he swears he didn't torch the bin. On the other hand, he knows too much for this to be one of his usual stories . . .'

'Agreed,' Rebus eventually conceded. 'Which is why we're back to the point I made earlier – he's been hearing things, or he scoped the place out. He needs questioning about both of those. He also needs to be warned what this is going to mean for him now Darryl Christie's got his name.'

'Then he's safer in custody, wouldn't you agree?'

'Only if he's in solitary.'

They sat in silence for a few moments, concentrating on their drinks. There was another tap at the window, a further invitation for Rebus to step outside. He shook his head and mouthed, 'No.'

'Am I really seeing this?' Fox said. 'You've packed in the cigs?'

'Call it a trial separation,' Rebus replied.

'Bloody hell. I need to sell my tobacco shares.'

'I think it's great,' Clarke said.

'Though it wipes out about the only hobby he had,' Fox countered.

Clarke turned to Rebus. 'Speaking of which . . .'

'What?'

'The files I gave you – any help?'

'Some.'

'What's this?' Fox enquired.

'John's looking at a society murder from the 1970s. Wish I'd been around at the time, actually.'

Rebus stared at her. 'You studied the contents before handing it over?'

'Just the summary. But then I went online. There's not much, but a few writers have used it in books about famous crimes.'

'So tell me,' Fox said.

'Woman by the name of Maria Turquand,' Clarke recited. 'Had a string of lovers behind her husband's back. He was the wealthy banker type, worked for Sir Magnus Brough. Maria ended up strangled in a bedroom at the Caledonian Hotel. Her latest lover – one of hubby's old pals – was chief suspect until another of his conquests provided an alibi. But the hotel was filled to bursting with musicians, hangers-on and the media. You've heard of Bruce Collier?'

'I don't think so,' Fox confided.

'That's because you don't like music. He was huge at the time. Local success story who'd come home to headline the Usher Hall. Story was, he'd been seen chatting up Maria. Pal of his was around, too – and Maria had bedded *him* in the past. Then there was the road manager . . .' She looked to Rebus for the name.

'Vince Brady,' he obliged. 'Whose room was next to Maria's. And there were connecting doors.'

69

'I didn't know that,' Clarke said.

'I had a word with Robert Chatham.'

'Who's Robert Chatham?' Fox asked.

'Ex-CID,' Rebus explained. 'Now retired. He headed a cold-case review a few years back.'

'And this has come on to your radar because . . .?'

'As you rightly said, a man needs a hobby.'

Fox nodded his understanding. 'Sir Magnus Brough was the power behind Brough's, wasn't he? The private bank?'

'That's right.'

'Is he still around?'

'Long dead.'

'The bank got sold on, didn't it? Any family members still involved?'

Rebus was staring at him. 'I've never been a customer. What's this about, Malcolm?'

Fox's mouth twitched. 'Nothing.'

'Liar.'

'You're amongst friends here,' Clarke added, leaning in towards him so their shoulders touched.

'Really?' he asked, his eyes fixing on her.

'Really,' she stated, while Rebus nodded his confirmation.

'It's just that his name came up,' Fox eventually confided.

'At Gartcosh?'

It was Fox's turn to nod. 'Not Sir Magnus, but his grandson.'

'In connection with what?'

'I can't tell you that.'

'Why?'

'Operational reasons.'

Rebus and Clarke shared a look. 'I keep forgetting,' Rebus drawled, 'that you move in higher circles than us these days, Malcolm. Got to keep all the good stuff locked away. Wouldn't do for lesser mortals to get a taste – might go to our heads.'

'It's not that I don't trust you – either of you. But I was sworn to secrecy. And by the way, the fact that you've not asked me why I'm back in the city tells me Siobhan's already told you. I'm not sure I like being ganged up on.'

'Aye, well. It's nice to know where we all stand, eh, Siobhan?'

Fox's shoulders had grown hunched as he gripped his near-empty glass, head angled over it.

'I'm sure Malcolm knows what he's doing,' Clarke replied coldly.

'First time for everything,' Rebus agreed.

Clarke had finished her drink. She started to get to her feet. 'You sticking around, John? I could give you a lift.'

'A lift home would do the trick,' Rebus said, lifting up the coat folded next to him.

'What about me?' Fox complained. 'My car's back at Gayfield Square.'

Clarke was already heading for the doorway. 'You,' she called back towards him, 'can bloody well walk.'

'It'll do you good,' Rebus added as he passed, patting the top of Fox's head.

Every Edinburgh pothole was torture, even in a car with the suspension of Darryl Christie's Range Rover. He sat in the passenger seat, trying not to flinch. Harry, his driver, had the knack of finding the road surface's every bump and crater. But eventually they reached Merchiston – probably not by the fastest route, as Harry was relying on the sat nav.

'Which house?' he was asking Christie now.

'Number twenty.'

'This one then.' Harry slammed on the brake, producing a gasp of pain from beside him.

'Sorry, Darryl. You okay?'

But Christie was paying him no heed. Instead he was staring at the For Sale sign. Slowly he clambered from the car, straightening up with effort. Then he pushed open the gate and walked down the path. No lights on within. One set of curtains open, allowing him a view of a gutted drawing room.

'You thinking of buying?' Harry asked.

'Go back to the car and wait there,' Christie snapped.

He walked down the driveway – so like his own – towards the rear of the property. A sensor picked him up and a light came on, illuminating the garden with its separate coach house, where Cafferty's one-time bodyguard had slept. Cafferty had paid the man off eventually, services no longer required. A red light blinked from the alarm box above the back door. Christie reckoned it would not be fake.

His phone buzzed in his pocket and he lifted it out. Joe Stark was calling him. He pressed the phone to his ear.

'What can I do for you, Joe?'

'I heard you got jumped.'

'It's no biggie.'

'Trust me, it's a biggie – means every fucker knows you *can* be jumped.'

'I'm dealing with it.'

'You better be.'

'And I appreciate your concern.'

'My *concern*?' Stark's voice was rising as Christie retraced his steps down the driveway. 'All I'm concerned about is my fucking money – when do I get it?'

'Soon, Joe, soon.'

'You better hope I believe you, son.'

'Have I ever let you down?'

'Saying that gets us nowhere, Darryl. I've already gone easy on you.'

'Are you saying you ordered that thumping?'

'You'd be talking through a wired jaw at the very least if I had. Money or your head, son. Money or your head.'

The phone went dead. Christie dropped it back into his pocket. Harry was holding the gate open for him.

'Back to the ranch, boss? Or do you fancy a drink somewhere?'

'I'm going home,' Christie stated. But he paused before getting into the car, turning to cast his eye over Cafferty's old house again.

You thinking of buying?

He wondered what his mother would say to that . . .

Day Four

7

The previous night, Rebus had taken Brillo for a late walk on Bruntsfield Links before settling down at the dining table and opening his laptop, searching for the name Anthony Brough. All of this after Siobhan Clarke had dropped him off.

'I mean it about Craw,' Rebus had reminded her. 'He's a dead man walking unless you can convince Darryl he's not the one.'

'I'll do what I can. But remand's probably not going to be an option, not even if he's charged.'

'Then hold him for psychological assessment.'

'It would be nice to have a more likely suspect in our sights.'

'Has anyone spoken to Joe Stark?'

'I thought Joe and Darryl were buddies?'

'Which should have given Darryl an extra layer of protection. But since that's not been the case . . .'

'They've had a falling-out and this is by way of Joe's punishment?'

Rebus had shrugged. 'Got to be worth a look, no?'

Just as he'd thought Sir Magnus Brough's grandson worth a look. In fact, he had dug out everything he could on the Brough family and its banking fiefdom. Established towards the end of the eighteenth century, a lot of its initial success coming from the financing of trade – slaves to America, cotton and tobacco back to the UK. From the Fife coalfields to tea plantations in India, via fine wines from Bordeaux, Brough's had been there. It had fallen out of family control for a brief period immediately post-war, but Sir Magnus had come in as a junior partner and worked his way up until he owned the whole operation. Rebus had wondered: what sort of man did you have to be to do that? He had found his answer in a handful of online essays and chapters from economic histories – ruthless, rapacious, hands-on, determined and tireless.

Sir Magnus's son had been none of these things, and had turned his back on banking, preferring to holiday the year round in far-flung destinations. Jimmy Brough had settled down eventually, marrying Lisanne Bentley. Two kids, Anthony and Francesca, both in their thirties now, orphaned in their teens when a car crash did for their parents, leaving Sir Magnus to look after them. Anthony had joined the bank, but hadn't survived the takeover. Drugs had sent Francesca off her rocker and mentions of her dropped away to nothing. But Anthony had set up Anthony Brough Investment Group and Brough Consulting, both of which had their headquarters in Edinburgh.

Rutland Square in Edinburgh, to be exact.

'Small world just got smaller,' Rebus had muttered, heading for bed.

So it was that after an early walk to the corner shop, followed by breakfast for dog and owner both, Rebus watched Brillo settle in his basket in the kitchen then headed out. Traffic towards Tollcross and down Lothian Road was its usual rush-hour crawl, not helped by the equally ubiquitous roadworks. He was starting to think he'd have been quicker walking, but then snorted at the very notion. There was a free parking bay on Rutland Square, so he decided to play the part of dutiful citizen and use it, even feeding a couple of coins into the meter.

From where he stood, he had a good view of one side of the red-stone hotel – the Caley as was. Rutland Square itself comprised four-storey terraces that had probably been residential when built but now had become mainly offices, at least at ground level. He wondered which of them belonged to Bruce Collier, and whether the internet would provide an answer. The elegant stone-pillared façades gave little away, though the occasional worker could be seen through a window, rising from their desk, paperwork in one hand, coffee in the other.

Rebus walked around the square. At its centre, railings protected a patch of neat lawn and a wrought-iron bench, the gate locked, accessible only with a key. A road off to the right led to Shandwick Place, where the passing of a bright new tram was announced by the clanging of its bell. Torphichen Street cop shop was a stone's throw away in the other direction. A couple of taxis sped by, having picked up fares at the hotel. One of the plaques Rebus passed announced that something called the Scottish Arts Club was based behind its door. But mostly he saw evidence that the square's occupiers worked in staid and sensible areas of commerce – chartered surveyors and solicitors, accountants and asset management.

Brough Investment was almost directly opposite the Scottish Arts Club. Rebus climbed its steps. The main door – solid wood, boasting gloss-black paint, polished brass letter box and knocker – stood open. Behind it, a vestibule led to a second door, of opaque glass. There were half a dozen buttons on the intercom, different company names beside each. Rebus studied the one marked ABIG, his finger hovering above it. What would he say? *I'm just wondering why DI Malcolm Fox is so interested in you*?

He smiled to himself. Instead, he stepped back on to the pavement and made a phone call.

'This'll be good,' Fox answered.

'Guess where I am,' Rebus said.

'Wild stab in the dark – Rutland Square.'

Brought up short, Rebus looked to left and right. No sign of Fox or his car. 'Clever lad,' he said, having given himself a moment to recover.

'You seemed too interested last night. No way you were going to let it go.'

'They're teaching you well at Gartcosh.'

'Not well enough, or I wouldn't have brought the name up in the first place.'

'Ready to tell me what this is all about, or should I just ring Brough's bell and ask?'

'Ringing won't help.'

'Why not?'

'He's not there. I phoned twenty minutes ago pretending to be a client. Secretary came in straight away with an apology. Said he'd been cancelling meetings due to being called away.'

'Called away where?' Rebus was studying the windows on each floor of the building.

'Seemed to me she didn't know. I think she's floundering.'

'Do *you* know why he's away?'

'Not really.'

'Meaning you've got an inkling? Maybe we should meet and talk this through.'

'John – no offence, but it's none of your business.'

'That's true, of course.'

'Most men your age would be content to put their feet up or go bet on the horses.' He broke off suddenly and Rebus's brow furrowed. Had Fox just let something slip?

'What is it, Malcolm?'

'Look, I need to call Gartcosh, let them know about Brough.'

'Because he connects to Darryl Christie? That's it, isn't it?'

'I didn't say that.'

'Of course not, Malcolm. Your secret's safe with me.'

Rebus ended the call, and didn't answer when Fox called straight back. He was tapping the corner of the phone against his teeth when a door opened further along the street. The figure who bounded out, unlocking a silver Porsche and manoeuvring himself in, was instantly recognisable, though Rebus had only seen him in photos and on a distant concert stage.

Hello, Bruce, he said to himself, walking towards the space the car had just vacated in a roar no doubt pleasing to its driver. He stopped outside Bruce Collier's front door. More gloss-black paint. But no nameplate of any kind, nothing to indicate that a man with a string of transatlantic number ones called the place home. The ground-floor windows boasted wooden slatted blinds, open enough to allow Rebus a glimpse of the interior. Gaudy paintings on cream walls; white leather sofas and chairs. No gold or platinum discs, and no hi-fi or musical instruments. Flamboyant in his day, Collier had learned to embrace a seemingly quieter life.

Rebus turned to watch as the Porsche exited the square. Quieter, yes, but not quite ready for complete anonymity . . .

Craw Shand had been charged, despite the Fiscal Depute's qualms.

'It's thin stuff, Siobhan,' she had warned.

'I know,' Clarke had acknowledged.

Charged, and then freed on bail. Shand had seemed satisfied with this result, thanking Clarke for her concern when she reminded him to keep his head down and maybe think about not going home for a few days.

'But wouldn't that be breaking my bail conditions?' he had asked.

'Not if you keep checking in at your local police station – trust me.'

He'd even wanted to clasp her by the hand, but she'd drawn it away and shaken her head, watching him as he made his way out on to Gayfield Square, where, thankfully, Laura Smith failed to be lurking.

Clarke got on the phone to Christie's house, where his mother picked up.

'He's not here,' she said. 'But that was quick work, catching the bastard. I'm sorry I doubted you.'

'Well, here's your chance to make amends,' Clarke said. 'I need a word with Darryl.'

'He's at work.'

'Any of his many businesses in particular?'

'The Devil's Dram, I think.'

'Thank you.'

Clarke knew the Devil's Dram. Named for the amount of whisky lost to evaporation in each barrel, it was a nightclub on the Cowgate, just along from the city mortuary. She'd last been inside on a girls' night out, organised by Deborah Quant. She was there within ten minutes, but couldn't find anywhere to park. Eventually she settled on the mortuary itself, tucking her Astra in next to one of the anonymous black vans in the courtyard.

The Cowgate was a canyon of a place, two lanes wide and with narrow pavements, steep gradients leading off. Not too long back, Clarke had chased a murderer up one of those lanes, until the effort got the better of her – not a detail she'd bothered adding to her written report. The graffitied metal doors of the Devil's Dram were locked tight. There were no windows, just stonework, similarly daubed – hard to tell if it was a design feature or the work of vandals. Clarke gave the doors a thump and a kick. Eventually she could hear them being unlocked. A young man was scowling at her, sleeves rolled up, arms colourfully tattooed. His immaculate hair had been swept back from his forehead, and he sported a luxuriant beard.

'You look like you probably work behind the bar,' Clarke commented.

'I *own* the bar,' he corrected her.

'On paper, maybe.' Clarke shoved her warrant card into his face. 'But it's the real boss I'm here to see.'

He managed a sneer but stepped aside eventually, just enough so she could squeeze past into a dimly lit vault that led to the main room. Plastic gargoyles leered from the ceiling, while bearded satyrs cavorted along the walls. Rock music was blaring from the speakers.

'I like a bit of Burt Bacharach in the morning,' Clarke said.

'It's Ninja Horse.'

'Do me a favour then and put it back in the stable.'

With a final sneer, the young man moved off. There was a glass staircase leading to a VIP balcony area directly above the long mirrored bar. As Clarke started to climb, the music cut off abruptly. The place was being readied for the night to come, vacuum cleaners busy, bottles restocked, chairs and stools repositioned. Darryl Christie was watching from his upstairs table, nose still strapped but eyes a bit less swollen, if no less bruised. He had paperwork spread out in front of him, and made show of turning each sheet so it sat blank side up as Clarke approached.

'I'm not Customs and Excise, Darryl,' she pretended to complain.

'Maybe it's my trade secrets I'm hiding – how to build a successful club from nothing.'

There was a glass of sparkling water next to him. He lifted it to his mouth, sipping through a bright red straw, content to wait for what she had to say.

'Craw Shand is back on the street,' she obliged.

'Is that right?'

'If anything happens to him, you'll have me to answer to.'

'The big bad DI Clarke?' Christie stifled a grin. 'Thing I've learned about getting even with someone, it's best to leave a bit of time. Could be weeks, could be months – there's still the anticipation.'

'Is that how it was with the man who killed your sister?'

Christie's cheekbones tightened. 'He killed more than one kid. He was never going to last long in jail.'

'Barlinnie, wasn't it? I'm guessing that means Joe Stark did the organising – his city, his sphere of influence. You and him still close, Darryl?'

'What's it to you, Officer?'

'Just because we've charged Shand doesn't mean we've stopped looking. That includes everyone you know, friend or foe.'

'So you'll have pulled Cafferty in, then?'

'Maybe after we talk to Joe Stark.'

'You can talk till you're blue in the face, won't make the slightest difference.' He was rising to his feet with effort, gasping a little as the pain hit his ribs.

'Your mum reckons you owe me for catching Shand so quickly.'

'And not touching him would balance the books between us? Nice try, Siobhan.' He was standing only a few inches from her. 'It was good to see you in here a few weeks back. Did you enjoy your evening? From the CCTV, it looked like you did. Seven G and Ts I think I counted.' He gave another grin, gesturing towards the staircase. 'Now if you'll excuse me . . .'

She stood her ground for a moment, and he gave a little bow of his head to tell her she'd made her point. So she went back down the steps, the smell of disinfectant heavy in the air. As she retraced her route across the floor of the main room, imps and demons staring down at her, the music started up again, setting her teeth on edge. Back out on the pavement, she paused to take a few deep breaths, then noticed her phone was buzzing. She checked the screen: her pal in the Police Scotland control room.

'What is it, Tess?'

'Body fished out of Leith Docks, not far from the *Britannia*.'

'Suicide?'

'Bit of a Houdini if it is. Houdini in reverse, I suppose I mean.'

'Spit it out then.'

'I'm hearing his hands were tied behind his back.'

'That *does* make it suspicious.'

'I thought so. But the reason I thought you'd be interested is one of our lot recognised the face.'

Clarke froze, eyes on the doors of the Devil's Dram.

Please God, she said to herself. But surely not so soon . . .

She realised Tess was spelling out a name, a name that meant something to her.

'Give me that again,' she demanded, then ended the call and found Rebus's number.

'Yes, Siobhan?' he answered.

'They've just fished Robert Chatham out of the docks,' she said.

'Fuck,' retorted Rebus.

She was thinking what else to tell him when she realised he'd hung up.

The Royal Yacht *Britannia* had a permanent berth to the rear of the Ocean Terminal shopping centre and the adjoining multistorey car park. At right angles to this berth stood a reception building used for passengers embarking and disembarking the smaller classes of cruise ship. With no such ships in the vicinity, the building was kept locked, but it had been opened now and was a hive of activity as police, forensic specialists, photographers and an assortment of ancillary staff buzzed around, under the supervision of the crime scene manager. The corpse itself lay dockside, a makeshift tent erected to protect it from general view.

Rebus caught sight of Deborah Quant and one of her colleagues, both in protective overalls, headgear and elasticated overshoes. She had eased up her face mask so it sat against her forehead, her hand cupped to her mouth to keep the conversation private. Nearby, a small white van had parked. Its rear doors were open to reveal rubber diving suits and oxygen tanks, two men waiting, arms folded, to be told what to do.

The crime scene manager's name was Haj Atwal. He carried a clipboard with him and used it to gesture towards Siobhan Clarke.

'Signed in?'

'At the cordon,' she confirmed. 'You know John Rebus?'

The two men shook hands. Rebus asked how long the victim had been in the water.

'Exactly what our medical friends are discussing. From what I've heard so far, the autopsy will answer a few questions.' Atwal paused, staring at Rebus. 'Thought you'd been put out to pasture?'

'I'm here for a bit of a graze,' Rebus replied.

'John spoke with the victim only yesterday morning,' Clarke explained. 'Always supposing he is who we think he is.'

'Facial recognition by the first uniform on the scene,' Atwal stated. 'Plus his wallet was in his pocket – credit cards and driving licence. We got his phone, too.'

'Anything strike you as missing?'

'Not a thing.'

'So not mugged for his belongings, then?'

Atwal's look said he wasn't about to start a guessing game. His strengths were the procedural and the verifiable. Clarke watched as another van trundled into view. Bigger than the one belonging to the dive team, with a black paint job. It might even have been the same one she'd parked next to at the mortuary.

'Everybody's itching to get on with it,' Atwal commented.

'Only natural,' Rebus said, nodding in the direction of the victim. 'That's one of our own lying there.'

'He was retired, though, same as you – so the two of you weren't meeting to talk business?'

'Problem is, that's *exactly* what we were doing – a case everyone else thought was extinct.'

'Seems to me it might just have become active,' Atwal concluded, moving away to answer a question from one of his team.

Rebus and Clarke kept their distance from the body, watching everyone work. Eventually Deborah Quant spotted them and, after

82

a word to her colleague, headed in their direction. She lifted her mask again. No smiles or greetings; all business.

'Suspicious death,' she stated. 'More than that, I can't say right now.'

'Any cuts and bumps?' Rebus enquired.

'None that couldn't have been sustained from an amount of time in the water.'

Rebus studied their surroundings. 'High fences and security cameras. Not the easiest place to dump a body.'

'Someone will have to check tidal currents. He could have gone in the water anywhere between Cramond and Portobello.'

'He lived across from Newhaven harbour.'

Quant stared at him. 'Why am I not surprised you knew him?'

'Spoke with him only yesterday, Deborah.'

Her eyes softened. 'He was a friend?'

'Only our second meeting,' Rebus corrected her. 'You've no idea if he drowned?'

'I'd say it's likely. No obvious wounds, and he wasn't strangled or anything.'

'So he'd probably have been yelling for dear life?'

'That's feasible.'

'Meaning someone could have heard,' Clarke stated.

Quant studied her. 'Are you in charge, Siobhan?'

'Not until someone tells me so.'

'Bloody hell,' Rebus interrupted, peering past Clarke's shoulder. 'Looks like word really has got around.'

Malcolm Fox was striding towards the group, trying to arrange his face so it was friendly but respectful.

'Detective Inspector Fox,' Quant said. 'Thought we'd lost you to Gartcosh.'

'I managed to get a tourist visa.' Fox checked something on his phone. 'Is the CSM here?'

'The Italian-looking guy,' Rebus said, gesturing towards Atwal. Fox nodded his thanks and moved off again.

'Haj's parents are Indian,' Deborah Quant said.

'I know that.' Rebus offered a thin smile.

'What does Malcolm want with him anyway?' Clarke enquired, frowning.

'I think Malcolm's tourist visa has just been revised. Like I say, Robert Chatham was one of our own ...' Rebus stared at Clarke until the truth dawned on her.

'Gartcosh are claiming it,' she announced.

Rebus was nodding slowly. 'With Malcolm in the vanguard.'

Quant was studying Fox's retreating figure. 'You mean he's in charge?'

'Looks like, wouldn't you say?'

'Thanks for the spadework, Malcolm. But I'm in charge now.'

Fox stood in front of Detective Superintendent Alvin James. He was a few years younger than Fox, wiry, with jutting cheekbones and a freckled face, his reddish-blonde hair neatly trimmed and parted. Fox reckoned he probably ran long-distance; it was that sort of physique. Maybe played competitive five-a-side, too. Sporty and clean-living and always amenable to promotion.

'Yes, sir,' Fox said, hands clasped behind his back.

James gave the thinnest of smiles. 'Call me Alvin – and I mean it about the spadework.'

They were standing in an unaired office on the first floor of Leith police station, at the corner of Constitution Street and Queen Charlotte Street. The building, which had once been Leith's town hall, was solid but shabby, its operating hours restricted. The office they were in had been set aside for this use and this use only – unlocked only when the Major Investigation Team came to town. Alvin James was the senior investigating officer, hand-picked for the role by ACC Lyon at Gartcosh. His team comprised CID officers and admin staff. They were already busy, plugging in laptops, sorting out the Wi-Fi, and trying to open the windows so the place was a bit less stuffy.

Fox recognised none of the detectives, which meant they were almost certainly not local. James seemed to read his mind.

'I know a lot of our colleagues this side of the country think Police Scotland is just Strathclyde with an aka, but it's not like that. Okay, so I've spent most of my professional life in Glasgow, but there are people here from Aberdeen and Dundee, too. On the other hand, none of us know this place the way you do – that's why you'll be my go-to guy. Does that sound reasonable to you?'

'Thing is, I'm working another case right now.'

'ACC Lyon said as much, but she's checked with Ben McManus and he seems to reckon you're a dab hand at multi-tasking. You're here when I need you, but otherwise you can be beavering away on your other inquiry. How does that sound?'

'It sounds . . . workable.'

'Terrific. So what do I need to know?' James watched as Fox wrestled with the question, then broke into a toothy smile and wagged a finger. 'Just kidding. But one thing I *would* like you to do is think about local bodies – warm ones, I mean. Preferably CID. We may need to co-opt a few if things get busy.'

'The best DI in the city is Siobhan Clarke. She has two first-rate DCs under her.'

'See? You're already more than pulling your weight – thanks for that.'

James turned on his heel and, rubbing his hands together, began dishing out orders to the rest of his squad. Having no role to play, Fox stood there shuffling his feet. His ringing phone came as a relief. Without checking who was calling, he pressed it to his ear.

'It's me,' Rebus said.

'Thanks a bunch for that joke you played earlier,' Fox said, keeping his voice down.

'Which one?'

'Telling me the CSM was Italian.'

'I only said he *looked* Italian. Have you got a minute for a chat?'

'I suppose I might have.'

'Last night in the pub, remember me mentioning Robert Chatham?'

'Not really.'

'No, because you were too busy thinking about Sir Magnus Brough and his grandson.'

Fox strode from the office into the empty corridor. 'Chatham's who we've just pulled from the water.'

'Exactly so.'

'He was killed the same day he talked to you?'

'Yes.'

'Christ, John . . .'

'Are they setting up the MIT room at Leith?'

'Pretty much ready to go. A detective superintendent called Alvin James is SIO.'

'Can't place the name. I'm guessing he's Glasgow, though.'

'How do you know?'

'Gartcosh chose him – stands to reason.'

'I've put in a good word for Siobhan.'

'She might not thank you for it. Now off you go and tell Alvin and his Chipmunks that a retired east-coast cop knows more than they do, and he'll be there to tell his story in about twenty minutes.'

8

'So this is the brave new world I keep hearing of?' Rebus sauntered into the room, hands in pockets.

'You'll be John Rebus?' Alvin James said, rising from his desk to shake hands.

'And you'll be Superintendent James.'

'*Detective* Superintendent James.'

Rebus acknowledged the correction with a movement of his mouth. He nodded towards Fox, who had the desk next to James. There were four other faces in the room. They had obviously worked together before and gave him a collective stare of professional scepticism. James gestured towards each in turn.

'DS Glancey and DS Sharpe; DCs Briggs and Oldfield.'

Just the one woman, DC Briggs, trim and businesslike. Glancey overflowed from his chair. He had dispensed with his jacket and was dabbing sweat from his face with a pristine handkerchief. Sharpe had a wise but wary look, an owl to Glancey's bull. Oldfield was younger, cocksure and primed for action. Rebus turned from them towards Fox.

'All feels very familiar, eh, Malcolm?' Then, for James's benefit: 'We had a crew in from Glasgow not too long back. It got a bit messy.'

'We're not all from Glasgow, though,' James felt the need to point out. 'What we *are*, Mr Rebus, is a unit whose focus will be to find whoever did for Robert Chatham.' He folded his arms and rested his backside against the corner of a desk. 'Malcolm says you might have some information that would help. So we can keep this at the playground level or rise above that and get some actual business done.' He paused, angling his head slightly. 'What do you say?'

'I say a spot of milk and no sugar, *Detective* Superintendent James.'

'Please, call me Alvin.' Then, turning to Fox: 'One thing we forgot about, Malcolm. Can you rustle up the necessary?'

'Me?'

'You're the one person here who's already heard John's story,' James reasoned.

Grins were being hidden behind hands around the room as Fox stalked out, heading next door to where the support staff were gathering.

'Is there a kettle anywhere?'

'You'll probably find one in Argos,' he was told.

Muttering under his breath, he left the building and made for Leith Walk. An electric kettle and half a dozen mugs in one shop, supplies of coffee, tea, sugar, milk and plastic spoons in another. The whole sortie took no more than twenty-five minutes, just long enough for Rebus to get to the end of his tale. Thing was, Fox had no way of knowing what – if anything – he had held back. Rebus being Rebus, the truth would not have been the whole truth; the man always liked to know just a wee bit more than anyone else sharing the stage with him.

Fox dumped both bags on DC Oldfield's desk.

'You can be mother,' he stated. Oldfield looked to James for advice, but James just nodded. With a scowl directed at Fox, Oldfield got up, lifting the kettle from its packaging and leaving to find running water.

'So everyone's in the loop now, yes?' Fox enquired, slumping into his chair.

'And highly intrigued,' James said. He was seated behind his desk, tapping a biro against one cheek. He had jotted down notes on an A4 pad of lined paper in front of him and was studying them as he spoke.

'Without discounting anything you've just told us, John,' he said, 'there are certain protocols that we'd be unwise to ignore. That means getting the results of the post-mortem examination, interviewing Mr Chatham's partner, and doing a bit of digging at his place of work.'

'Bouncers probably make more enemies than most,' Glancey commented, refolding his handkerchief and beginning to dab again.

'And he'll have upset a few undesirables during his CID days,' Briggs added, drumming a biro against her own notes.

'So we'll need to look at his record as a DI in Livingston,' James agreed. 'When you spoke with him, John, he seemed okay?'

'He was fine.'

'Didn't say what else he was up to after your meeting?'

'No.'

'No phone calls or messages while you were in the café?'

'I appreciate you have all these hoops you feel the need to jump through, but it can't be coincidence, surely? The same day I get him talking about Maria Turquand's murder, he ends up in the drink.'

James was nodding, but Fox could tell the man wasn't completely sold – and that was starting to grate with Rebus.

'You need to bring us all those files,' Sharpe said quietly. 'Files you shouldn't have taken from SCRU in the first place.'

Rebus made brief eye contact with Fox, letting him know the score. He had fudged the truth to keep Siobhan Clarke's name out of it. As far as James and his team were aware, Rebus had swiped Chatham's review notes from SCRU during his tenure there.

Over in a corner of the room, Oldfield was making as much noise as possible while plugging in the kettle and sorting out the mugs.

'Remember what I said about the playground, Mark?' James scolded him.

There was a knock on the open door. Haj Atwal was standing there.

'Finished dockside?' James asked.

'Done and dusted, as it were.' Atwal ran a hand over his shaved head. 'Everything I've got so far will be in your email folder by end of play.'

'Thank you. And the divers?'

'Had a quick look, but as there was no weapon as such . . .'

'And he'd probably drifted along the coast anyway,' Rebus couldn't help adding.

'You're saying we shouldn't have bothered?' James seemed to require an answer, but all Rebus could do was shrug. 'And what makes you so sure he didn't enter the water where we found him?'

'Big tall fences and surveillance.'

'But then we've not checked the surveillance yet, have we?'

Fox saw where this was headed – James was wondering how far to trust Rebus: was he trying to misdirect them? He could see Rebus coming to the same conclusion, shoulders tensing, jaw clenching.

'You about ready to interview me as a suspect, Alvin?' Rebus asked.

James tried to look disbelieving. 'Not at all,' he offered.

'Then we're done here? I'm free to leave?'

'Of course.'

Rebus headed for the door, managing a final glance towards Fox before brushing past Haj Atwal.

'Victim's clothing will be sent for analysis,' Atwal was telling the room at large. 'Autopsy's the next step.'

'Thank you,' James said, busying himself until the crime scene manager had retreated into the corridor.

'Should have asked who's doing the autopsy,' Sharpe commented. His voice still hadn't risen much above a whisper – Fox wondered if it was a ploy; the man spoke so quietly, you had to give him your full attention.

'Professor Quant,' Fox answered. 'Deborah Quant.'

Alvin James was giving him an appraising look. 'And is there anything we should know about Professor Quant, Malcolm?' he asked.

'She's highly qualified, personable, unshowy.' Fox pretended to think for a moment. 'Oh, and she and Rebus are an item.'

James raised an eyebrow. 'Are they now?'

'So if John Rebus is your killer, maybe she's the one who'll make sure he gets away with it.'

Alvin James threw back his head and laughed. 'A bit of humour always helps defuse the tension, eh?'

Fox pretended to return the half-sincere smiles being directed at him.

'I've got a question for you all,' Oldfield interrupted.

'What is it, Mark?'

'Tea or coffee?' Then, to Fox specifically: 'And how do you take it?'

'Without saliva, preferably,' Fox said. 'Though as I'm about to go for a slash, you might find yourself tempted beyond reason . . .'

Rebus was tugging the parking ticket from beneath one of the Saab's wiper blades and looking up and down the street for the culprit.

'Bad luck,' Fox offered.

'And me on a pension.' Rebus stuffed the slip into his pocket. 'You think this guy James is up to the task?'

'Too early to say.'

Rebus had started chomping on a piece of chewing gum.

'Does that help?'

'Barely,' Rebus stated. 'Remember: you don't let on Siobhan got me that file.'

'Message received. Anything else you brushed under the carpet?'

'I don't remember.'

'Then how will I know not to blurt it out?'

'Maybe if you try keeping your trap shut for once.' Rebus glowered at him. 'Can't say young Alvin fills me with confidence. Too shiny by half.'

'His suit or his face?'

'Everything about him, Malcolm. Only thing he's got his sights on is the next rung of the ladder.'

Fox couldn't disagree. 'I don't think he's dismissing the Turquand connection out of hand.'

'It's the only connection there is.'

'Then he'll get round to probing it.'

'Aye, once he's been through his bloody "protocols". Keep at him, Malcolm. You've got to make him see what's going on.'

Fox nodded slowly. 'Who else knew you'd started looking?'

Rebus considered this. 'Deborah got a sneak preview. And Siobhan, of course.'

'Plus whoever gave Siobhan the file.'

'True.'

'And anyone Robert Chatham might have gone running to.'

It was Rebus's turn to nod, albeit distractedly. 'We've got to get his phone records – see who he spoke to after I left him.'

'Where *did* you meet him?'

'A greasy spoon not too far from Ocean Terminal. He liked the bacon rolls there.'

'The condemned man ate a hearty meal then, as Professor Quant will soon discover.'

'Do you think I'd be allowed in to watch?' Rebus asked, brow furrowing.

'Might not be wise.'

'True enough – the James Gang are already trying to put a nice big frame around me.'

'I think you may be exaggerating ever so slightly.'

'You have to be my eyes and ears, Malcolm. Promise me that.'

'I'd better go back in. They'll be phoning Guinness World of Records to measure my bladder.'

Fox turned and pushed open the door, letting it creak shut behind him. Suddenly he was everyone's eyes and ears . . . which reminded him. He found Sheila Graham's number and hit the call button as he began to climb the imposing staircase.

'Thought it would be you,' Graham said.

'News travels.'

'ACC Lyon told ACC McManus and ACC McManus was good enough to pass it along.'

'I can still keep tabs on the Christie case.'

'You sure?'

'In fact, I've got something for you. According to Anthony Brough's secretary, he's AWOL – meetings cancelled, et cetera. Seemed to me she was in the dark about where he's gone or why.'

'Chickens may be coming home to roost.'

'How do you mean?'

'I need to give this some thought, Malcolm. Anything else to report?'

'I've been a bit busy since lunchtime.'

'Your first Major Investigation Team?'

'I used to head the Professional Standards Unit, Sheila. I've played with the big boys before.'

He could sense her smile at the other end of the line. 'We'll talk later,' she said, ending the call as he reached the door to the MIT room.

Alvin James gestured towards the mug on Fox's desk.

'I've kept watch, so fear not.'

'Thanks,' Fox said.

'Though we're all a bit disappointed in you, Malcolm.'

'Oh?'

'No biscuits,' Briggs said.

'No biscuits,' Alvin James agreed.

'Plus the longest piss in recorded history,' Mark Oldfield added.

'Not that we think that's what you were doing,' James added slyly.

'Well, you're right – I was on the phone to Gartcosh. I can give you a name if you want to check.'

'We're all friends here, Malcolm. Nothing more to be said.'

'Except for this,' Briggs interrupted. 'Next time – biscuits. Digestives, for preference.'

'Chocolate digestives,' Sharpe corrected her in a whisper.

*

The autopsy was booked for 4.30, soon after Chatham's partner Liz Dolan had identified the body. Fox had been tasked with accompanying her. Her legs had gone from beneath her, and he'd struggled to get her back to her feet.

'Oh God,' she kept saying. 'Oh God, oh God, oh God.'

Fox had been there before and he offered the usual crumbs of sympathy, none of which she seemed willing to hear. She was shaking, clutching at him, holding him in a tearful embrace.

It's not easy, Liz.

It's a hellish thing.

Is there a friend I can contact? Family?

Somebody, in other words, to pass the responsibility to.

But they'd never had children, and none of their parents were alive. She had a sister in Canada; Chatham's brother had predeceased him.

'What am I going to do?' she said, voice quivering, strings of bleached saliva at the corners of her mouth. 'Such a good man. Such a good man.'

'I know,' Fox agreed, steering her to the waiting room and a chair. 'I'll get us some tea – how do you take it?'

But she was staring at the wall opposite, eyes fixed on a poster showing Edinburgh from the air. Fox leaned out into the hallway, checking to left and right, eventually catching the eye of a passing attendant.

'Got a family member here who could do with something,' he pleaded.

'Valium maybe?' the man offered.

'I think she'd settle for tea.'

'Milk and two?'

'I'm not sure she takes sugar.'

'Trust me, they all take sugar . . .' The man moved off again in his calf-high rubberised boots.

Liz Dolan was leaning forward in her seat, looking as if she might be about to throw up. She wore black leggings under a knee-length patterned skirt. Her fingers were worrying away at the skirt's hem as she took in erratic gulps of air.

'You going to be okay, Liz?' he asked.

'Not for a long time.'

'Tea's on its way.'

'That's all right then, eh?' For the first time, she met his eyes, so he'd know she was being sarcastic. He sat down slowly, leaving one chair vacant between them. 'So what happens now?' she asked eventually, wiping her nose with her sleeve.

'You'll want to arrange things – the funeral and such like.'

'I was meaning you – Rab was murdered, so what do you do next?'

'Well, when you feel up to it, we'd like to maybe ask you a few things, find out his movements.'

'He had breakfast with someone – an ex-cop.'

'Yes, we know about that.'

'He was in a right flap after.'

'Oh?'

'Snapped at me when I asked him what was wrong.'

'Did he give you an answer?'

She shook her head. 'But he was upset right up until the minute he went out.'

'When was that?'

'Early afternoon. I told him he hadn't had enough sleep.'

'He worked evenings, didn't he?'

'Five till midnight, sometimes a bit later if it was the weekend.'

'Had the pair of you known one another long?'

'Six and a half years.'

'Since before he retired, then?'

She nodded again. 'He'd been married twice before. Woe betide those witches if they try to gatecrash the funeral.'

'No love lost?'

'You're a cop, you know what it's like – long hours, cases that get under your skin but you don't want to talk about them . . .' She looked at him until he nodded. 'Both his wives ended up going off with some other poor sod.'

'Did he ever talk to you about the job?'

'A little bit, after he'd retired. There'd be reunions, and some-times he'd invite me along.'

'You'll have heard a few stories, then.'

'A few, aye.'

Their teas arrived and Fox offered a nod of thanks to the atten-dant. The man paused for a moment.

'Sorry for your loss,' he said to Dolan.

'Thanks.' She seemed mesmerised by the boots as the attendant trudged back to work. 'Christ,' she said, softly.

'Deborah Quant's the one looking after Rab,' Fox said. 'She's very good, very respectful.'

Dolan nodded and fixed her eyes on the poster again, the mug held in both hands. 'Being a doorman ... well, there were a few stories there, too.'

'I don't imagine it's an easy job.'

'It's fine when they're all behaving themselves, but Rab found that boring.'

'He liked a bit of a ruck?'

'Came home with a few cuts and bruises. The girls were the worst, he said. They'd use nails and teeth.'

'The weaker sex, eh?'

She managed something that was almost a smile. 'They chatted him up too, though – he liked that bit quite a lot.'

'Just a normal guy, then.'

'A normal guy,' she echoed. But then she remembered there was nothing in the least normal about the way her day was unfolding, and tears started to trickle down her cheeks again.

'Oh God.'

And although she'd already waved the offer away once, Fox reached into his pocket for a handkerchief.

9

It was almost seven by the time Deborah Quant emerged from the mortuary's staff door. She had showered and changed and was searching in her bag for her car keys when the figure emerged from behind one of the parked vans.

'Jesus, John!' she gasped. 'I was about to karate-chop you there.'

'You do karate?' Rebus said. 'I didn't know that.'

She stomped over to her car and unlocked it. Getting in, she waited for Rebus to pull open the passenger door and join her.

'So?' he asked.

'He was alive when he went in the water. Stomach contents: bacon and bread dough. DC Briggs said you'd had breakfast with the deceased.'

'MIT sent their only woman to the autopsy?'

Quant glowered at him. 'We manage childbirth fine; a dead body's neither here nor there. Anyway, turns out that roll was the last thing Mr Chatham ate.'

'No lunch or dinner?'

'Not so much as a packet of crisps. Whisky, though – a fair whiff of the distillery as we opened him up.'

'Enough to incapacitate him?'

'Blood tests will give us the answer.'

'So when can we expect those?'

'Your guess is as good as mine.'

'Anything else?'

She half turned towards him. 'Is this becoming personal, John?'

'How do you mean?'

'You saw the man the day he was killed. Maybe you think you're somehow responsible.'

'Could be I touched a nerve.'

'With the victim?'

'Or someone he met later in the day.'

'It's not your problem, though. DC Briggs was clear on that.'

He stared at her. 'What did she tell you?'

'She knows we're . . . friendly.'

'Friendly?'

'That's the word she used. And I happen to think that you should be concentrating on yourself right now instead of old cases and new.'

'I'm fine, Deb.'

'I don't think you are.'

'Who have you been talking to?'

She shook her head. 'I've not gone behind your back, John – and no doctor or consultant would dream of discussing a patient with a third party.'

Rebus stared out of the side window: nothing to see except one of the vans, maybe the one that had transported Robert Chatham from the quayside. 'I can handle this,' he said softly.

She reached for his hand and gripped it. 'You're a stubborn old bastard and you'd rather go to your grave than let anyone see a weak spot in that armour you think you put on every morning.'

He turned towards her. Her eyes were moist. Leaning in towards her, he kissed her cheek. She pressed her forehead against his and they sat like that for almost half a minute, no words needed. Then she straightened up and took a deep breath.

'Okay?' Rebus asked.

'You know I'm here for you? Any time you need me?'

He nodded. 'And I need you right now, Professor Quant.' He watched as her eyes narrowed, knowing what he was about to say. 'Tell me about the way Robert Chatham's hands were tied.' He paused for a moment. 'You'd be making a stubborn old bastard very happy . . .'

Craigmillar was cleaning up its act, at least on the surface.

A lot of the damp, unlovely housing had been bulldozed, replaced by shiny new apartment buildings. The shops still rolled down their metal security grilles of an evening, but a Lidl and a Tesco Metro had arrived. Clarke wouldn't quite call it gentrified – Craigmillar

96

still seemed to exist in most minds as a conduit between the city and routes to the south. She knew traffic was busiest at the weekend as shoppers headed for Fort Kinnaird with its Next, Boots and Gap. But Fort Kinnaird was also home to garages selling Bentleys and Porsches, something she knew only because she had for a short time considered getting a Porsche of her own. Why not? She made good money and had few outgoings. Her mortgage rate was low and likely to stay that way. She had given the Cayman a test drive and had loved it, before deciding against. No way she'd feel safe parking it kerbside. There were gangs in the city who preyed on cars like that. Plus she'd be the talk of Gayfield Square, and the comments would all revolve around her being on the take or in someone's pocket – someone like Darryl Christie.

Stopping on a Craigmillar side street, she got out and patted the roof of her Astra.

'You'll do,' she told it, before heading to Craw Shand's door.

It was a 1970s terrace, paint flaking from its window frames. There was neither a bell nor a knocker, so she thumped with her fist, then stood back to watch for movement behind the curtains. Nothing, but she could see that the lights were on. A dog was barking nearby, someone screeching at it to shut up. Kids passed on pedal bikes, hoods up, faces muffled. Clarke knocked again, then bent down and pushed open the letter box.

'It's me, Craw. DI Clarke.'

'What do you want?' his voice called from within.

'Just checking you're all right. I see you didn't take my advice.'

'What advice?' Shand's speech was slurred. With her nose to the letter box, Clarke could smell neither drink nor dope.

'To keep your head down, somewhere other than your home address.'

'I'm fine.'

'Let's hope it stays that way.' She pushed one of her business cards through the slit. 'You've got my mobile number if you need it.'

'I won't.'

She studied the door frame. 'One good kick and they'd be inside before you knew it.'

'Then maybe I should be in protective custody.'

'I've thought about it, Craw, but my boss says no.'

'Then you'll both have to live with the consequences if anything happens.'

'At least we'll still *be* living, Craw. Tell me how you really know so much about Christie's house – did you go there when you heard the news, is that it?'

'Off you go now, little piggy.'

'That's not very nice, Craw. I'm about the only person in the world who's on your side right now.'

'Off you go,' Shand repeated, turning off the light in the living room as if to signal the end of the conversation.

Clarke lingered, even tapping softly on the curtained window. The curtains looked thin and cheap. It was a life, she supposed. Who was to say he was less contented with his lot than anyone else she knew? Anyone else in the city, come to that? Half his life he'd been seeking a crime he could take credit for, and he'd finally struck gold.

Clarke hoped he'd live to enjoy the victory.

Back in the Astra, she watched in her rear-view mirror as a car crawled towards her. As it passed, she caught the licence plate. Darryl Christie's Range Rover. She started her car and followed. Rather than make for the main road, it seemed to be doing a circuit, heading further into the estate before turning at a few junctions, a route that would lead it past Shand's house again. Clarke flashed her lights, but the driver ignored her, so she waited until the road was wide enough and put the foot down, passing him and slamming on the brakes. She got out, making sure the driver could get a good look at her. As she approached, the driver's-side window slid down halfway.

'Best-looking carjacker I've seen in a while.'

Tattooed arms, groomed hair, beard. The 'owner' of the Devil's Dram.

'What are you doing in this car?' Clarke demanded.

'It's Darryl's.'

'I know that.'

'He's not up to driving it, so he said I could.'

'Wouldn't have thought Craigmillar is its natural habitat.'

'I've a mate lives round here somewhere. I was planning to show it off.'

'The mate wouldn't be called Craw Shand?'

A shake of the head.

'So what's your mate's address?' Clarke persisted.

'That's the trouble – I can't quite remember. Thought I'd know it when I saw it.'

'Got your story all worked out, eh?'

His face hardened. 'Fuck's it got to do with you anyway? Did I wander into a police state when I wasn't looking?'

'I want you out of Craigmillar and I don't want you coming back. Tell your boss that Craw's being watched night and day.'

'I don't have a clue what you're talking about.'

'Then I'll tell him myself, while *you* drive this crate away from Craigmillar.'

'There seems to be a heap of junk blocking the route, Officer.'

Clarke already had her phone out and was finding Christie's number as she got into her car and pulled it over to the side of the road. The Range Rover growled past with a parp of its horn. At Christie's house, her call was answered by a male voice she didn't recognise.

'Is that Joseph or Cal?' she asked.

'Cal,' she was told.

'Hi there, I'm looking for Darryl.'

'Hang on then.'

She watched as the Range Rover's tail lights receded, and listened to Cal walk into a room filled with music. She half recognised the tune, some current R&B hit.

'For you,' Cal was saying.

'Who is it?'

'Dunno.'

'What did I tell you, Cal? You always *ask*.' The phone was handed over and the sound system's volume faded away.

'Yes?' Christie enquired.

'It's DI Clarke.'

'I'm off duty.'

'You seem to be forgetting – you're the victim this time, Mr Christie. We're supposed to be on the same side, though that may just have come to an abrupt halt.'

'Why's that?'

'I've been talking to your pal from the Devil's Dram.'

'Harry?'

'He's quite distinctive-looking, with the beard and everything. Not exactly stealth-bomber material.'

'What are you on about?'

'He was scoping out Craw Shand's house.'

'Is that right?'

'Drove past it twice in that car of yours – which, incidentally, likewise lacks camouflage.'

'I loaned him it.'

'That's certainly the story he gave me.'

'It's also the end of the story.'

'I don't think so.'

But as if to prove her wrong, Christie had already hung up. She stared at her screen, knowing there'd be no answer if she called back. Instead, she tossed the phone on to the passenger seat and drove off in the same direction as the Range Rover. What harm could it do to tail it for a while, just so that bearded Harry got the message?

She was two cars behind him at the Cameron Toll roundabout when her phone's screen lit up. It was Malcolm Fox. She pressed the Bluetooth button on her steering wheel.

'Thought you'd be spending the evening with your new best buddies,' she said. After a moment's silence, she heard his voice over the car speakers.

'What do you want me to say?'

I want you to say you're sorry the new regime takes all the best, most interesting cases!

'Is there something I can do for you, Malcolm?'

'Are you in your car?'

'Brilliantly deduced.'

'On your way home?'

'Slowly but surely.'

'I just thought, after the day we've both had, maybe I could buy you a drink.'

'Is that because you want to hear all my news, or so you can tell me yours?'

'It's just a drink, Siobhan. We don't even have to talk shop.'

'But we will.'

'I suppose that's true.'

She thought for a moment. The Range Rover was definitely heading back into town. Job done. 'How about food instead? Curry at Pataka?'

'Fine by me.'

'I'm less than ten minutes away.'

'I'm more like fifteen.'

'Last one in pays,' Clarke said, smiling for the first time in hours.

*

Rebus stood at the door and pressed the bell. After a moment, the intercom crackled.

'Yes?'

'Good evening, I'm wondering if you've seen your neighbour across the way recently.'

'Which one?'

'Anthony Brough.'

'Never heard of him – you sure he lives here?'

'His office is the other side of the square. We've some concerns about his welfare.'

The person on the other end of the intercom weighed up Rebus's phrasing. 'You the police? Hang on a sec . . .'

Rebus made sure that when the door swung open, his gaze was everywhere but on the person who'd just unlocked it.

'Thank you,' he said. 'As I say, it's just that he's not been seen for some time and there's growing . . .' He broke off as his eyes met those of the man standing one step above him. He pretended surprise. 'Sorry, but you look a lot like Bruce Collier.'

'That's probably because I *am* Bruce Collier.'

Open-necked denim shirt, suntanned face. A bit of a paunch, the leather belt tied perhaps a notch too tight. Shiny brown leather shoes, and gold chains on both wrists as well as around his heavily creased neck.

'I'm a big fan,' Rebus said. 'Right back to Blacksmith days.'

'You must be a palaeontologist then.' Collier's face was all crinkles when he smiled.

'Mind if I . . .' Rebus stretched out a hand, which Collier grasped.

'Come on in, Officer,' he said, leading the way. Inside, the place was a mix of the traditional and the modern – stone floor, wooden coat stand, recessed ceiling lights. Rebus nodded towards a Warhol print on one wall.

'Is that an original?'

'Oil sheikh gave it to me after I'd performed at his birthday party. I won't tell you who the headliner was, but they got a Rembrandt. What did you say your name was?'

'Rebus. John Rebus.'

'Well, my name's Bruce and it's nice to meet a fan who's still got all their faculties. Fancy a beer?'

'Maybe a coffee?'

Collier studied him. 'I always thought that was a cliché – no drinking on duty.'

'I could do with the caffeine.'

'This way then.'

They headed down a curving staircase into the basement. The kitchen was long and narrow, fitted with the latest gadgets and boasting a glass extension to the rear with views over a neat walled garden lit by halogen.

'Supposed to deter burglars,' Collier said, gesturing to the lights. 'Instant okay for you?'

'Fine.'

Rebus watched as the man tipped a spoonful of coffee into a mug, then held the mug under a tap at the sink.

'Instant boiling water,' Collier explained. 'So who's this fellow who's gone walkabout?'

'His name's Anthony Brough. He runs an investment firm.'

'Any connection to the bank?'

'He's Sir Magnus Brough's grandson.'

'I had a run-in with that old bugger once,' Collier said with a snort. 'Used to have an account with them – they charged an arm and a leg for the privilege. Thing was, you were supposed to keep a hundred K in your account and I fell short for a month or three. Next thing I know, the phone rings and it's the old boy himself. Can't imagine that these days, can you? In fact, I think I'd had to present myself in person at their HQ just to open the account.' Collier pulled himself up short. 'Sorry, I'm burbling on. Been too long in my own company.'

'Are you married, Bruce?'

Collier fetched milk from the fridge and handed it to Rebus, along with the mug. 'She's in India, travelling with a pal of hers. That's why the place is so clean – no cooking here since she left.'

'I'm just remembering something,' Rebus said, while Collier returned the milk to the fridge. 'Wasn't there some scandal about Brough's back in the seventies?'

'Scandal?' Collier had swapped the milk for white wine. He unscrewed the bottle and poured a slug into a waiting glass.

'A murder at some hotel.'

'That was right around the corner!' Collier exclaimed. 'The dear old Caley. I was staying there at the time.'

'Usher Hall, 1978? I think I saw you there.'

'Supposed to be the ticker-tape-parade homecoming celebration. Local lad made good and all that.'

'But there was a murder instead?'

Collier studied him above the rim of his almost-full glass. 'You must remember it. When did you join the police?'

'I'm not as old as I look. So are you still recording, Bruce?'

Collier's face creased. His hair was unnaturally brown and unnaturally thick. A weave, a wig, or good genes and a dye job? Rebus couldn't decide. 'Bits and pieces,' he said eventually.

'Do you have a studio?'

'I'll show you.'

Rebus followed him out of the kitchen and across the hall. It was a small room with no natural light. Behind a window was a smaller room again. Rebus could make out the mixing desk.

'If I need a grand piano or drums, we do those elsewhere, but this is fine otherwise. Some bands these days record straight to a laptop and sort it all out with apps and the internet.'

'You've not quite gone that route yet,' Rebus commented, studying the dozen or so platinum and gold discs framed along three walls. A selection of electric and acoustic guitars sat on stands. Collier grabbed one and settled on a stool. He played a few chords, eyes on Rebus.

'That's "A Monument in Time",' Rebus said.

'How about this?' More chords, Collier making a mistake and starting again.

'"Woncha Fool Around With Me",' Rebus stated.

'You know your stuff,' Collier said. He made to replace the guitar on its stand, then held it out towards Rebus instead.

'I don't play,' Rebus informed him.

'Everybody should learn an instrument.'

'Did you start at school?'

'Our music teacher played in a jazz band. I used to rib him about it, so he got me to go along one night – I was underage but he sneaked me in.'

'You loved it?'

'I *hated* it. Took up guitar the very next day, determined to learn stuff he would loathe.'

The two men shared a smile. Collier was still smiling as he took a step towards Rebus. 'You're not really here about this investment guy, are you?'

'Actually, I am. But it's a bit of a coincidence . . .'

'What?'

'You and the Broughs and the Caley.'

'And why's that?'

103

'A man called Robert Chatham was pulled from Leith Docks this morning.'

'I heard about it on the news. Suicide, was it?'

'The name doesn't mean anything to you? Robert Chatham? Detective Inspector Robert Chatham?'

Collier thought for a moment, then began to nod. 'Shit, yes, he grilled me a few years back! Your lot had reopened that bloody case because my road manager wanted to make as much trouble as he could before he pegged it – bugger had just had the first of his heart attacks. So now this Chatham guy has gone and topped himself? I suppose that *is* a coincidence.'

'It wasn't suicide, sir. His hands had been tied behind his back.'

Collier's eyes widened as he puckered his mouth.

'I don't suppose you've had anything to do with him recently?' Rebus asked, placing the half-empty mug on the stool.

'Not in however many years it is.'

'Eight,' Rebus reminded him.

'Eight years, then.'

'Your friend Dougie Vaughan – do you still see him around?'

All previous traces of humour had left Collier's face. 'I'm going to ask you to leave. And if you don't, I'll be straight on the phone to my lawyer.'

'You invited me in, Mr Collier.'

'Because *you* lied and said you were interested in one of my neighbours – something I doubt your bosses will be happy about.'

'I'm what you might call self-employed.'

'You told me you were with the police.'

'I really didn't.'

'Well, cop or no cop, I want you out.'

'But I can still bring a few LPs round for an autograph?'

'You can fucking whistle, Mr Whoever-you-are.'

'I'm really not very good at whistling.'

'And I'm not very patient when it comes to people who've conned their way into my house.' Collier had taken hold of Rebus's forearm. Rebus just stared at him until he released it.

'Good boy,' Rebus said, exiting the studio and making for the stairs. 'Thanks for the coffee and the tour. Maybe I'll see you at a concert one of these days.'

'I'll make sure your name's on the door – to be admitted under no circumstances.'

Rebus paused on the staircase. 'That's interesting,' he said, without turning back towards Collier.

'What is?'

'Robert Chatham worked as a doorman all over the city – maybe you did happen across him without knowing it.'

'I don't drink in places that need doormen.'

Rebus had started climbing the stairs again. 'Nice talking to you, Bruce,' he said.

Rebus had texted Siobhan Clarke from his flat, suggesting a catch-up. Her reply – *Bringing doggy bag* – had puzzled him until he opened his door and saw her holding up the carrier from Pataka.

'And soft drinks all round,' Fox added, hoisting another carrier filled with cans.

'It's like New Year came early – go on through, then.'

Brillo was waiting in the living room. Clarke and Fox gave him plenty of attention while Rebus filled a plate. Fox was browsing the Maria Turquand file when Rebus returned from the kitchen.

'This has to go to Alvin James,' Fox reminded him.

'First thing tomorrow,' Rebus promised.

'Malcolm tells me you kept my name out of it,' Clarke added. 'Thanks for that.'

'I'm a lot of things, but a grass isn't one of them.' Rebus settled in his chair and started scooping up curry with a spoon. Fox eventually joined Clarke on the sofa and she offered him an Irn-Bru.

'Actually, I got the San Pellegrino for me,' he complained.

'Tough,' she informed him, having nabbed it for herself.

'So how are things in the big school?' Rebus asked, eyes on Fox.

'I've not had to report any bullying yet,' Fox replied.

'Team seem decent enough. Talk me through them.'

'The two DS's are pretty hard-nosed. Sean Glancey's from Aberdeen originally.'

'He's the one who keeps sweating?'

Fox nodded. 'Cut his teeth on hairy-arsed oilmen fighting their way through Friday and Saturday night. Wallace Sharpe is a Dundonian. Parents worked for Timex and wanted him to go into electronics. He reckons that if he had, he'd have designed a million-selling game by now and be living on a yacht. When he speaks you can hardly hear him, but he's sharp as they come.'

'What about the DCs?'

'Mark Oldfield's the one who seems intent on getting me wound up.'

'Maybe because the first thing *you* did,' Rebus reminded him, 'was turn him into the tea boy.'

Clarke swivelled to face Fox. 'Did you?' He shrugged a response, attention still on Rebus.

'Which leaves Anne Briggs. Like Oldfield, she's west coast through and through. The pair of them talk in a code only they can decipher. Why the wry smile?'

'There's a folk singer called Anne Briggs.' Rebus gestured towards the rack of LPs beneath his hi-fi. 'One or two of her albums in there if I looked hard enough.'

'Probably not the same person,' Fox commented.

'Probably not,' Rebus agreed. 'But it's been my night for musicians.'

'You went to see Bruce Collier?' Clarke guessed.

'He happens to live across the street from Anthony Brough's office,' Rebus said for Fox's benefit, watching as Brillo curled up on the sofa in the gap between Fox and Clarke.

'And?'

'And he didn't have much to add, though he did recall being interviewed by Chatham.' Rebus paused. 'So Malcolm and I have both been busy – how about you, Siobhan? Feeling a bit left out?'

'This is the thanks I get for bringing you curry?' She watched him hold up a hand in apology.

'Malcolm says he's put a good word in for you, though.'

She tried out a scowl, but Rebus only grinned and tipped another spoonful of rogan josh into his mouth. 'I've been busy too,' she eventually stated. 'Went to check on Craw Shand, and he's not budging from his house.'

'That's the last place he should be.'

'I did try telling him that. And I was proved right when I saw Darryl Christie's car cruising past.' She saw she had both men's full attention. 'Darryl wasn't driving, though; it was a guy called Harry, who supposedly manages the Devil's Dram.'

'Checking out the lie of the land?'

'Looked like. I pulled him over for a word.'

'No weapons on view? No smell of petrol?'

Clarke shook her head.

'Why would there be . . .' Fox broke off as comprehension dawned. 'To pour through the letter box.'

'With any luck, Darryl will surmise we're watching Craw round the clock.'

'We're not, though, are we?' Rebus said.

'I've flagged the address up to the patrols – they might manage one pass every hour or so, unless something kicks off elsewhere. Pretty much the same coverage Darryl Christie himself is getting.'

'Not much more we can do, then,' Rebus commented. He caught the look from the sofa. 'And by "we", of course I mean "you".' Having finished the food, he placed the plate on the floor. Brillo had one eye open, watching. Rebus stifled a belch.

'They say it's toughest after a meal,' Fox said. 'Is that true?'

'Depends what you mean.'

'Nicotine craving.'

Rebus gave him a hard stare. 'You'd make a good torturer, Malcolm, has anyone ever told you that?'

'Someone I know,' Clarke added, 'says acupuncture can help. They just press their ear lobe whenever they feel the need.'

'Well the pair of *you* are starting to give me the needle, which means it's almost chucking-out time.'

Fox and Clarke finished their drinks and got to their feet.

'Know what doesn't quite compute?' Clarke asked. 'Darryl Christie's reaction. I mean, if Craw turns out to be in the clear, then his attacker is still out there. Shouldn't he be at least a little bit spooked?'

'What makes you think he isn't?'

She thought for a moment. 'When I phoned him, he was at home listening to music. At least one of his brothers was there with him. It all sounds too normal, don't you think?'

'Maybe he's got guards surrounding the place,' Fox suggested.

'Oh now you've done it,' Rebus said. 'You've planted a seed, which means Siobhan's going to have to drive over there and take a look for herself. Am I right?'

Clarke considered this. 'It's practically on my way home,' she eventually conceded.

The Christie house was in darkness by the time she reached it. No Range Rover visible in the driveway and no muscle securing the perimeter or parked kerbside, ready to spring into action. A typical suburban street in one of the wealthier enclaves of the city, places where crime remained rare. Clarke stopped her car across the road, the engine idling while she watched and waited. A single-word text arrived from Rebus.

Anything?

She typed in her own single-word reply – *Nada* – and, yawning, headed for home.

Day Five

10

Craw Shand wasn't a complete idiot, despite what everybody seemed to think.

He checked the outside world from his upstairs bedroom, even opening the window so he could peer to left and right. Then another check from behind the downstairs curtains, just in case anyone was stationed on his doorstep. Having assured himself that the coast was clear, he shrugged into his coat, stuffed a shopping bag into one pocket and headed out.

He kept his collar up and his head down, offering little more than grunts to the few neighbours who greeted him. He was off to the Lidl, where his mission was to stock up for the next few days. He had twenty-six pounds in cash, which would be more than enough. Tinned soup and ravioli, bread, a few beers. Salted peanuts as a treat maybe. Not the big packets – he always seemed to finish those at one sitting and felt queasy after. And no wine – these days it furred his brain as well as his tongue. He had to stay sharp. So just the beers to complement the tablets stashed away at home. The tablets had come from a pal. Happy pills, doled out for depression. They got him nicely buzzing, washed down with a couple of beers.

Buzz, buzz, he said to himself as he entered the store. He'd be in and out in five minutes – knew the layout like the back of his hand. Unless they'd moved stuff around. They did that sometimes. He'd complained once at the checkout.

'We call it a "refresh",' he'd been told.

'I call it messing with my head,' he'd retorted. But then the manager had come over and asked if there was a problem. So that had been that.

This morning was fine, though, everything in its right place. Five minutes in and out, like a pro. Craw was turning from a shelf when he bumped into the man.

'Didn't see you there,' he apologised.

'Problem with getting to my age,' the man replied genially, 'you mostly become invisible.' He was smiling, his hands empty – no basket, no shopping. 'How you doing, Craw?'

'Do I know you?' Shand looked around, but security was nowhere.

'You might know the name – it's Cafferty.'

Shand's face couldn't help registering surprise. 'Mr Cafferty,' he stuttered.

'So you do know me then?' The smile broadened.

'I've heard plenty about you.'

'And I've been hearing about *you*, Craw.'

'Oh?'

'Darryl Christie used to be someone I considered a friend. Well, maybe not a friend exactly, but someone I could do business with. That all changed, of course. Darryl started stepping on a lot of people's toes, mine more energetically than most, if you take my meaning.' Cafferty waited, but Shand had nothing to say. He gestured towards Shand's basket. 'Nearly done?'

'Nearly.'

'Maybe we could go back to yours and talk a bit.'

'Talk?'

'There's nothing to worry about, Craw. Whoever thumped Darryl maybe thought they were doing me a favour. I have to admit, I almost wish I'd had a ringside seat. If it was you, well, I just want to shake your hand.'

Shand looked down. Cafferty had extended a hand wrapped in a black leather glove. When he reached out his own, Cafferty clamped it so hard, Shand couldn't help but wince. The pressure stayed on as Cafferty spoke.

'But if it wasn't you, Craw, then I need to know the who and the why, because secret benefactors make me almost as nervous as out-and-out scumbags. So we'll go back to yours, have a cup of tea and a chat.' Cafferty reached past Shand with his free hand and grabbed a packet of biscuits. 'My treat,' he said.

'It was me that hit him,' Shand blurted out. 'I've been charged and everything.'

Cafferty released his grip. 'Maybe you did and maybe you didn't. Could be you're covering for somebody or you heard something you shouldn't. I watched you on your way here, Craw. You're almost as invisible as me. Means people don't even notice you when you're practically under their nose.' He wrinkled his face. 'Though the whiff coming off you might offer them a clue.'

'There's no hot water.'

'Not been paying your gas bill, Craw?' Cafferty dug in his pocket and lifted out a roll of banknotes. 'I might be able to help you there. Let's go have that chat, eh? Somewhere a bit more private than here . . .'

Forty minutes later, Cafferty closed the door of Craw Shand's house and walked down the overgrown path. He had called for a taxi, but preferred to wait for it outside in the cold. He had kept his gloves on throughout, mostly to avoid skin contact with any of the greasy furniture. He hadn't bothered with tea, either, reckoning the mugs would be less than pristine. Shand had broken open the pack of biscuits and he'd eaten one of those, while watching the damaged cogs of Shand's brain try to find some purchase. Stories had come – version upon version of something probably not even close to the truth. But Cafferty had probed, and Cafferty had been patient, and Shand had played a final hand.

A bar in the Cowgate . . . Craw couldn't be sure which one. The man had turned a corner into an alley to keep the call more private. Gone midnight and students were on the prowl, chanting and singing. Shand was just walking. He'd scored a cigarette and paused to smoke it. And had heard snatches of the phone call. A few details that stuck. About a man given a pasting in his own driveway. Next morning he had headed to Inverleith and found a street that seemed about right, a house that seemed about right. And he'd made up his mind to say he'd done it.

No, he hadn't caught sight of whoever was on the phone. Male. Probably a local accent.

It wasn't much and Cafferty doubted it was the whole story, but it was something.

'You're sure it was a local accent?' he had asked.

'It was noisy and late, I'd had a few beers . . .'

Cafferty rubbed at the underside of his jaw as he stood on the pavement. He knew this part of town, had spent some of his early years here. It had been feral then, a place where you learned quickly or perished. These streets had been his teacher, and the education gained here had sustained him. But there were probably plenty more like Craw Shand, victims of circumstance, floating on the surface and buffeted by every passing wave. Cafferty had encountered enough of them in his time.

He had thought those days were over. Maybe he would have been content to drift into retirement if anyone but Darryl Christie had come along. He had thought of himself as Christie's mentor, and the lad had played along for a while, all the time planning to barge Cafferty aside. His business had grown quickly and he had grown with it. No please or thank you – just alliances with each and every one of Cafferty's adversaries in the other cities, until Cafferty's own territory had withered.

Could he just sit on his hands and allow them to get away with that? So far they'd let him be, but history suggested this was a state of affairs that wouldn't last. Cafferty thought of it as a reckoning. And it was coming.

When the black cab arrived, he climbed into the back, his face almost as dark as the sky overhead.

'Snow later maybe,' the driver informed him.

'I didn't know I was getting a weather forecast,' Cafferty growled. 'Just fucking drive.'

There was a white Range Rover parked further along the street, most of it hidden behind a rusting transit van. Its driver was using the hands-free option as he watched the taxi head for Peffermill Road.

'That's him leaving now,' he said. 'Do I stay here or what?'

'He didn't take Shand with him?'

'No.'

'Maybe follow him then. I wouldn't mind knowing where he calls home these days . . .'

When Siobhan Clarke arrived at Gayfield Square, she was told that her visitor had already gone up.

'Thanks,' she said.

She climbed the stairs to CID, but the only people in the room were Christine Esson and Ronnie Ogilvie.

'Two doors along,' Esson stated.

Clarke headed along the corridor and into another of the offices, where John Rebus was busy at the photocopier.

'I might have guessed,' she said.

Rebus half turned towards her and spotted the beaker of coffee. 'I hope that's for me.'

'Not a chance.' Clarke watched him tidy up the sheets he'd just printed. More were churning from the machine. 'The file I brought you,' she commented.

'Of course.'

'You're giving James's team the originals but keeping copies for yourself?'

'Yup.'

Clarke rested against the nearest desk. 'I shouldn't really be surprised.'

'It was always going to happen, Siobhan, and I reckoned I could do it here for free.'

'Knowing I would know.'

'I'm always going to assume you're on my side.'

'Plus I was bound to find out one way or another.' She took a slurp of the coffee.

'Been back to Darryl's house this morning?'

'I'm not *that* much of a masochist.'

'So what's on the cards for today?'

'We're supposed to show Darryl some photos and voice recordings.'

'To see if he can pick out Craw as his attacker?'

'Waste of time, right?'

'Right.'

'What about you – I'm guessing you've got something planned?'

'Dropping this lot round to Leith.'

'And after that?'

'Irons in fires, Siobhan.'

'Make sure you pick up the end that won't burn you.'

'I'm always careful.'

'Robert Chatham probably thought he was careful, too.'

Rebus paused, then nodded. 'You'll be checking on Craw later, I dare say.'

'If I get time.'

'No trouble last night?'

'Patrol cars managed three passes in his neighbourhood. Believe it or not, they even got out and did a bit of walking.'

'You reckon they really did?'

'They wouldn't lie to CID, would they?'

'Perish the thought,' Rebus said, before cursing under his breath. 'Another paper jam,' he muttered. 'What is it with these things?' He looked to her for guidance.

'All right, let me look at it.' Clarke placed her coffee on the desk and walked over to the machine, sliding out the paper tray and easing the stuck sheet from between the rollers. When she glanced over her shoulder, Rebus was stealing a slug of coffee.

'Don't worry,' he assured her. 'I'm not infectious . . .'

One thing he hadn't considered was that an eleven o'clock consultation might not get under way until at least quarter to twelve. The hospital waiting room wasn't the most inspiring of spots. He hadn't bothered to bring a paper, and the day-old one he found on a chair kept him occupied for not much more than ten minutes. He was just about to tell the receptionist that he was a busy man and would need to make another appointment, but his name was called before the words came out.

And afterwards . . .

After the local anaesthetic, the CT scan, the needle biopsy . . .

Probably nothing to worry about, but better to be safe than sorry . . .

A shadow on the lung sometimes means little or nothing . . .

We do have some reading matter for you, and there are websites we can suggest, just to put your mind at ease . . .

Words that rolled from the consultant's mouth like a script she'd learned by heart long ago. How many patients had sat where Rebus sat, hearing but not really listening? Then released to the fresh air and a world that couldn't comprehend how they were feeling, accompanied by a dull pain and some medication to see them through.

Buck up, John, he told himself as he reached the car park. You're not for the crow road just yet.

Fox had been given the task of going through the cold-case notes. He would bet a pound to a penny that Rebus had kept copies, but he wasn't about to tell Alvin James that. Half the stuff he already knew from Siobhan's summary in the Oxford Bar two nights back. James wanted Rebus to come in and be interviewed formally, with the session taped, so they could have a record of his conversation with Chatham. Mark Oldfield had been dispatched to the café to make sure Rebus's story about breakfast checked out. Sean Glancey and Anne Briggs were interviewing Liz Dolan at her home. Wallace Sharpe was at his desk, studying the autopsy report with furious intensity while Alvin James took a phone call. The milk from the previous day had gone sour and not been replaced, meaning black tea or black coffee. Fox was the only one of the three who seemed not to mind.

He had done an internet search on Bruce Collier, even watched a few clips of the man in his prime. There was plenty of archive material about his 1978 homecoming concert. The show had gone on, of course, but Maria Turquand's murder had been mentioned in a couple of the reviews. There was much less online information concerning Collier's musician friend Dougie Vaughan, or the other players in the drama, most having lived out the bulk of their lives in the pre-internet age. A few photos of Maria and John Turquand on their wedding day and at subsequent society balls. Sir Magnus Brough, of course, captured in tweeds as he prepared to blast grouse or pheasant from the Perthshire skies; bowler-hatted in pinstripes on the steps of his bank's Charlotte Square premises; at the well-attended funeral of his son and daughter-in-law, a hand on the shoulder of each of his teenage grandchildren.

Which, of course, led Fox to search for Anthony Brough himself. Not for the first time, but you never could tell what detail you might have missed – and Fox was nothing if not diligent. It was all flotsam, though, no real depth or insight. The drowning of his friend on Grand Cayman. The aftershock felt most keenly by Anthony's 'sensitive' sister Francesca. A couple of business puffs regarding the setting-up of his investment company, but nothing, naturally, about shell companies or Darryl Christie.

Nothing to suggest why he hadn't been seen of late.

Fox watched Alvin James end his call. He seemed to have been given a small but effective jolt of electricity. Wallace Sharpe had noticed, too, and was waiting for his boss to share the news.

'Toxicology report,' James obliged. 'Our victim had imbibed the best part of a bottle of whisky.' He started composing a text as he spoke. 'I'm asking Sean to check with the widow how much he regularly took of an afternoon or evening.'

'Wasn't he supposed to be working the night he died?' Fox enquired. 'Would he have downed that much prior to starting a shift?'

'Good point, Malcolm. There was some on his clothing, too – lab seems to think so anyway.'

'Like it was forced down his throat?'

'Or else something had scared him witless, giving him the shakes.'

'Any news of the ligature?' Sharpe enquired in a whisper.

'Blue polyurethane,' James said, reading from the sheet in front of him. 'Cheap guy ropes use it – meaning tents and stuff. I'm not sure that gets us much further. Basic double knot, but tied tight enough to cut the circulation.'

'He was alive when he went in the water, but do we know if he was conscious?' Fox asked

'After a bottle of hooch?' James rubbed a hand across his forehead. 'I'd have been KO'd. How about you?'

'I don't drink,' Fox admitted, 'so I doubt I'd be exactly chipper.' He watched as James studied his phone, a text having newly arrived.

'Well guess what, Malcolm – our chap was off the sauce, too. For the best part of a year, according to Ms Dolan.'

'So person or persons unknown,' Sharpe mused, 'got him incapable, then tied him up and chucked him in the Forth.'

'Or tied him up first,' Fox countered. 'Easier that way to force the whisky down him.'

Sharpe signalled his grudging acceptance of this. James was studying the chart they'd fixed to one wall – a timeline of Chatham's final day, as yet hopelessly incomplete.

'We need those phone records pronto – home and mobile. Plus CCTV from around the city. Everywhere he worked, we need to see their footage for the past few days. I want to know everyone he spoke with, every place he frequented. Co-workers, buddies, anyone who came on his radar. All we seem to know right now is that he had breakfast with John Rebus, headed home afterwards for a few hours, seemed anxious, then sloped out without a word of goodbye. After which, it's like he doesn't exist. It's down to us to find out where he went. Twelve noon till whenever he died – all those gaps need to be filled.' James was looking at Fox. 'So where would you start, Malcolm?'

Fox thought for a moment. 'I'd start with a map,' he said.

'This better be me having a bad dream,' Cafferty said, staring at the figure on his doorstep.

'You never sent a change of address card,' Darryl Christie said with a shrug.

'So how did you find me?'

'Tried a couple of buzzers until someone answered. Told them

I'd a delivery for Mr Cafferty. Nice place . . .' He made to enter, but Cafferty blocked him. They stayed that way as the seconds passed, but then Cafferty stepped aside. 'In you come, then.'

The hallway led to a large open-plan room, all pale wood and unadorned white walls. A glass door led to the balcony. Christie opened it without bothering to ask permission and stepped outside.

'Quite a view,' he said, peering down at the usual array of students, cyclists and joggers criss-crossing the Meadows. Raising his head, he took in Marchmont, with the Pentland Hills behind. 'Can't quite see Rebus's flat, though – bet you wish you could.'

'I thought you were laid low, Darryl,' Cafferty said.

'My body's not quite as bruised as my ego.' Christie dabbed the tips of his fingers against the skin around his nose. The strapping was gone, but there was still discolouring and slight swelling. 'Hurts to take a deep breath, if that's any consolation.' He paused. 'Someone takes you down, you start to wonder why they're not as afraid of you as they ought to be.' He kept his eyes on the vista. 'You've had a bit of experience in that direction yourself, so I'm not telling you anything you don't know.'

'You think it's something to do with me, is that it?'

'You personally? No.'

'Me paying someone, though?'

'Yes, well, that *had* crossed my mind.'

'And what does your friend Joe say?'

Christie seemed to consider this. 'Mr Stark has been a bit quiet.'

'That's not like him.'

'He did phone to commiserate, of course.'

'But no bedside visit? Looks like things might be cooling between you, Darryl . . .'

'The beating made me look weak. Joe Stark can't abide weakness.' The two men were leaning against the balcony rail, hands clasping it. 'If you really wanted rid of me,' Christie went on, 'this is as good a chance as any – one shove and I'm a goner.'

'Think of the witnesses, though.'

'It would be your word against theirs.'

'There isn't a hit out on you, Darryl – not one that came from me. Not *this* week, at least.'

The two men shared a wary smile.

'You know they've charged someone?' Christie said, turning at last towards Cafferty. 'He's called Craw Shand.'

'Oh aye?'

'You've not come across him?'

'Name doesn't—'

'This morning, for example. At his house.'

Cafferty's eyes narrowed. 'You're having him watched?'

'Of course I am.'

'But you don't think he's your attacker?'

'He tells lies for the fun of it. But he knows stuff he shouldn't, which means that whoever hit me, Shand knows them.'

'Not me, son.'

'No?'

Cafferty shook his head slowly, maintaining eye contact throughout.

'Then why pay him a visit?'

'Same reason you just gave – he knows something.'

'And?'

'And he stuck to his story,' Cafferty said, making sure not to blink, not to give *any* tells.

'Why's it so important to you?'

'Because my name's on two lists – yours and CID's. I'm as interested in finding out as you are.'

'So you can give them a hug of thanks?'

'So I can *know*.'

Christie considered this. 'I think I remember you saying as much once – back in the days when you thought you could mould me. Something clichéd about knowledge being power.'

'It's a cliché because it happens to be true.'

Christie nodded, pretending to be interested in the view again as he spoke. 'It might be all to do with a guy called Anthony Brough.'

'I'm listening.'

'We had a business arrangement that didn't work out. Now he's nowhere to be found.'

'Local, is he? Scottish, I mean?'

'Yes.'

'So what does he do?'

'He's an investment broker, offices in Rutland Square.'

'Does he owe you money, or is it the other way round?'

'I'd just like to know his whereabouts.'

'And you think I can help?'

Christie offered a shrug. 'I'm not having much luck on my own.'

'Did you think to ask Joe Stark or any of your other old pals?'

'Like I say, I seem to be on my own.'

'So I get to be your best friend now, is that it?'

Christie met Cafferty's eyes. 'Joe Stark is an old man. One day soon he's going to topple.'

'And you step into the vacuum?'

'I wouldn't mind taking over his show, leaving Edinburgh to someone else. It's a beautiful city, but it's starting to bore me.' He paused. 'At least say you'll think about it – for old times.'

'Of course I'll think about it.'

The two men shook hands and began to move indoors.

'Have you seen my house?' Christie asked.

'No.'

'It's a bit like your old place. This is very different – what changed?'

'Eighteen rooms and I used about four of them. At least you've got a family to fill yours.'

Christie nodded. 'You'll put the word out?' he asked, watching Cafferty close the balcony door.

'About Anthony Brough? I don't see why not.'

'I knew you'd still have ears on the street.'

'The fruits of a lifetime spent doling out drinks and the odd banknote.' Cafferty paused. 'You should get a bit of personal protection – seriously.'

'You mean a bodyguard?'

'Either that or a weapon – I'm assuming you'll know someone who could help.'

'Never really been my style, but thanks for the advice.' Christie was making for the hallway and the front door. Cafferty leaned past him to open it.

'By the way,' Cafferty asked. 'Seen the Russian lately?'

Christie stopped on the welcome mat outside the door. 'What Russian?'

Cafferty held up a hand, palm out. 'Have it your way, Darryl.'

'No, I'm serious – what Russian?'

'Just something I heard.'

Christie gave a shrug and a shake of the head.

'Must have misunderstood,' Cafferty said, beginning to close the door.

Christie walked to the lift, jabbed the button and waited, hands clenched at his sides, eyes staring at his blurry reflection in the brushed aluminium doors.

'He's Ukrainian, you prick,' he said under his breath.

11

Fox had to admit it – he was impressed.

The MIT room was all focused activity, with Alvin James at its centre, keeping it that way. A map had been found and pinned to the wall. On it, coloured pins showed the spot where the body had been found, the victim's home, and other locations associated with him, from the café where he'd met Rebus to the bars and clubs he worked and the gym where he spent much of his free time. James had already said it: the man would have been no pushover, meaning they were probably looking for two or more assailants. The currents of the Firth of Forth had been scrutinised. Western Harbour, where the body had ended up, was hemmed in by two breakwaters, leaving a narrow access channel. According to the expert they'd consulted, the body had most likely either been thrown into the harbour itself or put in the water somewhere in the vicinity. That still left them a lot of coastline, and aerial photographs had been sourced and pinned up next to the map. The highlights of the autopsy report were there, too, as were lists of the deceased's friends and associates. But the timeline of Chatham's final day was still far from complete.

Anne Briggs was transcribing the interview with Liz Dolan, while the others were on their phones, arranging to talk with the names on the lists. Fox had a list of his own to work through. It had just arrived from Chatham's mobile phone provider, and sat on his desk next to a similar sheet detailing the past month's landline activity. Internet browsing and downloads were only given as totals, but numbers called and texts sent were laid out in more comprehensive terms. The phone Chatham called most often was his home land-line, usually in the evening – probably bored and cold as he waited to see some action at work. One number interested Fox – a mobile number. No calls to it, but over a hundred texts in a single month. Fox had tapped it into his own phone, but it went to an automated answering service. He hung up, and asked Briggs for Liz Dolan's mobile number. Briggs told him. Not a match. And he could see Dolan's mobile now – Chatham had texted it a couple of dozen times during the month. Fox put a question mark beside the mystery number and kept working.

Less than five minutes later, he had something. James could see it in his face, and strode over to the desk.

'Gimme,' he said.

'Each and every Saturday, around twelve noon,' Fox obliged, tapping his finger against the number called. 'A two- to three-minute call to the same landline.'

'Yes?'

'I just phoned it myself. It's a betting shop called Klondyke Alley.'

'So?'

Fox kept his eyes on the list. 'It's just . . . we didn't know he was the betting type, did we?'

James got Anne Briggs's attention. She slipped off her headphones as he asked her the question.

'Yes,' she said. 'Partner told us that – he'd have a regular bet on the horses.'

'Enough to get into trouble?' Fox enquired.

'I didn't get the feeling they had money worries.'

'Malcolm has a point, though – we need to look at Mr Chatham's bank accounts.'

'I don't recall bookmakers being quite so fierce,' Briggs said sceptically, 'even with punters who owe them big.'

'No stone unturned, Anne,' James warned her. He had turned his attention to the cold-case file, the one Rebus had delivered. Fox had given him a two-minute briefing on it, and James hadn't seen any cause to prioritise it at this stage.

'I could go take a look at Klondyke Alley,' Fox offered. 'I checked and it's on Great Junction Street, not a ten-minute walk from here.'

James studied him. 'What's your thinking?'

'Could be Chatham placed bets in person as well as by phone.'

James considered this. 'Ten minutes, you say?'

'Each way,' Fox corrected him. 'I can bring back milk.'

'And biscuits,' Briggs called from her desk.

'And biscuits,' Fox agreed.

Klondyke Alley sat between a café and a charity shop, with a bus stop directly outside. Its brightly lit window showed an oversized one-armed bandit, its reels turning slowly and constantly. Fox stepped inside. It was almost identical to Diamond Joe's and Diamond Joe's Too – one bored-looking cashier; a few glazed-eyed punters seated in front of their favoured machines; TV screens fixed to the walls. Fox stood in front of the cash desk, waiting for the bulky man behind the glass to finish the text he was composing on his phone. It took a while. The cashier gave Fox an unwelcoming look.

'Help ye?' he barked.

'I don't meet many novelists,' Fox said, gesturing towards the man's phone. 'I assume that was a chapter you were finishing.'

'I'm going to guess you're not here to place any bets.'

'You'd be right.' Fox held out his warrant card in one hand and a recent photo of Robert Chatham in the other. 'Know this guy?' he asked.

'Nope.'

'He was a customer here.'

'Doubt it.'

'He phoned in a bet every Saturday lunchtime.'

'Then show me a picture of his voice.'

Fox gave a humourless smile. 'He never came in?'

'Not on my watch.'

'His name was Robert Chatham.'

'Oh aye?'

'You won't be taking any more bets from him.'

The cashier sighed and typed Chatham's name into his computer. 'He had an account,' he confirmed.

'How was he doing?'

The man studied the screen. 'Breaking even, more or less.'

'So does he owe you or do you owe him.'

'Nineteen quid in credit. You should let his next of kin know.'

'I'll do that,' Fox said. 'But he never placed bets in person?'

'Always by phone.'

'How about online?'

The man scanned the screen again. 'No sign of that.'

Fox turned the photograph over. On the back he had scribbled the mobile number, the one Chatham had texted all those times. 'How about this?'

'Is it supposed to mean something?'

'It's not a number you recognise?'

The man shook his head. 'We done here?' he asked. Fox realised there was a punter behind him, needing change. He nodded his agreement, pausing by one of the machines and sliding home a pound coin before realising it only gave him a single credit. He pushed the button and waited. When the reels stopped, he had done something right, because a light was flashing to ask him if he wanted to gamble or collect. He pressed gamble and the reels spun at a slower rate than previously. The machine wanted him to decide when to stop each one, so that was what he did. The light was flashing again. He decided to collect and was surprised when coins started coughing out into the metal tray beneath. Pound coins. Twenty of them.

'Fuck's sake,' the punter at the cash desk complained, as Fox scooped up his winnings and left.

He bought multi-packs of Kit Kats from the supermarket, as well as a litre of semi-skimmed, even splashing out fivepence on a carrier bag. Outside again, he paused and crossed to the opposite pavement, heading back in the direction of Klondyke Alley. He focused his attention on the unwashed windows of the flat above. The flat was accessed from a scuffed door between Klondyke Alley and the charity shop. How many companies had Sheila Graham told him were registered there? Fox crossed the road again and tried the door. It was locked. There was a bashed-looking intercom, but it boasted only flat numbers rather than the residents' names. With the remaining coins weighing heavily in one pocket, he started back in the direction of Leith police station.

He took the stairs two at a time. A discussion was happening among the Major Investigation Team. Oldfield was on kettle duty again.

'You spoil us, ambassador,' he said, as Fox produced the Kit Kats.

'What have I missed?' Fox asked, directing the question at James.

'Fitness trainer at Mr Chatham's health club. He's not a great one for gossip, but he felt we should know.'

'Know what?'

'That the deceased was quite friendly with a female client.'

'How friendly?'

'Cosy drinks together in the café after they'd finished their work-outs. Trainer thought it quite a coincidence how often their visits to the club coincided.'

'We have her name and address?'

'We do now.'

'And phone number?' Fox watched James nod. 'Can I see it?' he asked.

James had it written on a pad of paper. Fox studied it, then brought out the photo of Robert Chatham, turning it over.

'Are you some sort of magician, Malcolm?' James said.

'Chatham texted her four times as often as his partner.'

'So why didn't you tell me?'

'I got distracted by Klondyke Alley.'

'Speaking of which . . .'

Fox shook his head. 'Phone bets only. They actually owed him a few quid at time of death. What's her name?' He was studying the phone number.

'Maxine Dromgoole. Heard of her?'

'Should I have?'

James turned towards Sean Glancey. 'Tell the man, Sean.'

'Quick internet search only throws up one Maxine Dromgoole.' Glancey paused, bunching his handkerchief in a meaty paw. 'With a link to the Amazon website.'

Fox couldn't help but look quizzical.

'She's a writer, Malcolm,' James explained. 'Non-fiction, mostly crime.'

'Including unsolveds,' Anne Briggs chimed in.

'The Maria Turquand case?' Fox understood now. 'She's the reporter who got Bruce Collier's road manager talking?'

'The very same, it would seem.'

'Which means she was responsible for the cold-case review – the one headed by Chatham.'

'And that's why I've taken Rebus's folder from your desk and given it to Wallace.'

Wallace Sharpe tapped the folder to underline the point.

'Did you try calling her?' Fox asked.

'Did *you*, Malcolm?'

'Automated answering service.'

'Well, we could ring again and leave a message,' James said. 'But we *do* have her address. And seeing how you've just generously donated all those lovely Kit Kats . . . how do you fancy a wee trip?'

'Sure.'

'Good, because I could do with a translator – none of us seem able to pronounce the name of her street.'

Fox studied James's pad of paper.

'It's Sciennes,' he said.

126

*

Sciennes Road was in Marchmont, not too far from Rebus's flat. Fox was beginning to feel as if the city had become a labyrinth, its denizens and neighbourhoods all connected by knotted threads.

'The red building on the left is the Sick Kids hospital,' he told James, trying not to sound too much like a tour guide. 'Sciennes Primary School next along.' Then a run of shops with three storeys of flats above. A very different feel to Great Junction Street; a different part of the puzzle. Fox signalled and pulled into a parking space.

'You always do that?' Alvin James asked.

'What?'

'Signal.'

'I suppose so.'

'Even when there's no other traffic?'

'It's the way I learned.'

'You're a creature of habit, Malcolm. And you stick to the rules.'

'Got a problem with that, Alvin?'

'Not that I can think of.'

They got out and found the bell with 'Dromgoole' next to it. There was no answer from within. Both men stepped back as the door to the common stairwell swung inwards. One of the residents was emerging, hampered by a bicycle. James held the door open for him.

'Ta.'

'We're here to see Maxine Dromgoole.'

'Second floor left,' the man said.

Alvin James nodded his thanks and waved Fox inside with a sweep of his free arm.

They climbed the stairs and stopped at Dromgoole's door. Fox rapped with his knuckles. Nothing. James bent over and prised open the letter box.

'Anyone home?' he called.

Fox was just taking out one of his business cards and a pen when there was a sudden croaky voice from within.

'Please, whoever you are, come back later.'

'Can't do that, Ms Dromgoole,' James stated through the letter box. 'We're police officers.'

'I can't handle this right now.'

James made eye contact with Fox. 'I can appreciate you're upset, Maxine. Of course you are. But Robert would want you to help us, don't you think?'

The silence lasted almost half a minute. Then the door was pulled open with infinite slowness, revealing a woman in what looked like pyjamas, the top baggy and grey, the trousers identical in colour and tied at the waist with a drawstring. Maxine Dromgoole had almost cried herself out. She looked ready to drop, face blotchy, hair unbrushed, eyes bloodshot. She held a wad of paper tissues in one hand. The area around her nose looked sore from rubbing.

'Does Liz know?' she asked.

'About you and her partner? Not as far as I'm aware.'

'But she'll find out now, won't she?'

'Might not have to come to that,' James said, looking to Fox to back him up.

'We just need a few minutes of your time,' Fox added as solicitously as he could.

'It was revenge, wasn't it?'

'Was it?'

'Rab had to chuck some guys out of a club a week or two back. He told me about it after. Said they'd promised payback.'

'Tell you what, Maxine,' James said. 'Let's go take the weight off while my colleague makes us all a cuppa. Does that sound okay?'

She nodded distractedly and turned towards the living room. Fox got busy in the kitchen. Once the kettle was on, he stood in the living room doorway, making sure he caught the conversation.

'So how long had you known Rab?' James was asking, notebook out.

'Eight years or so.'

'This would have been around the time you published your book?'

'That's right. He wanted to ask me about it.'

'Because the case was being reviewed?'

She was nodding, her eyes fixed on the window and the sky beyond. 'I'd reworked my interview with Vince Brady and sold it to a newspaper. This was in the days when newspapers still paid their contributors. Anyway, because it was back in the public eye, there had to be a review.'

'And that was how you two met.'

'We got on well. I didn't really think about it afterwards, but he called me a couple of weeks later. I knew he was married but was on the verge of splitting up. He was already seeing Liz . . . Christ, that makes me sound like the scarlet woman, doesn't it? It was actually a few years until we became serious – not that I ever wanted . . .' She broke off, gulping and getting her breathing back under control. 'I

128

met Liz a few times. They have parties at the gym once or twice a year, partners welcome.' She paused again, lowering her eyes. 'She seemed very nice. You think it's possible she won't find out?'

Fox sped back to the kitchen and returned with a tray – three mugs, milk, sugar. He placed it on the coffee table and let them help themselves.

'Did you see anything of him that last day?' James asked when they had settled again.

'He sent a couple of texts.'

Yes, Fox thought, at 10.45 and 11.10. Sent from home, with his partner either in the room or else not far away.

'How did he seem?'

'He was just letting me know he might not make it to the gym later.'

'Did he say why?'

'He'd been talking to someone about Maria Turquand.'

'And that's why he couldn't come to the gym as usual?' Fox probed.

'I don't know.'

'Can we see the texts?' James asked.

'They're . . . some of them are personal.'

'I think I understand. Maybe just those two from the day itself?'

She lifted her phone from the coffee table and opened it up, eventually turning it round so they could see the screen, but not about to let them take the phone itself from her.

Don't be cross, Hot Buns – can't watch you sweat today. ☹

She had sent a reply a few minutes later:

Tomoz? Everything okay?

And then his response:

In other news, Maria T is back! Ex-cop on the prowl. Maybe I should be insulted my brilliant investigation wasn't the end of it . . .

The last text ever sent by Robert Chatham.

'Would he be at the gym most afternoons?' James asked, sitting back down.

'He had a good body. He liked to keep it that way.' Dromgoole had turned the phone back towards her so she could stare at the texts. 'He told me they used to tease him in CID, call him "Fat Rab". He decided to do something about that.'

'It was the Turquand case that threw you together,' Fox interrupted. He was perched on the arm of the sofa, not quite ready to get comfortable. 'Did he ever share the findings of the review with you?'

'Would that have been against procedure?' She placed her phone on the arm of her chair.

'I'll take that as a yes. What did you think when he sent you that text?'

She puffed out her cheeks and exhaled. 'I was a bit cranky that I wasn't going to be seeing him. I don't think I gave it much thought.'

'No?'

'Should I have?'

'It was a story that interested you at one time. I notice your book's still in Amazon's top thousand.'

She gave a snort. 'Top thousand True Crime. I doubt it sells fifty copies a year.'

'Are you working on anything just now?' Fox asked.

The question seemed to throw her. She studied his face, more or less for the first time. 'Very early stages,' she eventually admitted.

'Mind if I ask the subject?'

'Morris Gerald Cafferty,' she said. 'You'll know the name, I dare say.'

'How far have you got?'

'There are plenty of books out there about London gangsters, Manchester, Glasgow – I thought maybe it was Edinburgh's turn. There's a lot in the newspaper archives. Court reports, that sort of thing.'

'Have you mentioned any of this to Cafferty?'

'I've written requesting an interview. No news back as yet.'

Unhappy at this diversion, James leaned forward in his chair. 'Apart from that disturbance you mentioned, the one outside the club, did Rab seem worried about anything?'

'He'd been a bit on edge, but lovely, too. One night when Liz thought he was at work, the pair of us went to dinner at Mark Greenaway's. Wasn't cheap, but we loved it. At the end of the meal, he gave me a rose.' She nodded towards a bookcase next to the fireplace. On one of the deep shelves sat a slender glass vase with a rose protruding from it, long dead, its petals never having opened.

As she gazed at it, the tears started trickling again down Maxine Dromgoole's cheeks.

After a further ten minutes, they were done, Dromgoole promising to drop by the station and make a formal statement the following day. The two detectives descended the stone stairs in silence, footsteps echoing. They were back in the car before James asked Fox what he thought.

'I don't sense she's hiding anything.'

'I wouldn't be so sure. For nearly eight years she managed to hide the fact she was shagging a man who had another partner.'

'Which might say more about him than it does about her.'

'How do you mean?'

'Chatham was leading two lives and managing to keep the one hidden from the other.'

James nodded slowly. 'So who knows what other secrets he had?'

'Added to which, it's funny how Turquand keeps cropping up – and now suddenly Cafferty's in the mix.'

'I only really know him by name.'

'He's like a cannier version of Joe Stark. Hasn't managed to grace the front pages quite as often because he *is* canny.'

'I'm more interested in this group who threatened Chatham. They've not appeared on any of the CCTV yet, have they?'

'Only a matter of time, I'd think.'

James looked thoughtful. 'Did we miss anything in there, Malcolm? Anything we should have spotted or asked?'

'The only books on her shelves are ones she wrote herself,' Fox replied. 'Not sure what that says about her.'

'Would Chatham have kept feeding stories to her, do you think? They met eight years back and he's only been retired three . . .' James was staring at Fox.

'Are you telling me I have to buy her books?'

'Only if you want to maintain your reputation for absolute thoroughness.'

'When you put it like that,' Fox said, starting the engine, 'how can I resist?'

12

Joe Stark always dressed as if the clock had stopped in the 1950s – camel-hair coat, polished black shoes, suit with wide lapels and a mauve shirt with a tie of the same colour. He wasn't tall, but he had heft. As usual, he was flanked by his two oldest friends, Walter Grieve and Len Parker, the three having been in a gang since primary school. Cafferty had his back to them, studying the grandeur of Glasgow City Chambers, but he sensed Stark's approach and half turned, managing the briefest of nods before turning his attention back to the edifice in front of him.

'Got to be honest, Joe, it's a damn sight more impressive than its Edinburgh equivalent.'

'Bigger and better, that's the Glasgow way.'

'Well,' Cafferty said after a moment's consideration, 'showier anyway.'

'If it's sightseeing you're after, I'm happy to oblige.'

Cafferty faced the man for the first time. 'You're looking well.'

'I'm breathing.'

'That makes two of us – against all the odds.'

'That sounds like the Glasgow way, too.' Stark saw that Cafferty was studying the statue next to them.

'"Thomas Graham,"' Cafferty read from the plaque below the statue, '"brilliant experimental chemist." We've known a few of those in our time, eh, Joe?' He began to chuckle, but Stark was staring hard at him.

'Why are you here?' he hissed.

'I'm a pensioner like you. The buses are free, so why not use them?'

'You came on the bus?'

Cafferty shook his head and Stark stifled a snort.

'Someone lamped Darryl Christie,' Cafferty stated.

'The lad got careless.'

'Maybe he thought he was untouchable.'

'Nobody's untouchable.'

'You might have been wondering if it was my doing.'

'While you've been thinking it was me, eh?'

'But let's suppose it was neither of us . . .' Cafferty paused as a fire engine roared past, siren howling. 'You've not exactly leapt to the lad's defence.'

'He hasn't asked.'

'Might make him seem weak if he did, but that wouldn't stop you offering.'

'Who's saying I didn't?'

'It's just a feeling I get.' Cafferty waited for a response, but Stark remained silent. 'Now if I was a betting man, Joe, I'd say you're maybe being a bit cautious. And the reason for that could be you think Darryl's about to be toppled. Nobody wants to be on the losing side when that happens. No point making unnecessary enemies, eh?'

'Darryl's a good kid.'

'I won't deny it. But even good kids make mistakes.'

'What have you heard?'

'Just whispers. I didn't give them much credence until the attack.'

'Not much of an attack, was it? Amateur hour, more like.'

'Which is why we can rule one another out, but who does that leave? Reason I had Edinburgh to myself for so long is it's more like a village than a city – better money to be made elsewhere.'

'Lean times, Cafferty.' Stark sniffed and shoved his hands deep into his coat pockets. 'Plenty of jackals watching the watering holes.'

'Care to name names?'

'Usual suspects – you know them as well as I do.'

Cafferty nodded slowly. He placed a hand on Joe Stark's shoulder, fixing him with a look. 'You really don't have a clue, do you?'

Stark was still considering his response when Cafferty turned and walked away. There was a shiny silver Merc parked outside the City Chambers, and at his approach its liveried driver leapt out, holding open the rear door and closing it again after him. Stark's trusted lieutenants, who had moved to a discreet distance during the dialogue, appeared at either of the boss's shoulders.

'What was that all about?' Grieve asked.

'A little fishing trip,' Stark muttered, watching the car drive off.
'And?'

'And I need a drink.'

'So which were you – the bait or the catch?'

Stark glowered at Grieve until the message got through. Then the three men, marching almost in line, Joe Stark half a pace ahead, started in the direction of Ingram Street.

'This is nice,' Clarke said uneasily, and not for the first time. She was seated at a banquette table in the Voodoo Rooms, just upstairs from the Café Royal, where she'd made the rendezvous with Rebus. It was eight in the evening and a blues band were due to play in the ballroom.

'The devil's own music,' Rebus had said.

The bar area was busy and noisy – not the sort of place she would usually associate with her dinner companion.

'My treat,' Rebus said as their food arrived.

'So why do I feel like the sacrificial offering?'

He gawped at her. 'I'm trying to be nice here, Siobhan.'

'That's what's making me nervous.'

'Maybe a bit of a boogie later.'

'I'm deleting "nervous" and adding "terrified".'

'Oh ye of little faith.' Rebus picked up his lamb chop and bit into it. 'So how pissed off with Malcolm are you right now – say on a scale of nine to ten?'

'Maybe a three.' She plucked a chip from her plate and bit it in half.

'That's pretty generous. Any progress with Craw?'

'He's still in one piece, as far as I can tell.'

'When was the last time you checked?'

She made show of studying her phone's screen. 'I'm checking right now.'

'Squad cars, though – someone could be bludgeoning him to death and they'd struggle to notice.'

'I'm sure the lower ranks love you too.'

'First time for everything,' he said with a wink, tossing the bone on to his plate and sucking clean his fingers. 'Another drink?'

'Aren't you supposed to be going easy?'

He tapped his beer glass. 'Low-alcohol.'

'Are you serious?'

'Tastes like hell, but it's got to be doing me good. Gin and tonic, yes?'

'Just a tonic.'

'Sure?'

She nodded, then watched him approach the bar. He held up a ten-pound note and soon had the attention of the staff. Clarke tapped her phone again: no new messages. She had driven down Craw Shand's street herself just after 5.30. No sign of either Devil's Dram Harry or Darryl Christie's car. Curtains closed, house apparently unlit. She jabbed at a morsel of fish and popped it into her mouth. Rebus was in conversation with a man at the bar. He appeared to be offering to buy the stranger a drink, but was shown a nearly full pint of lager. The man was bald and overweight, dressed in faded denims, an unbuttoned leather waistcoat, and a black T-shirt featuring a band logo. Rebus nodded towards the table and gave a wave. Clarke nodded back, wondering what was going on. Eventually both men approached, one far less reluctantly than the other.

'Dougie here,' Rebus said, altogether too jovially, 'won't take my word for it that we're CID. He wants to see some ID – would you credit that?'

Clarke was still chewing as she fished out her warrant card. Having placed their drinks on the table, Rebus clamped a hand around the man's forearm.

'Happy now?' he enquired. Then: 'Sit down, why don't you?'

Clarke's eyes were demanding answers as the two men slid on to the banquette, the visitor effectively trapped.

'I'm on stage in quarter of an hour,' he complained, a sheen of sweat on his forehead.

'This is Dougie Vaughan,' Rebus announced by way of introduction.

'What's this all about?' Vaughan asked. A tic had formed in one eyelid. He tried rubbing it away.

'It's just that there's some renewed interest in the Maria Turquand murder,' Rebus explained.

'And what's that got to do with me?'

'You were there when she died, Dougie,' Rebus stated.

'Where?'

'In the next room along.'

Vaughan shook his head. 'Says who?'

'You had a key to Vince Brady's room, didn't you?'

'No.'

'I heard differently.'

'I crashed on Bruce's bed. This was all in my original statement.'

'But then Vince started letting a few things slip out . . .'

'Because that writer paid him to. After he ripped Bruce off, no-body would work with him. He was skint, his health was ropey, and he had a wife and kids at home.' Vaughan paused. 'That's the most generous interpretation, mind. Bruce would have another view.'

'We know there was no love lost latterly.'

'He ripped Bruce off, pure and simple.'

'Money's often at the root of it,' Rebus seemed to concur. 'But then there's lust, too. And envy.' He looked to Clarke. 'Help me out here.'

'Pride,' she offered. 'Sloth . . .'

'Money isn't one of the sins,' Vaughan said. Rebus stared at him, then at Clarke.

'Is that right?'

'Could be,' she shrugged.

'Don't suppose it matters,' Rebus conceded. 'Maria Turquand wasn't killed for the contents of her purse.' He had fixed his eyes on Vaughan. 'Ever wondered why she *was* murdered that day, Dougie?'

Vaughan shrugged. 'Crime of passion?' he eventually offered.

'Does look that way, doesn't it? And one person we know she shared a bit of passion with was you.'

'Hang on a second. That was strictly one night only. I was stoned and she was blootered – I'm amazed we managed to do anything. And I volunteered as much as I could remember to the original inquiry.'

'That's not quite true, is it, Dougie? You only went to the papers later with your wee kiss-and-tell – looks to me like Vince wasn't the only one making money out of the poor woman's demise . . .'

A man with a thinning silver ponytail stopped in front of the table.

'You about ready, man?' he asked Vaughan.

'He'll be there,' Rebus said, his tone sending the ponytail on a hasty retreat to the ballroom. Then, to Vaughan: 'You didn't bump into her at the hotel that day?'

'No.'

'But your pal Bruce did.'

Vaughan was shaking his head. 'Vince Brady's lies again,' he stated. 'Unless there's new evidence? Is that what this is all about?'

He tried hoisting his glass, but the tremble in his hand defeated him.

'Bloody hell,' Rebus said, 'better get a steadier nerve before you have to pick up your axe. But now you've asked, I might as well tell you.' He slid so close to Vaughan the two men looked joined at the hip. 'Here's the thing – a detective called Robert Chatham was in charge of the last review.'

'I remember talking to him,' Vaughan admitted.

'Well, now he's been done away with, and that's put a whammy bar up all our jacksies. So let me ask you this – when did you last clap eyes on him?'

Vaughan's shoulders twitched. 'Must have been a couple of months back.'

Rebus managed to look as though he'd been expecting no less. 'And where was that?'

'Right here, I think. He was with Maxine.'

'Maxine Dromgoole?'

Vaughan was nodding. Rebus looked to Clarke. 'She's the writer who got the whole case reopened.'

'Right,' Clarke said, clearly not having studied the file as closely as Rebus had.

'Maxine knows her blues,' Vaughan was saying. 'After she'd talked to me for her book, we kept in touch. I mean, she's on the mailing list for gigs.'

'And she was here with Robert Chatham?'

'Just that one time. They were at the back of the room, next to the door. I knew I knew him from somewhere, but it took me a day or two to remember.'

'You didn't talk to them that night?' Clarke asked.

'They were gone by the time we finished the first set.'

'Did you think that was odd?'

'What?'

'The two of them being together.'

'What's odd about it?'

'Did you ever see them together again?'

'No.'

'You never happened to mention to Maxine that you'd clocked who she was with?' Rebus watched Vaughan nod slowly. 'And what did she say?'

'I don't really remember. Maybe something about bumping into him on the street. Edinburgh's that sort of place, isn't it?' Vaughan broke off. 'I really need to go. Is that okay?'

Rebus made a gesture and slid from the booth, allowing the man to get out. Vaughan paused in front of the table. 'I crashed out on the bed in Bruce's suite,' he repeated. 'When I woke up, someone had taken all my cash.'

'Just the cash?'

'Well, the key wasn't there, but the state I was in, if I ever *did* have it, I could have left it anywhere.' He offered a shrug and moved off. Rebus watched him go.

'Why would she do that?' he asked Clarke.

'Sex with Mr Vaughan, you mean?'

'Well, that too. But I'm talking about Dromgoole. She's having a huge secret affair with Rab Chatham, and she brings him face to face with Dougie Vaughan.'

'They were having an affair?'

Rebus nodded distractedly. 'Malcolm phoned me with the news.'

'That was nice of him – so what's your thinking?'

'Maybe she was shaking the tree. That's feasible, isn't it? But it would mean she hadn't quite let the Turquand story lie, in which case it's also possible she had nudged Chatham into getting back into it too.' He began to scratch his throat with a fingernail, only eventually noting the look Clarke was giving him.

'What?' he asked.

'You needed me here in case he asked to see a warrant card,' she stated.

'Busted,' Rebus admitted, helping himself to one of her chips.

Fox's sister lived on a terraced street in Saughtonhall. A lamp was on in her living room and the curtains were open, so he watched her for a moment through the window. She was curled up in an armchair, an ashtray on her thigh, cigarette in one hand and phone in the other. Just as he was about to tap a greeting on the glass, she caught a glimpse of him and, startled, leapt to her feet, sending ashtray, phone and cigarette flying.

'Just me!' he called as she approached the window. Next thing, she was at the door.

'What are you up to?' she complained.

'I saw your light was on. I was about to knock.'

'Instead of which you stood out there in the dark like any other bloody pervert.'

She had headed indoors again and was picking up her phone and ashtray. Fox located the smouldering cigarette. It had left a burn in the oatmeal carpet – by no means the first. She plucked it from him and held it between her lips as she tidied up butts.

'I'll help you vacuum,' Fox offered.

'It needs repairing.'

'What's wrong with it?'

'It doesn't work,' she stated, settling into her chair again, eyes on the screen.

'Must be an important text,' he mused.

'It's a game.' She turned the phone towards him for a moment. All he could make out were coloured balls arranged in rows. 'And before you ask, I got it for free.'

'I wasn't going to ask,' he lied, looking for somewhere to sit that wasn't covered in sandwich wrappers, crisp packets or women's magazines. Instead, he opened the window an inch.

'Just letting some air in,' he said when Jude gave him another of her looks. 'So how have you been?'

'You mean since you found me in that gambling den? And come to think of it, what were *you* doing there?'

'A routine inquiry.'

'I bet you say that to all the women you stalk.' She exhaled smoke towards the ceiling.

'I really wasn't stalking you. I didn't even know you liked a flutter.'

'A girl needs something to occupy her time.'

'Yes, so you said.'

She glanced up from her phone. 'Did I? Sorry if I found our little chat instantly forgettable.'

'Do you ever use other betting shops?'

'You know me, Malcolm – a complete tart. One of anything is never enough.'

He chose to ignore her tone. 'How about on Great Junction Street?'

'I'm not often in Leith.'

'But if you were . . .?'

She either paused or finished her game, placing the phone face down next to the ashtray and studying her brother.

'Is this your latest crusade? People gambling their lives away? Last time I looked, it wasn't a crime.'

'Those fixed-odds machines, they're sometimes used to launder money.'

'You looking to recruit your own sister as a spy? Is that what this is all about?'

'No.' He paused. 'But if you did happen to see or hear anything . . .'

'Like any other upright citizen I'd come straight to you, Officer.' She paused. 'But how will I tell which are the bad guys?' She tapped her cigarette against the rim of the ashtray.

'Maybe the amount of money they're feeding into the machines, and the fact they don't look too bothered about risking it.'

'And say I go along with this – do I get something in return?'

'You mean apart from the gratitude of the law-abiding public?'

'Yes.'

'Was there anything in particular?'

'Maybe a moratorium on you nagging me.'

'Define "nagging".'

'Getting at me about my lifestyle, my laziness, my not having a job.' She stubbed out her cigarette. 'Oh, and all that holier-than-thou guff about the money you dole out.'

'It's to pay your rent and bills.'

'And because you needed a new charity case after Dad died.'

'Yes, you said that the other day, too.' Fox's own phone was buzzing. Caller ID: Sheila Graham. 'I need to take this,' he muttered, heading for the hallway, answering only after he'd closed the living-room door.

'Good evening, Sheila.'

'Is this a bad time?'

'Not at all. You're working late.'

'I was in Edinburgh for a meeting. I got to Waverley just in time to see my train pull away, so I just wondered if you were at a loose end.'

'I can be there in fifteen minutes. There's a bar called the Doric across the street from the back entrance.'

'I think I saw it when the cab dropped me off. I'll have a beer waiting for you.'

'I usually drink Appletiser.'

'Then you're a cheap date.'

'Fifteen minutes.'

He ended the call and went back into the living room.

'I've got to go,' he announced. Jude had lit a fresh cigarette and was busy on her phone again. She held up her hand and gave him the briefest of waves.

'The place I'm interested in is called Klondyke Alley,' he added.

'Klondyke Alley,' she echoed, eyes fixed on the screen. 'Always supposing I happen to find myself on Great Junction Street.'

'Always supposing,' Fox agreed, turning to leave. 'And thanks.'

After he had gone, Jude went over to the window just to make sure. Then she took a small piece of paper from the back pocket of her jeans and unfolded it, tapping the number into her phone.

'Hello?' she said when her call was answered. 'I need to talk to Mr Christie. Is there any way you can get a message to him?'

Sheila Graham was dressed for business – charcoal two-piece trouser suit with plain white blouse beneath. Earlier, the blouse might have been buttoned to the neck, but now it was open, as if to signal that she was off duty. She was at a table by the window and smiled as Fox walked in. Most of the other drinkers looked like people waiting for trains, wheelie cases and backpacks parked next to their seats. Graham had a laptop case and a shoulder bag and was drinking white wine. Fox's Appletiser was waiting. He perched on a stool across from her, lifted his glass and offered a toast.

'Rough day?' he enquired.

'Scottish Government stuff. I won't bore you with the details. How are things with you, Malcolm?'

'Slow but steady progress.'

'The guy arrested for the attack?'

'Is probably not who we're looking for. But I'm starting to wonder about Anthony Brough.'

'You doubt it's a coincidence that he's suddenly not around?'

'What do you think?'

'I think a number of Mr Brough's recent schemes have yielded big losses. A lot of his clients are out of pocket.'

'And baying for his blood?'

'I'm not sure about that. But these are people who can't always go chat to a bank manager about a loan to tide them over. Cash is their currency. They might need a lender who isn't going to ask too many questions . . .'

'Someone like Darryl Christie, you mean?'

She nodded slowly. 'But let's not make this about business, Malcolm. I appreciate you taking the trouble to keep me company.'

A slow smile spread across Fox's face. 'Oh I think this is *all* business, Sheila. There was a titbit you wanted to throw me and you've just accomplished that.'

'Am I so transparent? Well, maybe you're right. But that's done now, so we really can just have a drink and a chat.' She nodded towards his glass. 'Have you never been a drinker?'

'I was a drinker right up until the day I stopped.'

'What happened?'

'You know Jekyll and Hyde? That was me with alcohol.'

Graham tipped her head back, stretching her neck muscles. 'It just makes me nicely mellow,' she said. 'And some days I need that feeling.' She lifted her glass and clinked it against his. 'What about this other case you're working?'

'Oddly, it's beginning to connect to yours.'

'Oh?'

'The ex-cop who was killed, he ran a review of the Maria Turquand murder.'

'I don't think I know her.'

'She was found dead in her hotel room in 1978.'

'Here in the city?'

'Right here.'

'And they told me Edinburgh was safe for women. So where's the connection?'

'Maria's husband was Sir Magnus Brough's right-hand man. Fast forward to the present, and grandson Anthony has an office that pretty much looks on to the hotel where Maria was murdered.'

Graham puzzled over this as she sipped her drink.

'I'm not saying there's any *real* connection, of course,' Fox felt it necessary to qualify. 'It's interesting, that's all. But when Anthony's parents died, he and his sister were basically raised by Sir Magnus.'

'There may be something else,' Graham said quietly, resting her elbows on the table. 'One of Anthony's early clients was John Turquand. It was in the papers at the time. Brough used it as a sort of calling card to other would-be investors. Turquand's long retired, but his was a respected name in financial circles.' She broke off. 'We seem to be talking shop again, don't we?'

'Well, you did ask.'

'I suppose I did.' She glanced at her phone. 'Just checking the time.'

'How long before the next train?'

'Seventeen minutes.'

'Another white wine, then?'

'Why not?'

He went to the bar, wondering about Anthony Brough and John Turquand, and about Darryl Christie and Maria Turquand's murder. Placing the fresh drink in front of Graham, he asked what she thought of Brough's disappearance.

'Nobody's reported him missing,' she confided. 'Not much to be done until they do.'

'Is he married?'

'Still very much the playboy about town. He could be lying low in a hotel suite anywhere between here and Sydney.'

'The question is why.'

'Agreed.'

'Do you think Darryl Christie would shed any light?'

'I think he'd deny even knowing Brough's name.'

'There's no record of them working together or meeting up?'

'It's all an electronic and paper trail, Malcolm. And you'd have the devil's job finding Christie's name anywhere. Companies he's associated with, yes, but the man himself is bloody elusive.'

'Is there anything you *can* pull him in for?'

'You mean so we can fish without seeming to?' She considered this. 'Far as we know, his tax affairs are in order. There was a full audit two years back, and he ended up paying a few hundred quid.' She shrugged.

'But if he's lending money illegally . . .'

'It's not necessarily illegal to lend money. Besides which, we've no proof other than hearsay and guesswork. Our best bet is still this physical attack on him. It has to mean something and it must have shaken him up, made him wonder who his friends are and who might have it in for him.'

'Then you should talk to your boss, demand phone taps and twenty-four/seven surveillance.'

'The sort of thing that was meat and drink to you when you worked Professional Standards?'

'Damned right.'

'I suppose I could ask, though I'm in danger of sounding like a broken record.' She placed a hand on her stomach to stifle a sudden gurgling. 'Should have grabbed something to eat,' she apologised.

'It's not too late,' Fox said. 'There are places on Cockburn Street.' He paused. 'Always supposing there's a later train you can catch.'

She met his eyes. 'There's a later train,' she said. 'But on one condition.'

He held up a hand. 'I've got to insist on paying – my town, my rules.'

'How very gallant of you. But my condition is no shop talk. For real this time.'

'Pretend we're normal people, you mean?'

'Normal people eating a normal dinner on a normal night out.'

'It's not going to be easy,' Fox warned her. 'But let's give it a go . . .'

Day Six

13

The call had come at 6.30 a.m., hauling Siobhan Clarke from her bed. She pulled on some clothes, dragged a wet brush through her hair and headed for her Astra. The patrol car was parked outside Craw Shand's house, two uniforms waiting for her. It was just starting to get light and the street lamps were still on, bathing both men in a faint orange glow.

'Round the back,' one of them said.

She followed them around the side of the house into the handkerchief-sized garden. The door to the kitchen stood open, splinters of wood showing where it had been forced.

'You've been in?' Clarke asked.

'Only to ascertain there's no one home.'

'Have you called it in as a crime scene?'

'Can't really say that it is, unless you know different.'

'If it's not a crime scene, what is it?'

'Maybe he locked himself out,' the officer said with a shrug.

Clarke stepped inside, keeping her hands in her pockets so there'd be no temptation to touch anything.

'One thing the CSM hates,' she advised, 'is contamination.' She turned towards the two constables. 'Stay here while I take a look.'

She hadn't been in the house before, but it didn't look as though it had been trashed, and there was still a TV in the living room. Bottles of booze untouched, too. Upstairs: Shand's bedroom, plus a spare that was being used for storage. No sign of any violence; no ransacking. So what the hell had happened?

She padded back down the stairs to the kitchen.

'What do you think?' she was asked.

'I think a man charged with assault has just gone missing.'

'Somebody took him?'

'Or he left before they got here.'

'Could be they came looking,' the second officer proposed, 'but there was no one home. Shand returns later, sees the state of his door, and makes himself scarce.'

'Possible,' Clarke said, looking at the dishes piled up in the sink.

'So is it a crime scene or not?'

'Won't do any harm to dust for prints. Everybody leaves something behind – a hair, a bit of saliva, maybe a footprint . . .'

'You don't sound hopeful.'

'Lack of enthusiasm due to too little sleep,' Clarke commented, taking out her phone, scrolling to 'CSM' in her address book and making the call. While she waited for it to be picked up, she made sure she had both officers' full attention. 'We have photos and physical description on file – I want them circulated PDQ. Shand is a creature of habit. If he's out there, he's going to become visible.'

'And if he's running, we just have to find him before anyone else.'

'That, too,' Clarke said, as Haj Atwal answered her call and asked why whatever she wanted couldn't wait another hour.

Fox was seated at his desk, reading the copy of Maxine Dromgoole's book that had arrived from the library service. He had already noted that it had been last borrowed just under a year back. Judging from the date stamps in the front, it had been popular when first published. Its title was *The Ends of Justice: Scotland's Greatest Unsolved Crimes*. Bible John was in there, of course, as were the World's End murders and Renee MacRae, but by far the longest chapter was dedicated to Maria Turquand. Nothing more recent, though; nothing to suggest that Robert Chatham had been feeding other titbits to his lover.

Hearing his name called, Fox looked up from his work. Alvin James was the only other person in the room. He was gesturing towards him, so Fox crossed to his desk. James was watching something on his laptop.

'CCTV from outside a place called the Tomahawk Club, two Saturdays back. These must be the blokes Dromgoole was talking about.'

'No sound?'

'Just pictures, more's the pity, and grainier than I'd like.'

Fox watched as three figures confronted Chatham. There was a good deal of finger-pointing and what looked like shouting. The leader of the group rose up on his toes to make himself appear taller. Chatham stood his ground, though, and seemed implacable. He was not about to be goaded into a fight, even after another doorman arrived as back-up. Then a fourth figure appeared and seemed to calm things down further, slinging an arm around the most hot-tempered of the group.

'Looks like smoke rather than fire,' Fox commented.

'I still want to talk to them.' James shut down the file and opened another. 'And I've invited this ne'er-do-well in for a chat, too.'

Another grainy night-time video. Fox knew who he was watching, though he doubted anyone who didn't know him would have been able to identify John Rebus.

'They're just talking,' he said.

'That they are. But as soon as Rebus leaves, Chatham gets out his phone and makes a call.'

'Yes, it's on his billing statement. He was speaking to his boss.'

'But watch this.' Chatham forwarded the recording. 'See? Chatham asks his colleague to take over. Then he walks out of shot.'

'Headed where?'

James gave a little smile. He clicked on a third file. 'CCTV from outside a pub further down the street. See that phone box? Does that look like Robert Chatham opening its door?'

'I suppose it does,' Fox conceded.

'Man carries a mobile with him, why use a public telephone?'

'He didn't want the call to be traceable?' Fox offered. James nodded his agreement.

'I'd love to know who he was calling.'

'I doubt an interview with Rebus will give you any answers.'

'You rang, m'lord?'

The two men looked up as Rebus walked in.

'How did you get past the front desk?' James demanded to know.

'The front desk of a police station in my home city? As an ex-cop, I really haven't a clue.'

'I'm going to be having words with them,' James stated.

'So how goes it at the beating heart of the investigation?' Rebus asked as he made a circuit of the room, pausing at Fox's desk to pick up the copy of the Dromgoole book. 'Any good?' he asked Fox, waving it at him.

'When I left my message,' James interrupted, 'I specified that you should phone and make an appointment for the interview.'

'Well, I was in the area,' Rebus responded. 'But it looks like most of your crew sleep late, so unless one of you two wants the job, maybe I'll come back another time . . .'

'Now you're here, maybe you should take a look at this,' James said. Rebus walked around the desk, watching the film over James's shoulder and nodding afterwards.

'I've been wondering about that call.'

'Chatham's boss is called Kenny Arnott,' Fox explained. 'He runs a company supplying doormen to pubs and clubs.'

James was staring at Rebus. 'What about the phone box?'

Rebus shrugged. 'I wouldn't mind knowing who he was calling.'

'I'll be requesting that information, don't you worry.' James closed the file and leaned back in his chair. 'And while I'm doing that, Malcolm will be taking your statement.'

There was a momentary silence as Fox and Rebus made eye contact.

'Fine,' Malcolm Fox said.

He led the way to the interview room. There was a tape machine fixed to its table, plus a camera pointing down from one corner of the ceiling. Fox took a seat and motioned for Rebus to sit opposite.

'No notes?' Rebus asked.

'Not needed.'

'Recording?'

Fox shook his head. 'Let's make this quick. You're here because you twice spoke to Chatham in the days before he died. Once in the café, and prior to that outside a bar he was working.'

'I can't deny it. I also had nothing to do with his death.'

'We both know this is a waste of time, but one thing stands out – he was spooked by something you said.'

Rebus processed the information. 'Agreed,' he said.

'So who did he call, and why?'

'He used a public phone to keep things nice and private.'

'That's how it looks.'

'I wish I could help, Malcolm,' Rebus said with a shrug.

'The only thing the pair of you talked about was the Turquand case?'

'Correct.'

'It was a brief chat that first night?'

'You saw it yourself on the tape – I wanted it to be longer but he

150

said he was knackered. You've got the CCTV – does anyone rock up after I left, someone he might have arranged to meet?'

'Detective Superintendent James has been the one watching the footage.'

'Maybe I should take a look, too.'

'Feel free to ask him.'

'I'm asking you.'

Fox shook his head slowly. He was still shaking it as the door opened. James himself was standing there.

'Slight problem,' he said. 'I've been called to Gartcosh – got to brief the chiefs.'

'I think I can hold the fort till the others get back,' Fox said.

'Thing is, Maxine Dromgoole's just turned up at the front desk. You okay to do her interview, too?'

'Of course,' Fox stated.

James was looking at Rebus. 'Sorry we're kicking you out.'

'I'm devastated.'

James decided to ignore this, leaving the door ajar as he made his exit.

'He doesn't like to keep his masters waiting, does he?' Rebus commented.

'It's true what he says, though – we only have the one interview room, so . . .'

'Let me sit in.'

Fox stared at him. 'Why?'

'Because there's something I know that you don't.'

'It wouldn't exactly be following procedure.'

'Nobody'll know if you don't tape it.'

Fox leaned back a little and folded his arms, waiting for more, so Rebus obliged.

'One question – I just have to ask her one question.'

'And then I'll know what you know?'

'Yes. Though there is an alternative.'

'And what's that?'

'While you're stuck in here, I'm on James's laptop playing the CCTV.'

'He really wouldn't like that.'

'Hard to disagree.'

'What do you know about Dromgoole?'

'Apart from her being Chatham's lover? Well, she wrote that book on your desk. Her piece about Collier's road manager kicked off Chatham's review of the Turquand case. It was all in the file Siobhan gave me.' Rebus paused. 'And one more thing . . .' His voice tailed off.

'Which I'll only find out if I let you sit in on the interview?'

'Yes.'

'This is the thanks I get for calling you to tell you about the affair in the first place?'

'I'm a bad bugger, Malcolm, there's no denying it.'

Fox gave a sigh. 'One question?'

Rebus held up his forefinger. 'Scout's honour.'

'You stay here then,' Fox eventually said, knowing he was probably going to regret it, 'and I'll go fetch her.'

Two minutes later he was back. Rebus had vacated his seat and offered it to Dromgoole as she entered. She sat down and Rebus took up position by the door. Fox had started unwrapping a tape, but then remembered Rebus's words and left it next to the machine.

'My colleague here,' he said as carefully as he could, 'goes by the name of John Rebus.'

She raised both eyebrows, studying Rebus as though he were some new and interesting species. 'I know who you are,' she said. 'You've got history with Morris Gerald Cafferty.'

Rebus tried to think of a response, but Dromgoole wasn't about to wait. 'Could you get me a meeting with him?'

'A meeting with Cafferty?'

'I'm hoping to write a book – did Inspector Fox not say?'

Rebus gave Fox a hard stare, but she was talking again.

'I've tried writing to him, but he never replies. It's a book about Scotland in the seventies and eighties, about the criminals of the day and what they got up to. From my research, Mr Cafferty would seem the best candidate – most of the others of his ilk are no longer around to tell their stories.'

'Cafferty may even have hastened their demise,' Rebus said.

'Are you still in touch with him?'

'Not really,' he lied.

'But you could get a message to him?'

'I wouldn't like to promise anything.'

Fox shifted in his chair. 'To bring us back to the reason you're here, Ms Dromgoole . . .'

Chastened by his tone, she calmed, and even managed to look solemn. But she couldn't help glancing towards Rebus as she answered Fox's questions about her relationship with Robert

Chatham. After quarter of an hour, Fox was winding down. Rebus decided this was his cue.

'You met Mr Chatham because of the Maria Turquand case,' he said. She half turned in her chair so she was facing him.

'Yes,' she agreed.

'Did you retain an interest in it? After you'd published your book, I mean.'

'I suppose so.'

'Occasional chats about it with Mr Chatham? And maybe with others, too? People like Dougie Vaughan?'

'Have you been speaking to Dougie?'

'I was at his concert last night.'

'It was in my diary,' Dromgoole said. 'But I didn't feel up to it, of course.'

'You're a fan, though? You go watch him perform, probably buy him a drink after?'

'Or during,' she corrected him.

'And one night, you took Mr Chatham along too. I think you did that knowing Dougie would eventually place him. Were you hoping for something? Maybe a guilty look or a sudden bum note that would give the game away?'

'I suppose I was,' she eventually conceded. 'Rab was angry with me afterwards. If Dougie recognised him, then he might also work out we were lovers. Rab was scared Liz would find out.'

'But you considered it a risk worth taking?'

'Yes.'

'Because above all else, you can't let Maria Turquand go?'

She considered how to answer. 'Maria was an extraordinary woman. A free spirit in a world that demanded the opposite. All those boring money men and their dinners and clubs. She should never have allowed herself to be trapped. They couldn't deal with her, you see.' She stared at Rebus. 'You're interested too, aren't you?'

'A few questions had cropped up,' Rebus answered her. 'I spoke to Rab about them, and soon after that . . .'

'You're the ex-cop – he texted me about you.'

'Do you think he might have been doing some archaeology himself? Maybe so he could surprise you if and when he found anything?'

'I suppose it's possible.' She was still staring at Rebus. '*Is* there something new?' But Rebus wasn't about to answer that. 'Have you spoken to Maria's husband and her lover?' Dromgoole continued.

'They're both still alive, you know. When I asked for interviews, they resisted. I ended up posing written questions, but their answers were vague. I'm not sure either of them really loved her . . .' After a moment lost in thought, she became animated again. 'You really should question them! They can hardly refuse to answer a detective!'

'That's certainly true,' Rebus said, glancing in Fox's direction.

After a further five minutes, Fox accompanied Dromgoole to the station's front door, shaking her hand and asking if she didn't want a taxi. But she preferred to walk – she *needed* a walk. He climbed the stairs again to find Rebus at Alvin James's computer.

'Christ's sake, John,' he complained.

'I can't unlock it,' Rebus said. 'I don't suppose you know his password?'

'I wouldn't tell you if I did.'

Rebus slammed the screen shut and leaned back in James's chair. 'What do we do now, then? And where are the rest of the goon squad anyway?'

'Tracking down Chatham's friends and colleagues . . . talking to his employer . . .'

'Remind me of the name.'

'Kenny Arnott.' Fox sifted through the notes on his desk. 'There are two outfits in the city providing similar services – one run by Andrew Goodman, one by Arnott.'

'Either of them ever been in trouble?'

'Not that I know of.'

'Doesn't sound like it'll keep James's crew busy for long, then.'

'They're also going through Chatham's house, seeing if there's anything on his computer or tucked away in a drawer somewhere . . .'

'While you're left here to read a library book?'

'Playing to one of my many strengths.'

'What? Basic literacy?'

Fox managed a smile, and Rebus joined him. 'So how will you be spending *your* day?' Fox asked.

'If I had a warrant card on me, I'd probably be heading off to talk to a couple of antiquated rich white men.'

'Turquand and Attwood?'

'One in St Andrews and one in Perthshire – not a bad afternoon out of the office.'

'But you've not got a warrant card, have you?'

'The only flaw in my plan.'

'I could come with you.'

154

'And why would you do that?'

'Because there's something I know that you don't.'

'And I'll only find out what that is if I take you?'

'One question, John. For Turquand specifically.' Fox was holding up his forefinger. Rebus mirrored the action as both men's smiles broadened.

Harry's full name was Hugh Harold Hodges. He'd had his first spot of bother with the police at the age of eleven: shoplifting from a supermarket. A dare, apparently. His parents were professionals – one a doctor, one a teacher – and they were paying for him to attend a good school. But he started truanting, and the shoplifting continued. Harry liked hanging around older, less privileged kids. He stole for them, fought alongside them and smoked dope with them. So his parents kicked him out. Slept rough for a while, then seemed to step off the grid completely until he cropped up in France, where the Parisian police took an interest. So it was back to Edinburgh and eventually work for Darryl Christie.

All of this Clarke had learned in the space of just over thirty minutes, thanks to the Police Scotland database. It had been two years since Hodges' last run-in with the law – stopped with a car full of untaxed cigarettes. He'd kept his mouth shut and paid the fine. But that should have prevented him owning or running a venue like the Devil's Dram, and a bit more digging had revealed that he neither owned nor ran it – not according to the paperwork. So what did he do?

Clarke was about to ask.

She thumped on the doors of the club and waited. Nobody answered so she tried again. There was a locked gate to the right of the building, leading to a narrow alley two inches deep in rubbish. To the left, a wider lane, paved with wonky-looking setts, led uphill and around to the back, where there was a door for deliveries. The door was open and cases of wine and beer were being unloaded from a white van with no discernible markings. The driver handed her a crate of twenty-four bottles, so she carried them inside. A young man she didn't recognise took them off her, eyes narrowing only slightly at the stranger's appearance.

'Harry around?' Clarke asked.

'Usual spot.'

Clarke nodded as if fully understanding, and walked through the storage area into a corridor, at the end of which was a door. Opening it, she stepped into the club proper. Harry's usual spot was the same one where she had found Darryl Christie on her previous visit. She was two thirds of the way up the staircase before he realised she wasn't staff.

'Who let you in?'

'A face friendlier than yours, Mr Hodges.'

'Oh, it knows my name.'

'And your record.'

'Rehabilitation is a great thing.'

'Is that what Darryl does – takes bad lads and turns them into paragons of virtue?'

'I'm a bit busy here, Officer.'

'Been out to see Craw Shand again? I'll be taking a look at the footage. Lot of traffic cameras along Peffermill Road.'

'Oh aye?'

'And that Range Rover does stand out.'

'You've still not said why you're here.'

'Mr Shand seems to have been abducted. That really wasn't a very good move on somebody's part.'

'I've already told you I don't know the fucker.'

'No need for bad language, Mr Hodges.' She paused for a second. 'Hugh Harold Hodges – your parents had a sense of humour, then?'

'Fuck you.'

'I want Craw Shand returned to me unharmed.'

'Good for you. Put it on your Christmas list.'

Clarke placed both hands on the table and leaned in towards him. 'It won't be a list I'll be carrying next time you see me. It'll be a warrant.'

Hodges looked her up and down. 'Your patter's as pish as your dress sense. The spinster look is *so* last year.'

'That hurts,' Clarke said, staring at his feet. 'What size shoes do you take? Looks like a nine. It's amazing what our lab can do with the impression of a sole – and one was left on Craw Shand's back door.' She paused to let this sink in. 'Tell your boss: Craw Shand belongs to me.'

'Tell him yourself. But do it somewhere else. And check out the gents' bogs on your way out – wee treat for you there.'

He got busy on his phone, checking messages and answering them with rapid movements of his thumb. Clarke held her ground for a few seconds longer, then walked down the stairs with as much dignity

156

as she could muster. As she made for the entrance, she paused and stared at the door to the gents. It was marked 'Warlocks' and wasn't giving anything away, so she pushed it open. There didn't seem to be anyone inside. She could see cubicles, sinks and a single trough-style urinal. And then something caught her eye. A large framed photograph, blown up from a video still. It was grainy, but she knew when it had been taken and who it showed. Deborah Quant's party. And there was Siobhan herself, in her short black dress, cut slightly too low at the neck. She had an arm around Quant's back and was leaning down to yell something in her ear, mouth and eyes open wide.

From the club's security cameras. Blown up and framed. Directly above the trough where the men stood in droves each evening.

She tried to shift it, but it had been screwed into the wall.

'Fuck,' she said under her breath.

'No need for bad language,' Hodges chided her, standing by the door, holding it a few inches open with one hand, a grin on his face.

'If you don't want us back here night after night, checking for drugs and underage drinkers, that'll be gone by the time I've reached my car.'

'Cops are always welcome here,' he said as she stormed past him. 'This'll be the highlight of their trip, wouldn't you say, Detective Inspector? And you should feel flattered – turns out even spinsters have a bit of life left in them when enough Happy Hour cocktails are poured down their throats . . .'

Forensics had finished at Craw Shand's. They had been satisfied with photos of the shoe print, so the door was still in place, a padlock added so the house could be secured before the team left. Although he had already been interviewed, the next-door neighbour came out to share his thoughts with Clarke.

'Never any trouble . . . didn't hear a peep in the night . . .'

The neighbour across the back from Shand had said the same. No shouts or yelps, nobody wrestling Craw Shand out from his kitchen. Nothing. Maybe the uniform had been right – the caved-in door had been waiting for Shand, and he'd taken fright and fled. Clarke had asked Laura Smith if she could place a story on the *Scotsman*'s website.

'Am I allowed to flag up the Darryl Christie connection?'

'Wiser not to.'

A patrol had last checked the rear of the property at 11 p.m., meaning the door had been forced sometime between then and six in the morning. Only one of the neighbours had seen Craw leave the house that day – a routine morning trip to the local shop. His TV had been heard through the wall in the afternoon – horse-racing commentary. As Clarke took a final tour of the rooms, she found little in the way of clues. A bag of groceries sat on the kitchen work-top – tinned soup, ravioli, peanuts. An open packet of biscuits on a chair in the living room. There was a large empty backpack on top of the wardrobe in Shand's bedroom. His drawers were half filled with clothes. Didn't mean he hadn't taken a smaller bag, maybe enough shirts and pants for a couple of days. The mail on the kitchen table didn't add much – a couple of overdue bills for his phone and his TV package, and one advising him that his gas supply was being disconnected. She had contacted his mobile provider. If he made any calls, she wanted to know about it pronto. The neighbours had been given her business card – they were to get in touch should Shand return home at any point, or anyone else pay a visit.

And that was that. Apart from one thing.

Christie picked up after three rings.

'I'm assuming you've heard from Harry?' Clarke asked.

'I only wish I'd been there when you saw that lovely photo. Now you know how it feels to be framed.'

'Is that what you think's happening to you?'

'Harry told you the God's own truth.'

'We're putting Craw's description out.'

'You know everyone will think I had something to do with it.'

'I don't suppose that'll do your reputation much harm.'

'If anything, it'll add to it, but that doesn't mean I snatched him. And by the way, I took your advice.'

'Oh?'

'Moved my mum and the boys into a hotel for a few days.'

'Has something else happened?'

'Cars rumbling past the house at odd hours . . . stopping outside, engines revving.'

'Recognise any of them?'

'No.'

'Maybe you got the licence numbers?'

'Sorry.'

'How about cameras? Have you got round to swapping your fakes for real ones?'

'I'm on it.'

'So with your mum and brothers gone, you've got the place to yourself?'

'You offering to babysit?'

'I'm just thinking how handy an empty house would be if you wanted to stash someone there.'

'Come take a look sometime.'

'Maybe I'll do that.'

'From what I hear of the man, you'd smell him long before you saw him. Bye bye, Inspector . . .'

Standing in his living room, staring out towards the park opposite, Christie realised that Cafferty now had a better view than him. Another black mark against the sod. Having ended the call with Clarke, he tapped in Hodges' number.

'Yes, boss?' Hodges asked.

'I just want to make sure we're clear on this – you didn't decide to use your initiative or anything? Maybe you've hidden Shand away and were planning to surprise me?'

'Absolutely not. Who's to say he's not just done a runner?'

'Did he maybe clock my car one of those times you did a drive-past?'

'That was the whole point, wasn't it?'

'I suppose so.' Christie ended the call and rubbed his free hand softly across his eyes. He was tired and knew he should switch off, if only for ten minutes. But how could he?

He was Darryl Christie.

People were out to get him.

He tried Anthony Brough's number again. The automated service picked up. It was sorry he could not leave a number but 'memory is full'.

'I swear I'm going to kill you,' Christie said into his phone. Then he heard a noise out in the hall.

Heavy footsteps descending the staircase in a rush.

Christie shook his head and smiled . . .

14

Maxine Dromgoole had sent Fox a text with addresses and phone numbers for Peter Attwood and John Turquand. Fox sat in the passenger seat of Rebus's Saab, checking maps on his phone while Rebus drove. A few miles south of St Andrews, however, Rebus started coughing and had to stop by the side of the road while the fit continued. His face had gone puce-coloured behind the handkerchief he was holding to his mouth.

'Christ, John.' Fox tried patting Rebus's back. 'You sure you're okay?'

Instead of answering, Rebus got out of the car, fumbling in his jacket for his inhaler. They were on a straight stretch of road, fields either side. He stood on the overgrown verge, bent over with hands on knees, until the coughing eventually subsided. He wiped tears from the corners of his eyes. Fox had emerged from the car and was standing a few feet away. A tractor chugged past, its driver watching them, trying to decide what they were up to.

'Sorry about that,' Rebus said, gasping for breath.

'No need to apologise. What's in the inhaler?'

'Some kind of steroids. They've promised me I'll be on the weightlifting team come the next Commonwealth Games.' Rebus patted his chest. 'Thought I was maybe getting over it – not that you *do* get over it.'

'This isn't just bronchitis, is it?'

'What else would it be?'

'Something that's got you fretting. I notice things like that.'

Rebus stuffed the inhaler back in his pocket. 'It's probably nothing,' he said.

'Okay.'

He met Fox's eyes and made his mind up. 'A shadow on one lung,' he confessed. 'They've done a biopsy. No results as yet. You're the only one I've told, and if it goes any further you'll be the second detective to be fished out of the Forth – understood?'

'Of course.'

'Last thing I need is anyone treating me as a charity case.'

'You mean Deborah Quant?'

'Deb . . . Siobhan . . .'

'But you don't think I'd do that?'

'You don't like me well enough.'

'I like you fine.'

'You're a terrible liar, Malcolm. When you were Complaints, you tried your damnedest to nail me.'

'You weren't exactly a model police officer.'

'Granted.'

'But that's history.'

'Besides which, you got your wish – I'm not a cop these days.'

'You still do a pretty good impression.' Fox paused, watching a car speed past on its way to St Andrews. 'So when will you have news?'

'About Hank Marvin? Any day – might even be an envelope or a phone message waiting for me at home right now.'

'Hank Marvin played guitar in the Shadows,' Fox said.

'You catch on fast, Malcolm.'

'I have my moments. Do you want me to drive? We're nearly there.'

Rebus shook his head. 'I need you to navigate, remember? Those bloody phone apps make no sense to me whatsoever . . .'

Both men had seen photos of Peter Attwood, but none of them recent. He lived with his wife in a modern detached house on the outskirts of the town. As the Saab crunched over the gravel drive- way, Attwood appeared at the door. He wore a baggy brown cardigan and brown cord trousers, and his thinning silver hair looked bril- liantined. A pipe was clamped between his teeth. He shook hands with both visitors as they made their introductions.

'Jessica's visiting a friend,' he said, leading them indoors, 'but I'm just about capable of making a cup of tea.'

While he was in the kitchen, Rebus and Fox explored the

living room. Bookshelves, a rack filled with classical CDs, a TV that wouldn't have looked out of place on *Antiques Roadshow*. There were a couple of squishy armchairs and matching sofa, plus an array of family photographs on the mantelpiece.

'Seems to come round regular as clockwork,' Attwood said, carrying in a tray and placing it on the small table between the armchairs.

'What does, sir?' Fox asked.

'Reopening the file on poor Maria's death. Help yourselves, chaps.' Attwood added a splash of milk to his own mug and sat down. Rebus and Fox did the same, settling side by side on the sofa.

'Eight years ago,' Rebus said, 'you would have been interviewed by an officer called Chatham.'

'That sounds about right. Then there was the ghastly journalist woman . . .'

'Maxine Dromgoole,' Fox clarified.

'The very same.'

'The thing is, sir,' Rebus said, 'Robert Chatham has been murdered.'

'Bloody hell.'

'And we just wondered if you'd had any contact with him.'

'Why should I?'

'Because he might not have been able to let the case go.'

Attwood considered this. 'Maria had that effect on men, but I haven't heard anything of the fellow in the eight years since he questioned me.'

'How about Ms Dromgoole?'

'She sent me a lengthy email, like something out of *Mastermind*. Did I know that musician fellow? Was I sure I hadn't visited the hotel earlier in the day?'

'Which musician did she mean?' Rebus asked. 'Bruce Collier?'

'Is he the one Maria had the knee-trembler with?'

'That'll be Dougie Vaughan.'

Attwood clicked his fingers. 'Exactly so. But you see, I definitely *wasn't* anywhere near the bloody hotel – that was the whole point.'

'You wanted Maria to get the hint? That you were breaking off the affair?'

Attwood screwed up his face. 'I'd tried telling her a couple of times, but then she would say something or do something and suddenly I'd change my mind. But Joyce had come along, you see . . .'

'The lover you left her for?'

'I really thought Joyce was the one.'

162

'Things didn't work out that way, though.'

'And then I met dear Jessica . . .'

Rebus knew from the photos on file that Attwood had possessed Hollywood good looks and a dress style to match. With the passing years he had lost both, and now he looked like any other pensioner. Which was to say: harmless. Forty years back, he would have been a very different proposition, something Rebus had to keep reminding himself.

'The staff member who said he saw you . . .' Fox prompted.

'Yes, that little bugger tried to dip me in shit all right. Know why? I'd never bothered to tip him. The mark-up on room service, why should I? He was sly with it, too – he only ever said he saw someone who looked "a bit" like me.'

'What did you think about Vince Brady's story?' Rebus asked.

'Is he the one who said Maria had been snogging the musician? Not the knee-trembler, but the other one?'

'Not snogging exactly, but she'd been talking to Bruce Collier in the corridor.'

'I think that's balls, if you'll allow a measure of frankness. Maria was expecting me to turn up at her door. She would have gone straight to her room, same as always – the first tap you gave, the door flew open and she was standing there, ready to pounce.' He smiled wistfully. 'She was some woman, I don't know if you can appreciate that.'

'She hadn't made a good marriage, though.'

'John was all right, I suppose. A decent type – too strait-laced, maybe, and not a huge fan of the physical stuff . . . intimacy, you know. They implied at the time that Maria was a nympho or off her head, but that was just to sell their papers.'

'You were friends with John Turquand, weren't you?' Rebus asked.

Attwood squirmed a little. 'Not so much that I wouldn't sleep with his wife.'

'You don't think he knew the two of you were lovers?'

'Not until the police told him.'

'Did you ever see him afterwards?'

'Once, some years later. We happened to be lunching in the same restaurant. He punched me square on the nose, and who's to say I didn't deserve it?'

'Did it ever cross your mind he might have killed her?'

'He wasn't that sort. Plus he was in meetings and such like.'

'Then who did?'

'If I had a fiver for every time I've been asked that . . . I think it featured more than once on Miss Dromgoole's questionnaire.'

'You don't have an answer?'

'Some psycho on the hotel staff? One of those musicians who were swarming through the place that day, high on drugs? Take your pick.' Attwood offered a shrug and slurped some of the weak tea. 'Whoever it was,' he eventually offered, 'they stole a beautiful spirit from the world. I'd never met anyone like her, and never would again.' He looked from one visitor to the other. 'But please don't tell Jessica I said that. She'd run me through with one of her knitting needles . . .'

John Turquand's country pile was reached by way of a half-mile private road bordered by rhododendron bushes. The house itself was probably Edwardian, with apparently endless crow-stepped gables and mullioned windows. The huge reception hall smelled of damp, however, and there was no sign of the army of servants such a place demanded, just the stooped, balding figure of Turquand himself. Fishing rods stood in an untidy line against one wall, while a stag's dusty head graced another.

'Whisky?' Turquand asked, his voice reedy.

'Maybe just a soft drink,' Fox responded.

'I think there might be something in the library.'

And that was where Turquand took them. He wore carpet slippers that, like their owner, had seen better days.

'Broke my hip last year,' he said, explaining his gait.

'Quite some place you have here,' Fox said. 'Takes a lot of upkeep, though.'

'You've hit the nail on the head,' Turquand agreed.

'You live here by yourself?'

'Yes.'

They were in the library now. Its floor-to-ceiling fitted shelves were mostly devoid of books, other than a few true stories of adventure. Turquand sported a tweed waistcoat and collarless white shirt. Two of the fly buttons on his trousers hadn't been done up. He had made for a drinks trolley. Next to decanters of whisky and gin sat a plastic one-litre cola bottle, a few inches missing from it.

'Might be a bit flat, I'm afraid,' he said as he poured, handing both men a glass covered in enough fingerprints to keep any crime scene manager happy. He poured an inch of whisky for himself, adding a splash of water from a jug.

'Down the hatch,' he said. The first gulp brought some colour to his gaunt cheeks and seemed to perk him up. Four chairs sat around a green baize card table. A deck of cards lay untouched in the middle. Turquand motioned to Rebus and Fox, and the three men sat down, the unpadded wooden chairs creaking in protest.

'We've just been to see Peter Attwood,' Fox said. 'He mentioned the punch you gave him.'

'I'd have done worse, too, but he's a bit bigger than me.'

'You know why we're here?'

'I saw it in the paper – Robert Chatham, it said. Retired detective. Dreadful thing to happen.' He shook his head. 'The only mystery is why you think I might be able to help.'

'Mr Chatham interviewed you eight years ago,' Fox recited. 'Had you heard from him in the intervening period?'

'Not a peep. Are you suggesting his death had something to do with Maria's story?'

'We're just trying to put together the complete picture.'

'I always thought Attwood must have killed her, you know.'

'He had an alibi, though.'

'Yes, the altogether convenient new lover,' Turquand said dismissively.

'While you yourself were locked away with Sir Magnus Brough,' Rebus commented.

Turquand smiled at the memory. 'Plotting the takeover of the Royal Bank of Scotland, no less.'

'Might have dodged a bullet there, if you'll pardon the phrase.'

'We would never have made the mistakes RBS did. What happened to that bank was a tragedy.'

'From everything we've discovered about your wife, Mr Turquand,' Rebus went on, 'she seems a remarkable woman.'

'She really was.'

'Were the two of you well matched, do you think?'

'I was making a lot of money, and a successful man needs to show it.'

'By investing in a glamorous partner?'

Turquand's mouth twitched at Rebus's use of 'investing', but he didn't deny the truth of the comment.

'I provided stability in her life, I suppose – that was the trade-off, or so I thought.' He stared at Rebus. 'Surely none of this can have any bearing on that poor man's demise.'

Rebus just shrugged. 'We have to keep an open mind, sir. Do you remember a woman called Maxine Dromgoole?'

'She wrote a book, didn't she? I remember giving it a quick squint – not very pleasant. She did want to interview me, but I think I told her to bugger off.'

'And she's not been in touch since?'

'No.'

'I'm sure you must have a few theories yourself . . .'

'About who killed Maria? The guitarist, I thought for a long time.'

'Dougie Vaughan?'

'I think he was infatuated with her, but she'd moved on and cast him adrift. When he saw her in the hotel that day . . .'

'He says he didn't see her, though.'

'And what else would you expect him to say? Why didn't he tell the inquiry he'd had a fling with her? Why wait until the trail had gone cold?'

'Have you ever confronted him about this?'

Turquand shook his head. 'I tried not to think about it at all, once the dust had settled – threw myself into my work instead. Some nights I'd dream about Maria, dream she was still alive. But every hour I was awake, I focused on money, how to make more and more of it for the bank and myself.'

'Where did it all go wrong, eh?' Rebus said, stretching out both arms.

'Mr Turquand,' Fox interrupted, glancing towards Rebus to let him know his 'one question' was coming, 'you were an early champion of Anthony Brough, weren't you?'

'For my sins.'

'Meaning what?'

'He was Sir Magnus's grandson. I felt I owed him a certain fealty.'

'You don't sound too enthusiastic.'

'Anthony lost me quite a lot of money. He talks a good game, but really that's all he does.'

'Are you in touch with him at all?'

'A six-monthly statement, if I'm lucky.'

'You don't visit his office or speak on the phone?'

'Not for quite some time.'

'You still have money invested with him, though?'

'The losses were such, it was pointless withdrawing what little was left.'

'That must grate,' Rebus said. 'You having been a hotshot money man yourself back in the day.'

'Don't I bloody know it.' Turquand got to his feet and poured another drink. He appeared not to mind that neither man had taken more than a sip of the stale cola. Once he had returned to the table, Fox started speaking again.

'Anthony seems to have gone missing. Could all those bad investments have caught up with him?'

'You'd need to study his books to answer that – even then, he's probably not above having two sets of accounts.'

'Do people still do that?' Rebus asked.

'They probably employ even more circuitous ruses, thanks to the wonders of the online world.'

'Do you know what SLPs are, Mr Turquand.'

Turquand turned his gaze from Rebus to Fox. 'Scottish limited partnerships?'

'Would it surprise you to learn that Anthony is involved with quite a number of them?'

'Involved in what way?'

'Setting them up.'

'In order to salt away money in them?' Turquand guessed. 'Well, I don't suppose it's illegal. If it were, HMRC would be on the hunt . . .' He broke off. 'Ah, now I see – that's why he's on the run?'

'I really can't say.'

Turquand tapped the side of his nose. 'Understood. Maybe I *should* try to repatriate the rest of my investment – always supposing he's not ditched Molly yet . . .'

'Molly being?'

'Secretary, receptionist, switchboard, personal assistant.'

Fox nodded, remembering the voice on the phone. 'She was *in situ* last time I rang.'

'Molly will know the score. I'll call her this afternoon. And thanks for the tip.'

'Doesn't count as insider trading, does it?' Rebus enquired.

'Not at all,' Turquand said.

'Pity . . .'

*

167

'Now we have a nice long drive back to Edinburgh,' Rebus announced as they got into the Saab and started fastening their seat belts. 'Which gives you plenty of time to talk me through Anthony Brough and these SLPs of his.'

'I've got a question for you first – what did you think of him?'

'Turquand? A bit eccentric, maybe.'

'I'd say he hasn't got two pennies to rub together. I'm betting he got rid of the staff. The grounds have seen better days. And the whisky smelled cheap.'

'All because he trusted his capital to Sir Magnus Brough's grandson?' Rebus mused. 'I wonder how many other clients are feeling short-changed as Molly fobs them off about her boss's comings and goings?'

'Darryl Christie could well be one,' Fox admitted.

Rebus's hands tightened around the steering wheel. 'You have my full attention, Malcolm. Make sure you don't waste it.'

'Darryl owns a betting shop and flat on Great Junction Street. Brough rents the flat and uses it as the address for hundreds of SLPs.' Fox saw Rebus looking at him. 'What is it?'

'When I called you from Rutland Square, you started to say something about betting, but then choked off the rest – now I know why.' He nodded to himself. 'Keep going,' he said eventually. 'And if you're talking company law and malfeasance, pretend you're explaining it to a complete idiot . . .'

Clarke tapped on the open door of the MIT room. Anne Briggs glanced up from her desk.

'I was looking for DI Fox.'

'He's not here.'

'So I see. My name's Clarke.'

'DI Clarke?'

'Siobhan will probably do.'

'I'm DC Briggs – Anne. Malcolm's mentioned you.'

'You holding the fort?'

'The super's at Gartcosh. Couple of the others are interviewing the deceased's boss. And one's gone to the shop for milk and biscuits.'

'Leaving DI Fox unaccounted for?'

'He was supposed to be in the interview room, but he isn't.'

'I'm guessing the tidy desk is his?' Clarke stood next to it.

'That's why you earn the big bucks.'

Clarke picked up *The Ends of Justice* and began flipping pages.

'That's who he was supposed to be questioning,' Briggs offered.

'Maybe I should phone him,' Clarke was saying as Mark Oldfield walked in, waving a carrier bag at Briggs. Briggs made the introductions as Oldfield switched the kettle on.

'I'm sure he won't be long,' Briggs said. 'Have a coffee first.'

'I might do that.' Clarke had moved from Fox's desk to the next one along. A pile of A4 sheets was lying on top of a closed laptop. The sheets were photocopies of stills from CCTV footage.

'What's this?' she asked.

'I've just finished printing those out,' Briggs said. 'Deceased had been threatened by the guys you see there.'

'The really blurry guys,' Oldfield added.

Clarke moved from group shots to close-ups of individual faces. She held one up towards Briggs.

'I think I know him,' she announced. 'I was talking to him only a couple of hours back. Name's Hugh Harold Hodges, but he prefers Harry. Works at a place called the Devil's Dram.'

Oldfield had come over to study the picture. 'You sure?' he asked.

'Fairly positive. It's the haircut and beard.'

'Every second guy I see these days has that beard.'

'Well, I reckon it's him.'

Oldfield turned towards Briggs. 'Do we call the boss man?' he asked.

'We call the boss man,' she said. '*After* we've had what turns out to be a well-earned cuppa.'

'Plus caramel wafers.'

'I love it when you talk dirty, Mark,' Briggs said with a grin.

Hodges was parked in the interview room when Alvin James got back. Clarke had gone with Briggs to pick him up.

'I'm glad you came,' Briggs had said at one point. 'These streets are a bloody maze.'

'Local knowledge is a wonderful thing, Anne.'

A sentiment Alvin James repeated almost word for word after Clarke had explained how she'd recognised Hodges. He even clasped her hand and gave it a shake.

'Malcolm was right to sing your praises,' he said. Then, looking around: 'Where is he anyway?'

'Nobody knows,' Briggs piped up.

James fastened his eyes on Clarke again. 'Well, since you're here and acquainted with the gentleman . . .'

'Happy to oblige,' Clarke said, following him to the interview room.

Hodges didn't look happy. He'd been stewing for the best part of an hour, and the club would be opening for evening business soon. Nobody had thought to tell him why he had been picked up. James dragged out the chair opposite and sat down, holding the photo so Hodges could see it.

'And?' Hodges said.

'It's you,' James stated.

'What if it is?'

'Outside the Tomahawk Club, just off Lothian Road. Two Saturdays back.'

'Maybe.'

'Oh, it's you all right, you and your mates having words with the doorman because he refused you entry.'

'Is that what he says?'

'It's what one of his colleagues says. The man in the photo isn't saying anything, Mr Hodges. Someone went after him and killed him. Big fit man he was, too, so we're thinking maybe more than one assailant.' James tapped the photo. 'There are four of you here. Care to name the others, or do we find out the hard way?'

'Did I hear you right? He's dead? Rab's dead?' Hodges' eyes had widened. 'We used him at the club a few times ourselves. Just once or twice.'

'You knew him?'

'Hardly.'

'But he was a bouncer at the Devil's Dram?' Clarke asked.

'Just when we were short of a body. On the really busy nights – like the night you were there.' Hodges fixed Clarke with a look.

'If you knew him,' James asked quietly, 'what was the argument for?'

'I'd stopped a bit further back along the pavement – had to make a call. The others are that bit younger, but they all had ID. Rab wasn't convinced, said two could go in but not Cal. Words were being exchanged when I arrived, but it all calmed down.'

'One of you – at least one of you – threatened to kill him.'

'I don't remember that,' Hodges said with a shake of the head.

'Quite an unusual name, Cal,' Clarke interrupted. 'Bit of a

coincidence that your employer has a brother called that. And I'm thinking Cal Christie wouldn't quite be eighteen yet.' She pretended to study the photos. 'Darryl had sent you out to babysit him, is that it? Him and a couple of pals and their fake IDs?'

Hodges glared at her. 'You've lost me again.'

'Let's go talk to Darryl then.' Clarke checked the time on her phone. 'Cal's probably home from college by now, too. We'll take the security footage to show them. I'll tell you something, though, Harry – Darryl's not going to be happy with you. He's not going to be happy *at all*.'

She knew she had got through to him when his shoulders sagged. He spoke with his chin tucked in against his chest. 'Is there another option?'

'You give us the other names so we can talk to all of them. Then, when we go to Darryl's house, we keep *your* name out of it – we tell him it was Cal we recognised.'

'He'll still know I was there.'

'You asked for options,' James stressed. 'That's what's on the table.'

Hodges thought for a few more seconds, then nodded.

'Let me fetch my pad for those names,' James said, exiting the room.

'One more thing, Harry,' Clarke said, once the coast was clear. 'That photo really does come out of the gents' toilet tonight. If it doesn't, I tell Darryl how wonderfully cooperative you were when you grassed up his little brother. You got that?'

'Got it, bitch.'

'Good,' said Clarke, as James walked back through the open door.

15

She was locking up for the evening when they arrived.

'Molly?' Fox asked, holding out his warrant card. 'I'm sorry, I don't know your surname.'

'Sewell,' she told him. 'Do you want to come in?'

'Thank you.'

She unlocked the door again and they followed her inside. She cancelled the alarm and switched on the lights. A small, tasteful waiting room led to a smaller office with no natural light.

'This is where you work?' Fox enquired.

'That's right.'

'And Mr Brough?'

'To the left as you come in the main door.'

'Mind if we take a look?'

'Whatever for?'

'Just want to be sure he's not hiding in one of the filing cabinets.' Fox tried to make it sound like a joke, but her oval face had grown stony. Rebus reckoned she was in her early thirties. Cropped black hair and bright red lipstick. Elfin was the word that came to his mind, but there was a toughness to her, too.

'You better tell me what this is about,' she said coolly, sitting down behind her desk. There was one chair for visitors, but Rebus and Fox stayed on their feet.

'Do you know the whereabouts of Anthony Brough, Ms Sewell?'

'No.'

'When was the last time you spoke?'

She had begun to tidy the surface of her already tidied desk, moving a stapler, a box of paper clips and a pen. 'About a week ago.'

'In person or by phone?'

'It was a text actually. He wasn't feeling great and wanted to cancel his morning meetings.'

'And since then?'

'I've texted and phoned, left messages . . .'

'Where does he live?'

'Ann Street.'

'Very nice, too. Does he have a partner?'

'Here, you mean?'

'In his personal life.'

'Not that I know of.'

'Big houses on that street – he must rattle around a bit.'

'If you say so.'

'You're not worried about him?'

'It's only been a few days.'

'All the same . . .'

She sighed and looked up from her desk, blinking back tears. 'Of course I'm worried. I went to the house, but there was no one home.'

'If he wasn't well, he probably wouldn't have gone far,' Rebus commented.

'I put a note through his door, but he still didn't call.'

'How well can you manage without him?' Fox asked.

'The paperwork is fine. I've rescheduled his meetings.' She looked around her. 'He's not here to sign cheques, but other than that . . .'

'How is business anyway?'

'Thriving.'

'That's not quite what we hear, Ms Sewell.'

'Then you're talking to the wrong people.'

'Do you know a gentleman called Darryl Christie?'

'Should I?'

'He's either a client or an associate of Mr Brough's – so yes, I'd say you *should* know him.'

'Well, I don't.'

'How about a flat on Great Junction Street, above a betting shop called Klondyke Alley?'

She shook her head. 'You've still not told me why you're here.'

'A few days after your boss went missing, someone attacked Darryl Christie.'

She gave a snort. 'Anthony would never do anything like that.'

'You're sure?'

'It's preposterous. I doubt Anthony's been in a fight since he left school.'

'How long have you known him?'

She glowered at Rebus. 'Long enough.'

'You must be about the same age as him – you didn't go to school together or anything?'

'Anthony was educated privately. I went to Boroughmuir.' She paused. 'And he's six years *older* than me.'

Rebus smiled an apology.

'It seems to me,' Fox said, 'that you know him *and* care about him. We think he's in some kind of trouble, Ms Sewell, and we want to help. So if you do know anything, this is your chance.' He paused to let his words sink in, handing her his business card.

She glanced at it. 'I don't think I saw *your* ID,' she said to Rebus.

'I don't have any on me.'

'Not a police officer then? HMRC? FCA?'

'Expecting a visit, are you?'

She ignored him and opened a drawer instead, dropping the card into it. 'I'd like to go home now, if that's all right with you.'

'Have you considered reporting him as a missing person?' Fox asked, as she started getting to her feet and buttoning her short woollen coat.

'If I don't hear from him in the next few days.'

'I'm assuming this is out of character for Mr Brough?'

'He has been known to take a notion – London for the night, a horse race in France . . .'

'He's a betting man, then?'

'That's something you'd have to ask him.'

'We will – if and when he turns up.'

'You really can't think anything's happened to him? Anything serious, I mean?'

'If he's had a falling-out with Darryl Christie,' Rebus said, 'it's entirely possible. Something you'd do well to bear in mind.'

They waited while she turned off the lights again and set the alarm. Rebus reckoned he knew which door must be Brough's office, so he tried it, but it was locked.

'Maybe bring a warrant next time,' Sewell told him.

'I'll be sure to,' he said.

*

Clarke had guessed that Darryl would have moved his mother and brothers into the boutique hotel he owned on one of the New Town's steep north–south streets. She explained as much to Alvin James, but when they got there the front desk denied any knowledge.

'We're police, remember,' Clarke told the fashion model who seemed to have ended up working as a receptionist. 'I know Darryl has to be cagey, but not with us.'

'They're really not here – both floors are closed for renovations.'

And sure enough, the carpet leading to the staircase had been covered with clear polythene, as had the staircase itself.

'Sorry about that,' Clarke apologised as she marched back out to her car.

'Not your fault, Siobhan,' James said. 'If you'd phoned and been given that story, you'd still have felt the need to come see for yourself.'

She glanced at him. 'How do you know that?'

'Any good detective would do the same. Where to now?'

'Darryl's house, maybe. It's five minutes away.'

'Lead on, then.'

She took him the long way round, so he could take in the Botanic Gardens and Inverleith Park. He gazed at the imposing detached stone houses.

'Could I get one of these on a CID wage?' he asked.

'Not even if you were Chief Constable.'

They parked on the street and got out. There were no cars in the driveway. 'I don't see his Range Rover,' Clarke said, preparing James for another dead end. But when she rang the doorbell, she could hear a noise from inside. The door opened and Gail McKie stood there. While Clarke was trying to hide her surprise, James asked if Cal was home.

'What's the story now?' McKie demanded.

'Just a couple of questions.'

'I've already told you he didn't see anything.'

James looked puzzled. 'She means the attack on Darryl,' Clarke explained.

'We'd still like to talk with him,' James nudged.

'With me in the room?' McKie paused. 'Or our solicitor?'

'You're free to sit in, Ms McKie,' James decided. 'Though Cal might not be too thrilled . . .'

They waited in the chintzy living room while she went upstairs to fetch Cal. He walked in looking sulky, shoulders hunched, avoiding eye contact. His black spiky hair looked dyed, and there were acne scars on his cheeks.

'Didn't see nothing,' he stated without preamble. 'Got nothing to say.' He dumped himself on one of the chairs, fingers gripping the armrests.

'That's not why we're here,' James said. Like Clarke, he had remained on his feet. McKie had lowered herself on to the sofa, curling her legs under her, staring hard at the two detectives. 'We're here about the Tomahawk Club. The night you and your pals were refused entry.'

Cal was trying to stop his face from reddening as his mother turned her gaze on him.

'What's this?' she asked.

'They're lying,' he spluttered.

James eased the CCTV prints from his pocket. 'We have evidence to the contrary. We already know one name – a Mr Hodges – but we need the other two.'

'Why?'

'Because a threat was made to the doorman, Ms McKie. Rather a serious threat.'

'By you?' Her eyes were drilling into her son. He shook his head.

'It was Dandy,' he said.

'I thought I'd told you to stop hanging around with that toerag!' Cal squirmed.

'He's nothing but trouble – always has been!'

'Can I assume Dandy is a nickname of some kind?' Clarke interrupted.

'His name's Daniel Reynolds. Lives in Lochend. He used to go to school with Cal.'

'Dandy's all right,' Cal added.

'He threatened to kill the doorman?' James asked.

Cal squirmed some more. 'He might've said he'd be back to cut him. He was just acting up – putting on a show.'

'There was one other young male with you?'

'Roddy Cape. He's a year above me at college.'

'Are you the only one who's underage, Cal?' Clarke checked.

Cal nodded. 'He was going to let the rest of them in – just not me. I think he wanted to see what we'd do. Like he was trying to get us worked up. Harry stepped in to keep the peace, and that was that.'

'Who's Harry?' Gail McKie demanded. Cal pursed his lips.

'He works for Darryl,' Clarke answered her. 'He was on baby-

176

sitting duty – is that right, Cal? Making sure the evening went smoothly?'

'I suppose,' Cal admitted.

'There we are then,' McKie said. 'A doorman was given some verbals, but not by my son. So you can go take your witch hunt elsewhere.'

'The doorman ended up dead, Ms McKie,' James informed her. For the first time, Cal looked up, his mouth opening soundlessly. 'So you can see that we have to look at anyone who might have held a grudge. Right now, I'd say that includes Daniel Reynolds.'

'Cal,' Clarke asked softly, 'does Dandy carry a blade?'

'How would I know?'

'Because he's probably the sort who'd want his mates to know.'

'He's mouthy, but that's as far as it goes. Besides, he knows when he's out with me he's got all the protection he needs.'

'Because your brother is Darryl Christie?' Clarke nodded slowly. 'But someone got to Darryl, didn't they? Someone proved he's human.'

'And what are the police doing about that?' Gail McKie snarled, folding her arms. 'They arrest the guy but then let him go and focus instead on *this*, because an assault on one of their own always takes precedence.'

'Murder rather than assault,' Clarke corrected her.

'You know what I mean, though – one law for us, one law for you. Always has been and always will.' She swung her legs off the sofa. 'Are we done here?'

'We need addresses for Dandy and Roddy,' James said, his eyes on Cal.

'We don't know their addresses,' McKie snapped.

'Cal's never been round to their house?' James sounded disbelieving. 'He'll have their phone numbers, though, won't he? He can let us have those at least.'

McKie's face darkened. She was on her feet now. She made a noise that was almost feral as she kicked her son on one ankle.

'Go on,' she said. 'And then you and me are going to have words.'

Cal was already sliding his phone from his back pocket, switching it on, readying to search his address book.

'Darryl's not home?' Clarke asked McKie, trying to make it sound like the most casual of enquiries.

'Back at work, despite his injuries – never relaxes for a minute, that one.' She seemed to be aiming this remark at Cal.

'Do you want the numbers or don't you?' he asked, holding the phone towards his mother.

'Not me, *them*,' she snapped back. As Cal began to recite, Clarke copied the details into her own phone.

'One more thing, Ms McKie,' she said when she was done. 'The suspect you mentioned – he seems to have gone missing.'

'Oh aye?'

'You wouldn't know anything about that, would you?'

McKie rolled her eyes, but said nothing.

James seemed pleased with the result as they headed to the car. Clarke wasn't so sure. Darryl had told her he was moving his family to a place of safety. Why had he changed his mind? Or had he lied in the first place?

'Back to Leith?' James suggested, opening the passenger door.

'Back to Leith,' Clarke agreed.

16

Fox stared from the doorway of the MIT room towards his desk. Siobhan Clarke was seated there, one leg crossed over the other, with a mug of tea in front of her and a chocolate biscuit protruding from her mouth. She had just said something that had the whole team chuckling – until they saw Fox.

'The prodigal returns,' Alvin James said, stretching out an arm in mock welcome. 'What happened? Did the interview with Maxine Dromgoole tire you out?'

Fox walked into the centre of the room. Rebus passed him on his way to the kettle.

'I had to check up on a couple of names she gave me – one in Fife, the other in Perthshire. Just in case you thought I was slacking . . .'

James held up both hands in a show of surrender. 'And you took a wingman, by the look of it. A member of the public, no less. That's bound to look good if these "names" are called at the trial.'

'The man has a point,' Rebus teased, filling his mug. 'No biscuits left?'

'Sorry,' Clarke replied, biting down on the last sliver of hers.

'Time to share,' James announced, slapping a hand down on his desk. 'You tell us yours and we'll tell you ours.'

'All right,' Fox said, his eyes on Clarke. She took the hint and eased herself from the chair – *his* chair. He squeezed past her and sat down. Mark Oldfield offered her his seat, but she shook her head and slid on to a corner of his desk instead, legs dangling.

'Let's begin,' Alvin James said . . .

*

Rebus had offered to buy the drinks, but Clarke had cried off, having already promised to share her favourite restaurant with Alvin James.

'Doesn't take her long to get her feet under the table,' Fox complained as Rebus returned from the bar to their corner table.

'Relax,' Rebus chided him. 'Shiv's not the one who got promoted to Gartcosh, remember?'

'She'd fit in there a lot better than I do, though – we both know it, so don't bother denying it.'

'How's your tomato juice?'

'A shot of vodka wouldn't harm it. How's your low-alcohol beer?'

Rebus screwed up his face.

'The state of the pair of us,' Fox muttered, causing Rebus to chuckle. They sipped in silence for a few seconds. Rebus rubbed foam from his lips with the back of his hand.

'It was interesting what Siobhan said, though,' he eventually offered.

'I was trying not to listen.'

'About Darryl Christie telling her he'd moved everyone out of the house when he hadn't.'

'Why tell the truth when a lie will suffice?'

'It's a funny lie to tell, though.'

'He may have his reasons.'

'Such as?'

'He's hiding behind his mum and brothers, betting that whoever wants him hurt won't want civilians involved.'

'Maybe.'

'Or else he just likes lying to the police – I get the feeling everyone I've spoken to recently has lied to me at least once: Dromgoole, Peter Attwood, John Turquand, Molly Sewell . . .'

'Me?' Rebus asked.

'Probably. Almost definitely, in fact. My dad used to drum it into Jude and me that we'd go to hell if we ever told a lie.'

'And did you stick by that?'

'I did my best.'

'Then maybe you won't be joining the rest of us in the fiery depths.' Rebus toasted him with his glass before taking another sip.

'Are you putting off going home?' Fox asked. 'In case there really is a phone message?'

'Nothing scares me, Malcolm.'

'Is that right? I'm the exact opposite.'

'That's good, though, means you err on the side of caution. Look at your relationship with booze – you saw it was becoming a problem and you stopped. Me, I should have stopped years back. Instead of which, I challenged the demon drink to a wrestling match, just the two of us sweating it out.'

'Only ever one winner in those contests.'

'Aye – mortality. Same thing that's waiting for me back at the flat, message or no message.'

'That's what I like about spending time with you, John – you never fail to light up a room with that positive attitude.'

'I'm smiling now, though.'

Fox looked at him. 'So you are. Why's that, I wonder?'

Rebus leaned forward and patted him softly on the shoulder. 'It's your round, lad,' he said.

Denise the barmaid had arrived, scouting for empty glasses. She glowered at Rebus.

'If this place goes broke, it'll be your fault.'

Rebus looked at Fox. 'You see where I get that positive attitude from,' he said.

Fox had turned down Rebus's offer of a bite to eat. He was wondering which restaurant Siobhan would have taken Alvin James to. There were three possibles, and he drove past each, slowing and peering through their windows as best he could. Then he stopped at a Sainsbury's and bought a ready meal, some bananas and the evening paper.

You'll survive, he told himself as he pulled into the driveway of his Oxgangs bungalow. As he lifted his shopping from the passenger seat, he heard a car door open and close nearby. Looking up, he saw it was Darryl Christie. Christie just stood there next to the white Range Rover, waiting for Fox to walk up to him. Instead, Fox unlocked his front door and went inside, placing the bag on the kitchen counter and pausing there until the bell rang. He opened the door.

'Was that you calling for back-up?' Christie asked. 'Because if it was, you better phone them with an excuse. Trust me, this chat has to be private.'

'I don't remember making an appointment, Mr Christie.'

'What I've got to say is important.'

'Then maybe you should drop by Leith tomorrow.'

Christie was peering over Fox's shoulder. 'We should step inside,' he said.

'I don't think so.'

'My car, then. This really does need to be kept between us.'

'You shouldn't be here.'

'Are you even listening to me?' Christie's face had hardened.

'Frankly, I've got better things to do with my evening.'

The two men studied one another. Eventually, Christie sniffed and ran a finger across the base of his nose. 'Okay then,' he said, half turning as if to depart. But then he paused. 'It's Jude's head on the block, though, just remember that . . .'

He walked down the path, hands in pockets, not looking back.

'Bluff,' muttered Fox, heading back inside. He took the ready meal from its cardboard sleeve and stabbed the film lid with the tip of a knife. Three minutes in the microwave, then leave for one more minute. Eat while piping hot. He opened the microwave door, then stopped. The newspaper was on the counter and he stared at its front page without really seeing it.

'Fine then,' he said, striding to the front door.

The Range Rover was still there, Christie drumming his fingers on the steering wheel. Fox climbed into the passenger seat and slammed shut the door.

'So tell me,' he said.

Christie took a deep breath and released it slowly, as if debating whether to comply. The movement of Fox's hand towards the door handle made his mind up.

'I didn't know she was your sister – not at first. I mean, I only ever knew her by her first name. Her first name and her address. Her address and her financial details.' He paused to let this sink in.

'She owes you money?' Fox guessed.

'She really does.'

'How much?'

'Before we get to that, let's talk about *you*. Let's talk about you being here on secondment from Gartcosh, asking questions about various betting shops, trying to pressure your own sister into spying for you . . .' Christie tutted. 'Cleaning up dirty money by putting it into fixed-odds machines? Do you really think you're ever going to pin *that* on me?'

'Are you saying it isn't happening?'

'I'm saying you'd have the devil's job proving it in court. And recruiting your own sister to the cause . . . a woman with a gambling problem – not quite the most reliable of witnesses, DI Fox.'

Fox could feel his jaw clenching, mostly because Christie was right.

'Sanctioned by Gartcosh, was it?' Christie went on. 'Or is this you using your initiative? In which case, I doubt your bosses are going to be too thrilled.'

'I'm going to ask again – how much does she owe?'

Christie turned towards the passenger seat for the first time, caressing the steering wheel with his fingers as he spoke. 'Twenty-seven grand – give or take.'

Fox tried swallowing, his mouth suddenly dry. 'I think you're lying,' he said.

'Then come to Diamond Joe's and I'll show you the figures. It's mostly from her online activities, of course. I'm almost as stunned by it as you are – I mean, the interest rate isn't even forty per cent . . .'

'I can get you the money.'

'You sure about that?'

'Given enough time.'

'But time's the one thing you don't have, DI Fox, because I want something from you right now.'

'The cashpoint will give me a couple of hundred.'

'It's not about money!' Christie snarled.

'What then?'

'Knowledge, of course. The knowledge stored at Gartcosh.'

'You want to know what they have on you?'

'Especially as it relates to this man.' Christie had lifted a slip of paper from the dashboard. Fox unfolded it.

'Aleksander Glushenko,' he read. 'Sounds Russian.'

'He's Ukrainian.'

Fox stared at the name again, then held the note towards Christie. 'I can't do this,' he said.

'That's a pity – Jude made destitute, your name dragged into it, the papers tipped off that you were using her as bait . . . and your bosses notified about all your various shenanigans.' Christie gestured towards the slip of paper. 'Am I really asking so much, Malcolm?'

'I can get you the money.'

'Hang on to the name anyway. That way, I may hold fire a few days before taking you and your sister to the cleaners.' Christie paused for a moment. 'Now get out of my fucking car.'

Fox knew how good it would feel to rip the piece of paper into tiny shreds and throw them into Christie's face. Instead, he opened the door and got out, the note pressed into his palm. The car was heading off before he'd even reached his front door.

Inside, he unpeeled the film lid from the ready meal before remembering that he hadn't yet cooked it. He swore under his breath and took out his phone.

'Oh Christ,' said Jude when she picked up. 'Look, Malcolm . . .'

'You're an unbelievable fucking idiot, Jude! Not just to get into debt like that – with a wolf like *him* – but then to toss me in his direction as a bone!'

'I know, I know, I know. I wasn't thinking straight. I wasn't thinking *at all*.'

'You were thinking about *you*, dear sister, same as always. Everybody around you can be hung out to dry, just so long as Jude survives . . .' He sighed and lowered his voice. 'Promise me you'll get help – Gamblers Anonymous, whatever it takes. Twenty-seven grand, Jude . . .'

He listened to her sobs, closing his eyes and resting his forehead against one of the cupboard doors. She was trying to talk, but he couldn't make out any of the words. It didn't matter anyway.

He ended the call and perched on a stool at the counter. Using a ballpoint pen on the blank side of the ready meal's cardboard sleeve, he began to work out how much he had, how much he could raise. The slip of paper was lying on the counter a little further along, crumpled but readable. An easy enough name to remember: Aleksander Glushenko.

Who the hell was Aleksander Glushenko?

If Fox found out, and discovered the connection between the two men, could he use that against Christie in some way rather than aiding and abetting him?

Maybe. Just maybe.

But to be on the safe side, he kept totting up numbers . . .

Three phone messages were waiting for Rebus at his flat on Arden Street.

'Press one or say one to listen to your messages . . .'

Instead of which, he had gone to the window, staring out at the night. Then he had walked to the record deck. *Solid Air* was still there from the evening Deborah Quant had stayed over. It was an album that had always been there for him, no matter the troubles in his life. And hadn't John Martyn been troubled, too? Johnny Too

Bad – hitting the booze, falling out and brawling with friends and lovers. One leg hacked off in the operating theatre. But barrelling on through life, singing and playing until the end.

Nice thing about an album – when it was over, you could lift the needle and start from the beginning again.

With the title track playing softly, Rebus finally picked up the phone.

'*Press one . . .*'

He pressed.

And heard a pre-recorded message telling him he didn't have long to claim for his mis-sold payment protection insurance.

Delete.

'*Message two . . .*'

The same automated caller. From further on in their spiel.

Delete.

'*Message three . . .*'

'*Did you know that a government-backed scheme can give you a new boiler at no charge . . .?*'

Delete.

'*You have no more messages . . .*'

Rebus stared at the phone for fully fifteen seconds before placing it back on its charger. He peered down at his chest.

'At this rate, my heart will give out before Hank Marvin gets me,' he muttered, turning the amplifier's volume control all the way up.

Day Seven

Day Seven

17

Next morning, Fox drove to Gartcosh. His night had been restless and he had nicked his chin while shaving. He'd woken up to four texts from Jude, three of them apologetic, one baleful and accusatory. Entering the main building, he climbed the stairs and walked past the HMRC office. Through the window, he could see Sheila Graham seated at her desk, so he headed back to the ground floor, got himself a coffee, and found a perch in the atrium where the upstairs floor was visible.

Nobody paid him any heed. He remembered that he was good at this – blending in, becoming invisible. He'd always enjoyed stake-outs and tailing suspects. With his suit, tie and lanyard, he looked just like everyone else. Only the most senior staff wore anything resembling a uniform. Remove them from the picture and he could have been in any corporate building in the country.

Graham had left her office and was walking towards the other end of the building, where the Organised Crime team were tucked away behind a locked door, one requiring a special keycard. It didn't really surprise Fox that Graham carried just such a card around her neck. She pulled open the door and passed through it, by which time Fox was halfway up the staircase. He walked into the HMRC office and looked around. Graham's neighbour was seated at his own computer, facing Graham's desk. Recognising him from his previous visit, Fox gave a nod of greeting.

'You just missed her,' the man said.

'Will she be long?'

'Bit of housekeeping to discuss with ACC McManus.'

Fox made show of checking the time on his wristwatch. 'I'll maybe wait for a bit, if that's okay.'

The man gave a shrug of assent and got busy on his screen again. Fox sat down in front of Graham's monitor. It was in screen-saver mode, and when he nudged the mouse, he saw that a password was required for access.

'Think she'd mind if I checked my emails?'

'You can't do it on your phone?'

'I can't always get a signal.'

'Try "GcoshG69".'

Fox typed it in. 'Thanks,' he said.

'I should have asked – making any progress in Edinburgh?'

'Slowly,' Fox said. He was studying a list of files. He couldn't see the name Glushenko, so entered it as a search.

No results.

Having stared at the screen for a few moments, he turned his attention to the desk itself. A three-inch-high pile of manila folders sat to the right of the console. He opened the cover of the first one, but the details meant nothing to him. Same for the one immediately beneath. To the other side of the console sat a tray containing A4 sheets of paper, some stapled or held together with paper clips, Post-it notes attached at various points. But again, no Glushenko.

The desk boasted two deep drawers. Fox slid the nearest one open a few inches. More paperwork, neatly filed.

'You okay there?' the HMRC officer asked, growing suspicious.

'Just wondering if she got the report I sent.'

'Easier to ask her, no?'

'Ask me what?'

Fox turned his head and saw that Sheila Graham had stopped just inside the doorway.

'Short meeting,' he said.

'McManus got called away.' She took a few more steps towards her desk. Fox rose to his feet, ceding the chair to her. But her eyes were on the screen. He looked too, and saw that the Glushenko search was still displayed. When he turned back towards her, she was staring at him.

'You and me,' she said quietly, 'need to have a little chat . . .'

He followed her out of the office and along the walkway towards one of the glass meeting boxes. She slid the sign on the door to IN USE and marched in, seating herself at the large rectangular table and taking out her phone.

'Sit,' she commanded Fox.

'I can explain.'

'That's exactly what you're going to do, but someone else needs to hear it too.' She waited for her call to be answered. When it was, she announced to the person on the other end that she was putting the speakerphone on. As she placed the phone flat on the table, a male voice said, 'What's up, Sheila?'

'There's someone here with me. Detective Inspector Malcolm Fox. I mentioned him to you.'

'You did.'

'We're in a private room and can't be overheard. Can you say the same?'

'Yes.'

'Then maybe you can start by identifying yourself to DI Fox.'

'My name is Alan McFarlane. I'm in charge of the Economic Crime Command at the National Crime Agency, based in London.'

'DI Fox has just come to me with a name – a name I didn't give him,' Graham said.

'Does it begin with a G?'

'It does.'

'Aleksander Glushenko,' Fox added, feeling the need to say something.

'How did you come across him, DI Fox?'

Fox leaned towards the phone. 'You can hear me okay?'

'Loud and clear.'

'You sound Scottish, Mr McFarlane.'

'Well spotted. Now, to answer my question . . .'

'I was asked to look into the affairs of an Edinburgh criminal called Darryl Christie and his connections with an investment broker called Anthony Brough. Brough's gone missing, by the way – his PA hasn't heard from him in over a week.'

'I wasn't aware of that,' McFarlane said. Fox watched as a little bit of colour appeared on Graham's cheeks.

'Brough rents a flat above a betting shop – both are owned by Christie. So I placed someone in the vicinity.'

'Someone you trust?'

'Of course. It was this person who heard the name Glushenko mentioned.'

'In connection with what?'

'The name was as much as they caught.'

'One more thing to add,' Graham said, her eyes on Fox. 'I found

DI Fox on my computer five minutes ago. He was attempting to access information on Glushenko.'

There was silence on the line for ten long seconds, during which time Fox held Graham's gaze.

'Why was that?' McFarlane eventually asked.

'Because,' Fox explained, 'I'd started to suspect Ms Graham wasn't giving me the whole story. Without being fully briefed, I could be putting people at risk – not least myself and my contact. And now that I know *you're* in charge, I'd say my hunch was spot on.'

'Can I assume you did an internet search for Glushenko?'

'Yes.'

'And found nothing?'

'Correct.'

'That's because he only became Aleksander Glushenko a year or so back. He had a number of other aliases before that, but his real name is Anton Nazarchuk.'

'Okay.'

'Sounds Russian, but he's actually Ukrainian.'

'And he's something to do with a flat in Edinburgh that's become a one-man dodgy Companies House?'

'Yes.'

Graham cleared her throat. 'I can give DI Fox the relevant details, if I have your permission.'

'It's a pity we're not face to face – I like to think I'm good at reading people.'

'If anyone should be having trust issues here, it's me,' Fox complained.

'You were told exactly as much as was deemed necessary.'

There was another lengthy pause on the line, then an exhalation.

'Brief him,' McFarlane said, ending the call.

Graham lifted her phone from the table and started passing it slowly from one hand to the other.

'I hope to Christ you're up to this, Malcolm,' she stated.

'Do we call him Glushenko or Nazarchuk?'

'Glushenko.'

'And what has Mr Glushenko done?'

'He went to Anthony Brough for a shell company.'

'And?'

'And fed a chunk of money into it, some of which seems to have gone missing.'

'Might explain why Brough made himself scarce.'

'But if Brough *has* gone to ground . . .'

Fox nodded as the picture became clear. 'This Glushenko character will be chasing his associates – including Darryl Christie.' He grew thoughtful. 'But the thing is, the way my source tells it, it's actually Christie who's looking for Glushenko.'

'Maybe he has something to tell him.'

'Such as Anthony Brough's whereabouts?'

It was Graham's turn to nod.

'So where did this money come from?'

'I'll get to that in a minute. Two things first. Aleksander Glushenko is connected to the Russian mafia, and that means he's somewhat dangerous.' She waited for this to sink in.

'And?' Fox nudged her.

'And the sum involved isn't far short of a billion pounds.'

'Did you just say *billion*?'

Graham slipped her phone into one of the pockets of her jacket. 'Which reminds me – I forgot my purse today, so when we break for coffee, you'll be the one buying.'

'A billion pounds passed through that little flat above Klondyke Alley?'

'Not in the form of notes and coins, but yes, that's pretty much what happened. And somewhere along the line, someone decided that skimming a few million here or there wouldn't be noticed.' She rose to her feet. 'Maybe we should get those drinks before I start. This story takes a while to tell . . .'

Cafferty was in the same Starbucks on Forrest Road. He signalled that he didn't want a refill, so Rebus queued behind half a dozen students.

'What's quickest?' he asked when his turn came.

'Filter,' the server announced.

'Medium one of those, then.'

He added a splash of milk to the mug and joined Cafferty at a table just about big enough for the purpose. The newspaper Cafferty had been reading was lying there, folded in half so only the masthead and main story were visible.

'You look like hell,' Cafferty stated without preamble. Rebus took a sip of coffee in lieu of responding. 'I know, I know – we *all* look like hell.' Cafferty chuckled to himself.

Rebus tapped the newspaper just where the date was displayed beneath its masthead. 'Is this today's?'

'Yes.'

'That's good, otherwise I'd have missed my birthday.'

Cafferty chuckled again. 'If I'd known, I'd have bought you something. How's tricks anyway?'

'Mustn't grumble.'

'You'd really forgotten your own birthday? No card from that daughter of yours?'

'I'm not a great one for opening letters.' Rebus took another slurp of coffee and lowered the mug to the table. 'Reason I wanted to see you is I promised someone I'd do them a favour.'

'Oh aye?'

'Her name's Maxine Dromgoole.'

'If you say so.'

'She's tried contacting you about a book she wants to write. The subject of the book would be you.'

'Me?'

'I'm thinking the same as you – nobody in their right mind would want to read it. But anyway, I said I'd pass the message on.'

'And what did she give you in return?'

'Contact details for a couple of people even older than us.'

'To do with the Turquand case?'

'Yup.'

'You've not given up on it, then?' Cafferty watched Rebus shake his head. 'Made any progress?'

'Bits and pieces, maybe.'

Cafferty stared at him thoughtfully. 'Today's really your birthday? Maybe I *will* give you a present, gift-wrapped and everything . . .'

'The Russian?' Rebus guessed. Cafferty smiled and shook his head. 'Craw Shand, then?'

'Craw?'

'I'm thinking maybe you've got him tucked away somewhere.'

'Why would I do that?'

'Because he can probably point you in the direction of whoever attacked Darryl Christie. This is always supposing it wasn't you. I reckon you'd want to know the who and the why. That way, you might have something you can use against Christie.' Rebus paused, eyes locked on to Cafferty's. 'It's only a guess, mind.'

'Do you do palm-reading, too?'

Rebus shrugged. 'So if not Craw or the mystery Russian, what am I getting?'

'That day at the Caledonian Hotel, the day Maria Turquand was killed – not every visitor was accounted for.'

'How do you mean?'

Cafferty leaned forward, elbows on knees. 'I don't suppose it can do any harm to tell you. In fact, maybe it'll tickle you . . .'

'You? You were *there*?'

'A touring band needs stimulants – too risky to travel with them, so there's usually a contact in each city they stop at.'

'You were the delivery boy?'

'Not quite a boy by that stage, but yet to scale the giddy heights. Actually, I'd probably have had someone else do it, but I wanted to meet him.'

'Bruce Collier?'

'Remember I told you I was at the Usher Hall show – Bruce himself put me on the guest list. Here's the thing, though. I was supposed to hand the stuff over to the road manager in his room. So I knock on the door, but no one's answering.'

'Vince Brady's room?'

'Right next to Maria Turquand's, though I didn't know that at the time.'

'Did you see her?'

Cafferty shook his head. 'The door at the end of the hall was open and there was music coming from it, so I went along there and found Bruce Collier and a couple of his band-mates. There were a few young women dotted about – girlfriends, groupies, who knows? I told Bruce why I was there, but he didn't know where Brady had gone – maybe to the venue or something. Bruce didn't have enough cash on him to pay for the delivery – offered me a signed album instead, but I wasn't having that. So he took me into the bedroom and there was a mate of his crashed out on the bed, reeking of booze. Bruce had a bit of a rummage and came up with all the money this guy had on him. It was just about enough, so that was that.'

'The guy would have been Dougie Vaughan.'

'Would it?'

'Tallies with his version. So what happened next?'

'I walked out of there with my money and the promise of a free ticket.'

'Nothing else?'

'Such as?'

'The key to Vince Brady's bedroom – Vaughan says he lost it. Did you see it in his pocket?'

'No.'

Rebus thought for a moment. 'What about when the story broke?'

Cafferty held up his hands. 'I was gobsmacked.'

'You didn't think about coming forward?'

'To tell your lot I was selling drugs in the vicinity? Oddly enough, it never crossed my mind.'

'And you could be pretty sure Collier and his entourage wouldn't bring you into the story.'

Cafferty nodded slowly.

'The photos in the papers at the time – her husband and lover – you must have seen them?'

'I didn't recognise anyone, John. Are they the OAPs you've just been speaking to?'

'Yes. I've talked to Bruce Collier, too.'

'And the mate with the emptied trouser pockets. You've been busy.'

'What is it they say about the devil and idle hands?'

'True enough.' Cafferty smiled. 'You don't really think nobody would read my life story, do you?'

'Want me to put you in touch with Ms Dromgoole?'

'I'll give it some thought. Might be nice to leave something behind.'

'Other than court reports and photos of you in handcuffs.'

'It's not much of a legacy, is it?' Cafferty appeared to concur. 'So did my trip to the confessional help you at all?'

'It might have – if Brady really wasn't in the hotel and Dougie Vaughan was unconscious.'

'Happy birthday then.' Cafferty held out a hand and the two men shook.

Outside, Rebus paused at the traffic lights. A birthday present? He didn't think so. Cafferty had given him the information for one reason only: to focus Rebus's efforts on the past rather than the present. Something was up. Something was brewing – and not just coffee . . .

After Rebus had departed, Cafferty tried to finish his paper but found he couldn't concentrate. That was the effect the man had on him. Instead he took out his phone and tapped in a number.

'Hello?' a voice answered warily.

'It's me, Craw, who else would it be? I'm the only one with your number, remember?'

'I liked my old phone.'

'Cops will be tracking your old phone, Craw. Best it stays in cold storage.'

'Can I come home yet? It's like I'm in a prison here.'

'You've got a sea view, haven't you? And it won't be long now. You've got to trust me, that's all . . .'

'I do trust you, Mr Cafferty. Really I do.'

'Well then, a few more days. Watch the telly, read a book – they're bringing you your newspaper every day? And feeding and watering you?'

'I could do with a bit of fresh air.'

'Then open a window. Because if I hear you've so much as tramped to the end of the street, I'll take a brick to your skull – understood?'

'I would never do that, Mr Cafferty.'

'Bear in mind, Craw, this is for *your* safety.'

'And only for a few more days, you say?'

'A few more days. It's all going to be sorted by then, one way or another.'

Cafferty ended the call and stared towards the café window as if everything on the other side of the glass made perfect sense to him. Then he picked up his paper again and began to read. Two minutes later, his phone buzzed.

'Yes, Darryl?' he answered.

'Just wondering if you've any news.'

'Anthony Brough, you mean? He's a money man, yes? I looked him up. Office in Rutland Square, home on Ann Street. How much has he cost you?'

'That's not why I need to find him.'

'No? Well, if you say so.' Cafferty paused. 'I *may* have a couple of sightings, but I don't want to get your hopes up.'

'Tell me anyway.'

'I'd rather wait for confirmation.'

'Sightings in Edinburgh?'

'Edinburgh and just outside – a fair few days back, mind . . .'

'How soon till you know for sure?'

'I'll be straight on the phone to you.'

'And this wouldn't just be you stringing me along?'

'I'm going to pretend you didn't say that.'

Cafferty listened to the silence.

'Sorry,' Christie said eventually.

'This guy's obviously important to you, Darryl. I appreciate that, and I'm doing my level best to help.'

'Thank you.'

'I'll be straight on the phone,' Cafferty repeated, ending the call as Christie was on the verge of thanking him again.

He shook his head slowly and went back to his paper.

18

Fox sat at his desk in the MIT room, staring into space. He had looked up Ukraine online to get a sense of the chaos it had been through and the chaos that still existed there, adding to the sum of everything Graham had told him. Glushenko's mafia friends had taught the man well, having previously laundered twenty billion dollars' worth of dirty money – money spirited out of Russia, moved via Moldova around Europe, and now sitting somewhere out of reach of the authorities, even supposing the authorities knew its exact whereabouts. Firms registered in tax havens such as the Seychelles became partners in SLPs, then once the money was in place those companies and partnerships were dissolved, making the trail more complex and much, much colder. Although there were plans to tighten the regulations, the UK was still a cheap and easy place in which to register a company – an agent could do it in an hour and charge around twenty-five pounds. These same agents were supposedly required to satisfy themselves that they weren't dealing with anyone shady, and they also had to know the identity of the true owner of the assets.

Fox couldn't be sure how Anthony Brough had come on to Glushenko's radar, except that Edinburgh retained an international reputation for probity and discretion, being home to institutions that looked after billions in pensions and investments. Glushenko brought with him just under a billion dollars stolen from a bank in Ukraine by way of loans arranged for non-existent companies, the paperwork signed off by executives who had been threatened or coerced. By the time the theft was noticed, the money was already a long way through its circuitous journey via the Edinburgh flat and beyond.

Sheila Graham had given Fox a short history of shady money in the UK. London's army of highly paid lawyers, bankers and accountants were, according to her, experts in dealing with it – using offshore accounts, trusts and shell companies to disguise the identity of any beneficial owner. There was plenty of regulation in place to attempt to stop money laundering, but banks often turned a blind eye when the price was right. The cash ended up transformed into pristine multimillion-pound apartments and even more expensive commercial assets. Tens of thousands of properties in London alone were owned by offshore companies, registered in the likes of Jersey, Guernsey and the British Virgin Islands – this last a favourite, as owners' identities did not need to be registered with the appropriate authorities. Offshore havens had their own distinct personalities: Liberia specialised in bearer shares, which provided absolute anonymity; setting up a company in the British Virgin Islands was cheap and quick, which explained why an island with a population of 25,000 was home to around 800,000 registered businesses.

'The sums we're talking about would give you vertigo,' Graham had said in conclusion, and after his own trawl of the internet Fox couldn't disagree. The thing was, gangsters such as Darryl Christie and Joe Stark were amateurs by comparison. Anthony Brough had climbed into bed with the worst of the worst. And something had spooked him.

Something almost certainly linked to the disappearance of around ten million pounds from the original chunk of money.

'So Brough's skimmed ten mil and done a runner?' Fox had asked Graham. 'Leaving his good pal Darryl Christie in the firing line?'

'It's one possibility,' she had replied.

'What do we know about Glushenko? Is he in this country?'

'He probably has aliases and passports we don't know about. Immigration have been warned to keep a watch at airports.' Graham had shrugged.

Now, seated at his desk, Fox was thinking through his options. Christie wanted information on Glushenko, and Fox could give him everything he knew. Or he could bide his time and wait for Glushenko to deal with Christie, after which Jude's debts might be history. He had considered telling Graham about Jude, about Christie's threat, but had decided against it. Not yet. Not unless it proved absolutely necessary.

'Penny for them,' Alvin James said, walking into the room.

'You wouldn't be getting your money's worth,' Fox assured him, fixing a smile on to his face. 'Anything happening that I need to know about?'

James shrugged off his coat and hung it up. 'Interviews with Roddy Cape and Dandy Reynolds,' he said, before noticing Fox's blank look. 'The two nyaffs who were with Cal Christie that night.'

'Right.'

'One thing we can't let happen is for this inquiry to stall. Got to keep up the momentum.' He clapped his hands together and rubbed them. To Fox's ears, it sounded as if he was trying to motivate himself.

'Will DI Clarke be joining us today?' Fox asked casually.

'She might. She's tip-top, Malcolm, you were right about that.'

'Did she take you somewhere nice last night?'

'Curry house – don't ask which street; this town still mystifies me.' James paused. 'You got enough to do?'

'I'm fine.'

James nodded distractedly and settled at his desk, booting up his laptop. Fox pretended to get busy on his own, doing a check of recent house sales in his neighbourhood. Following his divorce, he had bought his ex-wife out of her half of the mortgage. If he had to sell, he could clear what Jude owed. Downside was, he'd then be looking at renting, or else starting a fresh mortgage on somewhere a lot smaller, and perhaps in a less salubrious part of town.

Not yet, he repeated to himself. Not unless absolutely necessary . . .

He closed the property website and started a search for Anthony Brough instead. Although he knew about the man's recent exploits, he wanted to dig back a little further. It didn't take long to reach the tragic holiday in Grand Cayman, the one where Brough's best friend, Julian Greene, had drowned in the pool after consuming a cocktail of alcohol and drugs. The death had had a lasting effect on Brough's sister Francesca. She'd been hospitalised shortly afterwards, having gone from self-harming to a suicide attempt. The local newspaper in Grand Cayman had done its best to be diplomatic about the whole string of events, but the *Daily Mail* in London had been far less circumspect, going so far as to hint at a cover-up. Had Greene been alone, or were others poolside at the time? Had they failed to notice, failed to act? Had evidence of drug use been cleared away and the scene rearranged before an ambulance was called? The Brough family's solicitor had turned spokesperson, able to claim that 'these innocent young people' were in shock, and accusing the media of 'tasteless and tawdry tactics that do nothing but interfere with the grieving process'.

Fox sent a speculative email to the Grand Cayman newspaper asking if anyone working there might recall the drowning. He got an almost immediate reply giving the name of a retired journalist called Wilbur Bennett, along with a phone number. Excusing himself to James, he exited the room and headed out to the car park, where he made the call.

'I'm having breakfast,' a male voice snapped by way of answer.

'Wilbur Bennett? My name's Malcolm Fox. I'm a police detective in Scotland. Sorry to disturb you at such an early hour . . .'

'Are you really a cop?'

'Last time I looked.'

'Only when I worked Fleet Street, we often pretended to be. It was as good a way as any of opening a door.'

'I know someone a bit like that,' Fox admitted. 'But it's your time in Grand Cayman I'm interested in.'

'The drowning, then?'

'That's very perceptive.'

'I didn't do too many stories with a Scottish angle.'

'It happened at a house owned by Sir Magnus Brough, is that right?'

'Got it in one, though it was about to go on the market.'

'Oh?'

'The old boy had just popped his clogs. Always seemed rum to me that his two wards were cavorting on holiday so soon after the funeral. That's the way I always thought of them – "wards", like something out of Dickens. Best explanation I got was that the trip was already planned and it was what Sir Magnus would have wanted.'

'Odd to have two deaths in such a short space of time.'

'Isn't it, though?' Wilbur Bennett paused and took a slurp of something – coffee maybe, or something a bit stronger. From his voice – as rich and cloying as teacake – Fox got the impression of someone who might welcome the first drink of the day at an early hour. 'So why the sudden interest, Officer?'

'No real reason. Something's come up and it may involve Anthony Brough in a peripheral capacity.'

'You've been tasked with digging into his past? Well, what I saw of him I didn't like. He was too cocky by half – all that privilege and sense of entitlement. Probably why the *Mail* did a number on him – or would have if the lawyers hadn't started growling.'

'Did you feed them any titbits, Mr Bennett?'

'The *Mail*, you mean?'

'You worked Fleet Street before moving to Grand Cayman – I'm guessing you still had contacts there.'

'Well, you might be right. Here, tell you what – shall I pretend I've something juicy to tell you but I'll only do so face to face? You can fly out here for a few days . . .'

'I'm sorely tempted, but we have to think of the hard-pressed taxpayer.'

Bennett snorted. 'Not out here we don't!'

'Point taken. You're a tax haven like the Virgin Islands, aren't you?'

'That we are.'

'Which probably means dirty money has washed ashore at some time or other.'

'Caribbean's always been full of pirates,' Bennett's voice boomed. 'But to get back to that swimming pool . . .'

'Yes?'

'The inquiry – such as it was – never did get to the heart of it. Servants had heard raised voices. Then, questioned again later, they changed their story. The poor sod who died, he had plenty of booze and cocaine coursing through him, but not enough to knock him out. In fact, taking a dip should have revived him. Then there were the marks on his shoulders – nobody bothered trying to explain them. From what little I could glean, he'd had a major crush on the sister for a few months. And after he died, she went to pieces.'

'Who found the body?'

'Her and her brother. They were indoors allegedly, watching a film with the rest of the party. Took some time to realise Greene hadn't joined them. Found him floating in the pool. No drugs lying around by the time the medics and cops arrived. When the autopsy found cocaine in his system, they said they were unaware he'd taken any – usual story. And surprise surprise, the only place in the house where any was found was Greene's bedroom, a bag of white powder in a bedside drawer, never checked for fingerprints.'

'You've got a good memory, Mr Bennett.'

'Only because the whole investigation was a farce. You live as long as I have in a place like this, you see who gets away with things and who doesn't, and it can make you sick sometimes.'

'Are you telling me you think Julian Greene was killed?'

'I'm telling you it doesn't matter a tuppenny damn one way or the other – nobody paid for it then and nobody's going to pay now. But ask yourself why Francesca went off her rocker straight after. Some of us thought she deserved an Oscar, way she threw herself into it. I'm willing to bet she's still alive – thriving, even.'

'Alive, yes,' Fox conceded. 'But that's about as much as I know.'

'She wanted to see an exorcist – did you hear about that?'

'No.'

'That's what she told them after they'd pumped her stomach. Money can buy you a lot of things, but not always the one thing you really need – reckon I could get a self-help book out of that?'

'*Mindfulness for Millionaires*?' Fox suggested.

'You might be on to something, chum! I'm away to dust off the old typewriter, unless there's anything else I can help you with . . .?'

'Say Julian Greene's death wasn't an accident – who would your money be on?'

'Their parents died in a car crash, and from that moment on they were stuck together like glue with only their greedy old shit of a grandpa for moral guidance.' Bennett paused for a moment's thought. 'One or the other, or maybe even both. As I say, it hardly matters. Hardly matters at all . . .'

Ann Street was reckoned by many to be the most beautiful terrace in the city. Tucked away between Queensferry Road and Stockbridge, its two elegant facing rows of Georgian homes were separated by a narrow roadway constructed of traditional setts. The front gardens were immaculate, the black metal railings glossy, the lamp posts harking back to a more elegant age. Anthony Brough's house was towards one end of the street and not quite as imposing as those in the centre of the terrace. Rebus pushed open the gate, stood on the doorstep and pressed the bell. When there was no answer, he peered through the letter box. He could see an entrance hall and a stone staircase. Straightening up, he took a few steps to the window and peered into a modern living room boasting a TV and sofa but not much else. Back on the pavement, he was considering his options when he caught something from the corner of his eye – a net curtain twitching in the house opposite. Ah, Edinburgh. *Of course* a net curtain would twitch. Neighbours liked to know what was going on; for some, it was an all-embracing passion.

Rebus crossed the street, and was halfway up the path when the door opened slowly. The woman was in her seventies, stooped but immaculately dressed.

'Is he not at home?' she enquired in a lilting voice.

'Doesn't look like.'

'I've not seen him for quite some time.'

'That's why we're a bit worried,' Rebus informed her. 'His secretary says it's been over a week . . .'

The neighbour considered this. 'Yes, I suppose it must be.'

'Any other visitors?'

'I've not seen any.'

'Do you know Mr Brough well, would you say?'

'We stop and chat . . .'

'And you last saw him over a week ago?'

'I suppose,' she echoed, frowning as she tried to count the days.

'Had he seemed anxious at all?'

'Isn't everyone? I mean, you only have to switch on the news . . .' She gave a perfectly formed shudder. Rebus was holding out a card. It was one of Malcolm Fox's, lifted from the MIT office. He had crossed out Fox's phone number and email address and added his own mobile number in black ballpoint.

'Detective Inspector,' the woman said as she peered at the card. 'He's not dead, is he?'

'I'm sure he's not.'

'Francesca and Alison must be up to high doh.'

'Alison?'

'Francesca's carer.' The neighbour immediately corrected herself. 'No, her *assistant*. That's what she likes to be called.'

'You know Mr Brough's sister, then?'

The neighbour arched her back in surprise that he even needed to ask. 'Well of course,' she said. She nodded past Rebus towards the house. 'She lives there, doesn't she?'

Rebus turned his head to look. '*There?*' he asked, just to be sure.

'In the garden flat, directly below the main house. You just go down the steps and . . .'

But Rebus was already on his way. Yes, there was another gate, smaller, to the right of the one leading to the main house, with winding stone steps down to a well-tended patio. Rebus had been aware of it on arrival, but had thought it a separate property. The windows either side of the green wooden door had bars on – nothing unusual about that; many of the city's garden flats boasted the same.

'Garden' – when Rebus had first gone flat-hunting in the city, so many decades back, he had wondered at that word. Why not just 'basement'? That was what it meant, after all. Except that 'garden' implied you were getting a garden, too, and these flats did often lead directly into the rear garden of the property. He had looked at several before plumping for the second floor of a Marchmont tenement. His reasoning? No need to do any gardening.

The door was opened by a tall, well-built woman in her early thirties, her fair hair pulled back into a bun, one stray tress curling down past her left ear.

'Yes?' she asked.

Rebus held out another filched business card. 'I'm Detective Inspector Fox,' he announced as she took the card and studied it.

'Is it about the break-ins?'

'Break-ins?'

'There's been a spate recently.' She studied him closely. 'Surely you must know.'

'I'm here about Anthony Brough. Would you be Alison?'

'How do you know that?'

'One of the neighbours,' Rebus admitted with a smile.

'Oh.' She tried out a smile of her own.

'You'll be aware that Mr Brough hasn't been seen in quite some time. His secretary is becoming concerned for his safety.'

The woman called Alison considered this. 'I see,' she eventually said.

'She's been to the house to look for him – I dare say she spoke to you too?'

'Molly, you mean? Yes, she did. But it's not so unusual for Anthony to take off on some jaunt or other.'

Rebus was looking past her shoulder at the long, unlit hallway. There was a thick velvet curtain at the far end, which he guessed would lead to stairs, stairs connecting to the main house.

'Is Francesca at home? Could I maybe speak to her, Miss . . .?'

'Warbody. And yes, she's home.'

'You're her assistant?'

'That's right.'

'I'd imagine she must be fretting about her brother?'

'Francesca takes medication. Time doesn't mean as much to her as to some of us.'

Rebus tried his smile again. 'Would it be possible to talk to her?'

'She hasn't seen him.'

'Since when?'

'Eight, ten days back.'

'No phone calls or texts?'

'I think I would know.'

'And you're saying that's not out of character?'

'That's exactly what I'm saying.'

'Who are you speaking to?' The voice – thin, almost ethereal – had come from one of the doorways. Rebus could just make out the shape of a head.

'Nobody,' Warbody called back.

'I'm with the police,' Rebus announced. 'I was just asking about your brother.'

Warbody was glowering, but Rebus ignored her. Francesca Brough was walking towards the daylight, almost on tiptoe, like a ballerina. She had a ballerina's frame, too, albeit one wrapped in thick black tights and a baggy oatmeal sweater, its sleeves stretched so that her hands were hidden within. One of the sleeves was in her mouth as she reached the doorstep. Her hair was clumsily cut, the scalp showing beneath. Her skin was almost ghostly and her lips bloodless as she sucked at the wool. The material seemed matted, as though this was not an unusual ritual.

'Hello,' she said, voice muffled.

'Hello,' Rebus echoed.

'The inspector,' Warbody explained, 'is here because Anthony's gone off on one of his walkabouts.'

'He does that,' Francesca said, as Warbody gently pulled her hand away from her mouth.

'That's what I've just been explaining.'

'And you last saw him . . .?'

The question seemed to perturb Francesca. She looked to Warbody for guidance.

'Eight or ten days back,' Warbody obliged.

'Eight or ten days,' Francesca repeated.

'I assume you've been upstairs to check?' The two women looked at Rebus. 'You can get into the house?' he persisted.

'Yes, we can,' Francesca said softly.

'Could we maybe go take a look, then?' Rebus requested.

'He's not there,' Warbody stated. 'We would have heard him.'

Francesca was reaching towards a hook on the wall. She lifted down two keys, mortise and Yale. 'Here we are,' she said.

207

Rebus's eyes were on Warbody. 'There isn't a door behind that curtain?' he asked, gesturing.

'It's locked from the other side.'

'Why?'

She offered a shrug. 'Anthony likes his privacy.' Then: 'He really won't like it that we've taken a stranger inside.'

'I won't tell him if you don't.' Rebus's wink was aimed at Francesca. She giggled, holding her hands over her mouth.

'Let's get on with it then,' Warbody said with a sigh of defeat.

They climbed back up to street level and through the main gate. Both keys needed to be used. There was an alarm pad on the wall inside the front door, but Warbody knew the code.

Rebus had bent to pick up some mail from the floor.

'Put it with the rest,' Warbody said. There was an inch-high pile on an occasional table. Rebus sifted through it. 'Enjoying yourself?' she asked coldly. Francesca had padded into the room with the TV, but emerged again seconds later and headed down the hall. Warbody followed, Rebus bringing up the rear. They entered an extension to the original house. It was a bright kitchen, with sliding glass doors leading to a patio and steps down into the garden. An ashtray and wine glass sat on a small outdoors table. The kitchen itself was immaculate.

'Does Mr Brough have a cleaner?'

'Wednesday mornings,' Warbody confirmed.

'So the wine glass means . . .?'

'It means someone needs to have a word with her about standards.'

They paused and watched as Francesca opened the sink's mixer faucet and then shut it off again, only to repeat the process. Warbody approached and placed the palm of her hand against the small of Francesca's back. It was enough. Francesca's arms fell to her sides and her face took on a look of contrition.

'Can we go upstairs?' Rebus asked.

'Yes, let's!' And Francesca bounded out of the room, taking the stairs two at a time.

Two bedrooms and a large study. The bedrooms looking out over Ann Street, the study tucked away at the rear of the property. In the upstairs hall, Rebus looked for evidence of further floors, but he'd seen everything.

'He *was* meaning to renovate the attic,' Warbody offered, as if reading his mind. 'But it's not happened yet.'

'We *loved* attics when we were young,' Francesca blurted out.

'I'm not seeing an answering machine,' Rebus said, looking around.

'There isn't even a telephone – Anthony didn't feel the need.'

'You've called his mobile? Sent him texts?'

'A couple of times,' Warbody admitted. 'Not because we're worried, just to see if he wanted to join us for a meal or a trip into town.'

'You still don't think it's unusual not to get a reply?'

'He could be breaking the bank at Monte Carlo.' Warbody gave a shrug.

'Or pigging out at the Caledonian,' Francesca added. 'He likes to eat and drink there.'

'Any special reason?' Rebus asked her.

'It's handy for his office,' Warbody interrupted.

'Plus,' Francesca went on, 'it's where *she* was killed.'

'You mean Maria Turquand?'

The young woman's eyes widened. 'You know about her?'

'I take an interest in old cases. Your brother's interested too?'

'Look, Inspector,' Warbody said, manoeuvring herself between Rebus and Francesca, 'we'd help you if we could, but there's really nothing we can do.' She noticed that Francesca was dancing back down the stairs again, so made to follow. The two women were waiting by the front door as Rebus reached the hall.

'I appreciate your assistance,' he told Warbody. He took out his phone. 'I've given you my contact number – do you mind if I take yours?'

'Why?'

'In case I need to get in touch – saves me having to come back in the flesh.'

She saw the sense of this, so reeled off the number while Rebus entered it into his phone.

'Thanks again,' he said.

The net curtain across the way was twitching again as the two women headed for their own bolthole. Rebus called out to Warbody, who, after a moment's reluctance, joined him.

'I take it Mr Brough pays your salary?' he asked.

She shook her head. 'I work for Francesca. Sir Magnus made sure she was comfortable.'

'She got half the estate?'

'Not quite, but she got as much as her brother. And unlike Anthony, she's not a gambler.'

'He gambles?'

'Isn't that what all investment comes down to? No gain without risk.'

'I suppose so.' He thanked her with a nod and watched her march down the steps and close the door after her. As he walked towards his parked car, he saw another directly behind it. Malcolm Fox emerged.

'Fancy meeting you here,' Fox drawled.

'Great minds, Malcolm.'

'He's not at home, then?'

'His sister is, though.'

'Oh?'

'She lives in the downstairs flat, looked after by a woman called Warbody.'

'How did she seem?'

'The sister? Away with the bloody fairies.'

'I've just been discussing her with a—'

But Rebus interrupted him with a gesture. 'Let's continue this in my office.' He nodded towards the Saab. 'I just want to make a quick call first.'

When they were seated with the doors closed, Rebus phoned Molly Sewell, identifying himself and saying he had a quick question for her. He had put the phone's speaker on so that Fox could listen.

'Go ahead then,' she said.

'You told us you'd been to your employer's home and put a note through his door. I've just been in there, and I didn't see any note.'

'Maybe you didn't look hard enough.'

'I looked,' Rebus stated.

'Then someone must have moved it – maybe the cleaner.'

'Or Alison Warbody,' Rebus commented, listening to the ensuing silence on the line. 'Why didn't you mention that Francesca Brough lives directly beneath her brother?'

'I didn't want you bothering her. You've seen her?'

'Yes.'

'Then it can't have escaped your notice that she's incredibly fragile.'

'I managed to spend ten minutes with her without snapping a piece off.'

'What an unfeeling thing to say.'

'I did score pretty low on sensitivity at the police college. But it's not up to you to decide what we're allowed to—'

'John,' Fox interrupted.

Rebus broke off and stared at him.

'She's rung off,' Fox explained. Rebus studied his phone's screen and cursed under his breath.

'Your turn then,' he said, leaning back in the driver's seat.

Fox filled him in on the chat with Wilbur Bennett. Rebus took a few moments to digest everything he'd heard, then shook his head slowly.

'The whole family's something else,' he concluded.

'You think they're protecting Anthony,' Fox stated.

'Don't you?'

Fox nodded. 'What's more, I know why.'

Rebus half turned towards him. 'Go on.' But then he had another thought, and tapped at the screen of his phone once more, with the speaker still active.

'Hello?'

'Ms Warbody,' he said, 'it's DI Fox again.' He had turned his head so he wouldn't have to deal with the look he knew Fox would be giving him. 'Something I forgot to ask – Ms Sewell says she put a note through Mr Brough's—'

'I picked it up.'

'You did?'

'Yes.'

'That's okay then. Thank you, Ms Warbody.'

The phone went dead and Rebus turned his head to meet Fox's stare.

'You snatched some of my business cards,' Fox said eventually.

'Of course I did – sometimes people need to think they're talking to a cop.'

'But they're not, John, and impersonating a police officer is an offence.'

'I know guys who spent their whole lives on the force doing not much more than impersonating cops.'

'That's beside the point.'

'The point is . . . what did you make of that?' Rebus was waving his phone in Fox's face.

'What was I supposed to make of it?'

'You don't think she sounded like she'd just been told what to say by someone who knew I'd be asking the question?'

'Maybe. But to get back to what I was trying to tell you earlier . . .'

'What?'

'I know what's going on here. Not all of it, but a lot of it.'

Rebus stared at him. 'You do?'

'Want me to share?'

'I'm all ears . . .'

Fifteen minutes later, hands gripping the steering wheel, Rebus shook his head and gave a noisy exhalation.

'That's what he meant by the Russian,' he muttered.

'Who?'

'Cafferty. He told me to look for the Russian. I thought it was to do with the Turquand case, but all the time . . .'

'Glushenko's Ukrainian, though.'

'But the name sounds Russian – you said so yourself. Cafferty's information was just slightly less than a hundred per cent accurate. Thing is – how did he even come to know that much? He'd hardly have heard from Christie or Brough, would he?'

'Maybe this is still a town that talks to him,' Fox offered.

'You could be right.' Rebus nodded slowly. 'Or there could be something here we're not seeing. Did Darryl Christie look to you like he's sitting on a chunk of ten million pounds?'

'I'm not sure how someone like that would look.'

'Something we're not seeing,' Rebus repeated. Then he smiled for Fox's benefit. 'But thanks to you, Malcolm, we're closer than we were.'

Fox's own phone was letting him know he had a text.

'My absence has been noted,' he announced.

'The James Gang?'

'The very same.'

'How's the investigation going?'

'We seem to be making heavy weather. You really think it's all about Maria Turquand?'

'Odds-on favourite, I'd say.'

'Pity you've yet to convince Detective Superintendent James.'

'I lack your people skills.'

'You want me to keep nudging him?'

'With any blunt object lurking in the vicinity.'

'Thing is, I'm not sure you're right – not this time.'

'That hurts, Malcolm. You know you've got a very sick man right here in front of you? Added to which, it's my birthday . . .'

'It was your birthday three months back. Siobhan and me took you out, remember?'

'I forgot that,' Rebus said with a pained expression. 'Okay, off you go to dole out biscuits to your MIT chums – some of us have *real* work to do.'

'Such as?'

'Probably best you don't know.'

'Probably best *you* don't go pretending to be me any more.' Fox held out a hand. 'I want those business cards back.'

'I've used them all up.'

'Liar.'

'Cross my shadowed lung and hope to die.'

'Christ, John, don't joke about that. Any news yet?'

Rebus's face softened a little. 'No,' he admitted.

'You've still not shared it with anyone?'

'Just you.'

Fox nodded and started opening his door.

'Hey,' Rebus said, causing him to pause. 'Have you told me every-thing?'

'Everything?'

'About Christie and Brough.'

'Not everything, no.'

'Good lad,' Rebus said with a spreading smile. 'You're finally learning.'

Malcolm Fox couldn't help but smile back.

19

Siobhan Clarke hated herself for waiting on the phone call. Over dinner the previous night, Alvin James had said that he wanted her on the Major Investigation Team. It was just a matter of letting people know, including her boss. She had already found three excuses to visit DCI Page's cubbyhole office that morning, thinking he'd maybe just not got round to passing the news along.

But there had been no news.

Should she remind Alvin? A friendly text, perhaps, in the guise of wondering how the inquiry was shaping up?

You're not that needy, girl, she told herself, but she worried that she was.

The search for Craw Shand was ongoing, but with enthusiasm waning. Laura Smith had run the story online, repeating it several times to no avail. Clarke had texted to thank her. Christine Esson had commented that if someone had meant him harm, surely a body would have turned up by now. Clarke wasn't so sure – plenty of spots where a cadaver could be stored; lots of wild places within an hour's drive of the city. Craw hadn't used his mobile phone and hadn't been near a bank machine. The CCTV cameras across the city centre had failed to pick him up. Friends had been located and questioned, again without success. Meantime, Esson and Ogilvie had shown photos of Shand to Darryl Christie, who had shaken his head, making the same gesture when he was played a recording of Shand's voice. Nor had the photos meant anything to Christie's neighbours – no one had seen Craw Shand in the vicinity of Christie's home.

Clarke's phone sat on her desk, tormenting her with its stubborn silence. Esson was busy at her computer, while Ronnie Ogilvie took a call, using his free hand to stroke what there was of his moustache. Clarke pulled some paperwork towards her, but couldn't concentrate. Instead, she got up and put her coat on. Christine Esson gave her a quizzical look. Ignoring her, Clarke headed for the door.

Traffic was sluggish towards the city centre and she drummed her fingers to the music on her radio. Two songs and a news report later, she turned into Cowgate and parked at the goods entrance to the Devil's Dram. A delivery van was dropping off catering supplies, so she squeezed past the boxes and went inside. Darryl Christie was downstairs for a change, discussing something with Hodges. They stood behind the illuminated bar. The subject seemed to be flavoured gins.

'And here comes an expert,' Christie announced at her approach.

'Do you never give up?' Hodges added, eyes narrowing.

Christie ignored him. 'Pull up a stool – you can be our guinea pig. The rhubarb and ginger is a bit tasty, apparently.'

'I never accept free drinks.'

'Just Happy Hour ones, eh?' Christie said. 'We took your lovely portrait down, by the way. Harry reckoned it would be a bit too much for the clientele.' He paused, leaning across the bar, palms pressed down against it. 'That wasn't very nice, by the way, barging into my home when I was elsewhere.'

'You told me you'd moved your family out – I'm interested in why you changed your mind.'

'Is this about Craw Shand? You still think I've taken him out of the game?' Christie managed a thin smile. 'How often do I have to tell you?'

'If whoever attacked you isn't in custody, why are you acting like it's all gone away?'

'What makes you think I've not taken precautions?'

'And what precautions might those be, Mr Christie?'

He tutted. 'As if I'd tell you. My mum was livid, you know – she thinks I was condoning Cal's behaviour. Well, I was doing a lot worse at his age, and at least I sent a chaperone.' Christie focused his attention on Hodges, who began to look uncomfortable. 'For all the fucking good that did. Thing about a chaperone is, they're supposed to *be* there.'

'I was hanging back to take a call, Darryl. You know that. They were never out of my sight, swear to God.'

Christie squeezed Hodges' shoulder, but his eyes were back on

Clarke. 'I'd imagine you're winding things down, no? Other fish to fry and so forth?'

'Not until Craw turns up. He's been charged with assault, re-member – *your* assault. Procurator Fiscal tends to take a dim view when the main suspect vanishes.'

'Well, good luck finding him. Now, about these gins . . .' The uplighters below the bar cast half Christie's face in shadow, exag-gerating the other half so that he seemed to be wearing a Halloween mask. 'Are you quite sure I can't tempt you?'

'I'm sure,' Clarke said, turning and walking away.

The interviews with Cal Christie's friends had gone nowhere and the mood in the MIT room was grim.

'Maybe it's time to take Rebus's theory a bit more seriously,' Fox suggested.

'Give me a suspect, then,' Alvin James demanded, not bothering to hide his exasperation. 'Tell me which of these pensioners was able to overpower a bodybuilder and tip him into the Forth.'

'We're talking about people with a bit of spare cash,' Fox con-tinued calmly. 'Bruce Collier, John Turquand, Peter Attwood – any one of them could probably dig deep enough to pay someone.'

'And who would they pay, Malcolm? Give me a list of the city's hit men.'

Fox held up his hands. 'I'm just saying.'

'Saying what, though?'

'We've maybe not explored the possibility as thoroughly as we could. You come up against a wall, the best thing you can do is find reverse and try another route.'

James glared at him. The others in the room were looking away, pretending to be indifferent – Glancey dabbing at the nape of his neck, while Sharpe studied some of the dust he'd just gathered from his desk with a forefinger. 'What we're going to do,' James eventu-ally said, 'is go back to the very start. Crime scene, autopsy, victim's associates. We're going to fill in the gaps in his timeline and we're going to check the logs and records again. And just to remind you all – the man was a cop most of his life; we owe it to him to pull out all the stops. Got that?'

There were murmurs of acceptance from behind the desks. James flew to his feet and walked into the centre of the room, readying to dish out tasks. Five minutes later, Fox found himself with

Chatham's phone bills – landline and mobile – and the printout of calls made from the phone box he had used after speaking to Rebus. As Rebus had left him, having arranged to meet for breakfast the next morning, Chatham had used his mobile to call his employer, Kenny Arnott. When questioned, Arnott had stated that Chatham had wanted to discuss the following week's working hours. No, he hadn't sounded upset or flustered. He had sounded the same as always. And no, it wasn't so unusual to be called by an employee at 10 p.m. Those were the hours doormen worked, so they tended to be the hours Arnott kept too.

Their conversation had lasted just over three minutes.

As soon as it was over, Chatham had asked a colleague to cover for him and headed to the phone box, this time to call three different bars in the city: Templeton's, the Wrigley and the Pirate. None of them used doormen provided by Arnott, but as Arnott himself had said when asked, Chatham could have been touting for a bit of freelance work. When questioned, none of the staff at any of the three could remember anything. Hardly surprising: they weren't the most salubrious establishments, and all had suffered at the hands of the Licensing Board at some point in the past, meaning they had no love for the local police. As to why he had used a phone box rather than his mobile . . . Well, nobody had a ready answer. The colleague who had taken over for the duration didn't know. Kenny Arnott didn't know. Anne Briggs had offered a guess to Fox: battery died. Yes, perhaps. But scouting out new jobs at ten at night, when the pubs would be at their busiest and no manager available to chat for more than a minute or so?

Templeton's: ninety-five seconds.

The Wrigley: two minutes and five seconds.

The Pirate: forty-seven seconds.

Then back to his post until his shift ended at midnight. No more calls or texts that evening, nothing until the following morning, when, after the meeting with Rebus in the café, he sent the messages to Maxine Dromgoole. And after that . . . nothing at all.

'How's it going, Malcolm?' Alvin James was standing in front of Fox's desk, looking as if he'd had one espresso too many.

'Nothing new,' Fox conceded.

James spun back into the centre of the room. 'Give me *something*, people! We're supposed to be good at this – that's the only reason we're here. If I have to report back to the ACC that we're achieved the square root of hee-haw, it'll be the end of us. Somebody threw him in the water! Somebody saw! The whisky – was it bought locally? Check shops and supermarkets. Get the CCTV from the roads along that part of the Forth – they had to have used transport.' He clapped his hands together like the boss of a football team at half-time in a relegation play-off.

Fox watched as Glancey and Briggs pulled their shoulders back in a show of enthusiasm. Wallace Sharpe wasn't looking quite so keen. But then, as the surveillance expert, he'd be the one saddled with the hours of camera footage. Mark Oldfield was by the kettle, waiting for it to boil. James spotted him and shook his head.

'No, no, no, Mark – you get a tea break when I say so and not before. Time you all earned it for a change. Back to your desk, son. Give me names, give me ideas, give me something I can use.'

Fox had the timeline up on his screen. Chatham had headed out of the house without a word to his partner, having told Dromgoole he wouldn't be seeing her that day. So what did he do instead? He left his car in its usual spot. Liz Dolan had told police he often took the bus, but there was no sign of him taking one that afternoon. If he had been snatched off the street, surely there would have been a witness or two. So maybe he had gone somewhere willingly, in one of the thousands upon thousands of cars visible on the citywide CCTV cameras.

Bloody hell – 'needle in a haystack' hardly covered it. No wonder Wallace Sharpe looked so despondent.

Fox picked up his phone, which had started to vibrate. Caller ID: Rebus. He pressed the phone to his ear.

'Hang on a sec,' he told Rebus, getting up and moving into the hallway. Alvin James gave him a hopeful look, which Fox crushed with a shake of the head.

'What can I do for you, John?' he asked, leaning against one of the olive-coloured walls.

'The smallest of favours.'

'I'm not giving you any more business cards.'

'Business cards won't help – this bugger already knows I'm not a cop.'

'That's why you need me along?'

'In a nutshell.'

'Who is he? What do we want from him?'

'I like that "we", Malcolm. And to answer your question: he's a legend. I really think you'll get a buzz from meeting him.'

Fox checked his watch. 'When and where?'

218

'Right now would suit me.'

'There's a surprise.'

'Unless I'm tearing you away from anything urgent . . .'

Fox sighed. 'Not really. Okay, give me the address.'

'I'm waiting outside.'

'Of course you are,' Fox said, ending the call.

He didn't bother going back to explain or grab his coat. Rebus was double-parked across from the police station. Fox climbed in and Rebus put his foot down.

'So where *are* we going?'

'Rutland Square.'

'Bruce Collier?'

'Only fair I introduce you,' Rebus said. 'After all, you've met most of the other main players.'

'I pitched an idea to Alvin James – one of them paying to have Rab Chatham done away with.'

'What did he say?'

'He didn't seem keen.'

'The man lacks vision.'

'And yours is twenty-twenty?'

'With hindsight sometimes,' Rebus said with a smile.

'James has got us retreading old ground, starting from the beginning.'

'The mark of an inquiry that's going nowhere.'

'Exactly. So what's Collier going to tell us?'

'Wait and see.' Rebus watched as Fox slid down his window, breathing deeply. 'Too long behind a desk, Malcolm – it makes a man stale.'

'We finally tracked down the calls he made from the phone box. Three pubs. His employer reckons he was touting for business – but at that time of night? I'm not so sure. And the calls were short – not one of them over three minutes.'

'Telling you what exactly?'

'He used the phone box because he didn't want anyone to be able to check.'

Rebus nodded slowly. 'Makes sense.'

'And this was straight after you spoke to him, bringing up the Turquand case.'

'Right.'

'He told you he was going home straight after his shift, yes?'

'Said our little chat would have to wait till morning.'

219

'But according to his partner, there's a gap of almost two hours between him finishing work and her hearing the front door close.'

'Which pubs did he phone?'

'Templeton's, the Wrigley and the Pirate.'

'Well, there's not one of them couldn't use a doorman.'

'I felt sure you'd know them.'

'Templeton's is Gilmerton Road way, the Wrigley is in Northfield, and the Pirate is just off Cowgate.'

'Anything you can tell me about them?'

'Probably good places to do your Christmas shopping – hand any of the regulars a list of what you want, they'll be back an hour later quoting a very reasonable price.'

'Having just broken into someone's house?'

'Putting the "nick" into St Nick. Not too many places like that left in the city.' Rebus was thoughtful. 'So he talks to his boss, and then he starts phoning around.'

'Hardly the sorts of place that would cater to the likes of Turquand, Attwood and Collier.'

'True enough. And I don't think any of them has live music, so we can probably rule out Dougie Vaughan.' Rebus paused. 'Cafferty was there that day, though.'

'Where? In the hotel?'

Rebus nodded. 'And that sort of bar might just appeal to him. He used to own a few that were of similar calibre. Come to think of it, Darryl Christie owned some too, before he moved on to better things . . .'

Fox's phone buzzed and he looked at the screen. Speak of the bloody devil – a text from Christie. *The clock's ticking, don't forget.* He sent a three-word text in reply – *I'm on it* – and switched off the phone.

Rebus had pointed the Saab at Princes Street, then ignored the No Entry sign and kept on it where only buses, trams and taxis were allowed. 'Pain in the arse having to go via George Street,' he explained.

'How many tickets do you average a month?'

'Police business, Malcolm – you'll back me up on that.'

They took a sharp left on to Lothian Road, then turned right almost immediately and passed the Waldorf Caledonian before stopping outside Collier's house.

'That's his Porsche over there,' Rebus announced, gesturing towards the line of cars parked across the street.

'Very nice, too,' Fox said. He watched as Rebus reached into the back seat of the Saab, bringing out a red polythene bag, then followed as Rebus rang the doorbell and waited.

Bruce Collier opened the door, squinting into the daylight. He hadn't shaved, and looked as though he had slept in the black T-shirt and grey joggers.

'Not you again,' he barked.

'Show him the card, DI Fox,' Rebus said. Fox took out his warrant card, but Collier ignored it.

'Ought to be a law against this,' he complained instead.

'A law against the law?' Rebus pretended to muse. 'Interesting thought. Mind if we come in? The hallway will do, we're not staying.'

'Make it quick, then.' Collier ushered them in and closed the door, rubbing his hand through his hair. Rebus made show of sniffing the air.

'Nice sweet aroma, isn't it? Dope, I mean.'

Collier folded his arms and waited.

'Bruce?' A woman's voice, wafting from somewhere upstairs.

'Two minutes,' Collier called back.

'I thought your wife was in India, Mr Collier?'

'Just get on with it,' Collier snapped.

'There used to be a sort of religious police force in Edinburgh, you know. Back in stricter times. They were called the Night Police. There to uphold the morals when the lights went out across the city.'

'Fascinating.'

Rebus stared at him. 'The day Maria Turquand was murdered, a delivery was made to your suite. Probably not dissimilar to what I'm smelling now, plus some cocaine and who knows what else.'

'Oh aye?'

'The man who delivered it was called Morris Gerald Cafferty. He became a big player – the biggest in these parts by a long shot. Do you remember him?'

'Nope.'

'Name doesn't mean anything to you? You put him on the guest list for that evening's concert.'

'I'm not sure what you're getting at, or why *you're* doing all the talking when you're not even a bloody cop!'

'Mr Rebus,' Fox drawled, 'is working with Police Scotland at this point in time, sir. You'd be advised to answer any questions he puts to you.'

221

Collier puffed out his cheeks and exhaled. He looked weary, cling-ing on by his fingernails to a lifestyle that should have said goodbye to him a decade or more back.

'Anyway,' Rebus continued, 'the thing is this. You didn't have enough cash on you to pay Cafferty, and your road manager was nowhere to be found, so you rifled Dougie Vaughan's pockets while he was crashed out.'

'So what?'

'I'm just wondering if you happened to see the key to Vince Brady's room. Mr Vaughan says he lost it at some point.'

'You're asking me if I took it – well, I didn't.'

'Could Cafferty have lifted it?'

'He wasn't anywhere near the bed.'

'You do remember him, then?'

'Maybe.'

'When you handed the cash over, the key couldn't have been tucked in between the notes?'

'You're trying to set up this gangster Cafferty? That's what this is about? The key got mislaid, end of story. Now if you don't mind . . .' He had already opened the door and was gesturing towards the world outside.

'Thought you'd like this,' Rebus said, holding up the bag. The words 'I Found It At Bruce's' were printed on it in black lettering.

'I remember that place,' Collier said. 'Did signings there a few times. Rose Street, wasn't it?'

Rebus opened the bag and lifted out Blacksmith's first album. Collier stared at it for a moment.

'You really think I'm going to give you an autograph?'

Rebus shook his head. 'I just wanted you to know I was a genuine fan, back in the mists of time.' He pretended to study the LP sleeve. Its edges were frayed and there was a cigarette burn in one corner. 'Bit like yourself, Mr Collier – it's seen better days . . .'

Fox followed Rebus outside as the door slammed behind them.

'Good line,' he said admiringly.

'Better still if nobody could say the same about me.' Rebus stifled a cough and popped a piece of gum into his mouth.

'So what now? Back to Leith?'

'If you like.'

'What's the alternative?'

'You've got me thinking about all those phone calls Chatham made . . .'

'And?'

'And I have half a mind to go talk to Kenny Arnott.'

'Will he speak to you without a warrant card?'

'I don't know.'

Fox pretended to consider for a moment. 'Maybe best if I come with you, then.'

'Well, if you insist . . .'

As they got into the Saab, Rebus tossed the carrier bag on to the back seat.

'They any good?' Fox asked.

'Dogshit,' Rebus replied, starting the engine.

20

'Do we know if this guy Arnott connects to either Cafferty or Christie?' Rebus asked as he drove.

'Rab Chatham worked a few nights at the Devil's Dram,' Fox said. 'How come Christie doesn't use his own security? Wouldn't that make more sense?'

Rebus mulled this over. 'Darryl's a new breed of gangster. He buys in what he needs for as long as he needs it. An army of full-time heavies doesn't come cheap. Added to which, you're never sure when one of them's going to learn too much about you and sell you out to the competition.'

'Or else maybe start plotting a coup against you?'

'That too,' Rebus acknowledged. 'Back in the day, Cafferty was surrounded by henchmen. One of them – name of Weasel – turned out to be a major liability. Over in the west, people like Joe Stark want to be seen flanked by muscle – reminds them how big and important they are. Our Darryl isn't that way inclined. I doubt he sees himself as anything other than a businessman, providing services people require.'

'Drugs, gambling, dodgy loans . . .'

'And more besides.' Rebus was bringing the Saab to a stop outside an unloved brick of a building near Pilrig Park.

'It's a boxing club,' Fox commented.

'Brought your gloves with you?' Rebus enquired as he undid his seat belt and got out.

The door to Kenny's Gym was unlocked, so they walked into a busy room filled with male perspiration. Two heavyweights sparred in the ring, their arms, chests and backs heavily tattooed. Punchbags were getting good use elsewhere, and a wiry young lad was dripping sweat as he used a skipping rope in front of a full-length mirror. There were weights and a couple of rowing machines on the far side of the room. Three men who were watching the action in the ring seemed to be having a conversation comprised almost entirely of profanities.

'I'm sure your mothers are very proud,' Rebus announced, drawing their attention to him. He had stuffed his hands into his pockets and spread his feet.

'Anyone smell a big fat side of bacon?' one of the three said, scowling.

'Can't fault your nose,' Rebus answered. 'Which is pretty impressive, judging by its shape. How did the other guy look afterwards?'

The man had started to move forwards, but a hand on his shoulder stopped him. It was the man next to him who took a few steps towards Rebus. He had curly brown hair and a round freckled face, the eyes not unwelcoming.

'The other guy,' he answered, 'looked like Tam here hadn't managed to lay a glove on him. Went on to win a few more fights and make a bit of money.'

'With you as his manager?' Rebus guessed.

The man shrugged and stuck out a hand. 'Kenny Arnott.'

Rebus shook the hand. 'My name's Rebus. This is Detective Inspector Fox. Any chance of a word?'

'I've already been questioned about Rab,' Arnott said.

'This is by way of a follow-up. Is there somewhere more private?'

'My office,' Arnott said. He led the way to the door and back out on to the street, where he lit a cigarette, blowing smoke into the sky.

'This is your office?' Fox asked.

Arnott nodded and waited, eyes twinkling.

'You still in the game?'

Arnott looked at Rebus. 'Depends which game you mean.'

'Managing boxers.'

'There's a cage fighter I look after. You probably just saw him.'

'Skinny, all muscle, busy on the skipping rope?'

'That's the one. Donny Applecross.'

'Is he any good?'

'He's getting there.' Arnott held up the cigarette. 'When this is done, I'm going back in.'

'We're wondering,' Rebus said, 'about the call Mr Chatham made to you the night before he was killed. He was on duty outside a bar on Lothian Road. I spoke to him just before ten, and as soon as I was gone, he phoned you.'

'I've explained this already,' Arnott said, looking aggrieved. 'It was shop talk – shifts for the following week.'

'My name wasn't mentioned?'

'Remind me.'

'John Rebus. I'd just been asking Mr Chatham about the Maria Turquand murder.'

'News to me, bud.'

'You know the case, though?' Rebus watched as Arnott shook his head. 'When you took on Rab Chatham, you knew he was ex-CID?'

'Sure.'

'He never talked about cases he'd worked?'

'Nope.'

'I find that hard to believe.'

'Maybe he shared stories with the other doormen – you'd have to ask them. Only time I ever spent with him was at the initial interview. After that it was mostly phone calls and texts.'

'How was he as a doorman?' Fox asked.

'He was diligent.'

'What does that mean?'

'Always turned up to a job. Got stuck in when the need arose.' Arnott held up the cigarette again. 'Two more drags and we're done.'

Rebus batted the cigarette away with the back of his hand. It flew to the ground unheeded. Arnott's eyes had lost their sparkle, his whole face darkening.

'This is a murder inquiry,' Rebus told him. 'We don't measure it in fucking tabs.'

Arnott considered this and nodded slowly. 'He was one of your own, I get that. He was one of mine, too, don't forget, and if there was anything I knew that would help . . .' He shrugged.

'He spoke to you,' Rebus said quietly, 'and then he headed straight to a phone box and called three pubs – Templeton's, the Wrigley, and the Pirate. What was that all about, Mr Arnott?'

'I already explained to the other coppers – looking for a bit of extra work maybe.'

'Those pubs don't have security?'

'Far as I know they do – courtesy of my competitor.'

'Andrew Goodman, you mean? So your theory is that Rab Chatham was looking to work for Goodman? How likely does that sound? And wouldn't he need to talk with Goodman rather than phone the pubs themselves? You can see how we might find this all fairly implausible.'

'Then maybe he was looking to catch up with someone after his shift ended.'

In which case, thought Rebus, he must have hit pay dirt with the Pirate, his final call. Not the kind of bar he would have thought Chatham or any of his buddies would have frequented. Dregs and lowlifes comprised the more regular clientele. The great unwashed . . .

'Bloody hell,' Rebus muttered.

'What is it?' Fox asked. But Rebus was already stalking towards the Saab.

'Any time, lads,' Kenny Arnott called to their retreating backs. 'Nice of you to drop by . . .'

'What is it?' Fox repeated as he climbed into the passenger seat.

'Know who would drink at a hole like the Pirate?'

'Who?'

'Craw Shand.'

'Meaning what?'

'Meaning I need to do a bit of thinking, which necessitates muting you – sorry about that.'

'Muting me?'

Rebus reached for the stereo, pushing a button. Music burst from the speakers, filling the car as Rebus pressed his foot against the accelerator. Had Fox been any kind of a music buff, he might have recognised the guitar sound.

Rory Gallagher, 'Kickback City'.

From a corner of the street, Cafferty watched them leave, and kept staring as Kenny Arnott opened the door to his gym. The place looked busy, but that was okay. Arnott would still be there at closing time. Maybe he'd even be on his own . . .

'Does anyone have a photo of Glushenko or Nazarchuk or whatever he's called?' Siobhan Clarke asked.

She was seated with Rebus and Fox at a corner table in the back room of the Oxford Bar. The downstairs area was post-work busy, but the rest of the pub was quiet as yet. Rebus was nursing a half of IPA. He'd just texted Deborah Quant to suggest dinner somewhere, but she'd pinged a message back immediately saying she was due at some official function and how was his COPD?

Both hunky and dory, he typed, pressing send.

His personal demon was outside again, tapping on the glass and holding up a packet of twenty. Rebus pulled back the net curtain long enough to flick the Vs by way of answer.

'Not that I've seen,' Fox was telling Clarke. 'A few dodgy passport photos, but with different hairstyles, and wearing glasses in some but not others.'

'I don't get it,' she said. 'If this thug is coming for Darryl, why isn't Darryl worried?'

'Maybe he thinks we're watching over him,' Rebus commented. 'Cheaper than hiring bodyguards.'

'And another thing, shouldn't we be putting Anthony Brough's name out there? He's done a runner with mob money – how long do you think he's going to last?'

'Alan McFarlane down in London is checking if his passport's been used,' Fox said. 'Could be on a Caribbean beach by now.'

'Somewhere with no extradition treaty,' Rebus added, lifting his glass again. He'd had a coughing fit earlier, but had retired to the toilet with his inhaler. His shirt was damp, sticking to his back, but otherwise he was fine, so much so that he was beginning to think a second IPA wouldn't hurt.

'So he flees with all this money, leaving Darryl in the lurch,' Clarke said, watching Fox's nod of confirmation. 'And there's a big bad Ukrainian on his way here seeking some sort of vengeance . . . Cafferty would be lapping it up if he knew.'

'He *does* know,' Rebus corrected her. 'He knows some of it, at least. Only he thinks the Ukrainian is a Russian.'

'*How* does he know?'

'That's a very good question,' Rebus allowed. 'Maybe we should ask him.'

'You think he's involved in some way?' Fox enquired, elbows on the table.

'There's always that possibility.'

'He paid to have Darryl attacked?'

Rebus pondered this. 'Do we have photos of Craw Shand and Rab Chatham?'

'Back at the MIT room,' Fox said.

'Then we should go there.' Rebus checked the time. 'I'm guessing they'll have knocked off for the evening. All the same, best if me and Siobhan wait outside.'

'And after I've lifted the photos, what next?'

Rebus looked at him. 'We pay our respects at a den of iniquity, of course.'

'Of course,' Fox said, watching as Rebus and Clarke drained their glasses.

The Pirate was called the Pirate because it had been taken over in the 1960s by a man called Johnny Kydd. That was one version, anyway. Rebus regaled his passengers with others as they headed to Cowgate.

'You ever been to the Devil's Dram?' Clarke interrupted at one point.

'Thumping music and mass snogging? Not really my scene.' He glanced at her. 'But I know Deb was there not too long ago, with the hangover next day to prove it.'

'Darryl Christie runs it like something out of *Goodfellas* – has his own table upstairs, master of all he surveys.'

'Maybe not for much longer,' Fox said. 'HMRC reckon it's costing him more than it takes in. Same goes for his hotel.'

'You might have said something,' Clarke complained.

'I only found out this morning.'

'Even so.'

'Well, I'm telling you now.'

'When I went to his hotel, it was being renovated – that has to cost a few quid.'

'Builders should maybe have asked for the money upfront,' Fox commented.

'So what's the story?' Rebus asked. 'He must be making money somewhere.'

'His betting shops and online gambling,' Fox conceded. 'But he's using those to prop up everything else.'

'Doesn't he control most of the drugs in the city?' Clarke enquired.

'That doesn't exactly come under HMRC's remit.'

'I've been reading in the paper recently,' Rebus added, 'that Border Force Scotland have had a few success stories – big shipments stopped before reaching their targets.'

'Meaning supply could be limited?'

Rebus nodded. 'No supply, no money.'

'Might explain why he'd be keen to get into bed with Anthony Brough. Ten million split two ways . . .'

'Would certainly tide Darryl over.'

'He doesn't still have it, does he?' Clarke asked.

'If he did, why not hand it back to Glushenko?' Fox answered.

'So Brough's scarpered with the lot.'

'Somebody knows,' Rebus said quietly. 'The PA, the sister, her carer . . .'

'There is another alternative, of course,' Clarke piped up. 'Maybe Glushenko has Brough.'

The car fell silent as they considered this. Then Fox cleared his throat.

'You remember the friend who drowned in Sir Magnus's pool?' he said, his eyes on Clarke. 'I spoke to a journalist in Grand Cayman who said he wouldn't rule out foul play.'

'Is there no end to the stuff you've been holding back?' Clarke retorted.

'It's not exactly relevant to Darryl Christie or Craw Shand, though, is it?'

Clarke stuck out her bottom lip. 'And I thought we were pals.'

'Remember, children,' Rebus said from the driver's seat. 'Toys must remain in the pram at all times.'

'Easy for an OAP to say.'

Clarke and Fox were sharing a smile as Rebus pushed out his own bottom lip.

The Pirate was near the foot of Blair Street, just before the Cowgate junction. Rebus parked on a double yellow line and they got out. The bar was down some steps, its interior smelling of the same mould that would have lingered on its walls a few centuries back. The main room had a vaulted ceiling, which, like the walls, consisted of exposed stonework. Most of the bars in the vicinity had been gentrified, but not the Pirate. The framed prints – sailing ships of the world – were askew and mildewed. The floor would forever remain sticky, due to the amount of drink spilled on it. The solitary barman was entertaining the only two drinkers in the place to a sullen silence, the new arrivals doing nothing except darken his mood.

'Help ye?' he snapped.

'Bottle of your best champagne, please,' Rebus said.

'If ye want fizz, we've got cider and lager.'

'Both of them fine substitutes.' Rebus held out the two photos. 'Care to take a look?'

'What for?'

'Because I'm asking nicely – for the moment.'

The barman glared at him, but then decided to at least glance at the head shots. 'Don't know them.'

'Now there's a surprise.'

'You buying a drink or leaving me in peace?'

'I didn't know I'd walked into a quiz show.' Rebus turned the photos towards the two pint-drinkers. 'Help me out here,' he said, watching as they shook their heads.

'Craw Shand,' he persisted. 'He drinks in here sometimes, when he's not at Templeton's or the Wrigley. Places like this make him feel right at home.' He focused his attention back on the barman. 'His home's a shithole, by the way.'

'I want the three of you out.'

'Maybe you should call the police.'

'Come to think of it, where's your ID?'

Fox had started reaching into his pocket, but Rebus stopped him. 'We don't humour wankers like him,' he explained. Then, to the two drinkers: 'You'll want to see the rating we give this place on TripAdvisor. Thanks for your help, gentlemen . . .'

He led Fox and Clarke back to the door, opening it and ushering them through. 'The famous John Rebus charm,' Clarke said. 'It never ever fails.'

'Just you wait,' Rebus said, slipping his hands into his pockets and looking content to stand his ground.

'What is it we're waiting for?'

'My instincts to be proved right.'

Ten seconds later, the door behind them reopened, one of the pair of customers stepping outside. Rebus gave him a nod and the man held up a cigarette, asking if he had a light. Rebus took a box of matches from his pocket.

'Keep them,' he said.

'That's very kind.'

Rebus turned to Fox. 'You got a twenty on you?'

Fox frowned, then dug into his right-hand trouser pocket. Rebus plucked the note from his hand and gave it to the man, who offered a grin, showing yellow teeth. With cigarette lit, he commenced to suck the life from it.

'Craw hasn't been around for a few days,' he said as he exhaled smoke. 'Bugger owes me, too.'

'Why's that?' Rebus asked.

'The phone rang and Alfie was busy changing barrels, so I picked up. Man on the other end was looking for Craw.' He cast a glance back at the door, checking it was tightly closed. 'Said it would be worth his while to still be here around midnight.'

'And you passed on the message?'

The smoker nodded. 'Craw said he'd stand me a drink just as soon as he had some spare cash.'

'I don't suppose you stuck around?'

'Ah, no. I turn into a pumpkin at midnight.'

'Did the caller give his name?'

'Not that I remember.' Having pocketed the matches, the man had brought out his pack of cigarettes, making the offer to Rebus.

'I won't,' Rebus said.

'You're not a smoker?'

'I'm trying to quit. Relieving me of those matches has been a big help.' He patted the man's shoulder and turned to leave. The offer of a smoke was still there, but Clarke and Fox shook their heads and made to follow.

Back in the Saab, Rebus studied both photographs as he thought things through.

'Fine,' Fox said. 'Your hunch was right and Rab Chatham met with Craw Shand.'

'So Chatham attacked Christie?' Clarke added. 'And Christie retaliated by having him killed?'

'Doesn't quite add up, does it?' Rebus conceded.

'Someone must have arranged it and paid Chatham to do it,' Fox went on. 'When you walked up to him that night, you spooked him. He wanted someone else to take the fall, and he knew Craw's reputation.'

'But Chatham wouldn't be enough to satisfy Darryl,' Clarke added. 'He'd want to know who was really behind it. Did Chatham die before he could talk?'

'No sign he was tortured,' Fox said. 'Just the whisky and then drowned.'

'I thought it had something to do with the Turquand case,' Rebus said quietly. 'I was walking the wrong bloody trail all the time – so much for a copper's nose.'

'Do we talk to Arnott again?' Fox asked. 'He has to be part of it. Chatham spoke to him only minutes before he headed to the call box.'

'Maybe in the morning,' Rebus agreed. 'Right now, I think we all need a bit of a break. Well, I know *I* do – I'm not like you young things.'

'Some food would hit the spot,' Fox said.

'I'd be up for that,' Clarke added.

'Better be your shout, Siobhan,' Rebus said. 'Malcolm's already down twenty quid.'

'Aye, thanks for that,' Fox muttered.

'Fair's fair,' Rebus told him. 'Name your restaurant and I'll drop you off – cheaper than a taxi.'

'You're not joining us?'

'Watching my weight, remember?' Rebus patted his stomach.

'I'm starting to worry now,' Clarke said, turning towards Fox to see if he agreed. But he was staring out of the window, avoiding eye contact.

'John,' she said quietly. 'What's the matter?'

'Not tonight, Siobhan,' Rebus said, lowering his own voice to match hers. 'Not tonight.'

Kenny Arnott started switching off the lights. Donny Applecross had been the last to leave. Arnott liked that. The kid had attitude – attitude, focus *and* stamina. If he didn't get hurt, he would manage a few years in the cage-fight game. He wasn't as wily as some, and he needed to bulk up a bit, but that was something they could work on.

It was dark outside now, Arnott's favourite time of the day, as he switched from gym owner to security fixer. He had fourteen guys on duty tonight. It would have been fifteen if Rab hadn't got stupid. Still, best not to dwell – that was what Arnott's mum had always said when there was bad news, didn't matter if it was close to home or half a world away. Best not to dwell. He had a mind to take a drive, stop off and chew the fat with a few of his guys, just to remind them he was looking out for them. Then again, his girlfriend was waiting for him in the flat. The flat was new, and so was Anna. He'd already bought her too many clothes and too much perfume. What the hell else was he going to do? She deserved it, and she was always grateful. He wasn't so sure about her mates. They were loud and always talking about stuff he didn't understand – singers and actors, TV shows and celebrities. But then Anna was almost half his age. Stood to reason he'd be out of the loop some of the time. And one or two of her besties . . . well, he wouldn't say no.

With only one of the overhead strip lights still on, he readied to set the alarm. Not that there was much worth nicking, but the insurance had insisted. But someone was knocking on the door. Had Donny or one of the others forgotten something? They wouldn't knock, though. Those cops again? One way to find out . . .

The figure filled the doorway, silhouetted against the sodium street lighting. The arm swung down and Arnott staggered back at the impact of hammer against skull. His vision blurred and his knees went from under him. He was pushing himself to his feet when the hammer connected again. Gloved hands. Three-quarter-length black coat. A domed head above it all, the lips parted, showing teeth. Arnott held up his hands in a show of surrender. The door had been kicked closed. He could feel blood trickling down his forehead. He blinked it out of his eyes.

'Know who I am?' the giant said, his voice like earth filling a pit.

'Yes.'

'Say my name, then.'

'You're Big Ger Cafferty.'

'And what are these?' Cafferty dug in his coat pocket and started scattering the contents across the floor in front of Arnott.

'Nails,' Arnott croaked.

'Six-inch nails, to be precise.'

'What do you want?'

'I want you to tell me why one of your employees whispered sweet nothings into my friend's ear.'

'What are you talking about?'

Cafferty managed a disappointed look, towering over the crouched figure. Arnott couldn't meet the man's stare, so busied himself dabbing at the blood with his jacket sleeve.

'You want it done the hard way, that's fine by me. One way or another, you'll be spilling your guts.'

'I don't know anything, gospel truth.'

'I didn't know you were religious, Kenny.' Cafferty was slipping out of his coat. 'But if you are, wee bit of advice for you – time to start praying . . .'

Day Eight

21

Having been wakened by Brillo wanting a walk as the sky was just starting to lighten, Rebus had decided to drive to Kenny's Gym for want of anything else to keep him busy. He wasn't sure how early the place would open, but he arrived to see two ambulances parked outside and the door to the boxing club standing wide open. Cursing under his breath, he stopped behind the rearmost ambulance and got out.

Inside the gym, two green-suited paramedics were kneeling either side of a prone figure, while a third stood next to an anxious-looking young man. Rebus sought his name – Donny Applecross, Arnott's cage-fighting protégé. As he stepped forward, he recognised the figure on the floor as Kenny Arnott himself. His head partially encased in polystyrene to protect it, arms splayed. His palms were upwards, blood pooling between and beneath the fingers.

'This what I think it is?' Rebus asked.

The paramedic nearest him turned her head. 'Sorry, who are you?'

'I'm with Police Scotland. We were here yesterday to question Mr Arnott.'

Arnott had been given a painkilling injection. His eyes looked glazed as soft moans escaped from between his cracked lips.

'So,' Rebus went on, 'are you waiting for medical advice or the local joiner?'

The unused nails were strewn around the floor. Rebus stooped and picked one up, showing it to Applecross.

'What's the story here, son?'

'Like I was just saying, Kenny gave me a key. I often do an early

237

workout. He was . . .' He glanced down at Arnott's figure. 'He was lying there when I got here.'

'Door locked?'

Applecross shook his head. 'Shut but not locked.'

Rebus turned his attention to the paramedic. 'Is he going to be okay?'

'He's been beaten around the head. You can see the marks on his temples.'

'A hammer, yes?' Rebus guessed.

'Maybe,' she allowed. 'And to answer your other question, we're waiting for advice on how best to move him.'

'Anyone called the police?'

She stared at him. 'Isn't that why you're here?'

Rebus took out his phone and texted Siobhan Clarke. 'Wheels are in motion,' he told the paramedic. Then, to Applecross: 'What time would he have started locking up?'

'Eight thirty, nine. I left around eight.'

'Were you the last out?'

The young man nodded, tensing his fists. 'Be a different story if I'd stuck around.'

'You weren't to know.' Rebus paused. 'That is, unless there's something you want to tell me.'

'Like what?'

'For starters, who'd want to do something like this to a fine up-standing man such as Kenny?'

Arnott was mumbling something, one of the kneeling paramedics leaning forward so she could make it out.

'He's saying it was an accident,' she announced.

'Well of course it was,' Rebus said, his eyes on the young cage fighter. 'Because if it wasn't, you might feel honour-bound to do something about it that could lead to you getting hurt – and Kenny doesn't want you getting hurt.' He turned away and leaned down so that his face was directly over Arnott's. 'Give me a name, Kenny – a name, a face, a description.'

Arnott squeezed his eyes shut and filled his lungs. 'It was an accident!' he roared, almost weeping from the effort.

Rebus straightened up. 'Hard as nails, your boss,' he said to the young man. 'Which is just as well, really . . .'

He sat in his car, chewing gum and listening to the radio, until Clarke's Astra arrived. She had been preceded by a fire engine and a van with the name of a joinery firm on its side. Rebus explained the situation as he walked with a bleary-eyed Clarke back into the gym. Applecross had changed into shorts and a vest and, barefoot and hands strapped, was pretending the punchbag in front of him was responsible for his manager's anguish.

'Dedication for you,' Rebus commented to Clarke. She was focusing on the scene around Kenny Arnott.

'He was here all night?' she asked.

'Looks like.'

'Wouldn't he have been screaming fit to burst?'

'Not much foot traffic around here – and people might expect to hear noises from a boxing club.'

She seemed to accept this. The joiner, tools laid out in front of him, was deep in discussion with one of the firemen about how much of the floor was going to have to be sawn through.

'Even then,' he added, 'if the nail's gone into a joist, that might have to be cut away too.'

The man looked calm enough, though Rebus doubted he had been called to many similar jobs.

'Let's do it then,' the paramedic said. One of the ambulances had already left on another job, just her and her colleague left with the patient.

'Will he feel anything?' the colleague asked the fireman.

'We'll find out soon enough.'

'Maybe another dose of morphine first, then . . .'

Clarke turned away and, arms folded, walked towards the boxing ring, Rebus following.

'Who did it?' she asked in an undertone. 'Darryl Christie?'

'Not sure this is Darryl's style. Cafferty, on the other hand . . .'

She stared at him. 'What was he after?'

'Same as us – information.'

'How would he know, though? About Arnott and Chatham and the rest?'

'He's got Craw Shand,' Rebus stated.

She thought this over, then nodded slowly. 'Let's go talk to him.'

'We've been here before with Cafferty,' Rebus cautioned. 'You know the way he is . . .'

Her eyes met his. 'You can't go on your own, John. When all's said and done, you're a civilian.'

'I'm really not. And he'll open up to me.'

Her gaze intensified. 'Why is that, I've always wondered?'

'Because he likes to get my attention, knowing damned well that

I almost certainly can't touch him. He needs to keep reminding me he's in charge, not you or me or anyone else.'

Clarke said nothing for a few moments, then nodded again. 'Fine. But you bring everything back to me afterwards, agreed?'

'Agreed,' Rebus said, heading towards the doorway as an electric saw began competing in noise levels against the relentless thwock of Donny Applecross's fists and feet hitting the punchbag.

Cafferty wasn't answering. Rebus sent a text instead, then drove to the café on Forrest Road, but he wasn't there either. He tried pressing the bell at Quartermile, but to no effect, so he returned to the café and ordered a mug of coffee, seating himself at the table Cafferty liked, waiting. Someone had left a newspaper on a nearby chair; he turned its pages, his mobile clutched in his free hand. It was twenty minutes before the text arrived.

Another time, it said.

Rebus hammered back a reply. *Did Kenny Arnott keep you up late? Where have you stashed Craw?*

Two minutes later: *Craw's on holiday, a B&B and plenty spending money in his pocket.*

Rebus composed another text and pressed send. *He gave you what you wanted then? And that took you to Rab Chatham's boss.*

He waited two minutes, then five, then eight. With the coffee gone, he stepped back outside, holding the screen to his face. Ten minutes, twelve . . . He unlocked the Saab and got in, noting that a warden had given him a ticket. He got out again and snatched it from beneath the wiper blade, tossing it on to the passenger seat.

Still nothing.

Where are you?

Nothing.

What are you up to?

No reply.

He's Ukrainian, not Russian

Rebus's phone told him a text was coming. He watched it arrive. *What makes you think I wouldn't know that? Didn't want to make it TOO easy for you.*

Rebus's fingers got busy again: *Meet me.*

Send.

Wait.

Incoming.

He's lucky I didn't kill him.

Who? Arnott? Christie? Craw?

Everybody's lucky, even you – it wasn't really your birthday, was it?

But then you didn't really give me a present.

Should have seen the hunger in your eyes, though. Nice to see passion stirring in such an old crock.

Fuck you too. Meet me. Let's do this face to face.

Why?

My thumbs are getting sore. And I can't believe you don't want to gloat in person.

My gloating days are behind me.

I don't believe that for a minute. Let's do this.

I'll think about it.

It has to be right now.

Another wait, but this time he knew it was fruitless. Cafferty was a busy man with a lot on his mind, Rebus only occupying a tiny part of the game he was playing.

Playing? No, he was *controlling* it, like the croupier with his hand on the fixed roulette wheel, knowing the house was going to win in the end.

Rebus drove across town to Great Junction Street and stopped outside Klondyke Alley. The café where he'd shared bacon rolls with Rab Chatham was a short walk away. Chatham had placed regular bets at Klondyke Alley. Had he been aware of what was happening one storey above? Rebus peered up at the grimy windows of the tenement flats. Decision made, he got out and locked the car. There were five separate buttons on the intercom and he pressed each of them in turn. As he'd expected, the buzzer sounded, letting him know the main door had unlocked itself. He pushed it open and stepped into a shadowy hallway leading to the winding stone staircase.

The flat he wanted was one floor up. There were two doors. One had a name on it – Haddon. The other was anonymous. Rebus pressed his ear to the door, then eased open the letter box for a look. The place felt empty. He rapped on the wood with his knuckles, wondering if the neighbour who had buzzed him in would start to show any interest. But there was no sound of any other doors opening. He tried the door handle. A single Yale lock seemed to be the flat's only protection. Rebus put his shoulder to it without success. He tried again, then stepped back and lifted his right foot, slamming it into the wood. He felt a jab of pain in his hip, so swapped legs and planted the sole of his shoe hard against the door. There was a cracking sound. He had another go, and this time the door burst open a few inches. Rubbing his thigh, he shoved the door a little wider.

The problem was mail. It lay an inch or two deep on the carpet. Rebus squeezed through the gap and bent down to scoop some of it up. Holding it in his left hand, he checked the flat's interior. There was no bed in the bedroom, no furniture in the living room, nothing in the drawers of the kitchen. From the look of the toilet, it had last been used weeks ago by someone who hadn't bothered flushing. Back in the hall, he squatted down and sifted through the mail. There were the usual circulars, and a couple of cards to say the meter reader hadn't been able to get in. Most of the envelopes were plain white or brown. Most had little cellophane windows. Business post, addressed to dozens of companies Rebus had never heard of. He opened one. It was offering 'enhanced services at a special rate for your start-up company'. He doubted the others would be much different.

Moving into the living room, he stood in the middle of the floor. There were marks on the walls where pictures had been removed by a previous owner or tenant. A cable snaked in from a corner of the only window, waiting to be connected to a TV. There was a phone point on one of the chipped skirting boards, but no phone. Like the companies it served, the flat was nothing more than a shell. But then what had he expected – Anthony Brough, feet up on the sofa sipping Moët?

Well, it would have been nice.

'I've called the police,' Rebus heard a voice say from the landing outside. By the time he reached the doorway, the neighbour had retreated behind their own door. Rebus approached it and knocked. He heard a chain being slid into place, the door opening two inches. Above the chain he could make out a pair of bespectacled eyes. The man looked tired and unshaven, dressed in a string vest and jogging pants. Unemployed, probably.

'No need for that, sir,' Rebus said, trying to sound professional.

'Well I've done it anyway.'

'How long has the other flat been empty, do you know?'

'Ever since I moved in.'

'Anybody ever visit?'

The man shook his head. 'The police are on their way,' he felt the need to clarify.

'I'm with the police, sir,' Rebus explained.

'Is that right?' Clearly not believing a word of it.

'You've never seen or heard anything from that flat? No comings and goings?'

'Nothing.' The man was starting to close the door.

'I'll be on my way, then. Thanks for your help. You can always cancel that call-out, if you want . . .'

But the door had shut with a click, plus a turn of the mortise key to be on the safe side.

Rebus didn't know how long he had. Ten minutes minimum, forty-five max. But what was the point of lingering? He gave the envelopes another quick look in case anything anomalous stood out. After all, the last case he'd worked, a takeaway menu had been a crucial, missed clue. But there was nothing here for him. He traipsed back down to the ground floor, opening the door and exiting on to the pavement. A punter was coming out of Klondyke Alley, lifting a cigarette packet from their inside pocket.

'Got a light, bud?' the man asked.

Rebus patted his jacket, remembering he'd given his box of matches away. 'Sorry,' he said. But the smoker was already moving on to the next passer-by.

Rebus stepped into Klondyke Alley and took a look around. He rested on a stool at the machine nearest the door and stuck in a pound. Time was, he liked a bet – horses, even the odd night at the casino. Bandits not so much. But he won straight away, cashed out and decided to try again. The patrol car was pulling to a halt outside. No blues and twos – not taking the call-out too seriously. Rebus stayed where he was, even though he had now lost his pound and his three quid winnings. There was a woman at a machine nearby. He could see her back and half her face. He got up and stood next to her.

'Hello,' he said.

'Get to fuck.'

'You're Jude?'

She turned to examine him. 'Do I know you?'

'I met you at your dad's funeral. I'm a friend of Malcolm's.'

Jude Fox rolled her eyes. 'Malcolm sent you?' Rebus said nothing. 'He never ceases to amaze. You supposed to warn me off? Send me on my merry way back to my living room and the daytime talk shows? He knows I can have a flutter there too, right? I mean – he *does* know that?'

243

'He only wants what's best for you, Jude,' Rebus said slowly, trying to piece together what she was telling him.

'Everybody seems to want what's best for me – Malcolm, Darryl Christie, *everybody*.' She slammed more coins into the machine.

'How much do you owe?' Rebus asked as the truth dawned.

She scowled at him. 'Malky didn't tell you?'

'He said it was a lot,' Rebus bluffed.

'Everything's a lot when you've not got much, though, eh?' She started the reels turning, taking a deep breath and exhaling, trying to calm herself. She was concentrating on the machine when she next spoke. 'Don't tell me my brother doesn't have that kind of money salted away. But will he bail out his sister? Will he hell. Because what's in it for him? That's the trade-off – there always has to be *some*thing in it for Malcolm Fox.' She paused and turned to study Rebus again. 'I *do* remember you. You were at the church but not the meal. Malcolm and whassername were talking about you.'

'Siobhan Clarke?'

'That's the one. Malcolm was saying he tried drumming you off the force. And now suddenly the two of you are buddies? I swear to God this world makes no sense to me, none at all . . .'

'Does Darryl Christie know you're related to Malcolm?'

Her mouth formed a thin tight line.

'I'll take that as a yes. Does Malcolm know he knows?'

Her hand had paused over the array of flashing buttons. She was staring at the machine but not seeing it. 'Go tell him I'm here doing my duty – *he's* the one who asked. He's the whole bloody reason . . .' Tears were forming in her eyes.

'You need to sort yourself out, Jude.'

'Pot, meet kettle,' she sniffled, looking him up and down again, but Rebus was already heading for the door.

He had driven quarter of a mile before he made the call. Traffic was at a crawl towards a junction. Fox picked up almost immediately.

'Siobhan told me,' he began. 'She's at the hospital waiting for—'

'I know about Jude,' Rebus interrupted. 'How much does she owe Christie?'

The silence on the line stretched. 'Twenty-seven and rising.'

'And what does he want from you?'

'What do you mean?'

'Don't shit a shitter, Malcolm. He's got something he can use against you, no way he's not going to use it.'

'He wanted everything HMRC has on Glushenko. Don't worry – I took it straight to Gartcosh. We're trying to decide if we can finesse it somehow.'

Rebus thought for a moment. 'There's no way you told them your sister's in hock to him – if you had, they'd have had to pull you off the case.'

'That's true,' Fox eventually conceded.

'So when you say *we're* trying to decide if we can finesse it . . .'

'Okay, I mean me. Me on my own – unless you're about to grass me up.'

'Once Christie has a hold on you, he's not going to let go.'

'I can get the money. I just need to sell the bungalow. Until then, I'm stringing him along.'

'You sure *he's* the one on the end of the string, Malcolm?' Fox made no answer. 'How long has he given you?'

'A couple of days.'

'As from . . .?'

'A couple of days ago.'

'To give him the gen on the Ukrainian or pay off the twenty-seven K? Good luck with that.'

'What's your daily limit?'

'At a cash machine? Two hundred.'

'Pity.'

Rebus smiled despite himself. 'Jesus, Malcolm – for a really careful guy, you do seem to get into a few holes.'

'I like to think I learned from the best. How did you find out, anyway?'

'I was at the flat above Klondyke Alley. Nipped in for a look-see and Jude thought you'd sent me.'

'She was at Klondyke Alley?'

'Yes.'

'Why would she do that?'

'How do you mean?'

'Christie knows about her – he's hardly likely to let anyone launder cash at the machines while she's sitting there.'

'Maybe it's her way of trying to atone,' Rebus speculated.

'Aye, maybe.' He heard Fox give a lengthy sigh. 'So was there anything at the flat?'

'Brough and Glushenko were drinking tea and playing cards.'

Fox gave a snort. 'Siobhan says you were going to talk to Cafferty.'

'Hasn't happened yet.'

'Losing your powers of persuasion?'

'Maybe he just needed a rest after last night's exertions.'

'You don't think Arnott will speak?'

'Not a chance.'

'What do you think he told Cafferty?'

'Judging by the fact that he's still alive, I'd lay odds he told him *everything*.'

'Which would amount to what, exactly?'

'Chatham got the job from Arnott. Got twitchy when he realised who it was he'd thumped. Put Craw in the frame as insurance . . .'

'Arnott has to know who the original client was. And now Cafferty knows too. Which rules out Cafferty but nobody else.' Fox paused. 'Joe Stark?'

'It had crossed my mind. But Joe has his own guys, why not use them?'

'Because Darryl would know from the get-go who'd sent them,' Fox speculated.

'Maybe . . .'

'I'm not convincing you, am I?'

'Your persuasive powers seem to be matching my own today. Look, if Christie calls you or wants to meet . . .'

'He'll probably be taping it for future use. I'm not a complete thicko, John.'

'That's good to hear. We'll maybe catch up later, aye?'

'Say hello to Siobhan from me in the meantime.'

'How did you know?'

'You're nothing if not predictable, John.'

'I prefer "methodical".'

'Will you tell her about Jude and Christie?'

'Not if you don't want me to.'

'Then I owe you one.'

The line went dead. Rebus placed the phone on the passenger seat and turned up the music. Three cars ahead of him, the lights were red again.

22

Siobhan Clarke was in a corridor of the Royal Infirmary, phone held up to her face, when she recognised Rebus making his way towards her.

'You're limping,' she said.

'Just to correct you, I'm actually walking like John Wayne.'

'John Wayne had a limp?'

'Technically it's called "moseying".'

'So you didn't hurt yourself kicking in a door?' She waved her phone in front of him. 'Patrol car dispatched to Great Junction Street. Someone broke into a certain flat of our acquaintance. Neighbour described the intruder as a heavy-built man in his sixties with a local accent.' She paused. 'So what did you find?'

'Bugger all,' Rebus admitted. 'What about Kenny Arnott?'

'He's in the ward right behind me. They say he'll be okay, though he may not get back the full use of either hand.'

'Lucky he's not a pianist, then.'

'He's still sedated and there's talk of an operation if the surgeons think it would help.'

'So he's not been saying anything?'

'A few words here and there.'

'Did those words include "accident"?'

'How did you guess?'

'So what's next?'

'I'm meeting with Alvin James. He needs convincing that the two cases are actually one.'

'It's not like we have any hard evidence. Would it help if I was there?'

'I was just debating that – would you play nice?'

'I'll be yours to command, Siobhan.' Rebus watched as a bed was pushed past by two male orderlies, its occupier hooked to a saline drip. 'Christ, I hate hospitals,' he said.

'Had much experience lately? As a patient, I mean.' She waited for an answer she knew wouldn't come, then glanced down at an incoming text. 'James can see me in half an hour. Better skedaddle.'

'Is there anyone at Arnott's bedside?'

'His young cage-fighting pal is visiting. And Christine Esson's due to take over from me.' She peered over his shoulder. 'Talk of the devil.'

'Sorry I'm late,' Esson apologised. 'Stopped off for a bottle of water and a magazine.'

'He's in there,' Clarke said, gesturing. 'Bed three. Visitor with him is Donny Applecross. He uses Arnott's gym. Don't expect much chat.'

Esson nodded and made her way into the ward. Rebus was looking at Clarke.

'So am I invited or not?'

'You really promise not to start winding James up?'

'Cross my heart.'

Clarke exhaled noisily. 'Okay then. Let's go . . .'

'Is your head full of fucking mince?' Rebus asked Alvin James.

He was standing in front of the detective superintendent, Clarke alongside him. James was leaning back in his chair, one foot up on the edge of his desk. His team, Fox included, had been watching and listening. It had taken Clarke a full ten minutes to recount what they knew and what they suspected. At the end of which, after a few seconds' thought, James had said he wasn't sure, which was when Rebus had opened his mouth and asked the question.

'John . . .' Clarke cautioned.

'I mean,' Rebus ploughed on, 'if you can't see the connection, you're up there with Tommy.'

James's forehead creased. 'Tommy?'

'Deaf, dumb and blind.'

'I wouldn't say I'm any of those things,' James continued calmly, 'but as a police detective, I work on evidence, and that's the one thing you've not given me.'

'Then why not rally the troops and *detect* some?'

'We'll certainly interview Mr Arnott when he's available.' James looked down at the notes he'd made during Clarke's presentation. 'And Cafferty, too, though you don't sound hopeful that either of them will give us anything. The fact remains that there's nothing to prove Robert Chatham attacked Darryl Christie, or that this is why he was killed. We can ask Christie if he has an alibi for the night in question. From what you've told me, I'm guessing he will, and that it will be iron-clad.' His eyes moved from Clarke to Rebus and back again. 'You know yourself, Siobhan, what the Procurator Fiscal will say if I take this to her.'

Clarke was forced to nod in agreement.

'Okay, it's thin,' Fox piped up, 'but that doesn't mean it's not right. John has a point when he says we should dig further.'

'Not so long ago,' James said, 'your friend John here was telling us it all had to do with a murder back in the 1970s. There's a folder on your desk as proof, Malcolm. I dread to think of the hours you wasted going through it, plus reading the book that woman wrote, *plus* letting yourself be taken on a wild goose chase to St Andrews and Perthshire.'

'I'm right this time,' Rebus bristled. 'Siobhan knows it, Malcolm knows it.'

'Some of us haven't fallen under your spell the way they have,' James commented. He rubbed one cheek. 'On the other hand, we're not exactly making headway in any other direction . . .'

'This could be the lease of life the inquiry needs,' Fox stressed.

James looked at him. 'Reversing away from the dead end, eh, Malcolm?'

Clarke's shoulders straightened – she had won him over.

'Okay,' he went on. 'Let's arrange a new game plan, starting with the attack at the gym – neighbours, local CCTV, whatever we can get our hands on.' James had risen from his desk and was making a circuit of the room, pausing for a moment at each desk. 'Was the hammer new? Let's talk to DIY stores and hardware shops. Where's the weapon now? Did the assailant dispose of it nearby? Then there are the nails – if we get lucky, he bought everything at the same time. It wasn't forced entry, so maybe someone saw a stranger loitering in the vicinity. He might have popped into a local shop, or been parked kerbside for long enough that passers-by took note.' He paused and fixed his eyes on Clarke. 'Anything I've forgotten?'

'We need to see if Arnott will open up to us. Might help if we have leverage.'

James nodded. 'So we look at his business dealings, see if there's anything he's been hiding. Friends, associates – the usual drill.' He returned to his desk and fell into his chair, pulling a pad of paper towards him and turning to a fresh sheet. 'I need five minutes to decide on what order we do this in and which tasks you each get.' He had already started writing. 'And in case nobody's noticed, there's a member of the public in this room – maybe one of you could escort him out of the building?'

Rebus stared at the top of Alvin James's head. 'Your patter's shite,' he said.

'I'd say that's all you merit,' James replied, without looking up.

Glancey and Oldfield had risen to their feet, eager to haul Rebus outside, but Clarke placed a hand on his forearm.

'Come on, John,' she said. 'I'll see you to the door.'

For a moment, he refused to budge, then he allowed her to lead him out into the corridor and down the stairs.

'We got the result we wanted,' she reminded him as they reached the ground floor.

'Bully for us.'

'He's good at geeing up his team, though, you have to give him that.'

'No, *you* have to give him that – he's your boss, not mine.'

'In point of fact, he's not my boss either.'

'You just handed him your case, Siobhan.'

'I suppose that's true.' She followed Rebus out of the building on to the pavement. 'So what now?' she asked.

'I've got a dog to walk.'

'And after that? Maybe put some ice on your hip?'

'It's not that bad.'

'Just your body telling you something?'

'Aye, it keeps doing that – I wish to hell it would shut up. You heading back upstairs?'

'I think so.'

'On you go, then. And tell James something from me.'

'What?'

'That I've seen more arseholes than a proctologist, and he's a Grade A specimen.'

'Am I allowed to rephrase that?'

'I'd rather it was verbatim.' Rebus stared across the street to where his Saab was parked. 'And speaking of arseholes ...' He crossed the road and ripped the parking ticket from his windscreen.

'Almost got the full set,' he called to Clarke, waving it towards her as he opened the door and got in. He added it to the collection in his glove box and started the engine. If Hank Marvin did end up being the death of him, at least he could say he'd cheated the council out of their pound of flesh . . .

Rebus drove straight back to the Infirmary and told Christine Esson she could take a break.

'On whose orders?' she asked.

'All I need is five minutes. Maybe you could nip to the loo or something.'

'It's nice to see you too, John.'

'Sorry, I'm forgetting my manners. How are you, Christine? You and Ronnie still an item?'

'Not for much longer if he doesn't shave off that moustache.'

'I thought the hirsute look was in? Want me to drop a hint?'

'You think I've not tried?'

'I could hold him down while you take a razor to his face?'

She smiled and placed her magazine on the floor before getting to her feet. 'Five minutes?'

'Tops.' Rebus looked at the figure in the bed. The sheet had been pulled up to his neck, but with his arms lifted clear by a frame-work of splints and clamps, so that his bandaged hands sat mid-air, relieved of any pressure. His eyes were closed, but Rebus got the feeling he was awake. 'Has he said anything?'

'Not since I arrived. His other visitor left soon after.'

'Donny Applecross?'

Esson nodded. 'A nurse asked Mr Arnott if he wanted a drink. He tilted his head and she fed him through a straw.' Esson gestured towards the plastic tumbler on the bedside unit.

'Off you go then and stretch your legs.'

Rebus watched her pick up her shoulder bag and make her exit. The ward was full, but none of the men looked remotely interested in anything around them. Two were asleep, one with his mouth gaping, small snores escaping. Another was wearing headphones while watching a TV monitor. Each bed had a similar screen, but you paid for the privilege. He wondered if it was any more expensive than the car park, but surely that was unfeasible.

Rebus didn't bother sitting down. He walked around the bed to the other side and poured a little more water from the jug into the tumbler.

'Fancy some?' he asked. There was no response. He checked the chart as best he could. An intravenous drip had been fixed to Arnott's left forearm. Usually they used the back of the hand, but Rebus could appreciate that this would not have been an option with this particular patient.

'No family, Kenny? No mates other than your young fighter friend? That's a shame. You look okay, though.' Rebus paused. 'In fact, you look good enough to kiss.' He leaned over so that a shadow fell across Arnott's face. With their mouths no more than an inch apart, Arnott's eyes flew open. Rebus smiled and straightened up.

'I seem to have got your attention,' he said. 'So here's what I have to say. We are going after Cafferty on your behalf, with your help or without it. Either way he's going to think you talked, so you better start hoping we put together a strong enough case to lock him away for a while. Be a hell of a lot easier if you told us at least a little of what happened. And if you so much as whisper the word "accident", I swear I'll squeeze your bandages till you puke.' He paused again. 'Okay, that's me said my piece.' He rounded the bed again and angled the chair so it was facing the patient. Then he settled on to it slowly. Arnott was blinking. His eyes seemed moist and he was focusing on the ceiling lights.

'You're not a cop,' he said eventually, so softly Rebus almost didn't catch it.

'That's right, Kenny.'

'Then what are you?'

'One of Cafferty's oldest enemies, which is good news for you.'

'I can't help you. He'd kill me.'

'You told him everything, though? Just nod if you did.'

Rebus waited and watched Arnott angle his chin downwards and up again.

'You know who ordered that attack on Darryl Christie,' Rebus went on. 'They used you to find someone. You chose Rab Chatham, gave him the address but nothing else. After Chatham found out it was Darryl, he had a wobble and decided to use Craw Shand as insurance, knowing Craw would take the blame with a gladsome heart and Chatham would be safe from a vengeful Darryl. If I'm right so far, another nod would be nice.'

The head bobbed again.

'Thank you,' Rebus said. 'So now we're just left with the who and the why. The why isn't such a problem – I think we're slowly getting there. A name, Kenny, one little name and we can start building the case against Cafferty, always assuming the name you give me had Rab Chatham done away with . . . Am I safe to assume that at least?'

Arnott squeezed his eyes shut and a tear rolled down the side of his face towards his ear. 'He'd kill me,' he repeated, voice quavering. His whole body seemed to be shivering, and Rebus turned his eyes towards the readout on the monitor next to the drip.

'You okay, Kenny?' he asked.

Arnott's teeth were clenched and his face was turning the colour of beetroot. Rebus rose from his chair and leaned over the bed. Arnott's breathing had grown ragged.

'Want me to call for someone? Pain getting a bit much?' He looked around for a nurse but couldn't see one. The numbers on the digital readout were climbing. Then Arnott seemed to spasm, his face grimacing.

'Nurse!' Rebus yelled.

Two arrived out of nowhere, ignoring Rebus as they flanked the patient, assessing the situation. Words flew between them and Rebus backed away, giving them all the space they might need and more. He felt the presence of someone behind him and turned to find Christine Esson standing there, staring past him with widening eyes.

More staff were approaching the bed. The curtains were being pulled closed around it. The sleeping patients had woken up and were watching. The man with the TV slipped off his headphones and craned his neck.

'Jesus, John,' Esson hissed.

'I didn't do anything.'

'You did *some*thing.'

'I was talking and he was listening and then . . .'

A machine on a trolley was being wheeled in. Rebus could see the paddles attached to it. Someone else was bringing a syringe and a small bottle of clear liquid. A nurse was closing the curtains around all the other beds, to put paid to the spectacle. She pointed at Rebus and Esson.

'I'm going to have to ask you to leave. As in, right now.'

They took a few steps into the corridor just as more staff rushed past. 'What do I tell Siobhan?' Esson asked, looking in the direction of the ward.

'The truth,' Rebus advised.

253

'Mentioning you?'

'I suppose so.'

'She'll have my guts for garters, letting you have your five bloody minutes.'

'Maybe you had to take a toilet break. I saw my chance and crept in.'

Esson stared at him. 'Is this us concocting a story?'

'I suppose it is,' Rebus agreed. 'How is it sounding so far?'

'It sounds like you're saving my guts from becoming garters.' Esson peered around the corner of the nurses' station into the ward. 'Maybe he'll be all right, eh?' she said, trying to sound hopeful.

'I'm sure he will,' Rebus said, listening as the doctor with the paddles barked the single word *'Clear!'*

When news of Kenny Arnott's death reached the MIT room, there was a numbed silence that lasted fully fifteen seconds until Fox broke it with a question.

'What now?'

'We keep going,' James said.

'Was the cardiac arrest brought on by the torture?' Anne Briggs asked.

'We'll have to wait for the autopsy.'

'If it was, we're talking culpable homicide,' Siobhan Clarke added. She had been the one who'd broken the news, after stepping out into the hallway to take Christine Esson's call. She was still standing just inside the doorway, her phone in her hand. One detail she had left out was the presence of John Rebus at the bedside and the absence of anyone from CID.

'Which makes it imperative,' James said, 'that we redouble our efforts. Sean, how are we getting on with those DIY stores and hardware shops?'

'Biggest ones are all done. Staff are checking their recordings and even till receipts.'

'That could take a while.'

Glancey nodded. 'And I'm on to the fourth hardware shop on my list.'

'Good man,' James said. 'Wallace?'

'Door-to-door is about ready to go.' The room fell silent so Sharpe could be heard. 'Took a while to conjure up the bodies. There are a couple left over, and that'll comprise our search team until

I can drum up more help. I'll be heading out there in about ten minutes.'

'Thanks,' James said. 'How about you, Anne?'

'Tracking down the victim's friends and associates just got that bit harder. We could do with a search warrant for home and business premises, see if his computer is any help.'

'I'll sort it.' James turned to Mark Oldfield, who was busy at the kettle. 'You okay to help out with the doorstepping?'

'Sure,' Oldfield said, not quite managing to look enthusiastic.

'There'll be a café somewhere on the route,' Fox teased him.

'How about you, Malcolm?' James butted in. 'Managing to keep busy?'

'Absolutely.'

'Feel like applying for those search warrants?' Fox nodded and watched as Alvin James started clapping, his eyes taking in his team. 'All right then, people, let's get going. The crime may have changed but the investigation hasn't.' He turned towards Clarke. 'You know the pathologist, don't you? Find out how soon she can do the autopsy.'

'Easiest thing is to ask in person. If she's in the autopsy suite, her phone will be off.'

'Do that, then.'

Clarke kept her eyes averted from Fox as she made her escape. Striding towards her car, she called Rebus and pressed the phone to her ear.

'Thought I'd be hearing from you,' he muttered.

'What happened?'

'I was just talking to the man, Siobhan.'

Clarke got into her car and put the phone on speaker while she turned the key in the ignition and fastened her seat belt. 'Having sneaked past Christine while she was in the loo?'

'You can't go blaming her.'

'I *don't* blame her.' Clarke checked the road was clear and moved off. 'It's you I'm furious with.'

'All I did was tell him we were going after Cafferty big time, with his help or without.'

'And?'

'He said he'd kill him if he said anything.'

'Who'd kill him?'

'What?'

'Who'd kill him?' she repeated. 'Cafferty?'

'Well, yes, obviously.' But Rebus didn't sound sure. 'How's James handling it?'

'Very competently. He's got everyone working flat out.'

'Present company excepted?'

'I'm on my way to the mortuary.'

'To chivvy Deb into fast-tracking the autopsy? Reckon there's a chance we can pin culpable homicide on Big Ger?'

'Your guess is as good as mine. So where are you now?'

'Five minutes from the Cowgate.'

'You're going to see Deborah?'

'That was the plan – great minds and all that.'

'John ... for us to have even the slimmest hope of nabbing Cafferty, everything has to be done by the book.'

'No argument here.'

'You're not a police officer.'

'I'm not sure why people think they need to keep reminding me. How long till you arrive?'

'Ten, twelve minutes.'

'I'll be in the car park.'

The phone went dead as Clarke pulled out to overtake a bus.

'Fourteen minutes,' Rebus said, making show of checking his watch. Clarke had parked next to his Saab. She could see the regulation black vans but no sign of Deborah Quant's car.

'She's not here,' Rebus confirmed. 'I already asked. Teaching a class at the uni. Should be done in an hour or so, though. We could grab a coffee.'

'Where?'

'Caffè Nero at Blackwell's,' he suggested. Clarke shook her head.

'I meant what I said – think how you'd feel if we got Cafferty to trial and a technicality scuppered us.'

'The technicality being me?' Rebus nodded slowly. 'You know best, Siobhan. With me, it's always been about the outcome rather than the process.'

'Which is why you've lost a few along the way.'

'I can't just walk away.'

'Not even for a day?'

Rebus shook his head slowly, trying for a contrite look and failing. Clarke puffed out her cheeks and studied the tarmac, rubbing the sole of one shoe against it.

'You sure about that coffee?' he asked.

'She's coming here after the lecture?'

'Almost certainly.'

'Are we walking to the café?'

'Have you seen the hill it's up?' Rebus responded.

'My car or yours?'

'More room in mine.'

She looked towards the Saab. 'There's also half a chance it won't make it to the top.' Her phone was buzzing. 'James,' she told Rebus as she made to answer.

'Yes, Alvin?'

'Are you with Professor Quant?'

'She won't be here for a bit.' Clarke paused. 'You sound—'

'We might just have struck lucky,' James blurted out. 'Had to happen eventually.'

'Oh?'

'Are you going to hang around there or do you want to join the party?'

'I'll be there in fourteen minutes,' she said, ending the call.

James and his team were readying to brief a lawyer from the Procurator Fiscal's office. The Fiscal Depute's name was Shona MacBryer. MacBryer knew Clarke, and the two shared a nod of greeting as she arrived. Fox and Oldfield were handing round mugs. Someone had splashed out on a cafetière and proper coffee, and the biscuits were Duchy Originals. Nothing but the best for MacBryer, not when they were about to try persuading her they had a locked-down case requiring only her thumbs-up before the arrest was made.

'A hardware shop on Leith Walk,' James was saying. He was seated directly in front of MacBryer's chair, having hoisted himself on to his desk, hands on knees. With his legs spread, his crotch was at eye level, a fact he seemed unaware of but which had caused MacBryer to twist her mouth in displeasure. 'The owner had a man come in yesterday afternoon – well dressed, in his sixties, shaven head. A hefty bloke, three-quarter-length black coat and black leather gloves. Didn't hang about, knew exactly what he wanted – two nice big claw hammers and a dozen six-inch nails, same number we retrieved from the boxing club. So DS Glancey sends the shop-keeper a file photo of Morris Gerald Cafferty and the shopkeeper says he's sure it's the same man.'

MacBryer had opened an iPad, preparing to take notes. 'This would be easier at a desk,' she said.

'Take Malcolm's.'

MacBryer thanked him and shifted to Fox's chair, James shoving all Fox's paperwork to one side. James sat on his own chair and was preparing to continue his speech when MacBryer held up a finger to stop him.

'Can I just clarify – the shopkeeper has only been spoken to by phone so far.'

'DS Sharpe is fetching him here – shouldn't be much longer.'

'So a man who may or may not be Mr Cafferty buys two hammers and some nails. Do you have a forensic report?'

'Not as yet,' James admitted.

'If gloves were worn . . .'

James nodded his understanding. 'But there may be DNA at the scene. Forensics have given the floor a thorough swabbing, lifted all sorts of bits and pieces.'

'Which might prove Cafferty had visited the building, but not pinpoint his presence there at the time of the attack.'

'And if we put him in a parade?'

MacBryer glanced up from her typing. 'A positive identification would tell us nothing more than that he bought a hammer and some nails.'

'Not more than a five- or ten-minute walk from the boxing club.' James looked to Fox. 'Where does Cafferty live?'

'Used to be Merchiston . . .' Fox sought out Clarke.

'Quartermile,' she obliged. 'Quite the hike from Leith Walk.'

'Does the shop have CCTV?' MacBryer asked.

'No,' Glancey said.

'Proprietor's name?'

'Joseph Beddoes.'

'Did he seem lucid?'

'I'd say he's a reliable witness.'

MacBryer stared at him without blinking. 'On the evidence of a single phone call?'

'We're sure it's Cafferty,' James interrupted. He had angled his chair so he was facing MacBryer. Her mug of coffee sat untouched, as did the biscuit she'd been given.

'For a successful prosecution, we need a *bit* more than that, Detective Superintendent. Mr Cafferty is not unknown to the

Fiscal's office. We've had half a dozen previous cases fail. Recovery of the weapon would help.'

'We've officers scouring the neighbourhood.'

'Clothing could well be bloodstained,' MacBryer went on.

'In which case,' Fox interrupted, 'Cafferty will already have disposed of it. He's not exactly an amateur.'

'Even professionals have been known to slip up,' MacBryer commented. She had paused in her note-taking. 'Cafferty will be lawyered up – you can be sure of that. If your case rests on one witness and no forensic evidence . . .' She didn't need to complete the sentence. 'I imagine you'll be questioning Mr Cafferty?'

'We will.'

'And when he denies any involvement, as he surely will?'

'We keep building the case.'

MacBryer nodded thoughtfully. 'That's all you can do, and I sincerely hope that at our next meeting you can bring me more than this. Because *this*, Detective Superintendent, isn't nearly enough.' She closed the iPad's cover and got to her feet, looking for her shoulder bag. Fox handed it to her, and with a few nods and gestures of goodbye, she left the room, taking all the oxygen with her.

Fox reclaimed his chair and began to put the stuff on the desk back in order. Clarke stood just inside the doorway, watching James slump in his own chair.

'You summoned her for that?' Clarke asked.

James shook his head. 'She was coming anyway – an initial catch-up on whether Arnott's death changes things.' He picked up a biscuit, then set it down again. 'I just thought . . .'

'MacBryer knows what she's doing, and she's crossed swords with Cafferty many a time. It'll take more than the word of a single shopkeeper . . .'

'I *get* that, okay?' James glared at her. 'Now if you'll excuse us, DI Clarke, we're kind of busy here.'

'Malcolm has had dealings with Cafferty, too – if he has anything to say, you'd be wise to listen.'

James grunted, busy on his laptop. Fox gave a half-smile of thanks and tipped his head towards the hallway. Clarke turned to go, descending the stairs and pausing at the bottom, checking her phone for messages. She wanted to help James and the others, wanted them to pin the attack on Cafferty. For no other reason than that it would be a little gift to Rebus.

It was a couple of minutes before Fox appeared. He opened the front door and led her on to the pavement.

'That was my fault,' he said. 'I pushed them hard on Cafferty. The description sold them and the notion of a quick result stopped them thinking straight for a bit.'

'But they're back on track now?'

'Slow and methodical.' Fox's phone pinged. He checked the text message, his jaw tightening.

'What's up?' Clarke asked.

'Nothing.'

'Is something wrong, Malcolm?'

'No.'

'Remind me to play you at poker sometime.'

'Why?'

'Because your ears have gone red and you can't meet my eyes.'

'Sheila Graham told me I had a good poker face.'

'She was lying. So are you going to tell me what's wrong?'

'Nothing's wrong.'

'Whatever you say. But a trouble shared and all that . . .'

Fox nodded distractedly. 'I'd better get back in.'

'Wait a second – what about John? Is everything all right with *him*?'

'Why shouldn't it be?'

She tried staring him out, but gave up. 'Will we catch up later?'

'Sure.' He was already pushing open the door.

'Bye then,' Clarke said, without receiving an answer.

Climbing the stairs, Fox looked at the text again.

Tick tock.

Sent by Darryl Christie, of course. Fox had contacted a property solicitor. The man was going to recce the outside of the bungalow at lunchtime, and provide an initial valuation by close of play. One way or another, Jude would be all right.

And he, too, would survive.

23

The naked man had been weaving his way in a dazed state around the streets of West Pilton for maybe fifteen or twenty minutes. Photos had been snapped on camera phones and sent to the internet, with one young person even managing a selfie. As he approached a primary school, however – break time; kids gambolling in the playground – the alarm was raised and the police summoned. The officers in the patrol car managed to head him off before he reached the school perimeter, and threw a blanket over him. His hair was matted, and he smelled of sweat and faeces. His ribs poked out and he seemed unable to form a coherent sentence. Not knowing what else to do, they deposited him at Drylaw police station, where he could become someone else's problem. He would be charged with public indecency, just as soon as they got a name for him.

They had one soon enough. A dentist, checking his Twitter feed at lunchtime, saw a couple of the photos and recognised a man he'd played tennis with until they'd had a falling-out. He called the police and identified Anthony Brough. By this time, the detainee had been given a shower and some clothes. A doctor had been summoned and was of the opinion that the man shivering and babbling in front of him was a drug user of some kind.

'Probably taken something he shouldn't.'

An injection was prescribed and the man taken back to his cell and given a sandwich and a cup of tea, which he succeeded in keeping down for almost a minute.

It was Twitter again that led with Brough's identity, the dentist having posted his thoughts. After all, Brough had lost him a chunk of his savings, and here was revenge of a sort.

261

All of which led Christine Esson to inform Siobhan Clarke and Clarke to call Malcolm Fox.

'Where do you want him?' she asked.

'How about Gayfield Square?' Fox asked.

'Will do.'

Fox then called Drylaw and spoke to a sergeant, who told him Brough had been muttering something about being kidnapped.

'Where was he first spotted?' Fox enquired.

'Social media would know better than me,' the sergeant replied. So Fox tried Facebook and Twitter and the answer seemed to be Ferry Road Avenue. He called the sergeant back and requested that officers be sent to the street and surrounding area to see if any location could be found.

'Isn't it as likely he's spinning us a line? Gets blitzed and when he comes to his senses he whips out the first excuse he can think of?'

'That's possible.'

'Or else he was dumped here from a car or van?'

'Please just go take a look.'

There was a loud sigh on the line, and the sergeant rang off without saying any more.

A second doctor had been summoned to Gayfield Square and was waiting when Brough arrived. Fox and Clarke watched him being led into a makeshift examination room. The prognosis eventually came: Anthony Brough needed to be taken to hospital. He was malnourished, and whatever cocktail of drugs he had been fed – intravenously and by mouth – might have side effects. Blood tests were needed. Psychological evaluation might be required at some point.

'We need to talk to him,' Fox insisted, but the doctor shook his head.

'Not yet. Not for a while. I think I've found him a bed at the Western General.'

'Oh good, another hospital,' Clarke said, eyes on Fox.

They grabbed drinks and chocolate bars from the machine along the corridor, resting their backs against the wall.

'Glushenko had him but let him go?' Fox eventually offered.

'If you were Ukrainian mob royalty, would you be putting your feet up in West Pilton?'

'Maybe not. But one of his men might. On the other hand, the sergeant I spoke to reckoned it was more likely Brough had been dumped there.'

'In which case the question is: why? If he *was* abducted, why bring it to an end?'

'Maybe they got what they wanted from him.'

'The missing money, you mean?' Clarke nodded, allowing the possibility.

'Or he really *has* just been on a bender. You ever hear about that Scottish explorer, Mungo Park? Walked into the jungle with dozens of bearers, carrying countless trunks and bags. Staggered out again months later dressed in nothing but his top hat.'

'That can't be true.'

'I remember reading it somewhere.' Fox checked his watch. 'What do you want to do?'

'No point hanging around here.'

'We could get to the hospital early, beat the rush?'

'Or?' Clarke screwed up the chocolate wrapper and tossed it into a bin.

'Or join the search party in West Pilton, which is practically on the way.'

'Whose car?'

'I don't mind.'

'Mine then.'

'Go easy on me, Siobhan. My nerves aren't what they were.'

'Just for that, I'm playing Ninja Horse all the way.'

'Is that a game?'

'It's a heavy metal band.'

'One last thing – when do we tell John?'

Clarke considered this. 'Maybe not just yet.'

'Brough's sister and his assistant?'

'Ditto.'

'Any particular reason?'

'How crowded do you want it around his bedside?'

'Good point.'

'Besides which,' Clarke added, readying to move off, 'John seems to have a touch of the grim reaper about him today . . .'

Rebus just happened to have dropped in at Leith police station as Cafferty arrived for his interview accompanied by his solicitor, a skeletal man called Crawfurd Leach, who wore a three-piece pin-stripe suit and black shoes polished to within an inch of their lives. He was in his forties and almost completely bald, what hair he had left slicked back from the forehead and ears. He wore John Lennon-style glasses and there were always a few stray tufts of stubble on his cheekbones, no matter how clean-shaven the rest of his face.

Rebus was in the gents' toilet, washing his hands, when Cafferty pushed open the door and made for a urinal.

'You got my text, then?' Rebus asked.

'What's on your mind, John?'

'That was stupid. Stupid and overdramatic.'

'I've no idea what you're talking about.'

'I thought you'd outgrown the hands-on stuff. Shows how much I know.'

Rebus was drying his palms on a paper towel as Cafferty joined him at the sink. They studied one another in the mirror.

'You ever kill someone, John?'

'Only when there was no alternative.'

'Isn't that a bit boring, though?'

'Did you leave him to die or to live?'

'You miked up or something?' Cafferty had leaned in towards the mirror, studying his own face. 'It's pretty much done now anyway. You ever played bridge?'

'No.'

'Me neither, but I know the rules. There's a point where the bidding's finished and all that's left to do is let the cards fall. There might be a surprise or two, but the hard work's already been done.' Cafferty smiled. 'The shopkeeper, that's all they have?'

'I wouldn't know.'

'They're like kids playing snap. You and me are used to proper grown-up games.'

Wondering what was taking his client so long, Leach pushed his head around the door and scowled when he saw Cafferty had company.

'Don't fret, Crawfurd,' Cafferty said. 'We were just comparing manhoods.' And with a wink to Rebus, he followed his lawyer to the interview room.

Rebus made for the MIT office, where Briggs and Oldfield were pretending to be busy while actually sulking that they hadn't been chosen to partner Alvin James.

'He took Siobhan?' Rebus commented, surprised.

'She's not around.'

'Fox?'

'Likewise. It's Sean in there with him. Wallace is still running the search operation and door-to-door.'

'I like the new set-up,' Rebus stated, studying the cafetière and lifting the last Duchy Original from the packet.

'Was there something you wanted?' Briggs asked.

'Just kicking my heels really.' He beamed a smile towards her.

'I thought Alvin was going to make sure you didn't get past the front desk.'

'Must have slipped his mind. Any updates from the boxing club?'

'Forensics haven't found anything worth shouting about,' Oldfield admitted. 'Without the weapon, we're stuffed.'

'I wouldn't go that far,' Rebus reassured him. 'You've got the man who sold Cafferty the hammer. If Cafferty can't produce said hammer, that's going to look suspicious. And if he does . . .'

'Which he won't.'

'Which he won't,' Rebus agreed.

'Suspicions don't make a case,' Briggs said.

'Sounds like you've had the benefit of the Procurator Fiscal's wisdom. Hard to credit, I admit, but they don't always know best.' Rebus took another bite of biscuit. He had ended up at Fox's desk, sitting on Fox's chair, casting his eyes over Fox's paperwork.

'Alvin will blow a fuse if you're here when he comes back.'

'Nothing Big Ger likes more than a nice long chat,' Rebus explained. 'And as his lawyer is charging three figures per hour, he won't be in a hurry either.'

'Story is you know him almost *too* well.'

Rebus met Briggs's gaze. 'For the sake of my health, yes, that's probably true.'

'I've been checking his files. Seems this is the first time he's used a hammer.'

Rebus considered this. 'I think he may be regretting it. He walks past the shop and thinks, why not? He needs *some*thing. Kenny Arnott is twenty years younger than him and no pushover.' He offered a shrug. 'Besides which, a hammer and nails is old school – maybe he thought Arnott would appreciate that.'

'*Appreciate* it?' Briggs sounded appalled.

'It's hard to explain.' Rebus was about to anyway when Alvin James appeared in the doorway, his face like thunder.

'I was just leaving,' Rebus assured him.

'He wants you. He won't speak to me until after.'

'That's unfortunate.'

'Yes it bloody well is. Five minutes, he says. Then we can get back to questioning him.' James stabbed a finger towards Rebus's chest. 'You're going to report back every word he utters, understood?'

'Will you still be recording?'

James shook his head. 'Five minutes,' he repeated, spreading the fingers of one hand. 'So don't go getting too comfortable . . .'

Rebus knocked and entered the interview room, at which point Cafferty told Crawfurd Leach to stretch his legs.

'I'm not sure that's wise,' the lawyer drawled.

'Just fuck off, Crawfurd. Go try a proper shave or something.'

Cafferty watched his lawyer leave, closing the door softly after him. There was a beaker of tea in front of him, but nothing else. The tape recorder and camera had been turned off. Rebus sat down in what he presumed had been Alvin James's seat, on the opposite side of the table. Cafferty was studying his surroundings as if considering an offer of tenancy.

'We've been in a few of these down the years, eh, John?'

'A few, yes.'

'Craw tells me you roughed him up once – Johnny Bible case, wasn't it?'

'That was in Craigmillar, though.'

'Different rules back then. But you know what?' Cafferty puffed out his chest. 'I feel like I'm getting my second wind.'

'Why's that?'

'Because all those cards are landing just the way they should, and I'm so far ahead on points it's almost embarrassing.' He chuckled, fingers playing across the beaker.

'Superintendent James has only given me five minutes,' Rebus warned. 'Is that enough time for you to make your full and frank confession?'

'I just thought . . . we might not see one another again, *ever*, not in a place like this. Now that you've been pensioned off and everything. Is that cough of yours getting any better? Of course not. I seem to have this new lease of life, while everybody around me is falling apart.'

'Some of them helped along by you.' Rebus paused. 'You're not going to give them anything, are you?'

'Of course not.'

'What about me, though?'

'You?'

'I think I deserve something.'

266

'Is it your birthday again? I gave you Glushenko, isn't that enough?'

'You didn't give me Glushenko – all you did was dangle a "Russian" in front of me. You've known about him all along, though, haven't you? He's the card you've had up your sleeve.'

'You're a piece of work, John. I'm sure I've told you that before. This lot don't deserve you.'

'They're good cops.'

Cafferty snorted. 'Not nearly good enough.'

'You slipped up, you got identified.'

'Was that really me, though? One shopkeeper in his seventies who wears glasses like the bottoms of milk bottles? You know yourself nobody's going to trial on the weight of that.'

'Have they asked for your clothes?'

'I can give them clothes – they'll look exactly like the ones I was dressed in yesterday.'

'What did you do with the hammer? What did Arnott tell you?'

Cafferty gave a thin, almost rueful smile. 'Glushenko's close, John. He's very close. And when he gets here . . . game over.'

The door swung outwards. Alvin James and Sean Glancey stood there, Leach's head visible between their shoulders.

'Time's up,' James stated briskly. Rebus was already on his feet.

'He just wanted a walk down memory lane,' he explained. 'Five minutes of my life I'm not getting back.'

'Off you jolly well fuck then,' James told him, 'and let the professionals have a go.'

Rebus left the room, glancing towards Cafferty as he went, but Cafferty's eyes were on James, as he readied to continue the game.

Clarke and Fox arrived just in time to hear the news – a terraced house, its curtains closed but front door ajar, a single street away from the first reported sighting of Anthony Brough. A couple of uniforms had headed inside and were pretty confident. They were on the doorstep as Clarke and Fox approached. Clarke had her warrant card open.

'DI Clarke,' she said. 'Give me what you have.'

'Ground-floor bedroom, back of the house, next to the kitchen. Lock fitted to the outside of the door, but the padlock itself lying on the hall carpet. The room stinks. Window's been boarded up, nailed shut. There's a camp bed and a pail to piss in, bottle filled with what looks like water, but that's about it.'

'Pile of clothes just outside the door,' his colleague added. 'Suit, shirt, shoes.'

Clarke peered through the doorway. 'Is it a squat, or what?'

'There's stuff in the kitchen, and a mattress upstairs with a sleeping bag on it, plus more clothes in a couple of bin bags.'

'Toothbrush and razor in the bathroom,' the first uniform said.

'Anyone else been inside?' Fox asked.

'Just us.'

'Touch anything?'

'We know better than that.' The constable's face had tightened a little.

'I want to know who lives here,' Clarke said. A small crowd had gathered on the pavement, mostly kids on bikes. 'Ask the neighbours either side. Then we can check for paperwork. Probably some bills in a drawer somewhere.'

'Council will have a record of whoever's coughing up the annual tax,' Fox added.

Clarke studied the interior again before crossing the threshold. Fox didn't look so sure.

'Bedroom is the locus, Malcolm,' she assured him. 'Speaking of which . . .' She took out her phone and tapped in the CSM's number.

'Siobhan,' Haj Atwal said on answering. 'Is this by way of another contribution to the coffers?'

She gave him the address. 'It's nothing too nasty – person held captive. But we need the locus given a once-over.'

'Thirty minutes?' he offered.

'Someone will be here,' Clarke said, ending the call. Then, to Fox: 'Shall we?'

Fox followed her down the narrow hall. There was a tang of vomit in the air. They stopped at the bedroom door. The hook-and-eye fixings for the padlock looked cheap and flimsy, the padlock itself small and shiny.

'As new,' Fox commented.

Without stepping into the room itself, they could see that it was as the officer had described it. Nothing on the bare plaster walls. Plywood nailed across the entirety of the small window. Camp bed tipped on its side, a single blanket lying beneath it. Pail and water bottle. Some sick had dried to a crust on the threadbare carpet halfway between bed and pail. Fox had turned his attention to the bundled clothes near his feet. He nudged them with the toe of his shoe, dislodging a wallet from one of the suit jacket's pockets.

Taking a pen from his own pocket, he crouched down and flipped the wallet open. Credit and debit cards, driving licence. With his handkerchief covering his fingertips, he slid the driving licence out just far enough to determine that its owner was Anthony Brough.

Clarke peered down at it and nodded. Fox turned his attention to the brass padlock. It was unlocked, no sign of the key.

'Think the abductor just got sloppy?' Clarke mused.

'Looks that way.'

They moved into the kitchen. An ashtray by the sink was full of spliff remains. Clarke slid out a couple of drawers without finding any bills or other mail. Fox, on the opposite side of the kitchen, had pulled open two adjoining cupboards above the worktop.

'Hello,' he said.

Clarke turned and saw bags of white powder; bags of green leaves and buds; bags of pills of varying size and colour; vials and bottles with rubber-sealant caps, filled with clear liquid, obviously intended for injections. Fox studied the writing on one of the bottles.

'Might need a vet to tell us what this stuff does,' he advised.

'I don't think we're talking purely personal use here, Malcolm, do you?'

Fox had spotted something lying on the floor, in one dark corner. 'What does that look like?' he said.

'A padlock key,' Clarke said. 'Dropped by the kidnapper.'

'Unable to find it, he can't risk locking the padlock, so he takes a chance.' Fox nodded to himself.

The elder of the two uniforms was standing in the doorway. 'The occupier is Eddie Bates. Never any trouble, but gets a lot of visitors at all hours.'

'Anyone else live here?'

'Just him.'

'Run the name, see if he's known to us. We also need a description – he might just have nipped out and already be on his way back.'

'Do we send out search parties?'

Clarke considered for a moment. 'We lie low,' she decided. 'Pull the front door to and see what happens.' She led Fox and the constable down the hall towards the front door. 'Uniforms and marked cars, I want them at a safe distance.' She was already on her phone. 'Haj,' she said when the CSM picked up, 'hold fire on that. I'll tell you when it's safe to head over here.'

'So what's the plan?' Fox asked as they walked down the path towards the pavement.

'You and me in a car, eyes on the front door.'

'You really think this guy Bates has just "nipped out"? It's been at least a couple of hours since Brough escaped. That's a long time to leave an abductee . . .'

'Bates maybe thought he'd doped him to the eyeballs. He'd taken a couple of hits for himself, maybe a spliff or two, gets the munchies . . .' She saw Fox looking at her. 'Go on then, what would *you* do?'

'I'd be circulating a description of him – bus and train stations. If he *did* come home and find Brough had done a runner, he'd probably want to be gone from here.'

'Without taking any of the stuff from the kitchen with him? There's probably a couple of thousand quid's worth in those cupboards.'

'True,' Fox conceded.

They moved their car to the end of the street. When the uniforms and patrol cars evaporated, so did the spectators. Within a few minutes, the area was quiet. Clarke called Christine Esson and gave her Bates's name and address.

'Get me anything you can. Including Facebook, Twitter, Instagram. A recent photo would be perfect.'

'Will do.'

'Would a drug dealer really post pictures on the internet?' Fox asked after the call was finished.

'Everybody else does.'

'I don't.'

'That's because you're a freak, Malcolm.'

'While the people sharing their privacy with complete strangers are perfectly normal?'

'Weird, isn't it?'

Fox shook his head. His phone buzzed and he checked the screen. *Tick tock.*

'Your mysterious admirer again?' Clarke guessed.

'It's Darryl Christie,' Fox admitted.

'What's he after?'

'He wants me to use the resources of Police Scotland to track down Glushenko.'

'And why would you do that for him?'

'Because my sister owes him money.'

'How come?'

'Gambling debts.'

'You're not going to, though?'

'I'm stringing him along.'

'You can't just pay him off?'

'It'd mean selling my house. I'm looking into that, too.'

'Bloody hell, Malcolm. If it helps, I can lend you . . .'

Fox was shaking his head. 'I can do this, Siobhan.'

'Does your boss know?'

'Of course.'

'And you're only telling me this now because . . .?'

'It passes the time.'

'Well, seeing as you're in a chatty mood – what do you know about John's health?'

'Why would he tell me?'

'I just get the feeling I might be the only one who's in the dark.'

'I'm sure he's fine.'

'What about you, Malcolm – are *you* fine?'

'I wish you'd got that Gartcosh promotion, Siobhan. I was content where I was.' He paused. 'And I miss the pair of us hanging out together.'

Clarke was silent for a moment, before reaching over and squeezing his hand. 'Thanks,' she said.

'And you're sorry about how you reacted when I got the posting?'

She pulled her hand back. 'Let's not spoil the moment, eh?' They looked at one another and smiled.

Fox caught a glimpse of something in his wing mirror. 'Heads up,' he warned Clarke. A man was plodding along the pavement, a carrier bag full of shopping hanging from one arm. His steps had the careful precision of someone who was inebriated but trying not to look it.

'Daytime drinking is a wonderful thing,' Clarke commented as the man walked past their car without noticing. He had a roll-up in his mouth and was coughing. Thinning fair hair. Faded denims and matching jacket, scuffed brown work boots. He looked as though a sudden gust might blow him over. He paused at the right gate and opened it with one knee.

'That's him, then,' Clarke said. 'Let's wait till he's inside.'

The man was using a key to unlock the door. It took him a couple of goes. He disappeared inside, closing it after him.

'Okay,' Clarke said, getting out of the car.

They had just reached the doorstep when the door itself burst open. The man had ditched the carrier bag and looked suddenly

271

sober as well as shocked. Seeing the two figures, he tried shutting the door again, but Fox shouldered it open, sending him flying.

'I've done nothing!' he spluttered as he started getting back to his feet.

'We've got some lost property of yours, Mr Bates,' Clarke stated. 'Need to have a little word with you on the subject . . .'

24

The news from the Western General was that Anthony Brough was sleeping. Blood tests had been carried out and were being analysed. By evening, the patient might be awake and able to talk. With this in mind, Clarke and Fox were back at Gayfield Square. Christine Esson handed over a copy of Bates's criminal record. His history of petty crime went back to schooldays and included four stretches in prison. But his last brush with the law had been almost three years ago, and there was nothing to suggest he had climbed a few rungs of the ladder to the position of quantity dealer. Clarke handed the sheets over to Fox and let him read them while she studied Ronnie Ogilvie. He was behind his desk and busy on his computer, but there was something . . .

'You got rid of the moustache,' she announced.

He stroked his upper lip. 'Yeah,' he said, as Esson stifled a smile.

'In the two hours since I was last here,' Clarke went on.

'Took a sudden notion.'

Fox had finished reading. He placed the report on Clarke's desk. 'What do we do till the lawyer turns up?' he asked.

Esson had picked up her ringing phone. She placed her hand across the mouthpiece. 'Just arrived at the front desk,' she informed them.

'You ready?' Clarke asked Fox.

'Good and,' he replied, buttoning his suit jacket.

The solicitor looked overworked, the top button of his shirt undone behind the pale blue tie. His black-rimmed glasses kept sliding down his nose. Clarke nodded a greeting and loaded the recording machine with two tapes, while Fox made sure the video was working.

'My client—'

Clarke interrupted him, stating her name for the record and adding that of Detective Inspector Malcolm Fox. She paused and waited.

'I'm Alan Tranter, representing Mr Edward Bates,' the solicitor said, sifting what paperwork he had.

'And you are?' Clarke asked Bates, her eyes drilling into him.

'Eddie Bates,' he eventually muttered. 'No one ever calls me Edward.'

'I'll make sure the turnkeys have a note of that,' Clarke said. 'That's what we call them – the people who'll be keeping an eye on you while you're in the cells here.'

'What's the charge?'

'Abduction. Not sure we can call it kidnapping yet, since nobody seems to have received a ransom note. But abduction will do. It means holding somebody against their will, and it's quite serious. But when you add it to conspiracy to supply drugs . . .'

'I don't know anything about drugs.'

'They've been taken from your kitchen to our lab at Howden Hall. They'll be weighed, counted, identified. The packaging they came in will be fingerprinted – just like you, Mr Bates.'

'I'm telling you, someone must have put them there.'

'Right under your nose? Without you being any the wiser? Maybe they stuck Anthony Brough in that room, too, without you noticing the shiny padlock or the smell of shit and puke? Are you not the inquisitive sort, Mr Bates?'

'Is this tone really necessary, DI Clarke?' Tranter said.

'Your client is in a spot of bother, Mr Tranter. You'd do well to make sure that sinks in. We'll find his prints on the pail, the water bottle, the metal edges of the camp bed . . .'

'Not forgetting the padlock itself,' Fox added.

'You don't have those prints yet, though, do you?' the solicitor queried.

'Crime-scene team are there as we speak.' Clarke turned her attention back to Bates. 'I should warn you, they're *very* good.'

Tranter checked his notes again. 'Has this Anthony Brough said anything? Is it possible his stay in the house was voluntary? I learn from my client that Mr Brough is hardly of impeccable quality . . .' He broke off, meeting Clarke's stare.

'Meaning what?' she asked.

'My client has, in the past, supplied Mr Brough with a small quantity of certain stimulants.'

'How small?'

'Were this to go to trial, an answer might be forthcoming. Mr Brough works in the banking and investment sector, yes? Are you sure charging Mr Bates is in the gentleman's best interests? I mean, do you think *he'll* see it that way?'

'Doesn't matter if he does or he doesn't – we'll be the ones bringing the prosecution.'

The room was quiet for a few moments, except for Bates's chesty breathing.

Fox cleared his throat, unbuttoning his suit jacket. 'If you really did sell stuff to Brough,' he asked Bates, 'he'll be able to identify you if we show him a photo? He'll know your name?'

Bates looked down towards where his hands were gripping the edge of the table.

'I didn't sell to him directly,' he muttered.

'Who then?'

'Look,' the lawyer interrupted, 'I'm sure this can be fully explored when my client—'

'His secretary,' Eddie Bates blurted out.

Fox and Clarke shared a look. 'Give me a name,' Fox said, 'and I might even start to believe you.'

'Sewell,' Bates said confidently. 'Molly Sewell.'

'Is there no front desk you can't get past?' Clarke said, watching Rebus stalk towards her along the corridor. She was drinking lukewarm tea and had managed half a BLT sandwich. The sliced bread was damply unappetising, and the tomato had a slight fizziness to it.

'I'm like the cast of *The Great Escape* in reverse,' Rebus said. 'What's this I hear about Anthony Brough?' Clarke just stared at him. 'I have my sources, Siobhan.'

'Sources not too far from here, I imagine,' Clarke retorted, casting a glance through the doorway towards the desk where Christine Esson sat, eyes averted. Hearing voices, Fox emerged from the office. He too had a sandwich he was failing to make much progress with.

'Sorry to interrupt your lunchtime,' Rebus said. 'Or is it an early dinner?' He pretended to check his watch.

'Brough was doped to the eyeballs and being kept under lock and key,' Clarke began. 'His jailer is a dealer called Eddie Bates – know him?'

'Name sounds familiar.' Rebus furrowed his brow.

275

'His story is that Brough was just visiting. Wouldn't exactly be my destination of choice if I had plenty of cash and wanted to go on a bender, but that's what he's telling us.'

'Who – Brough or Bates?'

'Bates.' Clarke tossed the remains of her sandwich into a bin and brushed crumbs from her hands. 'Brough's still groggy and being pumped full of vitamins. We're going to talk to him soon.'

'Has Francesca been notified?'

Clarke nodded. 'And Molly Sewell.'

'So what is it you're not telling me?'

'According to Bates, Sewell was the go-between. She ordered the goods for her boss and handed over the cash.'

'Okay.'

'It doesn't stack up, though. Brough wasn't in anything re-sembling a party house. He was locked away, naked, in a room with its window boarded up, a bucket to piss and crap in. He'd been starved half to death and injected with God knows what.'

'People get their jollies in different ways,' Rebus commented, while Clarke shook her head. 'So you're thinking Bates saw a way to make more money by ransoming the boss? Have we seen any sign of a demand?'

'*We* haven't – how about you?'

'It's not the kind of thing I'd keep to myself.'

'John, it's exactly the kind of thing you'd keep to yourself.'

'I'm telling the truth.' Rebus paused. 'This guy Bates, does he seem the kidnapping type?'

'I wasn't aware there was a specific type,' Clarke bristled.

'I wouldn't say he was,' Fox interceded. 'He's not smart enough, for one thing. A kidnap requires a calculating brain.'

'Then why *did* he snatch Brough?' Clarke demanded, folding her arms.

'Maybe Brough will tell us,' Rebus suggested. 'When were you thinking of visiting?'

'Very soon. I take it you're angling for an invite?'

'I wouldn't be so presumptuous. But if you're offering . . .'

Fox's phone pinged to let him know he had a text.

'Christie?' Rebus and Clarke said in unison, staring at one an-other afterwards.

'Just for a change, no,' Fox answered. 'Alvin James is wondering why I'm not at my desk.'

'Tell him you're on Gartcosh business,' Rebus advised.

'That's exactly what I'm doing,' Fox said as he tapped his screen.

'Just one thing,' Rebus added. 'Whichever car we take, I can't sit in the back. I get queasy.'

'Always supposing we're letting you come,' Clarke retorted.

'Better an invited guest than a gatecrasher, don't you think?'

'Are you forgetting your recent record in hospital wards?'

'This time will be different, Siobhan, trust me . . .'

There was quite a gathering around Anthony Brough's bed. When Francesca spotted Rebus entering the ward, she bounded up to him like an excited child, squeezing his hand and standing on tiptoe, her mouth to his ear.

'My brother is the devil, did you know that?'

She had pulled her sleeves partway up her arms. Rebus could see old scar tissue.

Alison Warbody approached, tugging the sleeves back down again.

'No misbehaving,' she cooed. 'Remember what I said.'

Francesca allowed herself to be led back to the bedside, where Molly Sewell was standing. Francesca pointed Rebus out to her brother, who was sitting up, three pillows supporting his head.

'He's a policeman,' she intoned. '*Very* interested in Maria Turquand.'

'Can't you give her a Valium or something?' Anthony Brough was looking at Warbody as he spoke.

'Oh yes,' she responded. 'Drugs are just what she needs.'

Clarke and Fox were bedside by now and introduced themselves.

'Wait a second,' Warbody said, pointing at Rebus. 'He said *he* was Fox.'

Clarke gave Rebus a sour look. 'His name's John Rebus,' she informed Warbody. Then, to Brough: 'You look a lot better, sir.'

'Still got a head full of cotton wool,' Brough replied. 'Albeit cotton wool armed with a pneumatic drill.' He had the deep, sonorous voice of the Scottish gentry. His face had regained a bit of colour, the cheeks beginning to return to their natural ruddiness, and his wavy sandy-coloured hair had been combed, probably by a nurse. Brough ran a hesitant hand through it, as if trying to reshape it.

'You must have lots of questions,' he said, addressing the group. 'I know I do. But right now, everything's a muddle, so forgive me if I don't have the answers.'

'First thing we're interested in, sir,' Clarke ventured, 'is whether you were there of your own volition?'

'I don't even know where I was. It was like a bad dream, all of it. Running naked through the streets – that's what you have nightmares about, isn't it?'

'You were in a house in West Pilton, owned by a man by the name of Eddie Bates.'

'Never heard of him.'

Clarke turned her head away from Brough. 'How about you, Ms Sewell?'

'What?' Molly Sewell looked startled. 'No idea.'

Francesca had started repeating Bates's name under her breath, finding a rhythm to it.

'What has this got to do with Maria Turquand, anyway?' Brough was asking.

Clarke shook her head. 'We're not here about that, Mr Brough.'

But Brough was staring at Rebus as though his interest had been piqued. Then he screwed shut his eyes, gritting his teeth in pain. 'Wish they'd bring me some more bloody pills.' He plucked at his regulation-issue pyjama top. 'I've got the sweats, too. This place is like a furnace.'

'A *fiery* furnace,' his sister blurted out, eyes widening. She began to giggle. Brough's eyes were on Warbody again.

'Alison,' he said, 'it's not that I don't appreciate the thought and all, but shouldn't you take my sister home now?'

'I don't like hospitals,' Francesca explained to anyone who would listen.

'Nobody does,' her brother answered.

'She wanted to see you,' Warbody said.

Francesca looked puzzled. 'Did I?'

'You know you did.'

'I suppose so.' Francesca gave a huge shrug of the shoulders.

'Could we have a word, please?' Clarke was asking Molly Sewell. 'In private?'

'Can't it wait?'

'We'll only be five minutes. Mr Brough will still be here.'

Clarke led the way, with Fox to the rear and a reluctant Sewell in the middle.

'What's that about?' Brough asked Rebus.

'Do you mind if I sit? I'm not as young as some of you.' Rebus settled into the only chair.

'Yes, you're old,' Francesca stated. 'You're really *really* old. Are you going to die soon?'

'Francesca!' Warbody gripped her by one arm and gave it a shake.

'Take her for a walk,' Brough pleaded. 'The shop or something – maybe outside for a breath of air.'

'All right,' Warbody said, clasping Francesca's hand in her own. 'We'll come back in a while, though.'

'Can't wait,' Brough said, blowing a kiss to his sister, who bobbed down as if to dodge it. She was singing as she was escorted from the ward.

'She's a lot of work,' Rebus sympathised. 'I'm assuming you pay for everything?'

'Worth every penny.'

'Funny, I heard your sister pays for her carer out of her own pocket. Sir Magnus left her plenty – good job she didn't trust you to invest it for her, eh?'

Brough gave Rebus a hard stare. 'I really can't tell you anything.'

'Can't or won't?'

'Can't.'

'So what's the last thing you remember before you woke up in that room?'

'How many days was I there?'

'A bit more than a week, probably.'

Brough rested his head on the pillows, staring towards the ceiling. 'I was at home. Usual night-time routine.'

'And what's that?'

'Couple of whiskies and a few lines of coke. Or maybe some downers if I'm feeling like a nice long doze.' Brough thought for a moment. 'Started to feel a bit woozy; next thing I know I'm shivering on somebody else's fucking floor.' His eyes narrowed. 'Why did your colleagues take Molly away?'

'They want to know if there's been a ransom demand.'

'Is that what you think it was? A kidnapping?'

'What do *you* think, Mr Brough?'

'I've honestly no idea.'

'Must have crossed your mind, though . . .'

'What?' Brough turned his head towards Rebus.

'That it was Glushenko on the other side of the door, readying to slit your throat.' Rebus waited for Brough to say something. The mouth was working but nothing came. 'See, we know everything,' Rebus continued, rising from the chair, leaning over the bed with

279

his knuckles pressing into the mattress. 'You're not going to peg out on me, are you? I had that happen all too recently. Another would look bad . . .'

'Who's this Glushenko you mentioned?'

'The man you stole millions from. The flat above Klondyke Alley? You and your pal Darryl Christie? All those SLPs bouncing money around the globe, well away from the eyes of the tax authorities. Suddenly all this cash from Ukraine arrives. Your investments have been tanking and your clients aren't happy with you, so you skim some off before sending it on its way. But the deficit gets noticed and Glushenko is furious. He's coming to pay you and Darryl a visit. Then you do your vanishing act, leaving Darryl in the frame.' Rebus paused. 'How am I doing so far?' Brough remained silent. 'Oh yes, and your poor investors didn't get any of that skimmed cash in the end, did they? You kept it all to yourselves, you and Darryl.'

'That's not true.' Brough was shaking his head slowly. 'I wanted them to get their share, started arranging the necessary transfers. But the money wasn't there.'

'How do you mean?'

'It wasn't *there*.'

'Christie?' Rebus guessed.

'Who else?'

'You know someone attacked him outside his house?'

'Good. I hope they did him some proper damage.'

'I'm guessing it wasn't on your orders, then?'

'I wish I'd thought of it.' There were flecks of saliva at the corners of Brough's mouth.

'Does Glushenko really exist?'

Brough's eyes narrowed again. 'Of course.'

'You've met him? Spoken to him? He's not just some bogeyman who's been conjured up to get everybody antsy – Darryl Christie in particular?'

'He's real.'

'Then it's ironic, isn't it? All the time you were locked away, you were safe. But now you've managed to escape . . .' Rebus left the sentence unfinished. He could see that, headache or no headache, Brough's mind was racing.

'Can you help me?' Brough eventually said, his voice just above a whisper.

'Help you how?'

'I need to be two things – free, and safe.'

'Fine goals to aim for,' Rebus agreed.

'I have something to trade.'

'Oh aye? Got a bit of that non-existent cash you want to see go to a deserving ex-cop's pocket?'

'Maybe you're the sort of man who craves closure more than lucre.'

'First time for everything, I suppose.'

Brough ran his tongue along his lips, moistening them. 'I know who killed her,' he said.

'Killed who?' Rebus asked, knowing as he did so the name he was about to hear.

'Maria Turquand,' Brough said.

They found three seats in the foyer. The place was busy with staff and visitors, most of them on phones, no one paying attention to Clarke, Fox and Molly Sewell. They probably looked like family fretting about a relative in one of the wards. Fox moved his chair to form a sort of circle. Sewell's eyes were settling anywhere but on the two detectives.

'We need to ask you something,' Clarke said quietly. 'And we need you to start being honest with us.' She paused. 'Look at me, Molly.' The young woman complied. 'I'm going to ask you again: does the name Eddie Bates mean anything to you?'

'No.'

'Lying to us can get you into serious trouble,' Fox interrupted. 'You do understand that?'

'Eddie Bates seems to know *you*,' Clarke added. 'He tells us he sold you drugs intended for Anthony Brough. Are you saying he's lying?'

'He must be.' Sewell watched as, hand in hand, Francesca Brough and Alison Warbody strode past and exited the building.

'They make quite a pair,' Fox commented.

'Alison's absolutely heroic. Not everyone would have the patience she does.'

'Francesca certainly looks like hard work.'

'It's not her fault, you know.' Sewell's voice had grown colder. 'Too much tragedy and too many drugs—'

'Which,' Clarke interrupted, 'brings us back to Eddie Bates. Say we were to take you to Gayfield Square police station and put you in a room with him . . .?'

Sewell gnawed on her bottom lip. Her eyes were darting around again. 'Maybe I do know him,' she conceded.

'And you're sure you've never received any sort of ransom demand? A note of any kind?'

Sewell met Clarke's gaze. 'Are you telling me Eddie kidnapped Anthony?'

'I'm telling you your boss was kept locked away in Eddie Bates's house. Do you know where that is?' Sewell shook her head. 'Would Anthony have known?'

'The two of them never met.'

'But Bates knew who the drugs were for?'

Sewell considered her answer, then nodded slowly. 'Sometimes he came to the office.'

'How about Anthony's home address?'

Sewell shook her head again. 'Usually we met on the street outside the office. Eddie said it was handy because he had another client across the road.'

'Bruce Collier?' Fox guessed. Sewell just shrugged.

'Eddie *could* have found Anthony's address,' she speculated. 'Nothing is impossible these days.'

'Just to be clear, then – Anthony never knew the source of the drugs, nor where Bates lived?'

'You're thinking he could have run out, got desperate, and turned up there?' Sewell pondered this. 'Well, yes, maybe.'

'Except,' Fox said, 'you just told us your boss had no idea who his supplier was.'

'He might have found Eddie's number on my desk,' Sewell suggested.

'So how did it work? Anthony asked you to find him a dealer and you went and did just that?'

Sewell shrugged. 'That's what a good PA does.'

'What did you do – check Yellow Pages?'

'I go out clubbing some weekends. I asked a friend, who asked someone else, who gave me a phone number.'

'Any clubs in particular?' Clarke asked.

'Ringo's.' She paused to think. Maybe the Devil's Dram – is it important?'

'Probably not. So how long have you known Bates?'

'A couple of years.'

'Any idea where your boss got his stuff before that?'

'Someone who ended up going to jail.'

Clarke looked to Fox to see if he had any other questions. He was rubbing his jaw thoughtfully.

'Has Eddie actually said he was holding Anthony for money?' Sewell asked.

'We're still piecing it together,' Clarke admitted.

'Am I in trouble?'

'For scoring drugs for your boss?' Clarke considered this. 'Maybe.'

'Am I going to go to prison?'

'I wouldn't think so, though it would certainly help your cause if you told us anything you think we need to know.'

Sewell shrugged. 'There's nothing I can think of. Is it okay if I head back upstairs?'

Clarke took a notepad from her pocket and handed it over. 'Put down your home address and a couple of contact numbers. We'll need to talk to you again so we have a proper record of your version of events.'

Sewell bent her head over the pad, resting it on her right knee. Clarke took the pad back when she'd finished and checked she could read the neat handwriting.

'Can I go now?'

Clarke nodded, watching as Sewell sprang to her feet. Fox got up and moved his chair back to its original position.

'What now?' he asked.

'Maybe another word with Eddie Bates.' Clarke looked at him. 'Do you need to let Gartcosh know about Brough?'

'I suppose I should. Do we want to ask Brough a few questions?'

'Once the dust has settled.'

'I've just realised, we left John alone with the patient. I wonder if that was wise.'

'Why not ask him?' Clarke nodded towards the figure striding across the foyer. She waved, and Rebus noticed her. He offered a curt nod and signalled with his hand that there'd be a phone call later. Then he was out of the automatic doors and gone.

'What was all that about?' Fox asked.

'I think it means trouble for someone,' Clarke answered. 'Been a while since I saw him with that look in his eyes . . .'

25

When no one answered, Rebus rang the bell again. The sun was setting and birdsong filled the air. Not that he could see any birds – they were just *there*, present but largely invisible. He reached for the large metal knocker and tried that.

'Yes, yes, yes,' a voice announced from behind the door. 'It takes a while, you know, with this hip of mine.' As the door swung open, John Turquand took a second to recognise the man in front of him.

'You were here the other day,' he said.

'That's right. Mind if I come in?'

'It's really not convenient.'

'Now isn't that a fucking shame?' Rebus walked past Turquand into the hall, heading for the library. He poured himself a small whisky and had downed it by the time Turquand arrived. 'Long drive from Edinburgh,' he explained.

'You seem to be agitated,' Turquand stated. He was dressed in the same clothes as on Rebus's previous visit, and had failed to shave between times.

'Sit down,' Rebus ordered, doing the same himself.

The bridge table was still waiting for a game to be played. Rebus snatched up the cards and shuffled them, watching Turquand's performance as he edged towards the chair opposite and settled himself.

'Peter Attwood was a friend of yours – a good friend. Must have infuriated you when he started sleeping with Maria.'

'Well, yes, when I found out.'

'And that happened some time before she died, didn't it? Contrary to the story you told.'

'Are you about to accuse me of something? Should I have a lawyer present?'

'It was Sir Magnus's idea,' Rebus went on. 'He was worried that Maria's various flings were affecting your work. He needed you to be at your sharpest for the Royal Bank takeover. He told you to have it out with her. And you did try – you followed her, knew which room she stayed in at the Caley. You even tried phoning the room, but chickened out. Sir Magnus was adamant, though – something had to be done, and if you didn't speak to her, *he* would. So you steeled yourself and went to the hotel, stood outside her room and knocked. When she opened the door, she was expecting Peter Attwood. She didn't know he was breaking it off.'

'Stop it, please.' Turquand's top lip was trembling.

'The look on her face – radiant, ready to embrace her lover – it was a look she never gave you, and it sent you into a rage. You shoved her inside and put your hands around her neck.'

'No . . .'

'You throttled the life out of her.'

Turquand's head was in his hands, elbows on the table. Rebus kept shuffling the pack as he spoke.

'A crime of passion, they'd probably have called it – except that the passion was hers. And when it was done, you returned to your boss and confessed everything. He told you it would be all right, calmed you down, said he was ready to give you an alibi. You'd been in a meeting with him all afternoon. You became a suspect, of course, but so did a lot of other people. And eventually even the police lost interest. You were safe to make your millions and spend them.'

'How do you know this? Who told you?'

Rebus placed the cards on the table. 'On his deathbed, Sir Magnus confided in his grandchildren. He wanted them to know something.'

Turquand looked up from between his fingers. 'What?'

'That a certain kind of person can get away with anything – up to and including murder. He was moulding them in his own image, or thought he was. He wanted them tough, ruthless, venal – all the qualities to make a success of business and maybe even life itself.'

'That's horrible,' Turquand said.

'Your employer was a horrible man. It certainly rubbed off on Anthony. He's always had this hold over you. It's why you gave his investment company a glowing endorsement. It's why he was able to make you plough in so much of your own money.' Rebus paused.

'And it's why you're powerless now that he's lost all that cash. I look around me here and do you know what I see? A prison. A nice enough place to be incarcerated, but that's where you've been ever since Maria died. It's why you never remarried. You're serving a life sentence, Mr Turquand, with the Brough family standing guard.'

Turquand lowered his arms and leaned back in the wooden chair, which creaked in protest.

'There must be a reason why he told you.'

'Anthony's in hospital, recovering from an abduction. He's got no proof you were behind it, seeking long-deferred revenge, but he knows that financially you're an empty shell. Maybe you think you have nothing to lose by torturing him.'

'Abducted? This is the first I've heard of it, believe me!'

'I know it is,' Rebus said quietly, rising to his feet.

'So . . . what happens now?'

'Well, you could walk into any police station and confess. You might even get a book deal out of it, courtesy of Maxine Dromgoole. You'd be famous, which is better than nothing, I suppose.'

'And if I choose not to do that?' Turquand was pressing his fingers against the green baize of the table.

'If you were going to spill the beans, Mr Turquand, you'd have done it years back, just to be rid of Anthony's attentions. Pointless now really, isn't it, with the coffers more or less empty? The Broughs have already done their damage, one way and another.'

'You're not going to arrest me?'

'I'm not a policeman. And after all, it would be your word against Anthony's. Plus, deathbed confessions seldom hold much weight in court.'

'Yes,' Turquand agreed. 'Sir Magnus could have made up the whole story, couldn't he? One last little game with his grandchildren.' He was trying to get to his feet, looking to Rebus for help that wasn't about to be offered. The two men stood face to face.

'But we know the truth, you and me,' Rebus said.

'We do.' Turquand paused. 'Is Anthony going to be all right after his ordeal?'

'Already on his way to a full recovery.'

'I'm sorry to hear that,' Turquand said, shuffling along behind as Rebus headed for the hall. 'I did love her, you know, in my way. But that was never enough for Maria.'

'Is this where you tell me she was asking for it? Don't waste your breath.'

'I was just trying to . . .' The sentence died away, unfinished.

Rebus paused on the doorstep, watching the door close slowly. He sniffed the chill air. Mulched leaves and dewy grass. Some of the birds were still singing, but fewer than before. Fox had been right, he mused – the whisky in the decanter *had* been cheap. Taking a couple of steps back, he unzipped his trousers and began to urinate. After ten seconds, the door opened a couple of inches. Turquand must have been waiting for the sound of the Saab leaving. He looked horrified as the spray bounced off the doorstep, spattering the door.

'Long drive back to Edinburgh,' Rebus explained, zipping himself back up.

Clarke and Fox had gone for an early dinner at Giuliano's on Union Place. Across the road, the doors of the Playhouse Theatre had opened. A musical was playing, the keenest audience members readying to have their tickets checked. Others were enjoying a pre-theatre pizza at the tables around the two detectives, including one exuberant group of middle-aged women, each with a pink boa draped around her shoulders. More bottles of red were being ordered as Clarke and Fox waited for their food.

'What did Gartcosh say?' Clarke asked.

'Like us, they're keen to know two things – who ordered the abduction, and what happens now Brough is back on the street.'

'They don't think Bates could have acted alone?'

'I persuaded them that was unlikely.'

'Do they really know about the money Jude owes?'

'Would I still be working the case if they did?'

Clarke sipped her tonic water. 'Which raises another question – *should* you be working the case? Conflict of interest and all that?'

'Have you seen me do anything that would throw a spanner in the works?'

Clarke shrugged. 'Procurator Fiscal might think differently.'

'Procurator Fiscal doesn't view the world through our eyes.'

'You sound like a certain retired cop we know.' Clarke looked around, impatient for her food.

'I was sent here because of the attack on Darryl Christie,' Fox went on. 'Gartcosh wanted to see if it connected to his dealings with Anthony Brough – Brough was always the main target. But then with the death of Robert Chatham, the focus had to switch. Now it turns out the two were connected all along.'

'But Brough remains tantalisingly out of reach?' Clarke speculated. She was nodding to herself as her phone rang. 'It's that ex-cop
we were talking about,' she told Fox, picking up and answering.
Rebus sounded as if he were driving.

'Have you been to see Brough again?' he asked, not in the mood
for small talk.

'Not yet. We had another go at Bates and left him in his cell to
stew.'

'You should go to the hospital.'

'Why?'

'Because he's scared. I think he might be ready to talk.'

'About the SLPs?' Clarke's eyes met Fox's.

'About everything, as long as we promise to save his neck.'

'Tell me *you* didn't promise him anything?'

'How could I?'

'I doubt that would stop you.' She leaned back as her bowl of
gnocchi arrived.

'He's going to jail, Siobhan. For the wrong crime, maybe, but
that's where he's headed and he knows it. It's just a matter of what
class of prison and for how long.'

'Always supposing Glushenko doesn't get him first.'

'Always supposing.'

She listened to the silence. 'What did you mean about "the wrong
crime"?'

'He's a murderer, Siobhan. The second I've met in as many hours
who's got away with it.'

'What?'

'I'll explain later.'

'Where are you right now?'

'I'm just driving.'

'Driving where, though?'

'Are you with Malcolm?'

'Yes.'

'Indian or Italian?'

'Italian.'

'I wish I was there with you.'

'There's a seat at the table.'

'Maybe a drink later at the Ox – after you've been to see Brough.'

'What are we supposed to be saying to him?'

'Get Malcolm to check that with his friends at HMRC. The laundered cash that's gone walkabout . . . the days in that room in West

Pilton – Brough will bounce back, but right now he's fragile and hasn't a clue what his next move is. Your job is to show him the way.'

'A map might help.'

'You don't need a map, Siobhan.'

'What time at the Ox?'

'Maybe ten?'

'It's past my bedtime, but I'll try.'

'See you then.'

The line went dead. Clarke relayed the gist of the conversation to Fox. Before she'd finished, Fox had taken out his own phone and was tapping in Sheila Graham's number. While he was talking, Clarke's phone sounded again. She put it to her ear.

'Yes, Christine?'

'I'm halfway home,' Esson said, 'but the station just called me. They'd tried your number but it was busy.'

'What's up?'

'It's your friend Eddie Bates. Apparently he wants to talk.'

'We've not long finished with him.'

'Well, you must have passed the audition – he wants you back.'

'I was just about to go see Anthony Brough.'

'Toss a coin then, maybe? But I'm guessing Malcolm's treating you to Giuliano's, and last time I looked, that was a two-minute walk from Gayfield Square . . .'

Clarke rang off and gestured towards Fox.

'Hold on a sec,' Fox duly said into his phone, before holding it away from him.

'Need to drop in on Bates first,' Clarke warned him. When Fox looked quizzical, she offered a shrug and pushed away her uneaten food.

'Alan McFarlane's coming up from London specially,' Fox said as they entered the police station and headed for the interview room. Clarke had called ahead to make sure Bates was transferred from his cell.

'When will he get here?'

'Tomorrow morning, I'd think. Too late now for a flight.'

'Let's hope Brough is still feeling the jitters.'

'Nothing to stop us paying a visit after this,' Fox said.

'You're awfully keen – still trying to make a good impression?'

'Who with?'

'Anyone likely to notice.' Clarke smiled to let him know she was teasing, then pulled open the door to the interview room. There were two officers waiting with Bates. She nodded to let them know they could leave. Bates was twitchy, rubbing and scratching at his arms.

'Cold turkey?' Fox guessed. 'A good dealer never uses.'

'It pays to be sociable sometimes,' Bates said.

Clarke took the chair opposite him, leaving Fox to stand nearby. Next to the seated Bates he looked huge and threatening, which was the whole point.

'So just to sum up,' Clarke began, 'when we last met – oh . . . seventy-five minutes ago or thereabouts – you were sticking to your story. And *we* were sticking to the truth of your situation, which is that you are going to be put away for a very long time for false imprisonment and peddling drugs.' She broke off. 'Is your lawyer on his way?'

'I don't need a lawyer. I want to cut a deal.'

'Everybody wants something, Eddie,' Fox stated, folding his arms.

'Look, all that stuff I told you . . . I thought I was saying it for the right reasons. I do have a sense of honour, you know.'

'You're not a grass?'

'That's right! But a time comes when it's every man for himself, aye?'

'You'll get no argument from me.'

Bates looked from Clarke to Fox and then back again as he debated with himself. He blew air from his cheeks and focused on the scarred tabletop.

'It was Molly,' he said eventually.

'Molly Sewell?'

Bates nodded. 'She arranged it, even told me which room to use and how to kit it out. Like she'd been planning it for a while.'

'Molly wanted you to keep her boss prisoner? Did she tell you why?' Clarke was trying not to sound disbelieving.

Bates shook his head. 'She drugged his whisky. Went into his house and checked he was out for the count. Then we carried him out to her car, took him to my place.'

'Without anybody seeing?'

'We looked like we were helping a drunk mate.'

'How did she get into his house?' Fox asked.

'What?'

'Was the door unlocked?'

'Must have been, I suppose. Or else she had a key.'

'How long were you supposed to keep him?'

'Not much longer, maybe only another day.'

'And you don't know why?'

'She never said. I mean, yeah, I thought there'd be money at the back of it. Makes sense if you think about it – kidnap your own boss, pay the ransom, let him go.'

'But there never was a demand for money.'

Bates looked at Clarke again. 'Then I've no idea what it was about – you'll have to ask her. Far as I was concerned, I was doing a favour.'

'You realise this sounds like you're piling one porky on top of another?' Clarke said. 'We dismiss a story, you come up with a more outlandish one?'

Bates just shrugged. 'It's the God's honest truth – and I expect you to remember that.'

'Oh, we'll remember it – you aided and abetted a kidnapper and held the victim to non-existent ransom.' Clarke turned to Fox. 'What do you think?'

'Probably much the same as you. You've got Sewell's home address and phone number – let's ask her.'

Clarke nodded, her eyes on Eddie Bates. 'That'll give you time to conjure up another storyline – maybe try aliens next, eh?'

She exited the room, followed by Fox, and indicated to the waiting officers that Bates could be taken back to his cell. As he was led away, both detectives watched. Then Clarke took the pad from her pocket, the one with Molly Sewell's details. She tried her home number first. The receiver was picked up by someone with an American accent.

'Is Molly there?' Clarke asked.

'Think you've got the wrong number.'

Clarke held up the pad, reeling the number off.

'Okay, that's the right number, but there's no one here called Molly, unless one of my flatmates got lucky last night . . .'

Clarke apologised and rang off, then tried the mobile. An automated voice answered immediately.

'The number you have dialled has not been recognised.'

She tried again, same result. Fox was nodding.

'Let's go,' he said.

It took them only ten minutes to drive to the address. Duncan

Street sat between Ratcliffe Terrace and Minto Street. One-way traffic, meaning Clarke had to make three right turns before beginning the slow crawl along it, looking for number 28. One side of the street comprised a terrace of Georgian houses with imposing porticoes. The other side included a dental practice and an MOT garage.

'Only go up to twenty-four,' Fox said as they reached the Minto Street junction. Rather than go all around the houses again, Clarke reversed and drew into a parking space. She handed the notepad to Fox.

'Definitely says twenty-eight,' he confirmed.

'She's sold us a pup.'

Fox nodded. 'But not the *whole* pup. The tenement next to the pub is twenty-four, meaning the pub on the corner could be twenty-six. That's just shy of the address written here.'

'So?'

'So if she'd just been making something up off the top off her head, what are the chances of getting it so close?'

'She knows the street,' Clarke said, nodding.

'So maybe someone she knows lives here . . .'

'Or she's in one of these other houses.' Clarke turned her head to Fox. 'How does a bit of doorstepping sound to you?'

'I'm game if you are.'

They started at the Minto Street end, giving Sewell's name and description. A couple of householders said she sounded familiar but they didn't know the names of most of their neighbours. The grand building just along from the dental practice had once housed a publishing company but now boasted half a dozen bells for the occupants of its apartments. The first one they tried got them an invitation inside. The man was in his mid-thirties, bespectacled and wearing a green sweater, its sleeves rolled up.

'Yes, Molly,' he said, after Clarke ended her routine. 'She's in Flat Six.' He even showed them the way. Clarke tried the door, but there was no answer. There was no letter box – all the mail arrived at the main door and was picked up there. She tried knocking again.

'When was the last time you saw her?' Fox asked the neighbour.

'Not for a few days. I did hear a door close earlier tonight – could have been hers. There was a taxi idling outside.'

'A taxi?'

'Well, a vehicle anyway, but you get to know the sound they make.'

Fox nodded his thanks. Clarke's mouth was moving as she weighed up their options.

'You've been a big help,' Fox told the man, hinting that he could go. The man gave a little bow of his head and returned to his own flat.

'She took the money, didn't she?' Clarke surmised. 'And when Brough found out . . . No, that doesn't work. Maybe he was starting to get an inkling, though.'

'So why didn't she run *then*?'

'She needed somebody to take the blame. Maybe *Brough* was readying to run.'

'To get away from Glushenko?' Fox nodded slowly.

'When Glushenko hits town, that's when Bates lets Brough go, so he can stumble right into him. Meantime, Sewell tiptoes away and no one's any the wiser.'

'No one who's *alive*, that is.'

She studied him. 'How does that sound to you?'

'Feasible.'

'Likely?'

'It takes strong nerves, hanging around after the money's done its vanishing trick, Brough trying to work out who's got it and how they pulled it off.'

'He'd suspect Christie first,' Clarke said. 'That buys her some time. Then there are all the other villains on Brough's books.'

'But she'd have been on his list.'

Clarke nodded. 'But the very fact that she stuck around . . .'

'Might put him off the scent.'

They fell silent, running through the theory again, trying to find other possibilities.

'Another shout-out to airports, ferries and train stations?' Fox suggested.

'Where do you reckon she'll go?'

'With ten million tucked away in a bank somewhere?' Fox considered the possibilities. 'Center Parcs?' he offered.

Despite herself, Siobhan Clarke gave a snort of laughter.

26

Christie's white Range Rover was parked in the driveway, and there was a light on in the hall. Rebus rang the bell and waited, studying the fake cameras and burglar alarm. No answer. He tried again, then walked to the living-room window. It was curtained, but the curtains didn't quite meet at the top and he could see there were lights on in there, too.

He walked around the side of the house. A security light was tripped, showing him the rear door to the house, to the right of which sat the partially melted bin. He turned the door handle and the door opened inwards.

'Hello?' he called.

He stepped inside and called Christie's name.

Nothing.

He could see a modern kitchen off to his right, with a breakfast bar at its centre. Plates and pans were stacked next to the dishwasher.

'Darryl? It's Rebus!'

Into the main downstairs hall. He peered up the staircase and saw that the landing was in darkness. The door to the living room was ajar, so he gave it a push.

'Join us,' a guttural voice commanded.

The man was standing in the middle of the room, dressed in a three-quarter-length black leather coat, black denims, and what looked like cowboy boots. His head was shaved, but he sported a goatee beard. It, too, was black. The eyes were pinpricks, the nose hooked. Late twenties or early thirties? Not overly tall, but given added stature by dint of the curved sword held in one hand, revolver in the other.

Rebus looked towards Darryl Christie. He was seated on an armchair in front of Glushenko, hands wrapped around his chest in a hug, both knees twitching.

'Nice room, Darryl,' Rebus said, trying to calm his heart rate. 'Can I assume your mum was responsible for the decor?'

'Please,' the Ukrainian said, 'introduce yourself.'

'I'm in insurance,' Rebus said. 'I'm here to give Mr Christie a quote.' He turned again towards Christie. 'Family not around?' he checked.

'My guest was good enough to wait until they'd gone to the flicks.' Christie's voice was calm despite the body language.

'Are you a policeman?' Glushenko enquired.

'No.'

'Liar.' Glushenko showed gleaming teeth as he grinned. 'Give me your wallet.'

Rebus started to reach into his jacket, the Ukrainian gesturing that he should do so with infinite slowness. Rebus held it out.

'Put it on the mantelpiece.'

Rebus did so.

'Now pull a chair over next to the bastard.'

Glushenko watched as Rebus complied. He stood the sword against the fireplace but kept the revolver aimed between the two seated figures as he opened the wallet. A few business cards spilled out.

'Detective Inspector Malcolm Fox,' Glushenko intoned. 'Major Crime Division.' He glanced at Rebus. 'Impressive . . .'

'So I'm told,' Rebus acknowledged.

Glushenko nodded. 'Your phone, too, please.'

Rebus took it out.

'Slide it across the floor towards me.'

When it arrived, Glushenko stepped on it with the heel of one boot. Rebus heard the screen crack. The man's hand reached for the sword again.

'How did you get that past Customs?' Rebus asked.

'I bought it in your country. They are sold as ornaments, but I was able to sharpen it.'

'I think he plans to behead me,' Christie explained.

'Exactly so.'

'Leaving me for my mum and the boys to find.'

Glushenko nodded. 'Or,' he said, 'you could hand me the money you stole.'

'I don't have it. I never did have it.'

'For what it's worth,' Rebus added, 'I think he's telling the truth. It was stolen from the man who stole it from you.'

'Brough?' Glushenko looked like he might spit at mention of the name. 'The Invisible Man?'

'Actually, he's back in the land of the living,' Rebus said. 'As of earlier today. He'd been kept doped to the eyeballs by whoever took your money.'

Glushenko stared at Rebus. 'Who *are* you? How is it that you know so much?'

Rebus turned his head towards Christie. 'I know you ordered that beating you took. Even made sure Chatham was told the cameras outside were dummies. The slashed car tyres and the bin – those were your doing too. You thought maybe it would buy you some time – Mr Glushenko here might not interfere if he thought someone like Brough was already out to get you. Plus you'd be assured a lot of police attention, which likely would keep him at bay. But when Chatham found out who the victim had been and started blabbing to the likes of Craw Shand . . . you got on to the person who arranged the beating and told him Chatham had to be got rid of.'

Christie shook his head slowly. 'Kenny Arnott was only supposed to give Chatham a fright so he'd keep his mouth shut in future.'

'What went wrong?'

'They did too good a job. Chatham tried getting away, went into the water. They'd poured whisky into him because that was the way it would have gone down if he'd really been for the chop.'

'I'm guessing none of Arnott's guys could swim?'

'What we in the trade call a total fuck-up.'

'The condemned man's confession?' Glushenko seemed to approve. 'So now you can die cleansed of sin, yes?'

'Do you want me standing or kneeling?' Christie asked.

'This man has a certain dignity,' Glushenko said to Rebus.

'He also never had your money,' Rebus reminded him.

'But he was partner of man who did! And now you tell me Brough is in the city, he will be my next appointment . . .'

Christie had risen to his feet. He clasped his hands behind his back, looking suddenly calmer and more collected than any man Rebus had ever known.

'Ten million from almost a billion,' Christie said. 'It really makes that much of a difference?'

'If people learn that I can be cheated and do nothing? Yes, that makes a difference.'

Christie had angled his head towards the still-seated Rebus. 'I don't suppose he's going to want any witnesses, either,' he cautioned, sinking to one knee.

'I was thinking the same thing, Darryl.'

Rebus watched as Glushenko slipped the revolver into the pocket of his leather coat so he could grip the sword with both hands. He was raising it in an arc as Darryl's right hand whipped round from behind his back. The pistol must have been tucked in his waistband. He aimed it at Glushenko's face and pulled the trigger.

The explosion filled the room. A spray of warm liquid hit Rebus. Behind the billowing smoke, there was more blood on the wall above the mantelpiece. Rebus tried not to look at the damage to the Ukrainian as the man's knees buckled and he fell in a heap to the floor, the sword clattering next to him. Christie was back on his feet, the gun pointed at the prone figure. He stood like that as the smoke cleared. Rebus stayed where he was, attention focused on the pistol, unwilling to draw attention to himself until Christie had processed everything. The words that eventually escaped Christie's lips weren't the ones Rebus had expected.

'Look at the mess – Mum's going to kill me.' He turned towards Rebus and tried out a thin, sickly smile, his face and clothes speckled with gore. 'Bit of a stretch to make it look like suicide?'

'Just a bit,' Rebus conceded. 'Explains why you stayed put, though – you really *did* have insurance.'

'This?' Christie held up the pistol. 'I've got Cafferty to thank – he suggested getting tooled up.'

'Did he now?'

Christie's eyes narrowed. 'You think he meant for something like this to happen?'

'He must have known it was a possibility.'

'Glushenko kills me or I kill him – either way Cafferty wins.' Christie considered this. 'The sly old bastard,' he muttered.

'Any chance of you putting that down, now you're done with it?' Rebus nodded towards the pistol. Christie placed it on the mantelpiece and picked up Rebus's wallet, taking it over to him.

'Might want to give it a wipe, DI Fox.'

'And change my shirt,' Rebus added, studying himself. 'Why didn't you shoot him straight off?'

'He had a gun pointed at me. I knew my best chance was when he was focused on the sword, me kneeling, ready to meet my maker.' Christie paused. 'So what happens now?'

'You call it in.'

'Me?'

Rebus gestured towards the remains of his phone. 'Mine's out of action.'

'Self-defence, though, eh?'

'I can think of lawyers who'd have a good crack at that,' Rebus agreed.

'And you'll stand in the witness box and help me?'

'I'll say what I saw.'

Christie took a moment to ponder this. 'Three to five? Five to seven?'

'Maybe eight to ten,' Rebus said. 'Judges tend to frown when shooters are involved.'

'So out again in five years?'

Rebus nodded slowly as Christie settled back into the armchair. 'I'll miss the house,' he said. 'And Mum, of course.'

'She'll visit. Cal and Joseph, too.'

'Of course they will,' Christie said softly. 'Maybe I'll buy Cafferty's old place after all, move them in there. They won't want to live here . . .' He paused again. 'I *did* fuck up, though, didn't I? Walked straight into Cafferty's trap . . .'

'Traps most often look like something you want or need,' Rebus confirmed.

Christie was staring at the mantelpiece. 'Maybe I could pay a little visit before they come for me.'

'I don't think that would be wise, Darryl. Two murders looks a lot less like self-defence.'

Christie nodded his eventual agreement. There was a phone sitting in its charging cradle on a small table by the window. Rebus walked over to it, lifted it up and held it out.

'You do it,' Christie told him, sounding suddenly exhausted.

Rebus punched in the number and waited. He walked back to the window and pulled open the curtains, wondering if the gunfire would have brought out any of the neighbours – maybe they had already called it in. Hearing movement behind him, he turned in time to see Christie stalking from the room.

'Darryl!' he called out. Glancing towards the mantelpiece, he saw the pistol was gone. The operator had come on the line to ask him which emergency service he required.

'No time,' he said, dropping the phone. He was halfway out of the room when he remembered something. Diving back in, he removed the revolver from Glushenko's pocket, and reached the back door as the Range Rover was reversing out at speed, scraping one of the gateposts on its way.

Rebus ran to his car and got in, placing the gun on the passenger seat, butt towards him, muzzle facing the door. He was intending to phone while he drove, until he remembered he had no phone. The first pub he passed, he hit the brakes, squealing to a stop. The smokers gathered on the pavement looked bemused as he demanded a phone. A woman handed hers over.

'Where's the fire?' she said.

Rebus knew Cafferty's number by heart. An automated voice told him to leave a message after the tone. 'Get out now!' he yelled. 'Christie's on his way to blow your brains out!'

Next call: Siobhan.

'I've got news—' she began.

'Christie's just killed Glushenko,' Rebus interrupted. 'Now he's on his way to do the same to Cafferty!' He paused to let this sink in. 'Can your news wait?'

'Yes,' Clarke said.

Rebus tossed the phone back to the woman. 'Does that count as a fire?' he asked her, not waiting for her reply.

He ran every red light, stopping only when he encountered the immovable obstacle of a tram as it progressed at the usual stately pace along Princes Street. He took the opportunity to examine the revolver. It looked practically antique, but the bullets sitting snugly in their chambers were shiny and new. He snapped it shut and measured its weight in his hand. Slow and cumbersome – no match for Christie's pistol.

The road ahead had cleared. Rebus hit the accelerator and his horn and sped up the Mound.

George IV Bridge . . . around the one-way and into Lauriston Place . . . then left into the Quartermile development. The white Range Rover was parked on a double yellow line, lights on, driver's door gaping, engine idling. Rebus pulled up alongside and got out. The metal gate to Cafferty's block was open, and the main door had been hit by gunshots, the wood next to the lock splintered. Rebus toed it open and walked in. A uniformed guard stood in the hall, clutching a two-way radio. He froze at the sight of the revolver.

'I'm with the police,' Rebus tried to reassure him. 'Have you called it in?'

The guard nodded, eyes on Rebus's bloodstained shirt.

'I really *am* with the police. The guy upstairs is armed, too – best if you stay here.'

According to the illuminated panel, the lift had gone to the top floor. Rebus took the stairs rather than wait. He had to haul himself up the final few, heart thumping, breath coming in gasps. He choked back a cough and pulled open the door, entering the communal hallway. At the far end, the pistol had been used in place of a key again. Rebus breathed in the now familiar smell of cordite, pushed open the door and stepped inside.

'He's not here!' Christie spat. He was circuiting the large open-plan living space, the pistol hanging by his side. Rebus held the revolver behind him as he made his approach.

'Lights are on, but no one's home,' Christie continued to complain. There was a mug of tea on the kitchen worktop. Rebus touched it: still warm.

'You told him, didn't you?' Christie raged.

'My phone's in smithereens, remember?'

'You fucking did, though – I can see it in your eyes!' Christie pointed the pistol at Rebus's head.

'It's not me you want, Darryl,' Rebus reminded him. 'I'm not the one who got you into this mess, remember?'

'Maybe I should go see Brough, then – save Big Ger for later.'

'That's certainly a plan.' Rebus could hear a siren approaching. 'Best be quick, though – sounds like someone heard the shots.'

The pistol was still pointed at Rebus's head. The fiery look in Christie's eyes began to die back a little.

'You're a lucky man, Rebus – did anyone ever tell you that?'

'Brough's a different proposition, remember – cold-blooded murder isn't as easy to defend in court.'

'Fucker deserves to die.'

'We seldom get what we really deserve, Darryl.'

'Maybe I can change that for once – Brough first, then Cafferty.' Christie was backing his way down the hall towards the door. He didn't see one of the doors off to the right open slowly on its silent hinges. A hammer swung down, catching him on the top of his skull. As he flinched, he let off a shot. Rebus could feel it as it passed by him before smashing through the glass door to the balcony. Christie's whole body skewed, coming to rest against the wall before crumpling. Rebus walked towards him.

'Hiding in the toilet?'

'Didn't have time to do much else,' Cafferty said.

'The second hammer?'

Cafferty held it up for inspection, nodding.

'I meant to ask why you bought two.'

'They were on special offer,' Cafferty said. 'I'm not one to turn down a bargain.' He was studying the unconscious figure. 'You sure Glushenko's dead?'

'Shot in the face at more or less point-blank range.' Rebus gestured towards his spattered shirt.

'Did that belong to your grandad?' Cafferty meant the revolver.

'It was the Ukrainian's. He had a nice sharp sword, too. Lucky you offered Darryl that bit of advice.'

The two men stared at one another.

'I've always been generous that way,' Cafferty said eventually.

Rebus's flat.

Midnight had come and gone. Having given his statement at Gayfield Square, been swabbed for DNA and fingerprinted, and had his clothes bagged, Rebus was lingering in the shower while Clarke and Fox sat at the table in the living room, shovelling down food rescued from a chip shop just before it closed. Clarke's phone sat next to her, just in case there was news of Molly Sewell. Rebus finally entered, freshly dressed and rubbing a towel through his hair. He plucked a chip from Fox's carton.

'Thought you said you weren't hungry.'

'I'm not,' Rebus told him, drawing out a chair and sitting down. The Turquand paperwork had been pushed to one side of the table. He stared at it.

'Cafferty has a lot to answer for,' Clarke said, 'putting that idea in Christie's head.'

'On the other hand, if he hadn't, it would be Darryl on Deb's slab in the morning rather than Comrade Glushenko.'

'From what you say, facial ID is probably out.'

'It'll be DNA or distinguishing features,' Rebus agreed. 'Any news of Ms Sewell?'

'Nothing,' Clarke said, peering at her screen.

Rebus was thoughtful for a moment. 'Cafferty let me in on a secret, while we were waiting for the blues and twos.'

'What?'

'Eddie Bates was dealing with Cafferty's blessing – his blessing *and* his backing.' Rebus saw that he had two very willing listeners.

301

'Bates knew that Molly Sewell worked for someone with money. He told Cafferty, thinking Cafferty could maybe do something with it. So Cafferty met with Molly.'

'When?'

'A few months back. His idea was that she'd be good for information.'

'He already knew Brough and Christie were partners?'

Rebus nodded. 'But Molly explained the why and the how. Then, when she'd got to know Cafferty a bit better, she told him her plan. She'd met Francesca many a time and had got friendly with Alison Warbody. Alison told her how much she despised Brough. It was his fault Francesca was the way she was. It gnawed away at Molly until she decided to do something about it.'

'Namely, rip him off.'

'But handing half to Warbody. Francesca was down to her last half-million, thanks to low interest rates and expensive help. Relatively speaking, she was a pauper.'

'What did Brough do?' Fox asked. 'To Francesca, I mean.'

'On his deathbed, old Sir Magnus told them both that they could break any rule, get away with anything. The lesson was fresh in Anthony's mind when he stuck Julian Greene's head under the surface of that swimming pool and held it there.'

'With Francesca watching?' Clarke asked.

Rebus nodded. 'Anthony obviously didn't approve of Francesca's suitor. All of which sent her looking for oblivion.'

'At one point,' Fox said, 'she wanted an exorcism.'

'For her brother rather than her.'

'You got this from Cafferty?' Clarke asked Rebus.

'I sort of pieced it together,' he answered with a shrug. 'But I don't doubt it's the truth.'

'So did Warbody get her share?'

'I've no idea.'

'Shouldn't we be asking?'

'Sure.'

'But she's not likely to tell us, is she?'

The room fell silent again until Rebus spoke.

'Darryl even approached Cafferty to help search for Brough.'

'So he could offer Brough to Glushenko?'

'No – so Glushenko might get wind that Cafferty was on the lookout, and maybe start to think there was a link between the two.'

'So he'd target Big Ger rather than Darryl?'

'Not that Cafferty *did* help look, of course. But he strung Darryl along.'

'He's been stringing *all* of us along,' Clarke commented.

Silence again until Rebus leaned forward across the table. 'Say you do catch Molly and bring her in – what exactly have you got? Is Brough going to testify that his abduction revolved around money skimmed from an account filled to the brim with stolen cash, laundered by gangsters?'

'That's probably HMRC's call,' Fox said.

'And the best of luck to them. But if Molly keeps quiet, and Brough keeps quiet, and Cafferty keeps quiet . . .'

'There's always Christie,' Clarke countered. 'He's looking at a lengthy sentence. Maybe he'd cooperate?'

'You really think so?'

'Not really, no,' she conceded. 'What about Craw Shand?'

'Stolen away by Cafferty, making it look like force was used.'

'So we'd pile even more pressure on Darryl Christie?'

Rebus nodded. 'Craw's on his way home now from a bed and breakfast in Helensburgh, courtesy of his new friend.'

Fox looked from Rebus to Clarke and back again. 'So the only person going to jail is Darryl Christie?'

'You're forgetting Eddie Bates – but essentially, yes.'

'And what does that mean for the city?'

'It means,' Rebus said, 'Big Ger Cafferty just got a career-best result.'

'Every silver lining has a cloud,' Siobhan Clarke said with a sigh. 'Do we tell Alvin James tonight or tomorrow?'

Rebus was looking at Fox. 'Jude may be off the hook, Malcolm. Then again, if and when Cafferty steps into Darryl's shoes . . .' He shrugged. 'What you choose to tell her is up to you.'

'How do you mean?'

'If she thinks the debt's cancelled, might make her rethink her life – fresh start and all that.'

Fox nodded, then tapped a finger against the Turquand files. 'Just a pity *you* didn't get closure, John.'

'Ah,' Rebus said, leaning back in his seat, 'I was about to come to that . . .'

Day Nine

27

The Galvin Brasserie.

An early dinner, Rebus and Deborah Quant the only customers in their section of the restaurant. She'd ordered a Bloody Mary and downed it in three gulps.

'Tough day?' Rebus guessed.

'You ever seen someone who's been . . .?' She broke off. 'Sorry, I forgot – you were *there*. Come to think of it, didn't I hear you were bedside when Kenny Arnott passed away, too?'

'Guilty as charged.'

She pretended to move her chair a few inches further away from him.

'It's not contagious,' he said with a smile.

'So what are we celebrating? Until an hour ago, my dinner plan involved a microwave and a corkscrew.' She paused. 'You've got some colour in your cheeks, by the way. And the weight loss shows.'

'Maybe that's what we're celebrating, then. That and the fact that I got some news.'

'Oh?'

'Hank Marvin's not the threat I thought he was.'

She looked puzzled, but instead of an explanation, Rebus just smiled. 'Oh, and one other thing – that story I started to tell you?'

'Your locked-room mystery? Don't tell me you've come up with a new theory?'

The waiter was hovering to take their food order.

'I'll tell you over the main course.' Rebus looked at the menu. 'I think I'm going to have two steaks.'

'Two?'

'One to take home to Brillo.'

'If you're paying, be my guest.'

Another couple had walked in and were being greeted by the maître d'. Rebus recognised Bruce Collier, and wondered if the tanned, exotically dressed woman with him was his wife, newly back from India. He supposed there were people whose minds he should put at rest – not just Collier, but Peter Attwood and Dougie Vaughan. Didn't they deserve to be told the whole story? Maybe one of them would even do something about it.

Collier didn't notice Rebus. His attention was focused on his partner. Deborah Quant had finished ordering, so Rebus told the waiter what he wanted.

'Penny for them,' Quant said, once the waiter had left.

'I've just worked out what the music on the speakers is,' he said. 'It's John Martyn, "Over the Hill".'

'And?'

'And nothing. It's just, maybe I'm not there yet.'

'Nobody said you were.'

'I was starting to think it, though, before all of this.'

'All of what?'

'The last week or so, everything that's happened. It makes me realise there's unfinished business.'

'There's *always* unfinished business, John.'

'Maybe, maybe not.'

'You think you can do something about it?'

'As long as I've got some fight left in me.'

'This is Cafferty we're talking about, yes?'

'What makes you say that?'

'He's past it – you told me that yourself. Past it and long retired.'

'If you saw him right now, you might change your mind.'

'Why?'

'Because,' Rebus said, signalling to the waiter for more drinks, 'the old devil is back . . .'

Nine o'clock, and the revellers were making their way through the Grassmarket and the Cowgate, stopping off at selected pubs and clubs. Cafferty had left Craw Shand with a hundred pounds of credit behind the bar of the Pirate, making Craw suddenly very popular with the other regulars. Stepping out into the darkness, he pulled on his black leather gloves and walked the short distance to the Devil's Dram. Its doors were locked – no red carpet, no doormen. A group of half a dozen students looked as if they couldn't quite believe it, before heading off to find another room filled with noise and flashing lights.

Cafferty kicked the doors a couple of times, then went around to the back entrance and kicked and rattled that door, too. Eventually it was yanked open from within.

'We're shut,' the man snarled.

'Who are you?' Cafferty demanded.

'Who's asking?'

'People call me Big Ger.'

The man swallowed. 'I'm Harry.'

'And do you run this place, Harry?'

'Not really. It belongs to—'

'I know who it *used* to belong to, and we both know he won't be paying any bills for a while. But from what I hear, this establishment *could* be a goldmine with the right man in charge, and business has a way of evaporating if doors stay locked.'

'Yeah, but—'

'You've sent everyone home? The DJ? Bar staff? Chef?'

Harry nodded.

'Well get on the phone and haul them back here!'

Cafferty squeezed past Harry and stalked through the storage and kitchen areas, emerging into the club proper. He took it all in, the motifs of imps, demons and general bad behaviour, then climbed to the mezzanine, took one look at the nearest banquette, and sat down. Eventually Harry reached the top of the stairs.

'I don't see you making any calls, son,' Cafferty said with a growl.

Harry fumbled for his phone and started tapping the screen. Cafferty stretched his arms out along the back of the banquette.

'I want this place buzzing by ten thirty. Then you can sit down with me and tell me the ins and outs.'

'Of what?' Harry glanced up from his screen.

'Your old boss's empire. Isn't that what happens in any good company when there's a change at the top?'

'Yes, sir.'

'And fetch me a bottle of malt – best you can find. Time this place started living up to its name.'

Morris Gerald Cafferty watched the young man sprint back down the stairs, then closed his eyes, allowing himself the luxury of a

309

moment's relaxation, jaw unclenching, shoulders released of their tension.

It had been a long time coming.

A long time coming.

'But here I am again,' he said. 'And here I stay.'